THE
BURNING

BOOKS BY ANNA TODD

After

After We Collided

After We Fell

After Ever Happy

Imagines

Before

Nothing More

Nothing Less

The Spring Girls

After: The Graphic Novel (Volume 1)

The Falling

THE BURNING

A BRIGHTEST STARS NOVEL

ANNA TODD

w FRAYED
wattpad PAGES
books

Published in Canada by Wattpad WEBTOON Book Group,
a division of Wattpad WEBTOON Studios, Inc.

36 Wellington Street E., Toronto, ON M5E 1C7

www.wattpad.com

First Frayed Pages x Wattpad Books edition: August 2023

ISBN 978-1-99077-855-1 (Trade Paperback)
ISBN 978-1-99077-856-8 (eBook)

Library and Archives Canada Cataloguing in Publication and U.S. Library of
Congress Cataloging in Publication information is available upon request.

Printed and bound in Canada
3 5 7 9 10 8 6 4 2

Author Photo © Anna Todd
Cover design by Lesley Worrell
Cover image © sutlafk via Shutterstock
Typesetting by Delaney Anderson

To anyone and everyone who's ever felt lost,
let me help you find yourself.

THE
BURNING

PLAYLIST

SHAKE THE FROST (LIVE)
Tyler Childers

CHAMPAGNE PROBLEMS
Taylor Swift

I BURNED LA DOWN
Noah Cyrus

NARCISSIST
Lauren Spencer Smith

WHAT WE HAD
Sody

COMPLEX
Katie Gregson-Macleod

LITTLE BIT OF YOU
Kevin Garrett

DEAR READER
Taylor Swift

POSER
Grace VanderWaal

LOST ON YOU
Lewis Capaldi

SOMEONE WILL LOVE YOU BETTER
Johnny Orlando

FALLING
Harry Styles

WISH YOU THE BEST
Lewis Capaldi

HOLLOW (ACOUSTIC)
James Smith

LOST WITHOUT YOU
Freya Ridings

THE LIGHT
The Album Leaf

KEEP DRIVING
Harry Styles

MAKE IT RIGHT (FEAT. LAUV)
BTS, Lauv

FOR ISLAND FIRES AND FAMILY
Dermot Kennedy

MAROON
Taylor Swift

FORGET ME (ACOUSTIC)
Plamina

REST
Minke

THE OTHER (STRIPPED)
Lauv

UNSPOKEN
Aaron Smith

TRUTH UNTOLD
BTS, Steve Aoki

DOOMSDAY
Lizzy McAlpine

BETTER THAN FEELING LONELY
Olivia O'Brien

DRUNK TEXT ME
Lexi Jayde

EVERYTIME
GSoul

SOMETHING I HATE
ROSIE

I NEED YOU TO HATE ME
(PIANO VERSION)
JC Stewart

PART IV

I just started walking and ended up at the sea

        I'm looking at the coast from here

There's endless sand and the rough wind

      I'm still looking at a desert

I wanted to have the sea so I swallowed you up

But I'm even thirstier than before

     Is what I know really the ocean?

        Or a blue desert?

               -Kim Namjoon

If we're together, even the desert becomes the sea
만약 우리가 함께라면, 사막도 바다가 돼
Army ♡ BTS

PROLOGUE

Kael

The sea of black clothing makes my eyes hurt. It's been a while since I've been around such a uniformed crowd. I was so used to the camouflage I wore daily for years that even though I'm out of the Army, I still look for the camo out in the civilian world. Sometimes I miss not having to think about my choice of clothes every day. When I take one of my freshly dry-cleaned jackets off the hanger, I remembered my ACU jacket that had fabric so stiff from caked-in sand and dirt that it crinkled as we marched for hours in the Georgia heat. My hand reaches under my shirt to touch the dog tags hanging around my neck. For comfort? For punishment?

I'm not one of *those* soldiers who wear them as a prideful decoration or to get free drinks at local bars; I wear them because the weight of the metal on my chest keeps my feet on the ground. I'll probably never take them off. This morning at the coffee shop, I noticed Karina's eyes scanning my neckline and I knew she was looking to see if I had taken them off yet. The answer will always be no.

"It's a little cold in here," my mom says, as I drop the dog tag and bring my hands to my lap.

"Do you want my jacket?" I ask her. She shakes her head.

1

"They have to keep the body cool or it will start to smell," a familiar voice says.

"Still a sick fuck, I see." I stand up and hug Silvin. His body's a lot thinner than the last time I saw him. His jawline sticks out like the villain of an action film.

"Never gonna change, either." He hits my arm.

My mom looks at him with disapproval. "You better quit that." She hits him a little harder than he hit me.

"How many times have I heard that?" Silvin hugs my mom and she breaks into a smile.

She always liked him the few times they met, despite the fact that he could be an offensive prick with a crass sense of humor. His beyond dark sense of humor kept us all laughing through the lowest times in our lives, though, so I always liked him, too.

"How are you, man?" I ask casually, even though I know he's probably hurting more than most of the people in the church right now. Like I had been at the last one.

He clears his throat and blinks his red eyes. A puff of air blows from his cheeks before he answers, "I'm good. I, uhm—I'm good. I'd rather be in Vegas playing slots with a porn star and *her* money." He laughs awkwardly.

"Wouldn't we all," I joke back with him, careful not to add weight to his mind. Sometimes it's better to stay on the surface where you can stay numb.

"Come sit down with us? Or do you already have a seat?" I ask him.

"It's not a fucking concert, Martin," he says and laughs, coming to sit down next to my mom.

Even though it's masking deep sadness, Silvin's twisted laughter is the only inkling of happiness in the whole church. The ceiling is practically dripping with grief. The kind of sad that just bleeds into you and never washes away. It shows on you. The weight of everything you're carrying just flows through your blood and sits right on top of your shoulders.

Silvin sighs and leans back onto the wooden pew heavily, trying to give it some of the weight inside of him. His dark eyes stare ahead, lost in some memory that refuses to go away, denying him any chance of peace. He's too young to look so old. He's aged drastically since we all called him "Baby Face" in our best Southern accents. He's from Mississippi and had looked about fifteen during our first deployment, but now he looks older than me.

Baby Face had grown up a lot since he'd had chunks of what looked like raw tuna thump against his face as they fell from the sky. It took my brain another explosion to digest the horror of realizing the plague of chunks falling were pieces of human flesh, not fish. I was standing so close that a finger with a wedding band on it landed against the toe of my combat boot. Johnson's face had changed when he turned to look at him and realized that his battle buddy Cox was no longer standing there. I saw something in his eyes, the smallest gleam burning out as he lifted his weapon from his waist and kept on moving. He never mentioned him again and after that he sat in silence as Cox's pregnant widow cried at his funeral.

Come to think of it, this funeral feels eerily similar.

I look around for a clock. Isn't it almost time to start? I want to get this over with before I actually have to think about what we're doing here. Funerals are all the same, at least in the military; outside of it, I haven't been to one since I was a kid. Since I left for basic training, I've been to at least ten funerals. That's ten times that I've sat silently in a wooden pew and scanned the faces of soldiers staring ahead, the straight line of their lips well-practiced. Ten funeral homes full of shuffling kids who don't understand life, let alone death, crawling at their parents' feet. Ten times that sobs broke out in the crowd. Luckily, only half of the deceased soldiers were married with families, so that meant only five sobbing wives whose lives were ripped apart and changed forever.

I often wondered when the calls would stop coming. After how many years would we stop gathering like this? Would it continue until we were all old and gray? Would Silvin come to my funeral or would I go to his first? I always went, as did Johnson, whom I spot out of the corner of my eye. Stanson, too, who is holding his newborn son. He's still in the Army, but even the few of us who are no longer active duty still come. I flew to Washington State a few months ago for a guy I barely knew, but Mendoza loved.

There are more people today than usual. Then again, this dead soldier was liked more than most of us. I couldn't think about his name, or say it in my head. I didn't want to do that to myself, or to my mom, who I picked up in Riverdale and drove with me to Atlanta. She always liked him. Everyone did.

"Who's that lady there?" My mom coughs, her finger pointed at a woman I don't recognize.

"No clue, Ma," I whisper to her.

Silvin's haunted eyes are closed now. I look away from him.

"I'm sure I know that woman—" she insists.

A man in a suit walks on stage. Must be time.

I cut her off. "Ma. They're about to start."

I try to scan the pews for Karina; she must be here by now. She said she was coming straight here from the coffee shop. Next to me, my mom coughs again. She's been doing that more and more lately. She's had this cough for about two years now, maybe more. Sometimes it goes away and she's rewarded for quitting smoking. Other times it's wet and she gripes about how she might as well light up a Marlboro. I've argued with her half my life, since I was ten and I heard her doctor tell her she was going to lose a lung if she didn't quit. I look down at her as she rubs the tissue along her lips, coughing deeper. Her tired eyes close for a second before she goes back to staring blankly at the flower-covered stage. The casket is closed, of course. No one wants these children to see the barely recognizable body.

Fuck, I have to stop. I've spent God knows how many hours with medical professionals tasked with fixing me, so you'd think I'd be better at keeping those thoughts out. It never works, the techniques they teach us. The darkness is still there, unmovable. Maybe I should tell the government to get a refund on my therapy? They paid for it, as they should, but did it work? Clearly not. Not for Silvin, not for me, not for the body in the casket on stage.

Count down, they recommended when my mind got this way.

Count down and think of something that brings you joy or peace. Feel your feet on the ground, know you're safe now, they repeated.

I think of *her* when I need peace. I have since I met her. It only lasts so long until reality sets in and I want to punish myself for the fact that she's not in my life anymore, and I walk deeper into the darkness.

I don't get the chance to finish my self-therapy session.

"We're going to begin if everyone can take their seats now." The funeral director's voice is soft and unaffected. He probably does this a few times a week.

The room quiets and the funeral begins.

After the service, we stay sitting while some line up for a last good-bye. Silvin catches my eye and points upward, like he's trying to tell me something. As I look up, someone taps me on the shoulder. I'd be lying if I didn't admit that I briefly hope it's Karina. Even though I'm sure it's not.

And of course, it's not. It's Gloria, standing behind me in a black dress with white flowers stitched across the top. I think I've seen her in that dress at all ten funerals. Today has been a wild fucking ride already, from meeting Karina at the coffee shop this morning, to seeing Silvin again, to losing the bid on a hell of a deal on a four-plex apartment just outside Fort Benning—and now seeing Gloria, who always reminds me of her husband. I've been failing to come to terms with the situation with him. It's proven to be a lot harder than anything I've done in my entire life.

"Hey Gloria." I get up from the pew and hug her.

Gloria hugs me and pulls back, then hugs me again.

"How are you? I've been worried about you. You never answer my calls anymore." She makes a face. "Asshole," she whispers, looking me straight in the eyes.

"I've been swamped with work and you know I hate the phone."

She rolls her dark eyes. "The kids miss you, okay? And they ask about you a lot."

The kids. Acid that rises from guilt burns my throat.

"I miss them, too." I look at her feet where the littlest one usually clings. "I'll call more, I'm a shitbag." I smile at her and she nods, letting me off the hook a little.

"You are a total shitbag," she agrees with a smile on her face. "Uncle Shitbag still needs to call them once in a while." She looks up and down my face. "I didn't even recognize you at first because of this." She touches her palms to the stubble on my jaw.

"Yeah. I'm a free man now and decided to start acting like one."

"I'm glad. It's good to see you. Even if it's here of all places. And you—" She looks at my mom, and without breaking her conversation with the woman she recognized from earlier, my mom hugs and kisses her on the cheek.

"Karina looks great." Gloria purses her lips and stares into my eyes. "She always does but she looks . . . "

I look away as she pauses.

"She looks happy. That's what it is." She smiles.

Gloria always loved Karina, and I've heard through the grapevine that they still hang out; the gossip reached me even though I'd moved far away from post.

Happy?

She couldn't have seemed further from happy this morning, but maybe I would only get the cold, detached Karina now. It's not like I didn't deserve that.

I quickly scan the church for Karina's hair. It's brown again. That color that's "right between chestnut and chocolate," she told me once. It was her go-to color when she felt like she had her shit together. Controlling and changing her hair color was one of her rituals. She had many little things she did to exercise control while disguising it as luck.

"Yeah. I'm glad she is," I tell her. "I saw her this morning."

She doesn't have to tell me that she already knows. It's easy to gather from how unaffected she is.

"Anyway, the kids with you?" I change the subject. She gives me another eye roll and shakes her head.

"No. My mom's with them back at Benning. I figured they'd been to enough of these for a while."

"Haven't we all?"

"That's for damn sure."

A woman approaches us and moves to hug Gloria. She seems to know her, and they start talking. My mom is still in deep conversation, so I look for Karina again. How is it possible that I haven't seen her yet? The church isn't that big. Then again, she's good at blending in, hiding in the midst of a crowd. It's one of her "things."

My mom's voice cuts through the hushed greetings and condolences being shared around me while I'm lost in my own head.

"Mikael, where is it your sister is wanting to go to college again?" she asks, confusion in her eyes despite the hundreds of conversations we've had about it.

"MIT," I tell the woman talking to her, whom I recognize as Lawson's mom. I know she's a better person than her son, but that's not exactly hard to accomplish. After spending the last few years with him in my platoon, two deployments to Afghanistan later, I know Lawson better than even his own mother does. War brings people closer than anything can, except death. They go hand in hand in my world.

"That's it. MIT. She's the smartest in her whole class this year, and last. Two more years to wait, but they would be crazy not to accept her." My mom's black hair is falling out of the clip thing she always wears. The curls I helped her put in her hair this morning were fallen now. I reach down to push her hair back from her face.

The memory of Karina laughing at me as I burned my fingertips on a hot curling iron fills my mind. I knew she had to be the most thoughtful, selfless person I would ever meet when she offered to help teach me how to curl my mom's hair when we noticed burns on her hands. Some mornings mom's hands would shake so badly that she couldn't do it herself, but she was too stubborn to ask for help.

I don't travel home as often as I should, but my mom loves to have me curl her hair when I do. She says it will make me a good father one day. Karina said the same, with a look in her eyes like she could see the future. Turns out she couldn't, and neither can my mom, because she still hopes for grandchildren from me to pass on the family name. Not fucking happening. There's no chance I'd ever punish the world with another me.

I sigh and grab my phone from my pocket, checking it out of habit while glancing around the room. It's emptier now, so Karina will be easier to find. Eventually I'll either know for sure that she's not here, or she'll appear from whatever corner of the room she's hiding in. That's if she didn't slip out, and knowing her, there's a high likelihood—

"I'm right here, Dory."

Karina's soft voice sends both shock and relief throughout my body.

"There you are. Everyone keeps talking about you, and here you are," Ma says.

Karina's brows draw together and she shakes her head. "Gossip as always."

Her lips curl into a smile and she puts her arm around my mom's shoulders and squeezes.

Karina's fingers go to Ma's hair, and she unfastens the clip. Her delicate hands twist her hair, then clip it back exactly how she likes it and hell of a lot better than I can do. Man, they've come a long way since the beginning. It drives me fucking crazy with guilt that because of everything that happened, my mom doesn't have Karina in her life anymore. Unlike Gloria, who could drive to see Karina ten minutes away, my mom will never even sit behind a wheel again. Not safely, at least. The laundry list of mistakes I've made over the last several years just keeps growing. Even though now we are living separate lives, I've done too many unforgivable things to her.

"Do you want to go outside?" she asks Ma. "It's getting a little stuffy in here." The green of her eyes catches on the stained-glass church window.

My mom follows Karina and they both look back at me standing still.

"Well?" they say in unison.

"I'll go with you?" I look at Karina.

She stares back at me, her lips parting slightly, but she doesn't say anything.

As we turn, my phone vibrates in my hand. I go to answer and catch Karina's eyes. She's staring daggers at my phone, one of her worst enemies. She expects me to answer it, like I always do, so I ignore the call and keep her eyes on mine. She licks her lips and her eyes give away that she's surprised and that she sees this as a win. It was just one of my contractors, anyway.

"Shall we?" I ask her, digging in my position of at least trying to stay on her game board. She nods and leads us out of the church as the bells from its tower ring through the air.

CHAPTER **ONE**

Two years earlier
Kael

My truck roared down the small street. I continued to hit my hands against the steering wheel as I drove far enough down the dark road to be out of her eyesight. I slowed to a stop on the gravel pull-out a few blocks away and stumbled out of my truck. The ground was soaked with unforgiving rain and as I looked into the darkness, I couldn't see more than ten feet in front of me. It had only been a few minutes since I left Karina at her house, but the guilt weighed enough to feel like thirty years.

Reaching for my phone, I called Austin first. My hands were shaking intolerably, and the rain was soaking my phone as I waited for him to pick up.

"Hey man—what's up?" he asked in a casual tone. The nonchalant sound of his voice immediately triggered my anger. Even if I knew both of us did the right thing, I needed someone to be pissed at and I could hear women's voices and music in the background of wherever the fuck he was.

"Your sister found out," I flatly told him.

Silence.

"Found out what?" he asked. I knew he wasn't that damn clueless. He was in shock, not that ignorant.

"Where are you?" I was beyond impatient.

He paused, took a deep breath in before responding. "I'm at Mendoza's. What do you mean by my sister found out? Tell me it's not what I think it is."

"It's exactly what you think it is. I'm on the side of the road and I didn't call you for a heads-up, Fischer, I called you to tell you that your sister is devastated and could really use you right now."

"Did you tell her? I thought we were—"

Before I could help it, my fist slammed against the hood of my truck. "It doesn't fucking matter who told her, what are you going to do about her right now?"

"I don't even have a car, what can I do?"

"Are you drunk?"

"No . . ." He was lying. "Yeah, I mean, I'm not sober. But it's not like I knew this was going to happen and got plastered so you had to deal with her. Maybe call Elodie? She should be home—"

I ended the call before he offered another not-thought-out solution.

The rain took a short break, long enough for me to consider driving back to her house to beg for Karina's forgiveness, to explain why I did what I did. The weight of the world pushed against my shoulders as I imagined her at home alone, sitting in the dark kitchen feeling completely betrayed. I made the choice when I met her to try my best to take care of her, to make her life better, easier, but all I've done is fuck it up.

I still stood by, helping her brother get into the Army before he could tank his life in a serious way. That's what this was, the sacrifice was temporarily hurting Karina, but in the big picture of her life, her brother being alive and breathing would matter more to her than the feelings she thought she had for me. A year from now, she would be proud of him instead of mourning him. After a month or two she would barely think of me. She deserved to have that, and I didn't deserve to have her, so this was the way things would be. She will never leave my mind, but isn't love supposed to be about sacrificing? I didn't know—I had never loved anyone before, but it felt right. It felt wrong, but so right.

I hoped to God Elodie was home and could comfort her. I thought about calling her but I didn't want to admit what I had done. I knew Elodie lately had become attached to Karina's brother and she would be pissed at me too, so I took the easy way out, climbed into my truck and drove to Mendoza's. The solution wouldn't be there, but I knew a bottle of tequila would.

Mendoza's house was lit up with every single light on. All the other houses on the street were dark and quiet. I parked in the driveway right behind his van and took a breath before getting out. Soon, I wouldn't be able to come here when shit went wrong. Once I was out, I would probably only see him at funerals or weddings, or maybe never again. That's how it was in a soldier's life: you had unbreakable bonds, but when people got out, they usually moved back to where they came from and hardly ever looked back. Well, they looked back all the time, but physically never came back.

I heard his voice before I saw him.

"Your truck keeps gettin' louder. I can hear it a damn mile away." He greeted me with a soft smack to my shoulder.

"Yay, you're here!" Gloria hugged me. "What the fuck, you're soaked."

I tried to force a smile. Suddenly I wondered why the hell I was there. I didn't deserve the comfort of friends right now when I knew Karina had no one. Carefully moving out of Gloria's arms, I tried to think of an excuse to leave even though I had just arrived.

Fischer's voice rang through the living room. "Yoooo," he slurred.

ANNA TODD

He was lazily sitting there, his arm stretched across the back of the white sofa. His eyes were barely open.

"How drunk are you?" I questioned, moving closer.

He laughed a little, tilting his head. He looked so much like Karina that it made me want to throw up.

"Nah, I didn't drink." He nodded toward Mendoza and Gloria, who were being grossly affectionate in front of us.

Mendoza kissed Gloria's forehead. "He hasn't had a drink since he got here. But he's on some shit, that's for sure."

Gloria rolled her eyes and shot Fischer a look of disapproval. Fischer smiled and stretched his neck. He was definitely high out of his mind. "What are you on?" I pushed his shoulder and he moved like Jell-O.

"Some soldiers dropped him off here like that, but I don't know them. I think he bought pills from them."

"Again?" I groaned. This motherfucker was really driving me crazy.

I kneeled in front of him, and I saw Gloria and Mendoza leaving the room in the reflection of the window behind Fischer. There was a plastic baggie sticking out of the pocket of his sweats. I grabbed it and he tried to stop me, but his reflexes were too slow from the drugs. Long white rectangle pills and traces of white powder from them danced as I shook the bag in front of his face.

"You won't be able to do this shit soon. They're going to piss-test you regularly and they will kick you out or lock you up if you don't pass."

"I know, I know. I just wanted one last night to celebrate," he groaned. There was a sadness in his voice that almost made me feel for him. Almost.

"Your sister is completely destroyed right now and you're here high as a kite, not having to feel shit."

14

He closed his eyes. "You're here, too. Not with her."

"She wouldn't let me stay," I defended myself.

This irresponsible asshole gets to numb himself with drugs and I have to just deal with it, and so does she. It was unfair and infuriating. Times like this I wished I could show Karina why I helped her brother enlist, why his life was in danger, and why all of this was for her, whether she could see it yet or not.

"You and I both are the last people she would want around her right now." His voice was fading, his eyes bloodshot slits. "Maybe ever. And look, I know I'm a fuckup, but tonight just leave me alone with my mistakes? Please, bro." His desperation bled through his intoxication.

I didn't say another word as Fischer's head slopped to the side. I just sat at stared at him, hoping I was doing the right thing. I watched the rain through the window as he slept—or passed out— and Gloria and Mendoza never came back in.

CHAPTER TWO

"Whose food is this?" I tossed the dirty bowl into the overflowing sink.

No one answered and I didn't even know if anyone was home except me. Gunk-crusted dishes stacked in a chaotic pile filled my usually clean sink. There were beer bottles, half empty and fully empty on the counter, wadded-up potato chip bags, and crunchy pieces of instant ramen noodles in their foil wrappings with flavor packets torn on the corner and dotted with "chicken"-flavored crumbles of seasoning. For a couple of weeks now, things had gone downhill. I had never allowed my place to look this disastrous, but I couldn't find it in me to give a shit lately. I used my teeth to tear open another packet and pushed a pile of empty take-out containers out of my way. I was fully aware that the trash can was merely three feet away, but it didn't matter. Not much mattered these days.

I filled a bowl with water and pushed the noodles down enough to be covered before lazily putting my dinner into the microwave. I grew up eating these cheap ramen packets, ten cents apiece. Most of the time, I didn't bother to cook them and just dumped the uncooked noodles into a Ziploc, poured the seasoning in, and took it to school. I spent more time making my sister's lunch when she got tired of being in the "free lunch" line. Whatever I could do for her because she was the brains of the family and needed the fuel more than me. Our mom's work schedule of two jobs didn't allow the luxury of some families. Time-consuming lunch preparation, perfect packages strategically including every section of the food table, handwritten notes wishing us a good day, expensive sodas and name-brand chips . . . we didn't have any of that, but we had a mother who woke up before the sun and barely got a meal herself before her night job.

I used to be bitter about it and wish I had what the privileged kids I saw on TV or met during football game parties at the rich white schools had. Being what was considered talented at football gave me opportunities to mingle with kids who lived in wealthy Atlanta suburbs. I got invited to big houses with pools in the yard and once, a kid gave me a brand-new pair of Jordans just because he already had a similar pair. It would have been easy to feel like he was looking down on me, but I didn't really care since I knew I could sell the shoes and buy my sister a new school uniform and take her to the movies with the money. New cars and fancy new Nikes, but none of them seemed to know what sacrifice was. Not one of them knew what it meant to work for what they had, and it made me appreciate my mom more. Even though she couldn't go to my games often because of her work, I knew that the reason I could play was because of her. Karina melted into my thoughts. One of the things I respected about her the most was how hard she worked to have what she wanted. She could easily ask her dad for help, but she never did. If something was broken, she would fix it. She was proud that everything she had was from her own two hands, literally, and it made me feel connected to her because I valued working for what you have more than most people my age.

The familiar smell of the ramen made me want to call my mom or my sister, but I knew I wasn't in the headspace right now and they had more important shit going on in their lives than listening to me sulk on the phone and lie that my life was going great.

I heard the sound of the front door shut as I inhaled a mouthful of noodles. I knew every sound of this place, and most places.

"Yo! You home?" Fischer's voice rang through the duplex, bouncing from one wall to the other.

He walked into the kitchen before I bothered to answer him. His face was blotchy and his light hair a mess. Blue circles swollen under his normally bright eyes.

"You look like you feel like shit," I told him.

He nodded. "Because I do."

"Good."

Fischer lifted his T-shirt up and wiped his face with the bottom of it. "I am so out of shape. Basic is going to kill me." He plopped his head down on the counter.

He was leaving in about two months and had started trying to get into shape about a week ago.

"Yeah, and I'm sure the drugs help," I reminded him.

He shook his head. "You'd be surprised." His grin was sarcastic and charming, even if we were joking about something heavy.

"Have you talked to your sister yet?"

He groaned. "You ask me that every day."

"Have you?" I poked at his sweat-covered arm with my spoon. "Huh?"

He rolled his head, whining. "This is like having two annoying siblings annoy you at the same time."

"Good. You've completely ghosted her since she found out about you enlisting."

I was envious that she bothered him. She hadn't texted or called me once since that night. I kept checking her social media and for the first week it was great, but she eventually blocked me. I wondered if I had accidentally clicked something that gave away my stalking, or if she just didn't want to risk coming across me.

"So have you or not?"

He shook his head. "Every day that goes by makes it harder. I don't want to face her right now."

"Have you ever thought about how she must feel?" I sat my bowl down on the pile of dirty dishes as Fischer leaned up to face me. "It's for the best. You know that. If you explained to her why you did it, I think she would be more understanding. She wants the best for you, truly. She's probably so hurt now that it's been so long and you've avoided her."

"What does it matter to you how she feels? You hurt her, too, so don't give me that shit about thinking about how she feels when she's really probably more heartbroken by you than me."

A small hole opened up in my chest as he spoke. I knew he was wrong, but the idea of hurting her and betraying her trust had been feasting on my corpse for the last two weeks.

"This isn't a competition of who is worse. We both fucked up, but you're her brother, her twin brother, and I'm just a guy she halfway dated and hates now."

He stood all the way up. "Bullshit. You know you're not just a guy to her. We should have told her and you're right, I'll be the one who has to face her and deal with her pain, and you'll be able to run off to Atlanta soon. I'll have to see the disappointment in her face, and you'll never see her face again."

I reached for his shirt and balled my fist around the fabric. His green eyes went wide and he raised his hands up in the air.

"Sorry. Fuck. Sorry, Martin. I just feel like shit about it and am pushing it onto you. I'll go to her house tomorrow. I don't know how much longer I can avoid her, anyway. It's killing me day by day." He sighed and I let go of him.

"I don't think just showing up at her place without a warning is a good idea?"

"If I call her, she might be working or not answer. She's texted me too many times for me to say sorry over the phone. I need to just face the music." His voice was shaking and I knew even though his words sounded like he barely cared, he absolutely did and hated disappointing her. We had that in common.

As selfish as it was, I felt like I knew Karina more than he did, which I knew wasn't true, but it made something inside of me feel satisfied or fulfilled. Like the time I spent with her wasn't a dream or a waste of time. I would rather have felt that feeling at least once in my pathetic life than never at all, and since people like me didn't get a fairy-tale ending, I would take what I could get and leave it at that. I was already pushing my luck by having someone like Karina give me the time of day, and now the time had run out and I needed to get over her. Having her brother around me constantly didn't help me forget her, but maybe that's why I decided to spend my time helping him make his life better. I couldn't do that for her, so maybe doing it for him would help me repent for some of my sins?

I needed to work on controlling my temper and I knew my anger wasn't directed toward Fischer, just like his anger wasn't directed toward me. We both hated ourselves. That was the thing we had the most in common.

CHAPTER **THREE**

Karina

Ding-dong. The bell on the door of the spa rang and I sprang up from the rolling chair I was lazily circling in. We hadn't had a customer in almost an hour and not one of us had anyone on the books, so I was tending to the spa alone. I had dusted and vacuumed and filled up the oils in everyone's rooms. There was literally nothing else to do except scroll on my phone, and I was purposely trying to avoid that. I went through my typical pattern of typing Kael's name in, and as usual, there was nothing new. He had completely disappeared from my life. No apology, no trying to make excuses. Nothing. I blocked and unblocked him twice before tossing my phone onto the desk. The door opened forcefully and I had a potential customer to relieve my boredom. The man walking up to the counter had a sharp, square jaw like a pit bull, and an Alabama State cap covering dark hair and hooded dark eyes. He was tall, ungodly so.

"Hi, how can I help you?" I asked him, looking up at the clock on the wall and out the glass door behind him. It was dark and that gave me chills. I hated being in the spa alone lately. I couldn't tell why, but I'd had this anxious, dreadful-as-hell feeling in the pit of my stomach for the last couple of weeks and just couldn't shake it. All I could think about was my brother going to basic training and being screamed at by drill sergeants. I couldn't stop imagining him with his hair buzzed off, in ACUs doing push-ups and obstacle courses in the scorching sun. Visions of him dodging IEDs and gunshots overseas consumed me, making my brain even more chaotic.

By the time the man spoke, I had mentally left the lobby and was on a different planet. I was becoming so detached from my daily life that I wasn't sure if I was in the right headspace to be giving treatments to clients.

"Do you have any openings right now?" he asked in a husky voice.

My stomach dropped for the third time.

"Uh . . . " I thought about telling him no, that I was booked for the rest of the night, but I really needed the money and my electricity was due the next week. And he most likely wouldn't try to murder me. He didn't know I was alone here and that was good.

I wished I didn't have to think that way, and even though I knew that I was more paranoid than most people, I also knew as a woman there were dangers around me all the time.

"Yeah . . . what sort of treatment are you wanting?" I asked him, pointing up at the menu on the wall.

The laminated posters were all curled up at the corners, and some of the prices were barely legible because of Mali's scribbly handwriting that had been fading since the spa opened. Every once in a while, I tried to use a Sharpie to trace over the faded sign, since Mali couldn't care less about it. She rolled her eyes every time I told her I would gladly make a new one since it seemed to only bother me.

"Like, an hour? I need a massage bad. My back is all fucked up right here." He rubbed his hand on the top of his hip, twisting his body slowly.

"I can do an hour treatment. This is your first time here, yeah?" I recognized every regular client, mine and everyone else's.

He nodded and I slid the clipboard with the new client sheets over to him. His fingernails were dirty and his hands were so dry that his knuckles were cracked and had white rings around them. His face looked younger than his hands, but even looking straight into his almost black eyes, I couldn't guess how old he was. I could tell he worked hard and either was from Alabama or just liked the team.

As he filled out the paperwork, I slid my phone from my pocket and discreetly checked it. A notification popped up right as I went to unlock the screen. It was from Instagram; I had two new followers and three likes on my latest post, which was a picture of a dandelion peeking up from blades of grass. Two followers, huh? I might as well be an influencer with my three hundred followers and twenty likes on some of my posts. My fingernails on a chair got hundreds of likes, though, so it clearly didn't take much to impress the people of the internet.

"Here you go," the man said, interrupting my daydream of being paid hundreds of thousands of dollars to post aesthetically pleasing photos on an app.

"Thanks . . . " I looked for his name. "Thomas. When you're ready, I'm all set."

He nodded and I led him back to my room. When we stepped inside the small space, he felt even bigger to me. So big that I had to look up at him when I spoke. I turned the music on and circled around the table to light another candle on the shelf.

"Besides your lower back, do you have any problem areas for me to focus on?"

"My head," he said, and I waited to see if he was joking or not.

He smiled a little and looked way less murderous when his cheeks dimpled.

"They don't pay me enough for that, so anything else?" I smiled back at him, and he shook his head. He wasn't so scary after all.

"And for pressure? Do you want more Swedish, Thai style? Light, medium, deep tissue?"

He looked confused. "Don't know the difference, but I guess medium? I've never gotten a massage before."

I groaned internally. I would either turn him into a regular or ruin his first experience. I hated the pressure. Self-inflicted, yes, but it still made me anxious. Why did I always have to be like this? It was exhausting.

"Okay." I forced a small smile. "I'll give you a few minutes to undress to your comfort level and place your personal items in the basket. Go ahead and lie face down under the sheet and blanket when you're done, and I'll be back in about two minutes or so. Take your time."

I walked out of the room and tied the curtain closed. I found myself on my phone again, this time rereading my last one-way conversation with Austin. Three **where are you?** messages and one **if anyone should be pissed and not answering, it's me** later and still nothing. My twin brother and I had been through our share of fights and there had been times that we didn't speak for weeks, but this was different. He'd done something that he knew would put a huge crack in our relationship and didn't seem to give a single fuck about it. Unanswered calls, even more unanswered texts. He completely ghosted me. His audacity was at an all-time high.

He was a fucking liar now—no longer just a boy who fibbed sometimes to get what he wanted from our parents or from girls. He was a man now, one who fucking lied to me and joined the Army with the help of Kael, whom I should have known better than to trust in the first place. But of course I was charmed by him, just like he'd planned, and I allowed myself to be used in the game he was playing with my father. A game more involved and way more intricate than I could even think about right now. I scrolled the conversation all the way up to when Austin was on his way here from his short-lived stint in North Carolina with our creepy uncle. Everything had changed so much since then, it felt like a completely different reality.

"Uh, ma'am?" The voice scared me enough to jump from right where I was standing in the hallway back to reality.

"Shit," I whispered to myself. How long was I out in the hall-way? I had no idea.

"Coming!" I peeped, instead of just playing it off like he had been waiting the appropriate amount of time.

Pulling back the curtain, I rushed over to the table to attend to my neglected new client, who for sure was never coming back, not even to murder me, let alone to get another treatment.

"How is the headrest? Are you comfortable?"

He nodded and I pulled the sheet up to cover his entire back to begin. As my hands slid across his shoulder blades, my mind wandered out of the room, down the hall, and out the front door to the same place it always went lately.

CHAPTER **FOUR**

I got home just after ten. Thomas, my new client, was the last of the day. He rebooked with me for two weeks out, and I thanked my lucky stars that he didn't leave unhappy. The hour went so fast, while my mind ran through an entire lifetime, yet when I got home, time dripped as slow as room temperature honey. Elodie was asleep on the couch when I got there, so I turned the TV off, sat down on the chair, and stared into the darkness of my living room. I used to be so afraid of the dark and sometimes still ran and jumped over the side of my bed to avoid anything that could possibly be hiding under there. I wasn't as afraid of the ghosts anymore or the man who hid under the bed in the little girl's room in that *Urban Legend* movie that scared the hell out of me as a teenager, but that eerie feeling still hadn't fully disappeared. I spent my life with ghosts, alive and not.

Elodie lay there fast asleep. I was relieved as I'd tried to avoid conversation with her about all my drama these last few weeks. But I wondered how things were with her husband, Phillip, and what fruit her baby was the size of this week. I'd been working and sleeping and not doing much else. Of course I knew that I tried to detach from Elodie purposely—my pride was stronger than my curiosity. So I made plans to go on my own to my favorite little craft store the last two Saturdays and had then spent both Friday nights talking myself out of going the next morning.

The clock on the wall chimed. It was ten and I was both tired and wired. My body was exhausted, but my mind wouldn't stop moving. I sat back in the recliner as my head pounded. The house felt empty, even with Elodie on the couch.

Maybe it was me who felt empty? I'd had a lot of realizations lately, *that* being one of them. And also that I didn't have many friends, and truthfully never had. My closest one was pregnant and spending more and more time with her Army wife friends, which I understood, but it just helped exacerbate the feeling of loneliness that was already consuming me. I didn't have family at that moment. It had been weeks since I had seen or spoken to my father; the recent rupture in our relationship was far from repaired. Yeah, my brother and I were twins, so we would be bonded for life, but he was nowhere to be found, as per usual when he fucked up.

Time was another thing. Three months ago, my life felt completely different. Austin was in North Carolina. My dad and I had a functional if stale relationship. Kael was a stranger to me. And that was easier, simpler. It seemed impossible that I had known Kael for such a short amount of time and yet he'd managed to fuck up so much of my life. Even as I sat in my dark, lonely living room, he came to mind. I just couldn't stop thinking about him and it sure as hell wasn't doing me any good. I barely knew him, and the him I knew was a fucking liar. Why couldn't I get that through my thick skull? I kept repeating the same thoughts, ruminating on the fact that my life had been turned upside down, but no matter how hard I tried, I couldn't think of a solution and stayed in the vicious cycle.

It had only been two weeks since I found out that Kael had helped Austin secretly sign up for the Army—literally the worst possible scenario for me, and Kael *knew* that. He just didn't care.

My knees started shaking and I ran my fingers through my hair. The clock had barely moved, yet I had played through the entirety of our time together, from our first meeting to our last. The way the rain pounded against my skin that final day was never going to leave me, no matter how hard I tried to forget. Ironically, I could imagine that over the next few months, I would ultimately spend more time remembering Kael than I did knowing him. How fucked up.

I used to be good at forgetting things—sometimes I even made myself forget that I had a mother who ran out on us and didn't look back. I was that good. But there was something about Kael that just wouldn't leave me alone, and I was torturing myself with it. I'd never counted days before or stared at a clock just begging for it to move. I was becoming obsessed with time, I could feel it. I worried about becoming fixated, trying not to be as obsessive as my mother, but somehow that only made it worse.

I just ended up fixating on trying not to fixate and inevitably wound up back at the kitchen table, sitting and staring at the clock again, wondering if time would ever speed up. I hadn't had an appetite and had been living off a few bites of toast that Elodie forced me to eat earlier today, and a couple bites of Mali's noodles. Mali had watched in disapproval as I sat in the break room, slowly chewing while staring at the wall. I told her I had eaten before my shift, but she always knew when I was lying. I just couldn't stand how disappointed and pissed off I was at myself. I felt like a total fucking idiot around everyone. Elodie especially, but also Mali. Even with my clients who knew nothing of the situation, my mind convinced me that they did, and that they knew how gullible and just completely stupid I had been for falling for Kael's lies and bullshit. I hated myself even more for missing him, for spending hours every single day thinking about what I would say to him if I ever saw his lying face again. I loathed that at night I missed the warmth of his body and often woke up with tearstained cheeks and swollen eyes.

I wanted to get to the next phase of heartbreak, the one that everyone on Instagram claimed would compel me to go out with my friends and drink wine and laugh until we cried. Since I wasn't much of a crier, and I didn't have any friends, really, all of that seemed unlikely. If I could just get to a point where I didn't look at his Facebook or didn't think about the way his sweat tasted on his lips when he kissed me . . .

I pushed myself up out of the chair and went to the kitchen. My stomach growled at the sight of the fridge. I couldn't remember when I ate last. I grabbed a bag of bread from the counter and sat at the table. It was so dry, but not really having an appetite, I didn't care so much and at least Elodie wasn't here to overtoast it.

What felt like an hour later, I blinked out of a memory of Kael on my front porch speaking to me in poetry as we just stared at the stars and talked about them. It felt kind of good to remember those moments because they were some of the few memories from my life that I was happy to revisit, even knowing the pain that would follow.

I looked up at a crack in the ceiling, imagining it had turned into a huge lightning-strike shape that spanned nearly the entire kitchen. I stared through my roof, imagining the sky. Didn't the universe have enough sympathy to have the crack come next month, when it might not be raining nonstop like it had been the last few days? Knowing my luck lately, I wouldn't be surprised if it caused a problem with my roof that I didn't have the money to fix.

I picked at the skin around my fingernails. The polish was gone and I had started going for the skin. I tried not to and even did what my mom taught me when I got my first crush on a boy and started to care, which was to sit on my hands whenever I had the urge. I hardly did it, but the memory of her advice was there at least.

I remembered too the day she said that, our mom had smiled wide at something she had gotten in the mail. She had clenched the letter to her chest when she opened it, Austin and I watching from the stairs. She'd looked up at the sky, a light in her spirit shining brightly. It was because of the light in her that day, the way she was beaming, that Austin and I looked at each other instead of her. I think we were scared of the darkness that was surely to follow. The light never lasted long and we knew that.

CHAPTER **FIVE**

I was scared shitless when I first woke up with my cheek against the kitchen table. My neck hurt from the way I'd slept, hanging halfway off the table. As I cracked my neck and circled it around, my dreams came back to me: *Austin and I at the edge of the stairs, my mom making lasagna with us as she danced around the kitchen to Alanis Morrisette* . . . and then another dream about a crying girl with blood as tears. It had to be a metaphor for something, but I didn't have the capacity to analyze it right now.

At four in the morning, I had woken up with a plastic-wrapped loaf of bread next to my head, and closed the twist tie on the bag before dragging myself to my bedroom and flopping straight onto my bed without taking off my work clothes.

When I finally got out of bed, it took a long shower to make me feel somewhat human. Walking down the hall into the kitchen, I popped a coffee pod into my old Keurig and waited for my life-blood to pour into the mug. Outside the window, the sun was still hiding, and the sky was still crying as I sipped my coffee and picked at the stale bread still on a plate from last night.

Elodie appeared in the doorway of the kitchen. "I'll be back soon. Just grabbing some things from the store," she told me, hugging the back of my shoulders. She smelled like fruit and linen.

"You sleep well?" I asked, looking at her frail face. She was pink and glowing, but her eyes were puffy. She needed to rest.

"Kare, I'm sorry if you heard us arguing last night," she said, standing in front of me, her blond bob swaying a little. I looked into her big blue-and-bloodshot eyes and she bit down on her lip. "Phillip's just . . . he's stressed because he's not here. So, we're kind of fighting a lot. But he's fine. Everything's fine," she assured me, her hands fidgeting in front of her body.

I absolutely didn't believe her for one second, but I wanted her to feel comfortable and talk to me when she decided she wanted to.

"I didn't hear anything." I shrugged. "I slept at the kitchen table, though." I laughed a little to drown out the sound of the crying girl from my dream last night.

Elodie smiled, relief filling her adorable face.

"Okay. I'll be back in a little while. I have to work, too." She double-kissed my cheeks and rushed out the back door.

"Bye!" I yelled to her as the screen door snapped back after her exit.

I hated knowing they were fighting, and I hoped like hell it would get worked out for her sake, but if it didn't, I would be here for her and the baby in every way I could.

According to Elodie, she'd watched a YouTube video that told her the calmer she was during the pregnancy and the calmer the environment her baby was born into, the more calm the baby would be, so I was going to do my best to help make that happen.

I put a load of my laundry in the wash and went back into my bedroom. It looked so different with my mattress bare, so much bigger without the pillows across the top of my bed. I moved the junk on the top of my dresser around. I swiped my finger across the surface, through the gray dust, and scribbled a *K* and a heart, but caught myself and scribbled it out. I had always been an inveterate doodler, all the way back to my middle school agenda book. Dust collected so fast in my little house, I could never really keep up with it. That, or the succulent on my dresser. It was dead now.

Jesus, I couldn't even keep a cactus alive.

I sat down on my bed and pulled my phone from my pajama shorts pocket. I never got any calls, but I still checked my phone constantly. I wiped the screen off on my pajamas and set it on my dresser while I chose my clothes for the day. The humidity from the morning rain seeped in through the cracks around my windows and my room was like a sauna; it was miserable. I was nearly soaked by the time I finished getting dressed. I turned on the air conditioner in the corner, then turned it right back off, knowing my bills were high enough as it was. I needed to get out of my room before I spent the morning unnecessarily redecorating.

Dishes. I could wash dishes. I had to be at work in half an hour and was already dressed in my uniform, anyway. I went with an all-black, funereal pair of scrubs. I had time to kill, and I knew Elodie would do them if I didn't—and why should she have to be the one to scrape off the pan from the other night's failed attempt at a lasagna?

I turned on the water as her name popped up on my phone screen on the counter.

Do you want coffee? I'm almost back home

I looked at the empty mug and replied. The more caffeine I could have, the better the day would be. Around noon I'd get jittery, but that was just part of my routine these days.

I thought about inviting Elodie to spend uninterrupted time

with me tonight after we got off work. That would be my chance to confess everything that had happened, everything I'd been hiding from her. I could make a reservation at the only restaurant in town that actually took reservations. I knew she loved their steak. It would be good for us to hang out outside the house for once. It would also be good for her to know that I was actively trying to spend time with her, and not just occupy the same space, sitting on the couch while we both tried to stay awake with our phones in our hands. So far, I was able to get away with telling her that I ended things with Kael because he's being discharged soon, and I didn't want to get wrapped up into that. She knew my stance on being with a soldier, so I thought I had convinced her, but the more times she asked, I saw the doubt grow in her eyes when I told her half-truths. Elodie was great at not prying and she knew me well enough to know that pushing me to talk about what I wasn't ready to discuss wouldn't help our friendship in the long run.

Maya Angelou taught Oprah, who taught me, that when people show you who they are, you should believe them the first time. People are often less much complicated than they want us to believe—they seem predictable—but when they show their true colors, that's who they really are. I tried to give the Army wives the benefit of the doubt that their budding friendship with Elodie was honest and genuine, despite the prejudgment engraved into my brain. I hadn't really met them, but I knew how cliques of young Army wives could be. They could be sugar or salt. I was suspicious that this group of women wasn't the kindest to Elodie before, making her feel like an outcast at first, and then suddenly she was a part of their clique. I remembered the way my mom was treated like an outcast, and how that rejection made her rebel against her idea of the typical way an officer's wife was supposed to behave—the way my dad wanted her to be as the homemaker and bearer of his last name. My mom was never one to follow the crowd, but the pressure cooked her until she exploded.

Even Estelle, my dad's borderline Stepford wife, was at times the target of childish gossip, despite my dad being high up on the totem pole here at Fort Benning. They lived in the biggest model of house the post offered, and my dad bought her the nicest purses, tax-free, from the PX. She went above and beyond for acceptance from the women, from their bake sales and group trips to Savannah when tax season came. Still, no matter what she did, some of the wives still gossiped. They would say my dad's "crazy," "trashy" first wife took off and never came back. Some of the other wives had actually liked my mom and they would whisper that Estelle was probably having an affair with our dad before my mom left. Austin got in a lot of arguments, sometimes even fights with kids our age, over our mom and the mystery of her disappearance.

Elodie and my mom were completely different people, and maybe times had changed, but given the rhetoric I had grown up hearing, it was hard to release my judgment. Elodie felt like such an easy target for mean girls. So that didn't help. Her kindness and grace came so effortlessly and her sweet accent that always made everything sound much softer made her an outsider, in a way. One of them also recently accused her of hitting on their husband, whom Elodie had only double-cheek-kissed out of innocent habit. They turned on her quickly and had even made a post on Facebook talking about her in detail, but for some reason, they didn't say her name. It seemed they had all moved on since Elodie was hanging out with them again.

But poor Elodie, she was getting it from all sides; Phillip was calling more often from Afghanistan and their disagreements grew by the day, it seemed. She hadn't been sleeping much compared to the previous weeks when it seemed like that was all she did. She was so tired lately that by the time she got home from so-and-so's house, or from a Family Readiness Group meeting, she turned on Netflix and passed out on the couch less than halfway through an episode, but then she would be wide awake and on the phone at three in the morning. She continued to sleep on the couch, saying it was less lonely than a bed; she slept holding on to a body pillow and I started to wonder if I would be less lonely if I tried one, too.

I had a new philosophy of late: every single hour of sleep meant less time awake to face my shit show of a life. Less of a chance of confronting my brother. More time in my bed also meant less of a chance of running into Kael. Less of a chance of dealing with anything that I didn't want to deal with. By the time I got off work, and finished pulling the weeds that were taking over my yard, or cleaned the house, or even just stared at the crack in the kitchen ceiling, it was almost time to wake up and repeat it all over again. The problem was that all of those mind-numbing tasks actually had the opposite effect on me: my mind was anything but numb. My thoughts constantly churned and spun as I tried to make sense of everything that had gone down.

Prior to Kael, Brien was my only point of reference as an ex, and our breakups never bothered me this way. I was always the less emotional one, the one who didn't cry and didn't budge when I thought I was right. He was the apologizer . . . at least in the beginning.

Over the course of our relationship, he wore me down, and now, with him completely out of my life, I knew that our relationship had felt so big to me because it was the closest I had ever been with a man. In his case, a boy pretending to be a man, but most men that I'd met seemed to be in that class. But you know, daddy issues and all that. Given the man who raised me, it was only natural for me to attract men who weren't good for me.

Not Kael, though. Kael was an exception to nearly every rule. Every preconceived notion I had about men and relationships, he had proved them wrong.

Until he didn't.

What he did was reinforce that I should never trust people I barely knew. Well, trusting anyone was risky, since I couldn't trust Austin, my dad, or even myself lately.

I couldn't think about Austin, and how he was throwing his life away and was a coward for avoiding me. Or Kael, and how he was helping him do just that. Ugh, my mind was all over the place, making my heart race to try to keep up. It felt completely devastating at first, calling my brother at least twenty times, texting him long rants about my anger and even apologies about the rants. It became a cycle. I avoided my dad's stupid dinners the way Austin avoided me. I was growing tired of being the only person in my family who ever held themselves accountable. I was clearly still angry at Austin for not even trying to talk to me about it, or apologizing. The whole situation was completely unresolved and it made me sick thinking about it. Maybe it was time to cut him out of my life?

I couldn't decide today, but this total blackout of communication was driving me mad and I needed to keep my head as clear as possible by reminding myself daily that I couldn't change anything about this. I couldn't undo his contract with the Army, and I couldn't make him take accountability and have a conversation with me. I didn't even know exactly where Kael's house was, so I couldn't just show up there to force Austin to explain himself to me. I mentally had to come to terms with the fact that Austin was actively choosing himself over my feelings about his choices and that he didn't care about hurting me the way that I thought he did.

Water splashed on my feet, and I looked down to see it leaking over the edge of the kitchen sink, soaking my only pair of work shoes. I barely remembered turning the water on.

What the hell was wrong with me?

Quickly, I yanked the spout to shut the water off and let some of it drain while I grabbed a towel and threw it onto the floor, using my feet to dry the spillage. I added a ton of purple lavender dish soap to drown out the scent of the rest of the dishes. The pan from the other night was so blackened that I could still smell the burnt cheese. That, mixed with the humidity outside, did not create a good aroma in such an old house.

My fingers moved across a smooth ceramic plate. In the soapy water, I could feel the inscription of the date that Estelle and my dad promised to love one another until death did them part.

I was surprised that the fragile wedding gift had lasted so long in my chaotic little house.

CHAPTER SIX

The kitchen door opened and the sound of Elodie's native language glided through the room. She sounded upset, but I couldn't make out what she was saying. I had picked up a couple French words from her, but nothing that lead to actual understanding.

When I looked at her, she mouthed *Sorry* and made her way to the counter. Her arms were full of grocery bags and a coffee tray that she was about to drop. She was wearing her work uniform like I was, but had a rain jacket over it, with the hood pulled down. Her blond hair was dry, up in a little bun on her head. I grabbed a towel to wipe the soap off my hands and reached to help her.

The bags were heavier than they looked. One of them was filled with packs of construction paper, glue, and scissors. She really shouldn't have been carrying that much at once. The female voice on the other end of the line got much louder, almost barking out of the speaker, and Elodie took the phone away from her ear.

"My parents," she said to me as she set the bags down on the table.

I didn't know very much about her parents except that they weren't exactly thrilled when their daughter left France to marry an American soldier. It wasn't common to meet French citizens in military communities like this one. I had known a lot of wives from South America and Mexico, and one from Germany, but never from France.

Elodie had an entirely different life here in Georgia than what she had known in France; everything from the food to medical care to social norms was different in Europe than it was in the Southern U.S. In France, she lived with her parents in a town where everyone knew everyone. She often talked about how quiet life here was, how pleasantly boring it was. When Phillip got back from deployment in Afghanistan, her life would be easier and better, and things would run smoothly. Or so I hoped. But I worried about the anger in his voice that I heard during their Skype conversations and the way she was so defeated. I hoped their tension was just a phase and they were just having the standard newlywed, husband-is-deployed, wife-is-pregnant fights that many couples went through.

I knew my optimism was mostly feigned.

Elodie, still on the phone, moved toward the door and I stopped her.

"I'll get the rest. You can start putting them away?" I said.

She almost smiled, but whoever was on the phone said something that made her stop in her tracks and rest against the kitchen counter. She put the phone on speaker and dropped it onto the countertop. She spoke loudly, cutting against her mother's excessive volume and bite. I left the kitchen to get the rest of the stuff from the car, hoping that whatever was going on wasn't as bad as it seemed, and also hoping I would be quick enough to not get too soaked from the rain. I never had an umbrella or rain jacket when I needed one, and I had never owned rain boots. I was usually unprepared for regular life, and overly prepared for unlikely things. I had a full-on earthquake kit, for example, ready for the worst in southern Georgia, but no raincoat for the excessive rain that was the norm here.

I opened the screen door as Elodie stared at the phone with her tongue between her teeth. Dashing out, I yelped a little when the rain hit me and ran faster, trying not to slip in the mud next to the pavement. In the open trunk, just behind the few bags that were left, was a folded-up baby stroller. It was light green and looked almost new, but it wasn't in a box. Sometimes I forgot there would be another human in my little house in a few short months.

I reached in and touched the stroller, pausing for a moment before I grabbed the rest of the groceries and jogged to the back door of the house. The thick smell of wet soil filled the air; another unfinished project of mine was to finish the landscaping in my yard. The home improvements I'd been putting off for so long were slowly getting done, though. I'd almost completed tiling the bathtub and had changed all of my ancient silver doorknobs to sleek and modern black ones. All within a freaking week.

Neurotic or responsible? Maybe a little bit of both.

A truck drove through the stop sign and my stomach flipped. It wasn't Kael, it wasn't his truck, but it made me think of him and the sound of his loud Bronco and how the walls of my house would rattle when he revved his engine outside. The man driving the truck turned down the alleyway across the street, his big tires splashing rainwater everywhere.

I was wet now, just standing in the rain like a lost puppy. I shut the trunk, hurried inside, and slammed the back door. Elodie was off the phone and sitting at the kitchen table.

Her voice was brittle, her accent wrapping around her words more than usual. "I'm sorry about that." She sighed heavily, her eyes filling to the brim with tears. "They want me to come home."

"What?"

I sat down in the chair across from her and wiped the rain from my face. She looked a little stunned and the tip of her nose was red. She had the palest, clearest skin and rosy cheeks.

"What happened, El? Are you okay?"

"Someone . . . someone wrote my parents a stupid lie and they believe a stranger over me—"

"What do you mean? Who wrote to them?" I asked, beyond confused.

"Someone on Facebook wrote my mom a message saying that Phillip was cheating and these crazy things . . ."

"Who was it? Do you know them?"

She shook her head and didn't look at me as she said, "I think it was a fake account. It's all so stupid and not true. I don't know why someone would do that, or how they even found my parents."

I was at a loss for words. But I had so many questions.

"Why the hell would someone do that?" I asked the room.

"I hate this," she said, her shoulders beginning to shake. "And my doctor called on the way back and said my glucose test came back really low. It's just a lot of stress."

Her phone vibrated again, and *Papa* flashed on the screen. She flipped her phone over and pushed it away.

"I can't take much more. I can't." She pressed her fingers against her temples. Her chest rose and fell as her phone shook on the table.

"They don't think I can do this. None of it. Be married, be a mother. It's so much and the baby isn't even here yet." She started to cry. "I don't even have a place for the baby to live, I have no crib. Nothing. I don't know what I'm doing."

I inched my chair closer to her. "I'm sorry, El. You're going to make a great mom. I know you are. I'm not just saying that, either. I know you and your heart, and you're going to be fine. It will all be fine."

I tried to be as convincing as possible. The baby was on the way and Elodie needed a confidence boost. I meant it though, every word. I knew all kinds of moms, the good, the bad, and the really bad.

"Karina, I'm serious. I'm all alone here. If I have the baby and Phillip isn't home or gets hurt . . ." She was physically shaking. I leaned across the table and grabbed one of her hands. It was ice-cold.

"You're freezing," I told her.

She shrugged. "I'm okay. I don't care about being cold right now," she said emotionally. "My parents think I can't handle any of this. My dad pretty much just told me that on the phone and my mom agreed with him. They said they're scared. *Scared!*"

I was trying to process everything she was saying.

"Scared is a little much," I said, kind of pissed at her parents for saying that to her. It was too late for that conversation and their doubt only added to her stress. "I'm sorry they said that. They're wrong."

She barely looked at me.

"They also hate my husband now. They think he's a liar and having an affair while I'm *alone* here." She really stamped the word *alone*, and I felt like a bit of a failure for not making her feel like she wasn't alone. My heart broke for her because of their harshness. It reminded me of Kael saying, *People always have an opinion about others' choices and even if it's harmful, the selfishness of unburdening themselves outweighs the hurt it can cause.* More words of wisdom from the poet himself, Kael Martin.

"You're not alone," I told Elodie, pushing Kael to the back of my mind. I couldn't have guessed how many seconds had gone between us since she spoke. She looked at me and I knew that a defeated woman's eyes never lied. She was breaking, right then, and I could feel it in the air, see it in her body language.

"I have you. And I appreciate that and love you, but I'm used to my big family and my friends and my life back home." She paused and seemed to tell herself to redirect her words. Guilt lay heavy on her face. "It is better having more friends now. But my baby will not have any family here. And how will I work? I don't make enough money for daycare. There aren't enough hours at the spa."

"El. We live right here, I'll watch the baby while you work and we'll make sure our schedules aren't the same."

She was quick to remind me that our arrangement wasn't permanent. "Karina, my house will be far from work when Phillip's back."

"You could still drop the baby off here," I offered, trying to think of another fix for her problem.

"You can't solve this for me. I know you want to, but you really can't help me with this. Maybe I shouldn't have gotten married at all? I came here so fast, without knowing what it would be like and how much time I would be alone. My mom is right that I barely knew Phillip before I got on a plane, then was pregnant shortly after. I don't know what we were thinking?" Her voice broke and she lifted her hands into the air as if she was asking the sky. "What was I thinking?"

She started to cry harder. I could tell how hard she had been trying to keep it in, but this wasn't something she could hold back any longer. Her body seemed to need it, and she sank lower into the chair as she sobbed.

Tears spilled down her cheeks and her skin reddened even more. She touched her hand to her stomach and heaved. I didn't know what to say that could make this better and maybe she was right, I couldn't fix it. It was beyond me.

"I can't even afford a ticket home. God, what am I going to do? They are so angry and now they are making me doubt everything," she cried. A few seconds went by before she added, panicked, "I'm so scared."

She was full-on sobbing, choking into a heavy fit of coughing. I grabbed her a cup of water as quickly as I could and watched her gulp down the entire thing. She patted her chest.

"My chest hurts. My head feels like it's going to explode. I—"

The tears stopped falling from her eyes, but her body was still reacting as if she were hysterically crying. Her shoulders shook with dry sobs. Within a few seconds, her panic took over, and I watched her shift into worried-mom mode. Her hand flew to her stomach again and I tried to reach for her to offer her more water. She shook her head, taking deep breaths, hysterically, tearlessly sobbing.

Her sobs were almost loud enough to drown out the noise of the back door opening and Austin strolling through like we were even on speaking terms.

I got a little dizzy as I took the two of them in.

CHAPTER **SEVEN**

My brother looked like he hadn't slept in a week. And he also looked like a porcupine with his blond hair sticking up in the front and around the sides but soaked and dripping down his forehead.

There he was, in a blue T-shirt and black jeans ripped at the knees, looking dazed and confused.

His appearance made my anger toward him bite even more. His black sneakers squeaked across my clean kitchen floor.

I moved toward him, speaking in a low voice. "Why the *hell* are you here?"

"Kare, come on . . ." His tired eyes went from me to where Elodie was at the table, and he immediately rushed to her.

"What the hell? Are you okay?" he shouted, then turned to me. "Is she okay?"

My heart was racing and my chest lit up with borderline rage. I couldn't believe his audacity! He had our mother's nerve.

And our father's, too—this was insane.

Right then, he looked years younger than he was. He was never the kind of boy who was in control of his emotions—we were twins in so many ways, but that wasn't one of them. The way he was looking at Elodie reminded me of the little blue-eyed boy who cried when his dad's deployment orders got moved up by six months. He used to cry every time our dad would deploy. The opposite of me. As we got older, I felt relief when they came, even though I'd never admit that to anyone.

"Are you okay?" Austin asked Elodie again, as she doubled over as far as she could go. Her body was shaking, her arms wrapped around her stomach.

"My . . . my stomach, feels weird. The baby . . ." She shook her head. "I don't want to be dramatic if this isn't something serious."

"You're pregnant and don't seem fine. Let's just call your doctor or someone?" my brother insisted.

I tried to think of who to call to help us. It's not like I could call my mom and ask her what to do. Or Estelle.

"We need to take her to Martin right now," he said impatiently.

"What—" I started, then stopped.

"The hospital," he clarified as I nodded. Duh, my brother was talking about the hospital on Fort Benning with the same name as Kael.

"On a scale from one to ten, what's your—" Austin mocked in a voice that was supposed to mimic a doctor.

"Was that your doctor impression?" she asked him through labored breaths.

"Yep. Sorry I'm no Doctor Stewart or whatever the hell Patrick Dempsey's name is on that doctor show." Austin made Elodie smile, though the color of her face was getting more and more transparent as we all sort of laughed.

Inside I was panicking, but I was also trying to be outwardly calm by laughing with them. And it was genuine laughter. I felt empty and whole and concerned and like everything was fine. Emotions are funny like that, how we can feel so many things at once. The human power to be all the things at the same time, the pure weight of so many different things piling onto my chest, felt like an ancient and heavy punishment from a very unsympathetic and callous god. Feeling too much led to pain and problems and trauma and unrequited love and loss of control, all in one person, and then there was the fact that Elodie was possibly going into early labor in my kitchen.

My brain was all over the damn place and we were laughing about *Grey's Anatomy*?

"I'm more of a Doug Ross kind of girl, anyway," Elodie told him through heavy breaths.

Her hand held her stomach and she arched her back.

"I don't know who that is, but—"

She gawked at him. "What do you mean, you don't? It's an American series and it's George Clooney and you don't know?" Elodie arched again.

"Guys?" I said in my head about three times before I actually said it to them.

They both looked over at me. Elodie was ghostlike now.

"Okay. Okay. We should go." She agreed with me before I even had to force her.

"Elodie, can you stand up? Should we just go straight to the emergency room? Let me Google it. Just to check."

I knew that she was having a panic attack of some sort and it would probably pass soon or get worse, you just never knew, but with a baby growing inside of her, there were no chances to be taken, especially since she had gotten a call from her doctor about her blood sugar level just an hour ago. I Googled her symptoms and within seconds found confirmation that we should definitely be going to the emergency room at this point.

"Yep. We need to go. Let's go, El."

Her phone vibrated on the counter. I checked to make sure

Elodie wasn't looking at me and turned the phone over so I could see the familiar photo of her father filling the screen once more. I ignored the call while flipping the phone back upside down.

"We just need to make sure the baby is fine. It won't take long. I'll go with you."

"The ER won't be as busy right now. I'll come, too," Austin assured her.

"You don't need to come, Austin."

Elodie sighed and I watched the rise and fall of her chest. She sounded like she could breathe better than a minute ago, but she was clearly not okay. "Austin can come."

I looked at her quizzically, but it wasn't the time to question her. Elodie nodded as Austin bent down and tucked his arms under her legs, lifting her body into his arms like she was a bag of groceries.

"I can walk," Elodie protested, but didn't make a move to get down.

He shook his head and lifted the hood of her jacket back over her hair to cover it from the rain and she sighed. As Austin carried her across my yard to the car, I searched for my keys, which turned out to be in the pocket of my uniform the entire time. My hands were trembling even though everything felt pretty normal. Well, not normal, but not like in the movies where everyone is screaming and rushing and someone's crying and it's just completely chaotic.

My hands being in my pockets reminded me that I had to get to work, like right now.

Fuck my life.

Running past them, I opened the back door of my car, and Austin gently placed Elodie on the seat. When he finished and I ensured she was comfortable, it took everything in me not to tell my brother to sit in the back, or—better yet—to go back to Kael's house where he was likely still staying. His presence was clearly making Elodie feel better, maybe because she thought, rightfully so, that I would have no clue what to do here, but Austin wouldn't, either. Whatever her reason, she seemed to be calmer now that he had arrived. She had her face buried in her hands with her head leaning against the backseat.

As he opened the passenger door, I sighed dramatically, hoping he would hear me, and got in the car. Immediately I turned the music on and checked on Elodie again. Austin was staring out the window as she wept in the backseat. His leg was shaking like it always did when he was worried. I thought I saw his lips moving, but I couldn't hear anything over Ryan Seacrest's voice on the radio. I didn't know what to say to either of them, so I just drove the car.

When I pulled onto the highway, my service engine light came on.

When it rained, it poured.

Literally.

"El, do you have your military ID?" I called to her over the squeak of my windshield wipers, ignoring the engine light.

I hoped she did, because, depending on the gate guard's mood, being a woman in pain wouldn't stop them from turning us away without it. Even her blotchy, tearstained face and pregnant stomach most likely wouldn't sway them.

"I grabbed it from the entertainment center," Austin told us. "Kare, listen—" he started as I switched lanes to pass a semitruck.

"Don't," I snapped.

He put his hands together on his lap and I added, "Not now."

I glanced at Elodie in the rearview mirror. She was looking down at her stomach, tears streaking her face. She didn't need to get dragged into this building blowout between Austin and me.

Elodie caught my eyes. "I never had these attacks until I moved here. Everything is such a mess lately."

"Your life was way different before. You also didn't have a husband at war or a pineapple-sized baby in your belly."

Her eyes lit up a little and the corner of her mouth lifted for a quick second. "Yes. This is true. I'm sorry for ruining everyone's day."

She caught my eyes in the mirror again. She had stopped crying, but her shoulders were still shaking.

"You didn't ruin anything," Austin comforted her. Even though I was still unbelievably pissed at him, I was grateful he was helping Elodie.

"We'll be there in like ten minutes," I said.

Austin reached over and tried to touch my hand, something he used to do when our parents would bicker in the car. Usually on the way home from a "fun" family weekend that my mom forced on all of us. She couldn't stand being in the house much, just like my dad couldn't stand her. It was like our parents simply couldn't be around one another for the full two and a half days of a weekend, so by the time we drove home on Sunday from whatever escape my mom had talked my dad into, they would scream at each other in the car. It always started with a "joke" from my dad and ended with a slammed door or my mom sleeping on the swing on the porch. I swore she liked it better out there than inside my dad's officer-grade house, which she never felt was hers.

Sometimes our parents were the reason Austin and I bonded and clung to one another; at other times, they were why we pushed each other away. This time, when I jerked my hand away from his, Austin was fully the villain. He was just like our dad. And even though I was sure my dad had something to do with his enlisting, neither he nor our mom could be blamed for this. Austin had betrayed me, and I didn't want him to touch me. I didn't even want him in my car.

My brother leaned against the window in the passenger seat and stared ahead. I knew that look. That devastation and longing for forgiveness and approval. But I couldn't give it to him. He hadn't popped a tire on my bike, or knocked the head off my doll, like when we were kids. This was a sun-and-moon difference. Night and day. And it felt good to hurt him this way, to not give in and forgive him just because I hated when he was sad.

He'd made a choice, despite the promise we'd made to one another as kids. He would be shipped off to basic training. Then off to Iraq or Afghanistan, or whatever country we were invading at that moment. It was sure to be poison for him, as my experience with the Army had always been, and I wasn't ready to talk to him about it. No matter how many times I played out the conversation in my head, it wasn't going to change the reality of what was coming, whether I liked it or not, and I really wasn't ready to have that fight in this moment.

The three of us drove in silence, each quietly suffering in our own way.

CHAPTER EIGHT

We had been waiting almost an hour before the nurse called Elodie's name.

Austin had stayed with us the whole time, showing Elodie pictures of "ugly babies" on Facebook. He'd made her laugh, but that didn't mean he was suddenly a saint. Elodie stood and I followed her, past the children with red faces and snotty noses, past the soldiers in ACUs, past all the other people with phones stuck to their palms, including many, many worn-out parents and hyper children. The waiting area was huge and had been depressing us into silence the entire hour.

Before we left the room, Austin called my name from where he sat.

I turned around and gave him a look open for interpretation. It could have meant, *Fuck off* or *I'm busy, please hold . . .*

I didn't really care which one he chose to accept.

Beyond the door, there was a child coughing somewhere, a raspy, wet noise that sounded like something out of a horror movie. We passed three curtain-lined triage exam rooms, impermanent and lacking much dignity. I hated hospitals or anything that made me feel like I didn't have freedom. My stomach sank as the child kept coughing and began to cry.

When we got to Elodie's pseudo room, the nurse weighed her and took her blood pressure, then asked me to step out. I looked at Elodie and she nodded.

I needed to call Mali. When I got my phone out, I saw that she had called me three times. She was going to kill me. I also had a voicemail, but since I was going to call her to get chewed out anyway, I didn't need to listen to it. She was going to be furious. I was already forty minutes late.

Leaning against the only actual wall I could find, I called Mali but didn't get an answer. I sighed, feeling relieved that I could just talk to her voicemail instead. But right as the shop's voice message came on, I got the double beeping sound that meant Mali was calling in on the other line. I took a deep breath, switched over, and told her what happened. I explained to her that I could come in within an hour, but Elodie was surely out for the day. She told me we both cost her two new clients, but right as we were hanging up, she told me to tell Elodie she hoped she was okay. I smiled at her gesture.

I thought about slipping out the back door of the hospital instead of having a conversation with Austin in the waiting room. I wasn't ready to talk to him about why he'd done what he had and why he hadn't told me. I would eventually need answers, but I wasn't sure I was ready for them. If I knew Kael's involvement in getting him to enlist was some sick game to get back at me for whatever my dad did to Kael and his friends, I would feel better. Hopefully. At least it would make sense then. I sort of hated my dad for the things he had done inside our home, so now knowing what he was being held responsible for the things he did outside of it—and how evil he could be—almost made me welcome Kael's revenge. Almost.

Did I want to know the details? Not really. Would it make me feel better? In reality, probably not. Would I be able to avoid them both forever? Unfortunately, no. But today I could.

As if on cue, my brother burst into the hallway where I was standing. Fortunately, right then the monotone nurse popped out from Elodie's space and asked that I follow her through the curtain.

"She's asking for you two." She gestured to Austin, as well, which was fine because at least I wouldn't have to talk to him about our drama in front of Elodie.

Sitting on the bed with her shirt pulled up to just below her chest, her belly bare, Elodie looked so young. She had these strap-like things on her stomach with stickers on the end to hold little wires to monitor her baby. She wasn't crying anymore and seemed calm. Tired, but calm.

I sat on the edge of the bed and grabbed her hand. The deep blue of her veins showed through her paleness, causing her exposed skin to look grayish. As I got a closer look, it made me nauseous how sickly she appeared beneath the fluorescent lights. My stomach turned. I was used to a healthy pink in her cheeks and a brightness in her eyes that wasn't there.

She touched her hand to her stomach.

"The baby is okay. I just need to watch my stress level. The baby is completely okay." She pointed up at the IV bag hanging next to her bed. "I'm dehydrated, so they're going to give me these."

I breathed out, releasing some of my tension in relief.

"Hey, aren't you the Fischer boy?" asked a nurse, whom I hadn't noticed had been standing there all along.

I turned to look at him and saw he was looking at Austin, who stood in the corner with his arms crossed against his chest. Austin said "No" so nonchalantly and looked so genuinely honest that I almost believed him. What a good liar he was.

Elodie glanced down, avoiding the lie. I looked at the man's face, but didn't see anything familiar. Austin was looking at his phone, pretending the whole exchange hadn't happened.

The man seemed suspicious and annoyed, but just nodded.

"Why?" I asked him, my curiosity taking over.

Austin jerked his head toward me, clearly unhappy that I had engaged when he had dodged the question in the first place.

Another nurse popped her head in. "We need you. Broken arm," she told her colleague.

He looked at the two of us for a moment before exiting the room.

I glared at my brother. "Do you know him? What was that about?"

"I think he's Dad's friend."

"So why did you lie?"

He shrugged. "Like I said, I think he's Dad's friend." Austin looked at me as if that simple statement said everything I needed to know.

"You sure seem used to lying. Wonder where you got *that*," was all I could say.

Austin moved closer to me and lifted his arms in the air. "I didn't lie to you!" he whispered desperately.

His words hit me, right smack in the middle of my chest. I could feel that rumble, my temper shaking just below the surface. My brother tilted his head back and sighed. "Karina. I knew if I told you, you would freak out. Wonder where you got that."

I could feel anger budding around the sting of his accusation of being like our mother. We did that so much, comparing one another or ourselves to our parents as a way of inflicting hurt.

Elodie was looking patiently back and forth between my brother and me, unaware of what we were talking about. I gently squeezed her hand. The last thing she needed was more stress. I had to put her first, even though my temper was barely manageable.

"I'm so glad the baby is okay. I was worried about you. Both of you."

She nodded, lightly tightening her grip on my hand. "Me too. I'm sorry for all these problems. And this thing keeps checking the baby's heartbeat." She looked up at the beeping machines and the equipment lining the wall behind the head of her bed.

"There's nothing to be sorry about. You didn't do anything wrong," I told her.

Why do women always apologize for things they can't control? I did it, Elodie, my mom . . .

"Everything feels wrong. My parents. Phillip . . . he's . . ."

Elodie looked away from my eyes to the small television hanging in the corner. The thin curtain didn't really separate us much from the rest of the patients and I'm sure our neighbors could hear everything we were saying. I heard the bustle of nurses and that god-awful cough again. All of it was making me antsy, but I needed to be there for her.

I took in her frail body.

"Did something else happen with Phillip?" I caught her hollow gaze and hesitated with my brother there, and the other patients, and the lack of privacy in a place like this. "You don't have to tell me if you don't want to talk about it."

"The Facebook messages I told you about, well, they said that the woman my husband was cheating on me with is deployed with him. And married. And so I sent Phillip a message about it and he just replied." She looked at Austin before me.

She rubbed her baby bump over the thin hospital gown that draped over her body like cheap paper.

"How did he react?" I asked her.

ANNA TODD

"He said it's a total lie and he can't believe I had the nerve to even question him. He's really pissed off now."

I looked up at Austin, but he was staring at the floor. I imagined he was trying to make Elodie forget he was there so she would be more comfortable. Phillip's anger toward Elodie was a huge red flag to me. These kinds of stories were very familiar in a place where people got married well before they could legally drink. Married and deployed, then a baby, then deployed again. Underpaid, overworked, and underappreciated for enlistment after enlistment. It was a cycle, and Elodie seemed to be trapped in her own version of it. And this was just the beginning for her.

"When will you two talk next?" I asked.

"He was supposed to call me tonight, but he said in the message that now he won't be. He's basically punishing me for accusing him. Even though I didn't accuse him, I only asked a question."

Austin made a noise like a grumble, but didn't say a word. He looked up at the ceiling and rolled his eyes.

"Can I say something?" I asked timidly. I knew Elodie would say yes, but I felt like it was important to ask before giving my opinion.

In return, she smiled, biting down gently on her bottom lip as she nodded her head.

"The whole thing with the messages seems like an intentional personal attack and you should be able to ask your husband about it. You're the one here dealing with it and dealing with your parents on top of it. So, he should be more sensitive to that. His defensive response worries me if I'm being honest."

Elodie winced, but I kept going.

"Hear me out. I'm by no means saying that he's cheating on you, but that kind of thing does happen a lot. The lines are so often blurred and people spend a lot of time away from each other . . .

I'm not accusing him or saying I agree with your parents. I'm just suggesting that you investigate a little?"

"Seriously, Karina?" my brother interrupted.

"Investigate how?" Elodie asked me, and I was relieved when she didn't seem too offended, mostly curious.

"You could message the person's account yourself? Or keep asking Phillip. But asking Phillip might lead to more trouble than it's worth before you actually know if there's anything to be worried about. Plus, he might lie." I looked at my brother. "And if the guy who sent the messages is lying after all, and you ended up stressed out and in the emergency room because of it, I'm going to find him myself," I said, meaning every word. "And his wife."

Elodie didn't laugh, but I didn't really expect her to.

She jutted her chin out and up. "Okay, let's investigate. Even though I have faith in my husband, he's pissing me off right now."

Elodie and I smiled, and Austin shook his head.

She looked around a moment more. "How do we investigate again?" she asked, and our laughter filled the small space.

CHAPTER NINE

The lobby of the emergency room was even more packed than it had been two hours ago. The doctor wanted to monitor Elodie a little longer, and I had to go to work; I hoped that one of her Family Readiness Group friends might be able to drive her home when she was cleared to go. She seemed happy and even a little glowy after they pumped her full of whatever vitamins filled up the IV bag.

Austin offered to drop me off at work and drive her home later in my car when she was discharged. Around Elodie he seemed to become quite the gentleman, and we both appreciated the offer. At the same time, I didn't know how long it had been since he'd driven, and I didn't really want to leave him with my car, so I politely shot that down. Elodie sent a text out to her group chat to see if any of her Army wife friends would pick her up. They had all been texting or messaging or whatever for the last thirty minutes, her phone dinging and her fingers tapping on the screen from the hospital bed.

The group of wives on the receiving end all seemed eager to help, and she had multiple offers immediately. The woman who volunteered first was Toni. I thought I remembered her last name,

Tharpe, as Elodie had mentioned her more than a few times. Selfishly, I wondered who would pick me up if I was at the hospital and needed someone to depend on. Sometimes, like now, it felt like I was just floating around life alone, surrounded by humans who cared about everyone except me.

As I walked next to Austin, past the rows and rows of green uphol- stered chairs, beyond ready to get away from the smell of the hospital and the coughing children in the lobby, he asked, "Can I ride with you, or are you so mad that you're gonna make me walk home?"

"I haven't decided. Plus, you don't have a home," I reminded with a bite, one that he could not only handle, but deserved. Even though I knew he was living at Kael's, he was technically still couch-surfing.

"See, even more of a reason for you to pity me," he argued playfully.

I rolled my eyes, and he nudged my shoulder.

"We can talk about it on the way. I can get a ride from your place. I need to get my own car after basic training . . ." Realizing what he'd said, he looked down at me. "Kare, I—"

"Don't."

We stopped walking. I looked him straight in the eyes. "You're going either way, aren't you? What's the point of being angry now?"

Even my voice had given in to the reality of it all.

Realistically I couldn't resign myself to never speaking to my brother ever again. Especially since he would be going to what- ever state they shipped him off to soon. There was no way around it; that was the harsh reality of the military. Once you signed, the freedom of making choices was gone. I didn't want to lose him to the Army, but I also didn't want to lose him to my anger.

I hadn't thought much about what Army job Austin might have chosen for himself, and as I asked him, I hoped he would say something like dental hygienist, mechanic, any type of trade he could use in the civilian world.

"What's your MOS? Please tell me you're a paper pusher."

My dad always called anyone who wasn't in direct combat a paper pusher and I prayed that Austin would be one. It was also more likely that he would be able to get a job after he did his time in the Army that way. I knew from my father talking with his hands over a plate piled with chicken bones that the infantry soldiers worked long, unappreciated hours and were treated like shit most of the time. The abusive culture was something no one wanted to talk about. Not that other soldiers weren't mistreated, but infantry was mostly considered the bottom of the barrel by people, especially by those who abused their power.

Austin stuttered a little bit. "My MOS is infantry."

The most dangerous assignment.

Just like Phillip, Kael, Mendoza . . .

"Austin . . ." I continued walking, slowly. It was all I could think to do.

"I'm not as smart as you, okay? I was never good at school, you know that. I barely made it through high school. This was my only option. The Air Force wouldn't even take me, and even with the Army, I fucking failed the ASVAB the first time I took it. I'm lucky I even got in."

"*Lucky?*" I scoffed, eyeing the wide front door and looking through the glass wall to the parking lot. It was barely raining anymore.

My heart ached as it hit me that he had taken the enlistment test more than once. This wasn't a spur-of-the-moment choice. He had been trying to enlist for some time and obviously hadn't felt like he could tell me about it.

"When was that? When did this start?" I asked.

He sped up as I did, not letting me avoid him. "A few months ago. I've been going back and forth. I know I should have told you. I just knew you would be mad. It's not like I was going to keep it from you forever. It just happened, even Dad's reaction . . ."

I shook my head. "I'm not mad. Well, I am. It's more complicated than that. I'm confused why you left me out of a life-changing decision. Is Kael the only one who knew?"

I must have really pissed off something in the universe because right as I said his name, Kael appeared in the doorway of the waiting room. He clocked Austin and me immediately. His eyes went to my brother first, then quickly to me, confusion taking over his otherwise stoic face. His demeanor always showed that he knew exactly where he was supposed to be and exactly when he was supposed to be there. It was more than an Army thing; it was a Kael thing. We were at least twenty feet away from each other and I could already feel his energy consuming the space. I tried to fight it, to push down all the things that were happening to my mind and body as he got closer and I had no exit plan. I needed to look like I wasn't surprised to see him, even though we were in an emergency room, and I was very much surprised to see him.

I straightened my posture and took a step backward, shocked inside but not showing it, that he was standing there, right in front of me. It took me a few seconds to notice that behind Kael was Mendoza, and they were both dressed in civilian clothes. Kael looked so different in his everyday clothes than his uniform. Dr. Jekyll and Mr. Hyde. Except both sides of Kael were good, for the most part. Besides the fact that he was a liar and had completely betrayed me. If anything, he was more like Damon Salvatore from *The Vampire Diaries*, with two distinctly different sides when in love. Not that Kael was in love with me . . . and definitely not the way Damon loved Elena Gilbert. I wasn't even sure that type of love even existed in reality. And in reality, Damon would be in prison.

I had imagined that when I saw Kael again, it would feel like a gut punch. Instead, it was a slow pain, seeping into me. Processing my shock, I found myself fighting against my own emotions, needing to remind myself that he was bad. He was bad for me and he was a traitor. Looking at him standing in front of me, all I could think about was the way the sun hit his coffee-colored eyes and the way his quiet laughter filled my small living room.

I had planned out this scenario over and over in my head. What I would say, what he would say. What I would be wearing, which was far from the work clothes I was in now. In my dream scenario, I was beautiful, glowing with post-breakup pride and sleek hair, a pretty dress and high heels that made my short legs appear longer. Clearly my imagination was far-fetched and I'd had unrealistic hopes because I can't walk ten feet in high heels, but alas . . . there I was and there he was. I was heartbroken all over again and could almost feel the rain soaking me from the last time I saw him.

I wished Kael had been wearing his uniform instead of street clothes because it would have made it a tiny bit easier to pretend he was just another soldier and not mine.

Not that he was mine . . . anymore.

But in black Nike sweatpants and a fitted light T-shirt, part of me wished he was.

Finally, I looked at Mendoza, who was clear as day staring at me. His shirt was the same red color as his eyes, which matched the red of the blood seeping through what looked like a white T-shirt wrapped around his hand. The blood sent a wave of shock through me, but Mendoza's face was relaxed with no sign of tension or a care in the world.

"What the hell happened?" Austin asked them.

Kael looked back at Mendoza, down to his hand, and then met my brother's eyes. He was so calm considering where we were and the amount of blood coming from Mendoza. "His hand needs stitches."

"So he says," Mendoza said, a smile curling the corners of his lips.

"What the hell, man?" Austin's concern for his friend was obvious in the way he moved closer to him.

"It's not a big deal. Shit happens. People hit shit." He shrugged.

Austin chuckled. "Yeah . . . right. Looks like a big deal to me." He pointed at his hand.

Kael rolled his eyes and leaned his head back all the way, looking at the ceiling. He was doing everything possible to avoid looking at me and I couldn't seem to stop looking at him.

"This is just a regular Tuesday, man," he groaned sarcastically.

"It's not even Tuesday, bro." Austin smiled.

Were all men this ridiculous?

Mendoza lifted his hand a bit and a drop of red dotted the floor. He swiped it with his sneaker. I started to feel a little panicked, even though the three of them were being so causal.

"You guys should go check in, it takes forever." I kept my eyes on the sheet vinyl flooring and pointed at the now smeared drop of blood.

Mendoza used his free hand to tug at the T-shirt to tighten it. "Yeah, let's get this over with," he agreed with me and started to walk to the check-in desk with Kael.

"Wait—" Kael quickly turned on his heel and snapped his head toward Austin, again avoiding me. "What are you guys doing here?" His eyes narrowed to suspicious slits, looking my brother up down before his hand reached out for the pocket of Austin's jacket.

I froze. Why was he so worried about Austin, who was clearly fine, and not me? I guess I had already become a part of his past, though it had only been a few weeks.

Austin jerked away from Kael's grasp on him.

"Dude," he said defensively. "We're here because of Elodie, not me." He pressed his hands to his chest and tapped over his heart. "I'm good."

Kael glanced at me, then back to my brother. He hadn't looked at me long enough to actually see if I was okay, but it was clear he didn't give a shit.

"What happened to Elodie?" Mendoza was the one to react first.

As Austin's words sunk in, Kael snapped his head up again. The way he moved was so fast, so soldier-like.

"Wait, Elodie? What happened to Elodie? Does Phillips know?" He pulled out his phone and stared at the screen for a second, like he was going to call Phillip, but then realized that he couldn't because that's not how war worked.

Kael's eyes darted to and away from me so rapidly that a blink would have missed it. It was obvious that he was trying to avoid me, even though he was the one who'd fucked up. It pissed me off. If anything, I should be the one avoiding him. His body language would suggest to any onlooker that he and I were strangers—no, enemies. And that pissed me off even more.

I thought (well, hoped) that maybe if I could keep his eyes on mine for just a few seconds, if I used the sincere look that was reminiscent of the nights we spent lying in my bed with the box fan on my dresser whispering softly behind words and sounds that only Kael had ever heard from my mouth, I just knew I would see the sadness, the regret, that I wanted and expected to be on his face. I hoped he hadn't heard me mention his name when he appeared in the doorway. I wanted to be in control of our first encounter to keep him from manipulating me. I wanted him to hear my voice and remember those times the way I did. I cut off the rant inside my head to keep my temper at bay and my tone casual while my fingernails were digging into my palms.

"She's okay. We were here to check on the baby because she—" I started to say, but realized I shouldn't give him or Mendoza too much information about her personal life. Especially since they were clearly on her husband's team and he was directly responsible for most of the Elodie's stress.

"Because she what?" Kael prodded.

It wasn't my place to tell him anything about her and really, I should have just told him to mind his own damn business and worry about his friend who was currently bleeding through a T-shirt. But for whatever reason, we chose to stand there, wild west style, not making eye contact but not moving. It felt like he was waiting for me to walk away first and that just wasn't going to happen.

"Is anyone going to fill me in?" Kael asked, cutting off Mendoza, who was wondering the same.

"Really, what business is it of yours? You haven't seen her lately and you clearly have other stuff going on. You can either go ask her yourself or wait until her asshole husband tells you," I snapped.

Kael's face twisted and Mendoza's smile disappeared. Austin shifted awkwardly between us, deciding whether or not to take on the role of referee.

"We don't know anything yet but she's okay—" my brother told them.

I cut him off before he could add anything else. "And she hasn't talked to her husband yet, so you should do her a favor and wait until she does before running off to tell him yourself." I hoped and prayed that my voice sounded as harsh as I needed it to.

Kael simply nodded and looked from me to Austin. No reaction. Back to the cold, emotionless soldier I'd seen plenty of times before. What a fucking joke.

"Let me know when you find out and I hope Elodie is okay," Kael told my brother, affection wrapped around her beautiful name.

As Austin agreed, I studied Kael's expression. It was obvious that he cared about Elodie and her baby, but for someone left with so little detail, he was eerily composed.

"It was scary, but she's fine. I think." Austin paused. "I hope," he added, wiping his forehead.

Kael nodded coolly, the face of a soldier doing his duty. Why wouldn't he at least look at me? Why did I want him to so badly that it physically hurt? My mouth was dry as Austin asked him something I didn't hear because my thoughts were all over the place, beating loudly in my head.

"I'm gonna go check in. The tequila is starting to wear off." Mendoza walked away slowly, like he had a heavy rucksack on his back.

Austin and Kael were still talking, but I couldn't keep up. Their voices sounded like the teacher in Charlie Brown. My eyes focused on Kael's mouth, the sharpness of his square jaw. He was freshly shaven, looking youthful compared to me. My face had broken out, and I'd barely put any makeup on, hoping my skin would heal faster and honestly not really caring what I looked like lately. He looked like he'd slept at least eight hours and had coffee and didn't have a care in the world. I had too many. I should have brushed my teeth, changed my clothes, washed my uniform yesterday, plucked my brows. I should have worn at least a little makeup, but I hadn't expected to see Kael. Or to see anyone or go anywhere but my dim, candlelit treatment room at work. I had my hair tossed halfway up, the top part still powdery with half-rubbed-in dry shampoo and the roots slightly damp from the rain. My eyes were puffy from lack of sleep, lack of motivation to do anything, really, and Kael looked like he had never been better, which was probably true.

Even under the harsh light of the sterile hospital, his dark skin was glowing. The mint-green sweatshirt he wore looked great on him, as did his black cotton joggers. They were fitted to his body, clinging to the thickness of his thighs and hanging perfectly on his hips. I loved the way he always made street clothes look so good. I had been swooning over him—his outfit, his vibe, his everything. I wasn't worried about him noticing; it's not like he was paying attention to me, anyway.

My fingers twitched as I looked at the scar above his thick eyebrow and thought about how soft it had felt under my fingertips. It seemed like I hadn't seen him in months, not just weeks. His white sneakers looked brand-new as always. My work shoes were dirty and loosely laced up. I felt sloppy next to him. Even though I looked like shit, I wanted some sign that he cared enough to acknowledge me.

Mendoza came back over to us with an update that there were three people ahead of him. He said the hospital staff were probably tired of seeing him here, which made me wonder just how often he visited the ER.

"How you been, Karina?" he asked, his brown eyes slightly hooded. He gently rocked his shoulder into mine and glared at Kael and my brother. It made me smile that he seemed to notice my discomfort.

"Let's talk." Kael's voice sent a shock through me, but before I could react, I realized he was talking to my brother, not me. The two of them walked a few feet away from us and leaned against the white plaster wall. Ugh. I turned my attention back to Mendoza.

I swallowed, trying to wet my mouth. "Um, good, Mendoza. Just working. You? I mean, outside of your whole hand-massacre thing."

He let out a laugh that made my heart feel less heavy. Mendoza had that kind of energy that just made you feel warm, even in a place like the hospital.

"Hand massacre aside, I'm great. And who knows, maybe they'll give me a day or two off now since I'm hurt," Mendoza said, darkly laughing.

"What happened, anyway?" I asked him.

"I forgot my door was made of glass and felt like fighting it. I should have gone for the drywall, but I'm a dumbass."

The lightness of his voice and the way he seemed . . . happy . . . was equal parts off-putting and comforting. I felt an attachment to this man who was clearly running from some dark shit and battling demons that I would never fully understand, but I wanted him to be happy. I wasn't even sure why I cared, but I really, really wanted him to find peace.

"Hey, you're coming camping with us, right?" he asked after a few calm moments of silenced passed.

Camping?

"Um, I don't think I was invited?" I dug my fingernails deeper into my palms. One of the worst feelings was not knowing, but then discovering that you've been left out of something with people whom you thought were friends. I probably wasn't even supposed to know about the trip.

Mendoza's face was full of surprise. "Yeah, you were. It's for your birthday. Well, it's for your bro's birthday, but he said you were in. Gloria was looking forward to you coming so there would be more women for her to chill with instead of just a bunch of loudmouth soldiers."

I was so confused, but not entirely against it. I surprised myself.

"When is it?" I asked, sure the hesitation was clear in my voice.

"This weekend. You have to come. Plus, it's our send-off to Fischer before he's shipped off."

The words stung me but in a twisted way; I was relieved that no one had seemed to share my personal feelings about my brother and Kael's betrayal with Mendoza and he seemed blissfully unaware of the pain it caused me. I didn't want anyone walking on eggshells around me or feeling sorry for me.

"I think I have to work," I told him so he would stop looking at me like he was expecting an immediate yes. "But I'll try for sure."

"It's gonna be chill, don't worry. And don't worry about Martin either, he's a fucking idiot and will probably come up with an excuse not to come, anyway."

I wasn't sure if I should laugh or cry and the door seemed so far away, so I forced a smile.

"Tell Gloria I said hi, will you?" I didn't know her well, but had a feeling that if I had the chance to get to know her, I would really like her. A quick daydream of double dates with them and Kael caught me off guard, but I managed to push it away.

"She'll love that. She was looking forward to hanging with you before Martin . . ." as Mendoza opened his mouth to finish whatever he was going to continue with, Kael put his hand on his shoulder.

"Let's go," he said in a cold voice.

Mendoza didn't seem surprised or annoyed that Kael was bossing him around even though Mendoza was older than all of us and had way more responsibility. Honestly Kael did feel like the responsible one, but it was obvious that he didn't want Mendoza to talk about personal stuff with me. I had been cut out of their inner circle before I even had the chance to join.

"I think they just called for you," Kael said, nodding toward the main desk of the waiting room.

Austin promised to text Kael later and Kael mumbled something about Austin not losing the house key again. I waited like the pathetic lost puppy I was for the smallest smile or glance, or even acknowledgment from Kael, but it never came. He didn't even so much as look back as he walked away. Fuck him.

CHAPTER TEN

"How well do you know Mendoza and what's this about a camping trip that I'm allegedly going on?" I asked Austin as we crossed the parking lot.

The rain had stopped falling, but I was sure it would be back. The concrete was black with messy puddles scattered around the uneven pavement. The sky was the color of a river rock. Staring at it soothed me as the roller coaster of seeing Kael was wearing off and now brewing into anger. I opened the driver's-side door and sank into the seat. Holding on to the cold metal keys in my hand, I wasn't ready to leave just yet. I needed a second to breathe. As much as I usually preferred to avoid things and pretend they didn't exist, this time I wanted some answers from my brother. He huffed but didn't say a word and I wasn't having it. He had lived his whole life getting away with too much.

"Austin." I sighed. I wasn't leaving this parking lot until he told me. "How well do you know Mendoza?"

"Pretty well, I guess." He shrugged. "I don't know him as well as Martin does, but we're pretty tight. I met him before Dad shipped me off to our uncles." Austin rolled his window down a little bit to let in the cool air. Even with the humidity, the post-rain air felt good as it seeped into the car.

"What happened to him?" I paused. "To Mendoza?"

"You mean in general? Or right now, today?" he asked.

"Both? Either?" I looked around the packed parking lot.

"Well, right now, I'm not sure. Martin said he punched a window, or a door? Or maybe it was the glass window on the door? I can't remember honestly. But looks like he'll be all right. And overall, he's . . . well, he's got some fucking wicked PTSD. They went through some shit over there together and I think Mendoza is having a harder time than the rest of them."

I knew by saying *them*, he was including Kael. I was glad he didn't say his name; it somehow would have made it worse than the chill that blanketed my skin as I thought about the normalcy of all of this. Not one person in the ER seemed fazed by an intoxicated man bleeding through a makeshift tourniquet.

Austin ran his fingers through his sandy hair, which almost touched his ears. Long for him. It would be buzzed off Army style soon enough.

"Mendoza has been really fucked up lately. He's been like this since I met him, but Martin says he's gotten a lot worse. He's having a really rough time now and I'm sure having a new baby doesn't help the pressure he's feeling. Everybody's saying his wife is going to leave him if he doesn't get his shit together, but I don't think she would ever leave him. Their love is . . . just different."

Selfishly, I wondered if I would ever know how it felt to have a love like that.

"But it's hard. He's really struggling and what's he supposed to do about it? If he tells someone, they'll lock him up somewhere . . . and if he doesn't, he'll continue to do shit like this to cope." Austin sounded more mature than I've ever, in our *entire* lives, heard him sound. Maybe he was ready to be a soldier after all? Or maybe he really cared about Mendoza. Perhaps both.

"How many deployments did he have? He came back with Kael this time, right?" I asked.

My brother seemed to know way more about this group than I did. Sometimes the details of everyone's deployments confused me—the timelines, the last names, the drama—and Kael wasn't exactly a great interpreter. He didn't like to talk about the Army or what he had done or seen. When I thought about it, it felt like I had written and published an entire memoir for him and only him. It would have been nice to at least get a how-to pamphlet as a parting gift from him. Instead, I couldn't even get his eyes to meet mine for longer than a second inside the hospital, despite the fact that he's walking around full of my secrets.

"Yeah. Mendoza and Martin got sent home together because of their injuries. Phillip's weren't as bad I guess, but I heard when their Humvee caught on fire—"

"Injuries?"

Austin started to cough and rolled the window down more.

"Are you smoking still?" I asked him. Our conversation was bouncing all over the place, but so was my mind. I couldn't keep it in a straight line even if I tried.

"Shh. Doesn't have anything to do with anything. Anyway, I don't really know Phillips that well, but he was Martin's battle buddy. I don't love that El is married to him or how he is with her."

I sighed. Austin was slipping into soldier mode already. I started the car and pulled out onto the road, turning the radio on. And since when was Elodie's married life any of his concern?

"'Battle buddy'? You're already using the lingo—and, wait. So, is Phillip's last name Phillips or is his first name Phillip?" It had never occurred to me that Elodie was calling him Phillip this whole time.

Austin laughed. "You and I have been using the lingo since we were kids. And his name is Phillip Phillips." He laughed a little. "Like that girl from high school, Kristy Kristie."

I smiled at the memory of her. She was funny and loud but in a nonobnoxious way. I wondered what her life was like now. Austin turned the radio down so low that I couldn't hear it anymore.

"When you said injuries, did you mean he got hurt or *just* PTSD?"

"I wouldn't say it's just PTSD. You know mental trauma can be much, much worse than physical sometimes . . ." He pulled out a little cartridge from his pocket and took a drag of it. Vapor filled my car.

"Hey!" I rolled his window down all the way.

"I quit smoking cigarettes and weed. You should be proud."

I sighed as he took another hit. "I am, but you're still smoking."

"Why do you want to know so much about Mendoza, anyway?" he asked, licking his lips.

"I'm just—" I tried to think of an answer between the truth and a lie. "I just want to know. Especially if these are your friends now."

"Kare, a lot of shit goes wrong in the military, yes. And if you look for shit, you'll find it. But overall, life is easier there. There's structure, hot meals every day. I wish you would just think about the good things and not obsess over the bad."

And this was going to be our new dynamic: me, split right down the middle on how to feel. In order to have Austin be open with me, I needed to accept his decision and hope for the best. But I couldn't help how pissed I was, no matter how hard I tried to bury it.

"I'm asking because I want to know if he's okay. I'm worried about Mendoza. Kael is always with him, helping him through some kind of episode or talking him off a ledge. If his wife leaves him . . ." I paused to try to swallow the lump in my throat. "That will be awful."

"Yeah. He will go off the deep end for sure if Gloria leaves him but I'm telling you—she won't. They have three kids and have been together since high school. Plus, no one can handle him like she can. Except Martin."

I felt Austin's eyes on me, but I kept mine on the upcoming gate to exit the post.

"It can be fucking hard. This life. We grew up in it, so we know more than most," he continued. "But I'm only obligated to three years, and I'll get college money and have a place to live. I can get a car. So, stop worrying about me. Look, I'm sorry about the way I did it and if I could do it over, I would tell you the right way, but it doesn't change the fact that I'm still going."

"I just wish you would have talked to me before. At least warned me so I knew what was coming and wasn't the last one to find out." I rubbed my temples.

"Yeah, but honestly, you probably wouldn't have given me the chance to explain . . ." He trailed off, taking another hit of the vape pen.

I didn't know how to argue with him and really didn't want to right now. I was sad, pissed, still thinking about Mendoza and how Kael was wrapped into his life, and now that he was in my brother's, I'd never get him out of mine.

"I get the way you feel about the Army, Karina. I felt it too, you know that. But I don't have the money to go to school or any skills."

"We both had trade scholarships," I reminded him. "*I* used mine."

He rolled his eyes and leaned back against the seat. "Yeah. I know. You're also smarter than me. I'm not book smart, and I'm the fuckup. I'm the one who got arrested once and—"

"Almost twice. You nearly got Kael arrested *and* assaulted."

"That wasn't my fault!"

"It wasn't your fault the way they profiled him, no. But it *was* your fault that we were there in the first place. To save your ass."

Austin threw his hands up. "I'm sorry, okay! I wasn't going to let a girl get threatened and harassed by her boyfriend and I didn't know what else to do and some shitbags being racist isn't something I can control unfortunately."

I barely remembered the blurred faces of the young MPs that night, but as clear as day I remembered how they had drawn their black sticks into the air before a single question was asked. Kael's voice echoed in my head: *That's what happens when you train young men to kill, and not to restrain.*

Kael had tried to help get Austin out of the chaos, but was immediately targeted. It still made my blood boil that there was nothing we could do about it.

"I've said I was sorry for that and Martin knows I felt like shit about it. Look, Kare, I'm trying to do my best, okay? And yeah, I keep fucking up sometimes, but I'm doing a lot better than I was while living with our uncle."

I sped up to get in the fast lane and tried to consider what my brother was saying and to see things from his point of view.

"You have to learn to let things go, Kare. For real. I know you're pissed because I didn't tell you and you found out in a shitty way, but we aren't kids anymore and I can't keep promises that I made before I even knew what life would be like on my own. And not to be a dick, but this isn't your life."

I took a breath before responding. He was right in a way for sure, but that didn't help my anger and disappointment, and even worse, my fear—the deep fear that my brother might lose his life fighting someone else's war.

"I get that. But this isn't just getting a job at Kroger or something. And the fact that Kael helped you and didn't tell me. I thought I could trust him . . . this is a big deal"—I paused—"to me, anyway."

"You don't trust anyone. And that's what you're really mad about—that he was involved, not that I'm enlisted." My brother raised his brow, still smoking the USB-port-looking Juul.

He kept speaking while I contemplated his accusation. I couldn't say he was fully wrong.

"Martin, he's a good guy. I've told you before and I'll tell you again and again. He takes care of us. All of us. Look how he is with Mendoza. He's like that with everyone. He's the only reason I even got in with a good recruiter, one of his connections. Don't give him such a hard time. I know you're looking for a reason to hate him, but you won't find it through me."

"I don't think I need a reason," I argued.

Austin sighed, shaking his head.

And there, the sting of betrayal was back. I gave Kael access to me by sharing my insides and my secrets and he knew damn well how I would react if my brother signed his freedom away. Even so, Kael helped him anyway. I guessed he cared more about Austin than me and digesting that burned like hell.

"Well, I'm glad you've made such a good friend," I said sarcastically.

Part of me warmed over the way my brother felt about Kael. As he talked about him, I heard the security in his voice that I knew Austin needed. My brother was the kind of person who was at their best when around other people. We were different in that way; it was another thing he got from our mom.

"Kare. It's not like you were going to actually date him, anyway. He's getting out and moving and you always said you'd never date a soldier. I was shocked y'all were even hooking up."

I was glad we were almost home, because my brother was pissing me off the more he spoke and I was trying really damn hard not to slap the shit out of him.

"First of all, we weren't just hooking up and this isn't only about that. I'm worried for you. I don't give a fuck about him," I snarled at Austin and reminded myself. My cheeks were on fire.

He rolled his eyes and looked straight through my lie, but I continued, "Everything isn't black and white. You both lied to me, and now you're going away when you just got here. I'm going to be alone with Dad and Estelle, and sometimes Elodie until her husband comes home, and you're not just going off to college or a job somewhere—you're going to the fucking Army. And once you're in, you can't just quit or run away. The chances of you getting out once you're in are abysmal, you know that."

"That's not true. People serve one term and get out all the time. Besides, have you ever thought, even for one second, that this might be good for me?" Austin's lips pursed and he raised his voice louder. "You can feel however you want about the Army, and I know Mom leaving messed you up—and me, too—but some people are happy in the military; it even saves some people's lives," he said with a shrug. "Mom and Dad made zero sense together as a couple. Army or not, deployments or not. I don't think they would have stayed married either way. Everything isn't the Army's fault. They should have never been together in the first place if we're being really honest."

I blinked, and blinked again, thankful we had stopped at a red light. "But maybe it wouldn't have been the same," I said, though I was acutely aware that my argument was losing steam. "He wouldn't have been gone so much, and she wouldn't have been so lonely. That's what it was that did her in—the loneliness."

"Yeah, we can pretend that she and Dad didn't hate each other.

That she was just lonely," Austin scoffed, tugging at the hem of his T-shirt.

"Loneliness is hard, Austin. It can eat you alive. Feeling like you're always alone. No friends, no family . . . and no one to depend on." I took a deep breath. That had been the way I'd felt my entire life. Austin would never understand the toll it's taken on me. He had no idea how it felt . . . to feel loneliness to the bone.

Next to us, a woman pulled up in an SUV full of children. She smiled at the preteen in the passenger seat, who was gleefully handing out donuts from a green-and-white box. Judging from the ages of the kids in the car, and the fact that we were right outside Fort Benning, this was definitely an Army family. But the mom looked happy, car full of kids and all.

"Yeah, well, see, sometimes Army life works for some families," Austin countered, pointing to the SUV.

Maybe Austin had a point. I was nearly sure of it, but that didn't mean I wanted to hear it right then. *How could twins be so different?*

The light changed and I turned down the alleyway next to my house. We were both getting a little heated, but man, it felt good to be talking about things honestly and not ignoring them for once. We both must have been thinking about that as we drove down the street in silence.

"I'm lonely now," Austin said, as if admitting it haunted him. "I'm literally homeless, I don't have a car. And I'm walking away from everything and everyone that's familiar and the little bit of stability I have here. It's all about to change."

He laughed, changing the tone to make light of it, but it was the truth. I regretted thinking he didn't know what loneliness was. Without me saying anything, he continued.

"No offense, Kare, but I'm not like you. I don't want to be alone.

I'll have friends in the Army. Hell, maybe I'll get stationed here and you'll see me all the time, anyway."

I thought about that. Since he was joining the infantry, that likely meant either going to Fort Hood or staying here. At least, I'd heard that was where most infantry soldiers were being sent. I didn't know enough about the details of his MOS, so I was confused about all of it, but Austin's charm was working on me; I listened to the excitement in his voice and thought about him being close and having some structure and stability in his life.

"Hell, maybe I'll go to Hawaii, and you can come visit me on the beach and drink rum from coconuts?"

He smiled. The boyish smile from our childhood was all I could see. He'd changed so much since those memories, but no matter how much he looked like a man now, he would always be a mischievous teenage boy to me.

"I wish. But what if they ship you straight to deployment?"

"And what if you get hit by that truck backing out of that spot?"

I slammed on my brakes as Bradley, the mattress-shop owner, reversed in his huge silver truck less than ten feet away.

"What-ifs aren't real, Kare. You're going to what-if yourself to death."

I'd always been that way. I didn't know how to turn it off.

But I did know how to pretend that everything was fine when I wanted it to be, and Hawaii did sound pretty damn good.

"Fine. I'll stop being pissed at you if you get stationed in Hawaii or here. If you're sent to Texas, all bets are off."

"Texas would be good, too. It's not that far and the food is good as hell."

"No way. I'm not going back to Texas."

Slamming doors, screaming voices, my mom crying from the front porch and the creaking of the metal springs holding the swing up rang through my mind when I thought about the state with the biggest sky I'd ever seen.

"You loved Texas. Remember how much *fun* we had there?" he asked with a falsely innocent face.

Yeah, some fun. I remember tagging along to all the miserable parties. All the gross boys who were too old to be hitting on me. All the girls who stopped being nice to me after you ghosted them. Our mother nearly burning the house down and our father punching holes in the walls and patching them up every other month.

I filtered my thoughts instead of saying them. We were now parked in my driveway and I had to get to work.

I unbuckled my seatbelt. "Correction, *you* had fun there. I'm never going back."

He smiled. "Even Austin? It's my city, remember?"

"Ah, another one of Mom's tales. Don't try to distract me."

Our mother loved to tell us stories about the most random things. She should have been a writer with the way her imagination worked, sometimes so well that she floated between fiction and reality. This particular story was that Austin, the capital of Texas, was named after my brother when he was born. Her legend had it that the state had been in a drought for months until the moment he was born, making some mayor or senator name the city after him, even though we were twins and born only seconds apart.

Austin could have his city, though, because I had my own special island named after me. The beaches had white sand and there was a castle named after my mom. She told me these legends and secrets about our island, way past the age that I actually believed it. It was off the coast of Florida, she said. It was stunning, and the sun on your skin was as warm as the people. In a soft, wishful voice she would speak of a secret beach on our island where you could see the brightest stars hanging in the darkest sky. They lit up the night like nothing anyone had ever seen before, and she promised to take me there one day.

"Once we go, we can't come back," she would say, her fingers playing with the ends of my hair.

"Can Austin come with us?" I asked her once. I distinctly remember the way her face changed, the way she would always look back at the house from the porch swing.

"I don't think he can," answered, and I followed her eyes to the living-room window where my brother and father were watching a football game, talking, and smiling, shoving chips and dip down their throats.

She made me pinky swear not to tell anyone, even my brother, about our island. When I agreed, she made up more tales about a queen who shared not only her name, but who also had elaborate escape plans to leave her home island. It all sounded so stupid now, but as I thought about the trapped queen, I realized most of my mother's stories had meanings too deep for me to understand at the time. In tales told about Austin, he was always, always, always the savior. But mine seemed like an afterthought, as if Mom felt sorry and didn't want to leave me out; my tales were only woven from her fears, regrets, and worries.

Toward the end of her life with us, she stumbled up to my room more and more often. I would be tired as hell from school and my after-school job, but I would stay up just to have time with her, even with the smell of vodka on her breath and the shaking of her fingers as they brushed through my hair. Instead of making up the stories, she began to ask me to tell her about our island, how I was taking care of it. To be the storyteller instead.

How are the people?

Do we dance on the warm sand as the sun set across the ocean?

That's how she best coped with things. When I grew up and

became fascinated by psychology and why people were the way they were, I read books and searched the internet for facts, for reasons behind the human behaviors that I saw every day. The more I learned, and the more therapists I talked to, the more I realized that my mom *needed* to pretend everything was good to survive. She would always refer to a time when things were "better," back when I was a little girl. She wanted to live in the past because it was the golden time of her life, despite it being the darkest of mine. She had lived through a worse childhood than I had. Unthinkable things had happened to her at the hands of men in her family who'd claimed to love her, and no one had protected her.

When I was too tired and nodding off to sleep, she would beg me, alcohol thick on her breath, to take her away from here. I would start reciting the stories she had once told me, but she would always take over a few lines in.

She would cry too, sometimes. Silently, but I would feel her hot tears drip on my arm and her body shake in the darkness. When she was really disassociated from reality, I would talk in third person, telling her that I was glad she had visited again, that it had been too long. It made her smile when I said the island's water was warm and the people were thriving. I would pick up the stories where she left off and rub her hair right at her scalp line like she once did for me, until she spoke again.

The sadder she was, the darker the stories became.

It was hard to sleep afterwards, on the nights when her stories felt haunted, and she would usually stay in my room. Since it would invariably be the most attention I'd gotten from her in a while, I sort of longed for those dark tales.

A pang stung at the bottom of my stomach whenever I thought about my mom. The good memories felt so much clearer than the bad. For years, I'd been trying to hold on to them and pluck the bad ones out of my memory, one by one. It was like having two of her, like she had a twin. The bad times were becoming easier to drown out and emotionally detach from. The good times—the ones when we would laugh until our stomachs hurt while we ate peanut butter straight from the jar using sticks of celery—pulled me into missing her, which only made me feel more alone. That feeling of abandonment would follow me everywhere I went: Hawaii, Texas, Mars; the fact that I wasn't good enough for even my own mother to stay would always haunt me.

I looked over at Austin in the passenger seat. He was staring out the windshield, and I wondered which version of our mom he was thinking about.

"Where do you think she is right now?" I asked. I wasn't really asking my brother, or myself. It was more of a call to the universe.

"I don't know." Austin didn't look at me. "But she isn't here, and she sure as hell doesn't want to be found."

CHAPTER ELEVEN

"Is it okay if I stay here for a few hours?" Austin asked as he sat down on my couch, scratching his scalp. "I can go to Martin's later when things settle with Mendoza. I just need a shower and to sleep a bit?"

"Yeah. I'm going to work, anyway," I told him. "Just lock the door when you leave, and don't sleep in my bed."

I laughed lightly, but I was serious. I hadn't washed my sheets since Kael had slept in them, and I didn't want anyone in my bed for the small chance that the hint of his scent that was left would disappear.

"Thanks. I'll crash on the couch, or in the chair."

Kael's sleeping body spread across the chair flashed through my mind and I tried to ignore it, telling Austin to sleep there since Elodie would probably be home soon and she would only be comfortable lying on the couch. I needed to get to work. Today had been one of the most chaotic days of my life and I was ready for it to be over. What I really wanted to do was go into my bathroom, turn the shower on as hot as I could tolerate, and let my mind wander as the water soaked my body and hid my tears.

Austin's phone rang in his pocket. He showed me the screen as he ignored the call.

I rolled my eyes at seeing Kael's last name.

"He's a good guy and he's helping me a lot," Austin said defensively.

I snorted. "Yeah. Good guy. If he's so great, then why did he ignore me just now at the hospital? He didn't try to apologize to me. Or even talk to me. He acted like I wasn't there."

"As opposed to you doing what? Being so warm and friendly to him?"

Austin's comeback annoyed me. "He's in the wrong here. I didn't hide anything from him."

"Everyone hides shit. He did it for your own good, like I did."

I looked at him, a little stunned by the certainty of his words and the relaxed look on his face.

"It's not up to either of you whether it's for my own good or not. And not everyone lies, Austin," I said, rubbing the goose bumps prickling my arms.

He nodded. "Yeah. They do."

I didn't know what to say. There was definitely something different about the way my brother had been carrying himself in the short time since he'd been hanging out with Kael. He was more grown up than before. He still had his goofy, boyish demeanor, but I had to admit Kael's influence seemed good for him. Today, when Austin arrived at my house, his shoulders were slouched, his brows turned down, suggesting he was actually feeling bad for the way his recent choices had made me feel. He knew things between us weren't going to be normal for a while, but he also knew I would always have his back.

"I really, really have to go. I'm so late. Don't forget to lock my door." I ran my hands over my uniform pocket to make sure I had my phone and my keys.

"Why are you so worried about locking your door? You live

in a quiet neighborhood." My brother stepped in front of me as I made my way to the door. "Something happen that I don't know about?"

"No. I'm just being cautious. And Elodie is pregnant, so we have to be extra-safe." I stepped around him and onto the porch. I didn't have the time or energy to explain to him that I was generally paranoid and didn't exactly know why.

Austin looked me dead in the eyes. "Feels like you're lying."

I sighed, moving to the bottom landing of the steps. "Nothing happened. But some creep did come into my work a few weeks ago asking about Dad, and then that nurse today seemed to know you were his son. Shouldn't I be the one asking *you* what the hell is going on? I just feel like everyone around me knows something that I don't and it's making me feel . . ." I paused. I didn't think Austin would really understand the way my brain worked.

"Wait, what guy? Does Martin know?" Austin's voice was loud against the stillness of the quiet street. The sun was bright orange in the sky, breaking the rain.

"It was this guy named Niel, or Nate . . . Nielson? I think? Honestly, I don't know for sure. He looked sort of familiar, but I couldn't place him for the life of me. What's more I'm a woman living alone with another woman—who is pregnant. Haven't you seen the news lately? We need to keep our door locked."

"Nielson? Are you sure? What the fuck! What the hell was he doing at your work? Does Martin know about this?" Austin raised his voice and began pacing on the patch of grass next to the steps.

It was starting to feel like Kael was consuming my entire existence while simultaneously being absent. I refused to make this about Kael.

"He's the guy I was fighting that night with Kael and the MPs," Austin continued.

"It was that guy?" I tried to remember his face, but everything was a blur. "Do you know him?"

"Yeah . . . no. Not well, but . . . he definitely knows me."

Growing concerned, I asked, "Is he actually dangerous or is he just some dick who likes to start fights? What does he want with you? What did he want with me?"

"He's Katie's ex. She broke up with Nielson and he blames me."

It took me a minute to register who Austin was talking about. The girl from the party three weeks ago who'd heard me say that she was basically Austin's girl of the week. I had felt so bad for her. Now my guilt disappeared immediately.

Austin shook his head. "He also knows stuff . . . about Dad. I don't know if it's all true, and I've been trying to stay the fuck out of it, and you should too, but he's been spreading all kinds of shit around about Dad to anyone who will listen. I want you to stay the hell away from him."

"Like what, what is he spreading?" I knew I should be at work, not asking him about conspiracies about our dad, but this all felt too weird, too much like I was missing a piece of a puzzle. The way my brain works and Austin's half explanation didn't sit well with me. A hazy memory floated in my mind; the edges were blurry and I couldn't put it together, but I felt like I was missing something or forgetting something. I couldn't recall much of the night with the MPs, but there was an overly prickly feeling that coated my body when he showed up at my work. Had I seen him before? I couldn't exactly place him.

He hesitated. "Well, he was saying some crazy shit about Dad concealing a scandal involving civilian deaths or something, that his retirement is just a cover-up for what happened. It's spreading pretty fast around post."

Did my brother know more than what he was telling me about

our dad's secrets? I wasn't going to be the one to open that can of worms when I was already late as hell for work, and I was confused about the amount of truth there was to all of it. Investigating whether or not my dad was the villain responsible for innocent lives lost would have to wait until after work, or whenever I could force my brain to process just how heavy all of this was.

"What the hell does one of your little girlfriends have to do with Dad? This seems much bigger than that."

"I don't know what his hatred for Dad stems from, or why the fuck he showed up at your work or how he even found out where you work. Why didn't you tell me?"

"You're not exactly reliable, Austin," I snapped. "And I didn't know you knew him."

As his twin, I could feel that the truth in my words hurt him. Suddenly he looked so tired and so distraught, giving away that there had to be more to the story than what he was telling me.

"How does Nielson know Dad in the first place?" I asked.

"He was deployed with all of them on the last one to Afghanistan—in Dad's platoon and he just got back. I heard Nielson went AWOL. Just disappeared one day and months later they found him in a village living amongst the people. And when they tried to take him back, he said he didn't want to come. I heard he'd lost it completely and had even fallen in love with a local woman. After they found him, they locked him up for a few days, and then suddenly he was out, roaming the streets, which never happens, especially when someone goes AWOL and starts living with the so-called enemy. With smaller things, like drugs, sometimes you get shipped to rehab, sometimes you get kicked out with a dishonorable discharge slapped on you. But what Nielson did was so much worse. Something just doesn't add up."

Austin paused and looked at me, "I also heard—I don't know

if it's true or not, but the village he was in, along with the woman he was in love with, was completely destroyed." My brother's voice melted into sympathy. "I think he blames Dad for all of this, and now he's back at Benning, but his mind seems to be gone. I've heard all kinds of off-the-wall things about Nielson since he got back. He started seeing Katie, and when she broke up with him and went out with me, it sent Nielson over the edge."

My mouth was dry and my body felt like I had been carrying a backpack of stones. How did my life go from the most boring existence possible to this web of drama and secrets that I couldn't keep up with?

I glanced across the street, hoping my job would still be there when I finally arrived. I should have just called off work and dealt with the consequences later. I couldn't imagine being able to focus on my clients right now with all of this going on.

"So, a man who has it out for you and Dad after being locked up for going AWOL is roaming around and showing up at my work? Does Dad know about any of this?"

Austin rubbed his eyes. "It's a lot to explain."

"Well, I *want* the explanation."

"Don't you have to go?"

Austin tilted his head back and raised his hands in the air again before I could begin to go off on him. As usual, he opened the show, but wasn't able to close the curtain at the end.

"We can talk about everything later," he said. "Go to work, I need to sleep or I'm going to pass out standing here. I'll lock the door so your paranoid ass isn't worried about it your whole shift."

I nodded, even though I was far from finished with this conversation. As I crossed the street, I texted Elodie and told her I was heading to work in case she needed anything. During the brief walk to the shop, I thought about Kael again. Was he aware of any of this? In a fucked-up way, the idea of having him here to help, or hell, even to stop what was going on, made me feel more safe. But the reality, apart from my brother, was that he was already disso-ciating himself from my life. He barely seemed to notice me today and he was cold as ice.

Maybe he didn't want to cause a scene? Or maybe he didn't know what to say, or was too consumed by Mendoza's shit. Or maybe he just didn't care after all. It's not like he was the first or second, or even third, person who'd tossed me to the side. The more frustrat-ing part was not knowing when I would get used to it.

CHAPTER **TWELVE**

Work had flown by even though I'd stayed an extra two hours to make up for how late I was that afternoon. Mali had barely said a world to me, and the evening had been slow with no walk-ins and only one of my regular clients, Lisa, who spent the whole time talking about the laser hair removal she was getting next week. I listened to every word like it was the Bible so I could keep my mind distracted. It was ironic and funny in a fucked-up kinda way, just how different people's problems could be. I would kill to trade places with Lisa for one day. I'd love to worry about how my skin would handle thousands of dollars of laser hair removal, instead of worrying about how I was going to pay my electricity or fill my gas tank this week.

When I got back to my place after work, my neighbor Bradley was tying a bundle of wooden boards together in the bed of his truck. Ever friendly, he warned me it was going to rain again that night and the next morning. I thanked him and kept walking as Kael slipped back into my mind. The sound of his tires peeling out on the road as he drove away from me as I knelt on the wet grass, almost like I was praying for something, anything to take the pain away. It felt crushing then and still did.

Austin . . . Kael . . . Mendoza . . . now this Nielson guy. All of it gave me a headache. I missed the simplicity of my life before I met Kael. I hated that I missed him. When I got home, the house was eerily quiet. Austin had neatly folded up the blanket he'd slept with and left a half-rinsed-out bowl of cereal in the sink, colorful Froot Loops floating on top of the murky milk-water mixture. I checked my phone to see if he'd said anything about where he was going, even though I knew he was going to Kael's.

I wiped down the kitchen counter and sink, finally finishing the dishes I'd started washing that morning. The silence of my little house was deafening. I tried to hum a song, but the melody kept getting lost in my throat. Kael's deep, smooth-as-butter voice rang through my head on an endless loop. So I turned on music, then took a shower. Even my shower was tainted by memories of him.

Why the hell did I let him get so close to me so fast?

I tried to figure out the answer to that question while I towel-dried my body. The lotion on my palms reminded me of when he said my skin smelled like honey and licked his tongue down my bare shoulder.

I distracted myself from the memory by finishing the laundry. My hair was almost dry by the time I was done folding my clothes and putting the sheets back on my bed. And I was still thinking about Kael . . . how good he looked earlier. Not that it freaking mattered, but he'd looked better than ever. Though he hadn't been smiling, there seemed to be less weight on his broad shoulders. Maybe that weight from before had been caused by me?

Reality TV was a great distraction; I lay on the couch and turned on HGTV to watch Chip and Joanna Gaines turn a tiny dump of a house into a beautiful home. I rolled my eyes with envy when the big reveal came, and the husband picked his wife up off her feet and twirled her in the air in their brand-new kitchen.

Fuck them and their perfect life, and even better kitchen.

Elodie came through the door right as I skipped ahead to a new episode.

"I love this show. Oh, it just started!" she said, pointing at the screen.

Elodie sat down on the couch and kicked her shoes off. The color was back in her cheeks, and she had a bag with leftover take-out, so I assumed she'd eaten. I was relieved she was finally home.

"How are you feeling?" I asked her while a commercial for a sweepstakes played. One day I would pay for streaming without ads.

"Better. A lot better. I'm sorry for earlier. I'm sure Mali was pissed at you for being late." She winced.

"It's fine. Don't worry about Mali. We were slow, anyway. I'm so glad you and the baby are okay." I leaned against her knees, and she raised her small hand to pet my head, twirling strands of my hair between your fingers. Involuntarily my eyes began to sting. Tiny intimate gestures were not something I received often.

"Me, too." Elodie's voice had a hint of sadness in it. I looked up at her and she bit her lip, hesitating. "I talked to Phillip."

"What did he say?"

"He said he wishes I trusted him, and that none of it's true."

"But you do trust him?" Just because I didn't, didn't mean his wife felt the same.

"I did . . . I do. I trust him, but the way he handled it all bothers me. He said the person spreading this rumor is crazy and that I should ignore it all because it's nothing. The thing is, he wasn't surprised by any of it, and I just have this feeling . . ." She gently brushed the stray hair off my forehead as she spoke.

"What kind of feeling?" I asked, knowing Elodie probably couldn't articulate it. I wasn't sure what she was thinking, but if it were me, his response wouldn't have been enough. A stranger found her parents on Facebook—across the globe—and wrote them detailed messages accusing Phillip of having an affair. That didn't seem like something she should just sweep under the marriage rug. Watching my parents definitely taught me that in marriage, you have to pick and choose your battles; toothpaste in the sink is a very different battle than an accusation of cheating.

"I can feel it here inside. The feeling that something is wrong . . ."

"Did you tell him that?" I asked. Before giving her my opinion, I wanted to gauge where she was.

"I didn't . . . I lied and said I believed him. I can't ignore it now that my parents know. And the baby was in distress today because of it. It's not that simple to just ignore." She looked at me.

"I wouldn't be able to, either. I don't think anyone would," I assured her.

Her blue eyes focused on mine. "Would you believe him?"

"Me?" I tried to buy a few seconds. "I don't know him well enough to know, honestly. But someone contacting your family is a pretty big deal. And pretty ballsy to do if it wasn't true. Plus, I believe in trusting your gut, always."

"If it's true . . . what am I supposed to do? What if he *is* cheating on me? You told me that most military couples cheat." Her eyes started to water.

Man, did I regret saying that . . .

"Really, Karina, what can I do? Go home to France? Ask my parents to buy me a plane ticket? I don't have any money. Everything is in his name. And he says there is a law to stop me taking the baby away from him . . ."

I sat up and moved next to Elodie on the couch. "He said that today?"

She nodded. "He was very upset. He was threatening me."

I reached for her hand. I could feel her misery. It felt so familiar—even though our circumstances were so different, misery was misery.

"Don't think about anything but what's best for you and the baby, okay? He can't stop you from going home if that's what you want."

What an awful situation to be in. She could run home, but, realistically, would she? Would it even be for the best? I didn't know. The more I learned about Phillip, the more I realized I didn't actually know him at all. Kael was his only backer, which meant there had to be something good in him. Right? Or maybe they were two peas in one manipulative pod and that's why they were so close?

"I don't know what I want. He's so . . . he's become so angry. It is hard that he is not here. And hard that he is at war. And before the fight today, there have been more problems. I don't look forward to him calling me now," she said. "I know that sounds awful, but all we do is fight and I'm tired."

"It doesn't sound awful at all. It's understandable to feel like that. So, his advice as your husband was to ignore the whole thing? He didn't try to comfort you?"

Another nod.

"Is that what you want in your life, to be ignored when something is wrong?" I asked.

She shook her head. "I don't think I can live that way. And this feeling in my stomach . . ." Her hand rubbed over her belly. "Besides the baby"—she smiled a little—"is so strong that it's making me sick."

"I know he told you to ignore it, but like I said before, we can investigate on our own. Can you have your parents send you a screenshot of the message and we can figure it out?"

Elodie leaned forward to grab her phone from the table in front of the couch. She pulled up a pic and handed it to me. "They sent me a screenshot."

My eyes adjusted to the familiar face.

"It's . . ." I stopped myself from saying Nielson, the man Austin and I had talked about earlier today.

I zoomed in on his face, his beady little eyes, his tight jaw. It was the same guy from the shop asking for my dad, the same guy whose girlfriend my brother was sleeping with—and here he was, claiming his wife was sleeping with Elodie's husband. What in the hell was going on?

"Do you know him?" Elodie asked, looking at her screen again.

I grabbed my phone from my pocket and typed his name into the search bar on my Facebook.

"He looks like someone . . . I don't know . . . do we know him?" she asked, tilting her head a little.

I wasn't sure just how detailed I wanted to get with Elodie about the whole thing until I knew more—especially given her trip to the hospital today because of stress. But on the other hand, I knew very well how half-truths felt, and I hated that feeling.

"He's the guy who Austin was fighting in the street that night when the MPs were there."

She nodded, but I could tell she needed further elaboration.

"This is confusing," said Elodie, her fingers rubbed her temples and she sighed.

I agreed. "Very."

"Let's get some more information first. I don't want you to worry about it; you have enough going on. How did you leave things with your parents?" I asked, changing the subject.

She shrugged. She was still in her uniform from this morning; it was loose on her arms, but tight on her belly. "They want me to come home. Karina, am I a bad person if I don't want to go back?"

She took in a breath and slowly kicked her dangling feet back against the edge of the couch.

"I love Phillip. I do. And I've tried to be the best wife, and it has been hard. Even if we don't end up together, I want to stay here. Lately I've been thinking about it a lot. I know I don't have family in the United States, but I do like it here. The bigger houses, the people. The place I'm from is so small, and my parents aren't city people. They live outside of Paris, but don't visit the city, and anyway, I could never afford to live there. And I'm starting to make friends here. My friends back home have gone to university or have moved somewhere else."

I gently rubbed her shoulder. "First of all, no, it doesn't make you a bad person. And I get it. As much as I hated moving when I was young, some people thrive in new environments. My mom was like that. She always wanted to start over, to try new things. It's nothing to feel bad about. You're so young, Elodie. You can always move back if you want to. You have that freedom."

I thought about my mom dancing around the living room, raising her arms up high. She always dressed like she was straight out of Woodstock, her hair in a braid that she would let me decorate with colorful beads. I didn't know what it was about that particular memory that caused me to recall it so fondly. The music was loud, the windows were wide open for the whole neighborhood to hear Santana's electric guitar gliding through the air. My mom loved Santana before it was cool to love him. I remembered how the house smelled like pot roast when I got home from school that day. My mom grabbed my arms the moment I walked through the door, taking my book bag from my shoulders, and telling me to ignore my schoolwork for the night as she tossed the bag on the couch. She even wrote me an excuse the next day for my homework, something my dad would never agree with and never find out about. The sleeves of Mom's fringed suede jacket—brown and too big for her body—looked like wings as she flew around the room. She was like a bird trying to make the best of its metal cage.

Elodie leaned closer to me and snapped her fingers in front of my face. "Enough about me. I'm worried about you."

"Me? Why?" I shook my head, acting like I wasn't just spacing out of our conversation.

"You're so distracted lately. And sad. I can see it. You're just . . . how do you say, zoned out." She looked pointedly at my face.

I scoffed. "I'm not sad. Or zoned out. I was just . . ."

It was a terrible lie I didn't even bother to finish, and she rolled her eyes.

"Please! You are. And I know you don't like to talk about it, but I know you are very unhappy, very sad, and very lonely. And you saw Martin today . . . that must have been hard."

"Okay! Okay!" I put my hands up. "I get it. *Jesus*. Can't we go back to your life drama and not mine?" I smiled, trying to lighten things up.

We both laughed.

"It must have been hard. Are you guys speaking at all?" Elodie pursed her lips.

I loved the way the slight language barrier sometimes took the sugarcoating out of her words, especially when I really needed to hear something.

"Anyway. Back to *your* problems," I teased. "I'll find out more about this asshole, and you just focus on taking care of yourself and the baby. Please?"

She nodded and smiled, then sighed. "Thank you. No matter

what, I cannot leave you. I would miss you so much and you don't have any friends." She kissed me on both cheeks.

"I have friends! Plus, who decided that having friends was better than spending time with myself, reflecting on my own thoughts? Weren't we just saying that women should be their own best friend?" I did my best Samantha Jones voice. Elodie usually chose Charlotte as her favorite *Sex and the City* character to impersonate, but for me it was Samantha, the one I was the least like in real life.

"Mm-hmm, I don't agree. Life is about experiences with other people." She hummed, wiggling around on the couch before getting comfortable under her favorite blanket, the one her *grand-mère* made her.

"I have experiences." I pouted.

"Alone."

"And? I like to be alone. I like myself." I shrugged, lying a little, but someday that would be the truth.

"Yes. But Martin still likes you. I can tell by the way he was sulking around like a lost puppy when I saw him the other day."

"Shhh." I pressed my finger over my lips.

"And," she said, a mischievous smile growing as she spoke, "if my husband isn't cheating on me and you two can figure your problems out, we will have double dates with the two of you and be couple friends and do couple stuff together!"

She moved her eyebrows. I covered my face with a pillow from the couch.

"Don't count on it."

"You guys will work it out," Elodie said with certainty.

I groaned and pointed to the TV. "Look how beautiful!" I attempted to distract her with a huge white marble island being installed in a brand-new stark white kitchen. "Let's watch other people live perfectly and enjoy it and stop talking about my non-existent dating life."

"Fine, but only because I'm tired." Elodie yawned and leaned against me.

CHAPTER **THIRTEEN**

Kael

My place was freezing. I stepped into a familiar pitch-black darkness. The cold, dark nights in the desert sleeping on the ground were gone for now, but the reminders never stayed away long. I almost felt comforted by the chill.

Half of my life felt too good to be true; my freedom was right around the corner, supposedly. I knew the system better than that. To expect everything to go smoothly to the point that I could drive away from Fort Benning without consequences—shit never went down like that. But I was closer to freedom than I'd been in a while. Even if it wasn't guaranteed to be real. The other half, though: the harshness that I had always been aware of, but lately had been consuming me, that I wasn't a good person. I had done a lot of bad shit, but knowing that Karina knew it, that she was right all along to not trust me. I had my reasons, but she would see me as a bad person for the rest of her life, until she forgot me at least.

"It's fucking cold in here," Fischer bitched, his voice sending a shock through me as I flicked the lights on and saw him hugging his body. Sure enough, Fischer was on my couch wrapped in every blanket I owned.

"Why are you sitting here in the dark, you fucking weirdo?"

"I just got here and it's too fucking cold to move from here."

"Are you serious right now?" I could see my breath when I talked. "You're never going to make it through basic if you can't handle a little cold."

He waved his middle finger at me and snuggled farther into the couch.

"How bad could it be? You made it through, and Lawson's dumb ass did, too. Can't be *that* hard."

"No matter where they put you for basic training, your ass will get smoked for jokes like that," I warned him. "You can't just pop off at the mouth to anyone higher-ranking than you. Which would be me."

"Right," he said, laughing and saluting me.

Fischer thought it was funny now, but I had no fucking idea if he would be able to handle it. Smoking soldiers was no joke, and neither was running up and down hills until your lungs felt like they would explode and until your sergeant finally told you that you could stop, and barely being able to walk after. And basic training was just the start of it. Now that I'd been deployed, basic felt like a trip to the Bahamas in comparison. Not that I really knew what a vacation was like, but I watched enough TV to have an idea. Even if most of my impressions came from my ma watching the *Housewives of Every Fucking City* go on countless vacations with what seemed like endless money to blow.

I wanted to believe that Fischer would make it through and become a good soldier. Hell, even Lawson did, and I knew first-hand from basic how inept he could be. Fischer was tougher and more compassionate. From what I saw, he would actually make a pretty good soldier if he stayed with the right crowd and could get a handle on his addictions, which was way easier said than done. Problem was, in the Army, you had little control over your platoon, so the best you could hope for was just one person you could tolerate who wasn't a bad influence.

"A little running won't kill me," Fischer said, and his voice stretched with his body as he sprawled out all over my couch.

"Yeah, you say that now. You could barely make it through the physical."

I eyed the cold leather chair nearby. No way was I sitting on that. I needed more furniture, though maybe not since I was usually there alone, and I didn't want to waste the money. I didn't mind having Fischer's company. I wanted to be left alone, but not be alone. Whatever that meant. My mandatory discharge therapist told me that my independence gave me a false sense of freedom, but that really, I thrived with company. I was used to living in a small barracks room with a roommate when I was home, then sleeping in groups in a modified shipping container while deployed. I wasn't used to privacy or the concept of being physically alone.

In the container, my bunk was under the wall-mounted AC unit that only worked half the time. Before the heat got too bad, I got one of the guys to help me rig it with the random tools around our camp. It would be weeks waiting for a replacement, *if* we actually managed to get someone to order one. We made do with what we had most of the time while over there. When a lot of my meals came from MREs, the gross little packets of food, it was fucking Christmas every time someone in the platoon would get a care package from home.

Care packages helped a lot. Most of the dudes in my platoon weren't married, so if there were packages, they usually came from their moms. Like mine sending me Gummy Bears and Snickers bars. My ma couldn't send much, but when she did, it meant the damn world. When a box of the good shit came it was rare, but it gave us something to do while trying not to die. Lawson's wife would sneak vodka, moonshine, or a joint inside of a cereal box. Occasionally, letters from schoolkids would come, and most of the older guys would get fucked up over the Crayola-streaked reminders of their own kids back at Benning, who were living their lives without them. It was part of the sacrifice for their country, and we all knew that well—but it didn't mean it felt as good as the intention behind them or that a hand-drawn Memorial Day card couldn't bring a two-hundred-pound man to his knees.

While my mind was in the past, my eyes traveled around my living room. It was bigger than most quarters or barracks I'd had for the nearly three years I'd been in the Army. I was so fucking happy when I got promoted to sergeant just so I could move out of the barracks. I liked the convenience of walking across a lawn and being at work, but I couldn't stand having a roommate, especially in such a tiny room. I'd always been more of a lone wolf. I didn't like sharing space with people; I didn't like people touching my shit and sharing a bathroom and hearing when Phillips would bring home a girl from the bar and fuck her not even ten feet away from my bed.

There was no such thing as privacy in the Army, and Fischer being there didn't feel any different than being with one of my battle buddies, except now we were in my own space where I could take a piss in peace without having a half naked girl knock on the door, whining that she had to pee. At least with Fischer, he was the lowest-maintenance roommate I'd ever had. He was mostly on his phone or playing video games and didn't need to fill the quiet spaces in conversations. He didn't talk as much as his sister, although funny enough, he once told me once that Karina was quiet. It confused the hell out of me because it seemed like she never stopped talking whenever I was around. Though, she did apologize pretty much every time she rambled, which made me wonder who in her life had made her feel like what she had to say wasn't worth hearing. Subsequently, it made me want to fuck them up. Maybe it was her choice to shut herself off from the world? I would probably never know, but I did like the thought of Karina Fischer opening up only for me.

Having the brother of the only girl I'd ever loved living here was the worst scenario of all. There were times when his mannerisms reminded me of his twin, like the way he talked with his hands, huffed, and rolled his eyes—an ungodly number of times just like his sister. They were people who used their eyes, facial expressions, and hands to express themselves very clearly. Karina didn't look like her twin brother in a way that I would immediately think they were twins, but it was obvious that they were related. Good genes. Karina especially. Fuck, she was just one of those women who didn't need to try to stand out, but she did, and once you looked at her, you just couldn't fucking quit. And once she began to speak, her mind an endless ocean of intellect, it was impossible to stop listening.

The entire platoon noticed her when she began coming around more, and, with Elodie becoming friends with everyone through the FRG, Karina quickly became a constant topic of conversation. During PT every morning, between giving me shit about sitting out because of my leg, the guys would make comments about her—Elodie, too—but Karina was the single one, and no one wanted to fuck with crazy-ass Phillips's wife. The first time Lawson brought up hitting on Karina outside of PT, Fischer was there and made it clear as fucking day that she didn't date soldiers and never would. He said specifically that she didn't date *anyone*. He was pretty unfazed when a group of rowdy boys were talking about the way his sister's body was made to be fucked, though. When Lawson went on about her body, I looked at him, wondering if

Karina would even like him if he was single. I knew her enough to know she wasn't into married dudes, and I knew her enough to know she would probably cuss him out at minimum and knock his teeth down his throat at maximum.

She was the kind of woman who needed full, undying attention, even though she didn't see herself that way. The version of Karina Fischer I had come to know needed more than some stupid soldier who huffed cans of whipped cream in the backseat of a Humvee, returning from a mission that had nearly killed all of us. What she needed was someone who would fall harder for her the more she exposed her inner self, not an immature fucking moron like Lawson who wanted to use her body. She needed to be heard and understood without words being spoken.

The man she would end up with was going to have to have the patience of a saint and the ingenuity to figure out how she worked and what made her tick. If I, who somehow spoke her language no matter how different the two of us were, couldn't give her that, there was no chance Lawson or any dude I had ever met could. I didn't want to think about her, about other men and the way they wanted her body, and that one day, another man would come along who would be able to tap into her endless mind. That felt worse to me, someone hearing her talk about her feet aching at the end of the day or going on about how corrupt our government was. It created a hollow feeling in my chest in a way that was even more painful than a man putting his hands on her beautiful body.

While Fischer stayed quiet, staring down at his phone, typing away, I struggled to get his sister out of my head. God that woman drove me insane. Sharp, bright flashes of her eyes and laughter fought and defeated the part of my brain that was starting to hate her. It would be so much easier to hate her than to continue to ache for her and fantasize about her. The way drops of water stuck on her long eyelashes when she was first out of the shower. The way sweat dripped down her bare spine after I went down on her from behind, where I had a perfect view of her soft body. It wasn't only the physicality of her that I craved—it was hearing the way she could craft words like they were just for me. During my stroll down useless-memory lane, I felt my body grow restless and needed a reason to get out of the room.

I went into the kitchen to busy myself. I could eat. It had been a while since I'd eaten, so I threw something into the microwave. My stomach had been growling ever since I had to leave my fresh, hot, handmade enchiladas on the table at Mendoza's. Right as I had cut my fork into the food, Mendoza punched his hand through the glass on his back door. Gloria had spent hours cooking dinner for us, and everything was fine until it just wasn't. That's how he was. A ticking bomb in the most literal sense of the phrase. The smallest thing, a pop of oil on the stove, threw Mendoza into panic. And then things blew up.

I couldn't get his oldest son's face out of my head, the way it twisted as he grabbed his little sister and ran upstairs at the sight of blood spray. I looked at the frozen pizza whirling in the microwave and wished it was those enchiladas Gloria spent hours on. Her food was always so good. Mendoza was a lucky motherfucker; not only did he have a wife who loved him just the way he was—darkness, light, and all the shit in between—but she also took care of their entire family while he was gone and had never even looked at a man who wasn't him since they were sixteen. Made me gag sometimes, but I absolutely envied what he had. I'd take half of that, or even just the food. Hell's sake, I'd even take my ma's meatloaf over the shit pizza in my microwave. I knew I could use my mess hall card and still eat on post, but I couldn't be bothered, preferring to to stay inside my place as much as possible. I knew my whole life would change when my discharge went through, even if right now it seemed like it was never going to happen. I was slowly prepping myself for the new world, one with freedom. With freedom would come change, and I was sure as fuck ready for a change. Once I learned to cook for myself.

I really did need to start cooking for myself and maybe even eat actual food, but I had no damn time lately. Mentally or physically. Buying groceries, chopping and stirring and brining and shit—things people *do*—it wasn't happening. I had more time now than I had the last couple weeks, but I swapped the time I used to spend with Karina for going to my Army Transition Assistance program, where they attempted to teach me and a group of soldiers how to do basic things like fill out job applications, write a résumé, and use the VA healthcare system. They weren't going to let me run as far as I wanted away from the Army. In a lot of ways, I'd be a soldier forever. That's how they wanted it.

It all depended on what the hell was going to go down with my discharge. They weren't gonna keep me in, not with my fucked-up leg. It was so fucked up that they couldn't use my body anymore, but they would forever have my mind. I always came back to this. This wasn't the first time that I'd found myself standing in my drywall-dusted kitchen, using the noise from my microwave as white noise to drown myself in the past. Change couldn't touch some things in life. The fucking outrageous number of times I dug my boots into the sand of my past was enough torment to make up for my sins while there. I would never be able to forget how much blood had stained my hands.

I was always going to be that guy who had hemorrhaged the trust she'd had in me. Karina was the only person I'd ever met who made me feel like my life sentence was over and I was finally done being punished. She was the only one who knew some of what

I had done or seen, and she never, *ever* looked at me like I was the monster I had come to terms with being. She filled my ears and soaked my mind with bits of herself in a way that healed me. Listening to her talk was more valuable than any therapist I'd ever sat across from. Karina and work were the only things that took my mind off all the other shit. And since I'd lost her, I only had one thing left to lean on: turning this dump into a not only livable, but decent place. I had a shitload of work ahead of me if I wanted to try to make something of my life.

CHAPTER FOURTEEN

I needed to get my renovations done so I could start bringing in money instead of living in an expensive place that would burn through all of my basic housing allowance from being a seargent; I'd used my VA loan to get a run-down duplex and spent the rest of what was left after fixing it up to help pay my sister's tuition. It wasn't much, but I didn't waste money like most of my boys did. I put all of my extra pay during deployments into savings and bonds and lived off the bare minimum so I could stay afloat after I left the Army. I'd never admit it to any of my boys, but somewhere in the back of my head I knew I wouldn't be in forever. I wouldn't be able to stand it. I started moving the pieces a while ago.

Both sides of the duplex needed to be fully finished for me to get on my feet after my discharge. Phillips was going to be home soon and he wanted to surprise Elodie by moving into one side of the duplex. Things would be so fucking different if he were there. He would probably be hanging out with a case of beer, talking about how fucking terrified he was to become a dad soon. I sure as hell couldn't picture it, not with his temper. But babies changed people, at least that's what every couple told themselves. Not that I was stoked to have a screaming baby for a neighbor, but I had his back, and Elodie's. Not to mention the waiting list for post housing could take up to a year, sometimes longer, and I couldn't expect them all to live in Karina's box of a house. Karina's and Phillips's personalities weren't going to mix at all, so living together even temporarily wasn't an option.

The money he would save renting out my place would also help with the new expenses coming their way. Not to mention, the more I could keep my eyes on Phillips, the better. I trusted him. But I also knew what all our minds were like these days—his must be even more fucked since he's still there and is missing out on his wife's entire pregnancy.

Whenever I thought about him there, of any of us there, my leg hurt even more. It was fucking killing me . . . It had been all day, all week, all the time. The ache was tolerable enough to drive Mendoza to the hospital and get myself back home, but it was fucking throbbing now. I leaned against the counter and took all my weight off it. There was no chance I was going back to the doctor; that would only slow down the process of me getting discharged. He would prescribe another surgery, pump me full of pills that would not only fuck up my plan, but leave me ending up staring at the wall for hours: numb limbs, numb mind, exactly what they wanted. I'd done that before.

But on nights like this, the pain seemed extra-persistent. A constant reminder of my hurting inside and out.

I watched the microwave spin the pizza around and around. The cheese, crusted and burning at the edges of the folded box it sat on, melted all over the cardboard. I was so hungry that at this point, I'd eat the cardboard if I had to. I'd had worse. This microwave pizza was nicer than most of the food I grew up eating.

The pizza still had a minute and twelve seconds left. As a soldier, I could do a lot in seventy-two seconds. I leaned my head back and closed my eyes. I heard the phantom sound of rockets blasting in the distance the moment my eyes closed. Sometimes the blasts comforted me. This was one of those times. There were things about being a soldier that I knew I'd miss, like the routine and the adrenaline. I wasn't a BMX-riding, mountain-climbing kind of man, but every once in a while I had a nostalgic feeling when remembering the immense and exciting pounding in my chest as I ran for my life from the pop of gunshots. The first few months it was terrifying: the thought of never seeing my ma's or sister's faces again, but after a while, I became addicted to the thought of the fragility of life and how quickly mine could end.

The microwave beeped, making me jump back to the mundane. *Fuck*, I thought to myself. When would my brain function normally? Would it ever? Did I even care or could I coast through life barely thinking, barely living until it was over like most humans do? I leaned over to see if Fischer was still on the couch, still texting whoever he was talking to. I hoped she wasn't married or messy this time around. Fischer really needed something to get his priorities straight, or at least listed, and that was one of the endless reasons I had for doing what I did. I found control in the lack of freedom of the Army and that was good for me and for more people than they would care to admit. I knew what I was supposed to do every day, exactly when I was supposed to do it. There was order; there was a task to complete. In a way, things were just easier. I'd never had to choose between feeding my family or getting a tire for my truck. If I had a cold or needed a cavity filled, it wouldn't drain my bank account. Something that should have been free for every citizen but wasn't. Simple pleasures and necessities come at a cost for most people in the world. What a privilege it was not to have to worry about those kinds of things.

Fischer was going to be able to have a car, in his own name, a warm bed to sleep in at night, and three hot meals a day. His enlisting was going to hurt Karina, but at least I wouldn't be around to remind her of the person who had ruined her life and lied to her. I'd somehow become the villain of this story. To her, I'd be Rowan Pope from *Scandal*—the show that was on Karina's television every single time I went there. Remembering her living room was a reminder that I needed to get away from this town the very fucking second that I could jump in my Bronco and drive my ass to Atlanta. I couldn't risk finding a reason to stay, though at one point, I foolishly hoped she would give me one. That hope was gone now.

I had given myself and the paperwork a timeline of a few months. I still had some shit to do here, not only fixing up this duplex, but meetings and support groups so the Army could check off their list of mental and physical health surveys before they sent me out into the world. I needed to work faster on the repairs if I wanted to be able to sell or rent out my half of the place. The splintered wood on the counter edge was digging into my elbow, but since it distracted from my pain, I didn't mind. Plus, my guy at the flea market said he was getting a shipment of at least ten more slabs of marble for me, and I would cover the old wood on my counters with it. Since manual labor was getting harder and harder to do myself lately, with my leg acting up the way it was, having Fischer there as extra help was doubling my productivity. My own body was so damn worn out, but I had to keep going . . . I didn't have much of a choice. When did I?

There was less time to rest my mind or body than ever before, and I couldn't shake the feeling that I was running from or racing toward something. What was it? The Army? My future?

The ghosts of dead soldiers from both sides, friends and enemies alike with guns strapped to their chests shouting in languages I had only begun to understand. Maybe it was the fact that I was in love with someone whose father I despised for single-handedly destroying my battle buddy's lives. Or maybe it was pure narcissism and my own mistakes haunting me and making me want to blame someone so I didn't have to face reality. All of this would be easier if I could blame Karina for forgiving everyone's mistakes except mine.

She had secrets of her own and I didn't push her to reveal them. Her own brother warned me that sooner or later, she would run. She didn't believe in love, or lasting devotion. I wasn't sure that I did, either, but she made me come as close to the idea of it as I had ever come. Even if I hadn't done what I thought was best for Fischer, she would have found some other reason to push or throw me away. Just like my father and most other people in my life had, except my ma and sister and to some extent my battle buddies. Well, some of them. Despite all of that, something about knowing Karina made me want to get past all of this and live in real time, breathe live air, speak honest words.

The microwave beeped and the smell of burnt synthetic cheese filled my kitchen. A small cloud of smoke surrounded the metal-looking tray. I was so hungry; the day was nearly over and I hadn't eaten a single bite of food. Being alone with my thoughts was never a good thing for me, but it certainly was easier when those thoughts weren't about Karina, the brief time I had spent with her, and the taste of knowing how it felt to be alive.

I had assumed it would be a while, if ever, before we ran into one another. The post was huge and I knew she usually avoided it at all costs. I didn't even want to fucking see her again before I left—and at the hospital of all places. But life had taught me that shit never went the way I wanted it to.

I panicked at first when I saw her there, worrying something was wrong or that she was hurt. I assessed her quickly and when I realized that she was okay, I had to shut down. I didn't want her to see the concern in my eyes or hear the fear in my voice. I turned off my emotions, just like she had done. Fortunately, Elodie was okay, too, and Fischer's ass was lucky he wasn't the one fucking up again. Karina really didn't need to be worrying about her brother's mistakes or life choices when she could barely handle her own and there was enough tension between the two of them right now.

As she stood there, inside the entrance of the hospital, I could feel her green eyes burning into me. She'd wanted me to look at her so badly, but I couldn't do it. Only when she looked away. I knew I would see the challenge in her stare, waiting for me to say the first words, to apologize or try to explain myself. It wasn't going to happen, but she'd been testing me. That's what she'd wanted. I could feel it. There wasn't anything left for either of us to say. I was the dickhead soldier, and she was the victim. Arguing in front of a room full of people wasn't going to change that.

Still, being there face-to-face hadn't been an easy feat—seeing her brows drawn in worry and her pouty lips, hands on hips, ready to attempt to take me on. I couldn't shake the physical and mental reaction I was having to her; I couldn't get a grip. It sure as hell wasn't healthy, and no doubt one of my psychologists would analyze it all and agree. But the high I felt with her was addictive. It was something that only Karina, and being afraid for my life, could make me feel. As opposite as the circumstances were—being with Karina and being in combat—they were the only things that made me feel alive; I felt nearly numb to everything else lately.

How did I end up in this situation in the first place? I had no business getting into a relationship or promising anything to anyone. A woman should be the last thing on my mind. The only thing I needed to be worried about was getting out of this hellhole. And fast. No attachments. Maybe if I told myself that enough times, it would come true. I never wanted to be married or have kids or anything close to it.

My mind and body were worn down from the day, but I had to stay up for at least another hour. I felt like I could handle it; it was a soldier thing, to be so in tune with my body and to know when it could be tested, and when it couldn't. From the throbbing pressure on my kneecap to the pulse pumping at my temples, I clocked it all. I thought about the pain on a scale of one to ten, the way that doctors and specialists were always doing. Right now, I was at a heavy six, with ten being blown-the-fuck-up.

I was in constant pain tonight, but some knee pain and one of Mendoza's episodes were nothing compared to the shit I'd seen during my deployments. The sound of rockets slicing through the air and detonating in our camp was just as vivid to me now as when it had happened. The image of metal beams falling down like lightning bolts, and the ungodly pain that came with the metal striking my leg and crushing my bones was still there—and yet it was nothing compared to the fire that licked and ate my flesh while I waited for someone to pull me out of our burning camp. And the fire in the Humvee—

Fischer yelled, "Are you fucking alive? Bro—you've been in there for, like, twenty minutes. What are you doing?"

I came back to the world, to my apartment, where I was as far from fire and death as I could be. Physically, at least. My mind would stay burning, like always. I rolled my neck in a circle and felt the familiar ache. Karina's skilled hands working my sore muscles would feel incredible right about now. Karina, Karina, Karina, she always found a way to slip back into my mind.

"Hey, I'll pay you back for all this when I'm done with basic." Fischer's voice was slower now, and I opened my eyes to him grabbing a bag of chips from my kitchen counter. We bantered like battle buddies and I knew that he would have no problem with the constant fuckery soldiers were always slinging at each other. It was part of the lifestyle. The guys who couldn't take a joke had it the hardest; most of the jokes were so fucked up, beyond the standard of offensive, and would be considered highly, highly inappropriate in any other workplace, but when you're constantly on the edge of death, you find humor in things that most people don't.

"Speaking of pay. Your checks will go fast if you blow them before you even earn them. Watch everyone around you partying and buying the newest sneakers and random shit from Best Buy every time the check hits. Be smarter than them. If anything, put a down payment on a car if you feel like you *need* to spend the money right away. Only buy essentials and never, ever get a loan unless it's one hundred percent necessary."

"Look at you, Mr. Fucking Responsible. I'm just trying to eat Doritos," Fischer mocked, shaking the bag. "Saving money isn't that hard. I'll be getting paid every two weeks. I'll just put some back each time."

I laughed. Of course he thought that. I had heard many boys, men too, say the same thing before real life came into the mix. We would see how much money he managed to save in a year, and how much he owed the rent-to-own furniture stores. If I was wrong, I'd happily eat my words.

"Everyone thinks that. It can be pretty damn hard when your tire pops, or your electric bill is too high." I laughed. "Oh, you've never had *either* of those!"

"Funny guy." He opened the freezer and grabbed a Hungry-Man meal.

After removing the pizza, which had been done for several minutes, he popped his meal into the microwave, opened my fridge, and grabbed a beer. He wasn't old enough to drink, but I barely was myself and yet had already been to war twice. Plus, his twenty-first birthday was coming up, and truthfully, I didn't give a shit.

He lifted the bottle in the air toward me. "Want one?"

It took seconds to decide. "What the hell. Might as well."

Maybe it would help take the edge off my body and numb it a little. I needed something stronger to do the job, but even just a little mercy would be nice. I hated the unpredictability of the pain, how it came and went as it pleased. The unstable flare-ups were half the battle for me. The other half was sitting still long enough to heal, which wasn't possible for me.

"You good?" Fischer interrupted the brief silence. "I heard the microwave go off and you didn't open it." His eyes darted to where my pizza now sat, cheese already beginning to harden.

"Yeah," I said, my voice raspy. I cleared my throat and sat the empty beer on the counter. I wasn't going to tell him that I was going through the phases of longing for and loathing his sister. I thought quickly and lied, "Just thinking about Mendoza and Gloria. I really don't want to tell our platoon leader anything that's going on, but I'm running out of options if he keeps going to the hospital."

I had never purposely sought the attention of our platoon leader, but Mendoza wasn't getting any better, and today really made me realize just how much worse it could get. His PTSD was so out of his control that it was even out of mine now, too. I tried to help him every day, but today proved that no matter how much time I spent with him, no matter how often I kept my eye on him, it didn't change the fact that his trauma was not being dealt with. He was lashing out more and more.

"At least no one got hurt," Fischer said, concern in his eyes. Eyes that looked a lot like his sister's. His fucking sister. Mendoza was my priority.

Mendoza got hurt. He is hurting.

"Yeah," I said in a whisper.

I wished I could talk about it with Fischer, the way I wanted to with his sister. Instead, I just nodded. He wasn't ready to know the darkest parts of promising your life for the greater good of your country, and I hoped he would get through his enlistment without having to find out the meaning of the contract he'd signed. What was coming was too heavy for him and definitely wouldn't be good for his morale as a new soldier. He would have to try to survive, and I didn't want him to see Mendoza as a model for how that went.

His sister would get it. She would feel empathy and sorrow for my lost brother and his family. I never gave her much when she tried to ask about him, making me a huge hypocrite, but if I ever saw her again, I would tell her everything she wanted to know. I could use her wisdom right now. Standing there, I contradicted myself every fucking time I thought about her.

I shifted my weight between my arms so they wouldn't go numb as I leaned on the counter for support. I was hoping to make it to my room without Fischer noticing anything was wrong with me. I'd become a master at hiding my pain by now. His eyes followed my arms down to my legs. I knew Fischer wouldn't make a big deal of the injuries, but I didn't want anyone's sympathy or opinions, and I sure as hell didn't want him to tell his sister or mention it in front of his dad before I could get my ass out of the Army. I needed to get these last few appointments out of the way, none of them medical, so I could skate out and go to the VA hospital when my discharge went through.

"You good?" he asked.

I looked down at my legs and came up with a laugh. "Yeah. I'm good."

"Doesn't seem like it. You seem out of it," he replied.

I stretched out my aching leg. The Army doctors' job was to fix my broken body just enough that the Army could throw me back into a war that was supposed to have ended years ago. Their job wasn't to make sure I was healing right, just that I was healing fast. They were meant to speed up the process to save money, time, and paperwork. The VA was better and would treat me like a human. I'd done my research and I wanted to get out this way, to keep my benefits and leave with a good taste in my mouth after all the shit I'd gone through for the sake of "freedom."

"What will happen to Mendoza if they find out that he went to the hospital?" Fischer asked, taking after me and chugging his beer.

"Oh, they'll find out. I'm not sure what they'll do. It depends what kind of mood they're in."

"It's that fickle?" he asked, like he hadn't grown up as an Army brat.

I nodded. "You have no idea."

"Yikes." He ran his hand over his chin. "So, did you decide where you're going when you're out? You're leaving for real, to Atlanta?" Fischer asked, looking around the kitchen. It was full of supplies for the work I had to do on the duplex. Boxes of floor panels, buckets of paint. It was a fucking mess.

I nodded. "There's nothing for me here. I gotta get the fuck out of here. And fast. As soon as I sign that discharge paperwork, I'm out. Counting down the days." I finished off my beer.

"If I get sent somewhere cool, you can come with me. I'm hoping for Hawaii."

Fischer laughed when he said it, but I wondered if there was a real want behind his words. Soon he would be with a bunch of strangers who would become like brothers to him faster than he could imagine. We hadn't served together, and I felt a bond with him like a brother, but I knew it was kind of pointless since he was leaving soon, and I needed to keep my distance from his sister. I'd still worry about him getting himself in trouble and check on him every so often, but soon I wouldn't feel as responsible for him as I did now. He would be someone else's problem.

I half nodded. "We'll see. I'm only going if it's somewhere with sun, cheap property, and less fucking rain. Hawaii has none of those."

"Man, if I get stationed at Knox or Hood, I'm gonna be *pissed*."

I didn't blame him, and I sure as hell wasn't going to visit him in Kentucky or Texas.

"I'll be pissed for you. You might end up staying here after all." For his sister's sake, I hoped for that.

Fischer let out a laugh, clinking his beer to my empty one. "My sister would looove that."

Even though I was already thinking about her, at the mention of his sister, I opened the fridge and grabbed another beer.

"Sorry. I keep trying not to talk about her." Fischer reached for another, too.

"How is she?" It wasn't the most comfortable exchange in my life, but he was the closest source to Karina I had, and my curiosity got the better of me.

He looked at me silently for a second with the face of a preppy white boy who would always get off the hook for any trouble he caused, the kind of guy I usually couldn't stand. But I liked him more than I did most people; he had a good heart and an ease about him.

"I just saw her yesterday, for the first time since she found out. She's fine, I guess. Mad as hell and hates both of us right now." He shrugged, taking a bite of steaming, freshly microwaved food. "But that was to be expected. She'll be happy for me eventually. I hope. There's not much she can do now."

Fischer licked his lips and drank his beer. I couldn't bring myself to take a bite of my pizza, even though my body was fucking starving.

"She holds grudges for a while, doesn't she?" I asked, already knowing the answer but wanting him to drill it in.

He nodded. "Oh fuck yeah, she does. She remembers everything too, so even if you think you're off the hook, she'll bring some shit up years later like, *you kicked me once when we were twelve*." He was laughing, but I couldn't find the humor.

She would always hate me for lying to her. I guess I knew that, but didn't really let it sink in. She would always think of me as a liar now. I'd done it more than once and she would never let it go. Even before I lied, she barely trusted me, so there was no way I was ever going to get back into her good graces. Fuck it. I had come to terms with this, anyway—it was only because her twin was in my kitchen that I was thinking about her.

"Martin . . ." His voice was low, warning me. "I say this out of nothing but love for you, bro, but my sister isn't going to forgive you. I don't know how serious you guys were and I don't want to."

He sounded older than he was. The kitchen light flickered as an omen as he continued, his hands moving as I digested what he was saying. The honesty of it caught me off guard.

"Our parents really fucked her up. Me, too, obviously." He smiled. "But we took things so differently, and she just . . . well, she shuts down and I don't want to see you try and try only to fail in the end. I wish for her sake it were different, but I don't know if she's ever going to have a normal relationship with anyone. I worry about her, but don't beat yourself up over it."

Heat filled my chest. "That's a little far, don't you think? She's only twenty and you're out here fucking married women who are fucking married men. I wouldn't give anyone advice if I were you."

The way he looked at me after I said that made me want to grab him by his T-shirt and slam him into the wall. I didn't, but my fingers shook as I clenched my drink.

"Whoa, whoa. Don't talk shit about who I'm fucking—and I can speak of *my* sister any way I want. You don't even know her like that. Chill the fuck out."

His cheeks were growing red as his voice got louder.

"And you do?" I growled at him. We were getting heated over someone who wasn't here to chime in. Someone who would be cussing out both of our asses right now.

"Barely. That's what I'm trying to tell you. You'll never know her, either, and you're going to make yourself crazy trying to make sense of her. I'm looking out for you, both of you, but go ahead and ignore my advice and see what happens. She's been punishing our dad since the day our mom left. She doesn't give in."

I scoffed. It pissed me off that he thought he could talk to me like that, but he believed he knew Karina way better than I did, even though a part of me thought the opposite and that maybe he was the one who didn't know her.

"As if your dad doesn't deserve punishing."

He looked me over.

"What do you know that I don't?" he asked me.

We stared at one another. I wasn't going there with him. I couldn't. Even if Karina never spoke to me again, she had told me things I would never, ever repeat to anyone, even Fischer.

"What-the-fuck-ever. I don't want to talk about that shit, anyway." I ran my hand over my shaved head. "Anyway, maybe I'll go to Atlanta sooner than I had planned. I could work faster on renovating the house I just bought there and hope to make enough money in profit that I can look in and around my hometown, where the real estate's way cheaper than in a big city like Atlanta. The sooner

I pay back my VA loan on this duplex, the sooner they'll give me another loan."

The profit wouldn't be massive at first, but I had to start somewhere, and pretty much any soldier could get a VA home loan. As it should be. Serving your country should at least offer you the privilege of owning your own house.

"Hey, at least you have options, and a place to live. I don't even have a hometown. I'm jobless and homeless," Fischer said, not really complaining, just stating the facts.

He was such a contradiction: the most confident—and the least confident—dude I'd ever met.

"Haven't you ever heard you shouldn't compare yourself with others?" I laughed.

"Yeah, I think I read that on a T-shirt somewhere."

"Hey, at least you have a dad."

He laughed. "Fair. But not a mom."

"Well, shit. Touché."

We were both smiling, shaking our heads and joking about the heavy reality of our lives. It felt good for the time being, knowing everyone had shit that affected them that they fought to deal with. Taking the air out of the shit we couldn't control was our release. We had to have one. Well, outside of the beers in our hands.

"You have your sister," I said.

Both of our energies got a bit more serious. I felt on edge at my own mention of her. Austin's second beer was nearly empty.

"She's barely speaking to me. Not that she doesn't have every right to be pissed, but she tried to kick me out when I first got there. At the end of the day, she let me stay there and shower and shit, and, like I said, she holds grudges like you've never seen."

I looked at him, but my mouth outpaced my judgment before I could stop it and my instinct was to defend Karina.

"Yeah, you've made that clear, but against who? Your mom, who left her, or your dad, who doesn't act like he gives a fuck about her while simultaneously trying to control her, or you, who keeps trying to fuck your life up?"

Fischer looked at me like he wanted to deck me. "Fuck you. You're a part of this now, too." He pointed at me. "You'll be the one to get it now. I'm the one who asked you not to tell her, and she's never going to forgive you. She has to talk to me—we shared a womb. But don't be surprised when she acts like you never existed. So, like I said, my sister isn't like other girls who you can just say sorry to and get them flowers and they'll forgive you."

Karina and I seemed to have the same coping mechanisms. Grudges and self-preservation were our top priorities. People who forgave others too easily were weak and always taken advantage of. I wouldn't expect Karina to forgive and forget. I respected her more than that.

"I'm not asking her for forgiveness," I told him, sour regret filling my mouth.

Fischer's brows drew into a line and he rolled his eyes that were too big for his face, which helped his whole puppy-dog look. I knew he wanted to say something, but thank fuck for his sake—he didn't.

"I thought we agreed to stop talking about your sister." I rubbed my temples with my free hand. My beer was half full, sitting pathetically on the counter. I was increasingly jealous of the people around me who could numb with alcohol. It seemed to increase my emotional state, not dumb it down.

"You're the one who brought her up. But yes, please, for the love of fucking god, let's stop. I wanna hear what the hell there is to do in Atlanta that you love so much. I haven't been in years." He made a face like a lightbulb went off inside his head. "We should have gone there instead of this camping shit, but now everyone's obsessed with it, so it's too late."

"And cheaper, since you don't have to pay for any of it—you probably didn't think about it," I said with a bitter smile. "Well, not that you'll even know what I'm talking about, but for starters, there are a ton of movies being shot in and around the city because of the tax credits, so I want to get in before the real estate skyrockets any more than it already has. On top of that, there's always something to do. It's not sleepy like this place. I can live my life in silence." I waved the beer through the air.

"Silence in the city?" Fischer pondered.

"Yes. So many people around that no one will notice me. And the food. Nothing here, or anywhere in the States, compares to it."

I hadn't been to many places, so it wasn't like I had much of an elevated culinary opinion. I did try different things when I could, but I only traveled where the Army sent me, and there was no such thing as tourist shit when the Army shipped you somewhere. I'd been to Germany once, but never left the airport. I had a pretzel in the airport. And a bag of Skittles. But with food, there is an instinct that comes along with just knowing what works, from Skittles to culinary level.

"Also, how many times do I have to tell you, I'm not going on that fucking camping trip." I had already made up my mind when the group started talking about it. I've slept under the stars for hundreds of nights, why do it willingly?

"Come on. It's for my birthday. Our last time as a group for who knows how long?" I could see how Fischer so easily manipulated every situation; even I was beginning to be swayed.

"Not a chance in hell."

"My sister is coming," he said under his breath. My eyes shot up to his and I guzzled my beer. It was warm now, even more gross than before.

"Is she?" I couldn't help but ask.

"Elodie said she is. So, will you go if Karina does?"

"Stop asking." I gently pushed the nearly empty bottle against his shoulder. He was on his fourth—they were making the counter even more crowded with trash. Not that I really gave a shit.

"Whatever. You'll go, I bet you one hundred bucks," he said with certainty.

I looked at him with annoyance.

"Anyway," Fischer continued, "that's enough of that. Let's get back to talking about Atlanta and the food and shit." He smiled, eyeing his microwave meal. "How do you know all of this about the housing markets and real estate and movies?"

I laughed, readjusting my arm on the bare wood. "Imagine what you could do if you didn't spend all your free time sleeping with women and playing video games."

He scoffed, raised his beer to me, and chugged what was left.

"After basic, I'll try to be more like you. Grown up and shit." He grabbed another beer from my fridge and opened it with the buckle of his belt. "But for now, I plan on enjoying my last bit of freedom while it lasts."

I nodded, wondering if he knew how little freedom he would soon have.

I touched my bottle to his and we both took a swig. The beer was so cold that it hurt my teeth. I was still getting used to having a fridge at my constant disposal again.

"Have you thought about your last meal yet?" I asked Austin while dragging my teeth through the pizza dough. It was just as chewy as it looked.

He looked up from his phone.

"Is that something I'm supposed to do?" he asked. "It's not prison."

I said nothing. Sometimes it was worse than prison. At least in prison you're guaranteed a mattress and three meals a day, a toilet, no guns firing at you.

"But nah. Not yet. Probably a big-ass pizza. And beer. Lots of beer." The end of his sentence was slurred. He was fidgety, moving his body in the smallest ways, but never standing still.

"You good?" I asked, tipping my head to the fresh, cold beer in his hand.

He nodded, believing that he was. I looked at him and it took me a second to organize my thoughts and try to assess his sobriety. It didn't matter, anyway; he didn't have anything to do tomorrow.

"I'm not that drunk. I *want* to be. I hope my sister stops being so pissed at me." Then his voice went low, like he felt bad for saying it. "Sorry. Didn't mean to bring her up. Again."

I ran my hand over my mouth, pulling at my lips. "It's cool. It is what it is." I shrugged her off. Well, I tried to. "You did lie to her," I added.

"*We,*" he said, lifting the beer to his lips.

"We. I know, but you're her brother and you made that promise to her not to join. Not me. I only kept it from her because you were supposed to tell her."

As I said it, I started to get pissed at Fischer again. While he was cowardly, waiting to tell his sister about his plans, I'd had to lie to her. Kiss and lie. Try to gain her trust and lie. That's what I'd done.

"I know, but she doesn't get it. You still think I did the right thing. Right?"

I nodded, thinking of the empty baggie of pills I found in his pocket when he was unconscious and so fucked up that my dragging him from my yard into my house hadn't fazed him. I never found out who'd dropped him off. Not telling his sister was lying to her also. I seemed to do that a lot, even without trying.

"Do *you* think you did the right thing? That's the real question here, Fischer." I raised my brows, questioning his declaration.

"I don't know yet. Well, not the lying-to-her part. That was pretty stupid and made everything worse."

"Yep. I'd say." It gave her a reason to run from me. She was good at running. It was a habit of hers that she found comfort in.

"If I were you," Fischer began slowly, "I wouldn't push her to forgive you. She hates that. Ask anyone who knows her."

The thing was, I didn't believe that anyone who had met her truly *knew* her. I got close, but she bolted each time I neared.

"I'm not. I have plenty of other shit to worry about," I said.

He made a face at me.

Our conversations about Karina were usually one-sided, and I used them to learn what I could about her. It had to be the pull of her mystery that still had me obsessing over her. Even though I knew she was becoming a ghost in my life now, I couldn't shake her. Chance encounters like the hospital soon wouldn't be possible.

"I don't think you guys would've worked out, anyway. She can be difficult sometimes and needs a guy who can balance that. And she's shy with guys, anyway. It's because she's never really dated except that dweeb Brien, and he was such a dumbass."

It took a lot to keep up with even a conversation with Karina, intellectually and emotionally. She never said what I expected her to say, and she always kept me on my toes. With the mind games, the all-knowing explanations for everything under the sun. She was both right and wrong, forest fire and iceberg. She had her escape routes mapped out long before she even entered a situation.

She *was* difficult, but did Fischer realize the irony of him being the one to call her that? Shy was so far from what she was. Discreet, you might say, but not *shy*. Perhaps he had never seen her the way I had or gotten to know her like I did.

It wasn't that she was shy—it was that she was closed off because she doesn't trust anyone. I would never tell him that or expose any part of her to him—that's her own prerogative to share or withhold—so I had to think carefully about what to say to him.

"There are a million reasons why we would never work, and it's done now, anyway, so stop thinking about it and asking me weird shit about your sister."

I stood up straight, letting some of my body weight move back to my leg.

"I'll stop," he said through a mouthful of cheap stewed beef. "But you should stop thinking about her, too, because this is the third time we said we were going to change the subject." He paused, then said again, "You should reconsider the camping trip. It could be the last time we're all together."

I shook my head.

"I've had my share of camping with all of them in Afghanistan. Adding booze and girls would only make it worse."

He smiled, showing nearly all of his perfectly straight, bright-white teeth. "Booze and girls never make anything worse."

CHAPTER FIFTEEN

Karina

My day off started off uneventfully. I got my paycheck, which was nice and chunky with all the extra shifts I'd pulled. I made myself coffee and walked to the nail place down the street and came out with my nails and toes painted Lucky Lucky Lavender. I'd felt like getting black, but talked myself out of it. My nails didn't need to match my mood.

When I'd written my name on the waiting list, my nails were borderline embarrassing. But picking Lucky Lucky Lavender from a huge book full of painted fake fingernails, I knew things were about to get better. Plus, my luck was that the technician suggested that I add a layer of gel to strengthen my nails, so I did. The gel made them longer, and my hands just felt pretty and feminine in a way that they usually didn't. I kept them short for work, but this length wouldn't get in the way. The tech was such a good saleswoman that I paid extra for a ten-minute hand massage. Her fingers were magic on my overused muscles. As a massage therapist, I could tell she knew what she was doing and it was so, so good having someone else massage me for once.

On my way home, I passed the hair salon on the row and saw a woman I'd never seen before standing in the back doorway, lit

cigarette in hand. Pointing to the little hand-drawn wooden sidewalk sign, she told me they were having a special on highlights and
eyebrow waxing.

"I can add an eyebrow dye job for five," she told me in a raspy
voice while staring at my eyebrows for way too long.

Her forehead was shiny with sweat. The sun was going to be
unforgiving today. It was barely 11:00 a.m. and the sidewalk was
already heating up. I could feel it under my flip-flops as I walked
through the alley. It was cold yesterday, hot today. Freaking
Georgia couldn't make its mind up whether fall was ever coming
to stay or not.

I declined her generous offer as politely as I could, without
actually having to talk to her and without making much in the
way of eye contact. She flicked the cigarette onto the ground right
before I passed and then walked back inside the shop, letting the
heavy metal door slam behind her. I glanced at the door before I
mashed her cigarette butt into the sidewalk to make sure it was
out, picked it up, and put it in a nearby trash can.

I couldn't help but stop and look into the side mirror of a van
parked in the alley. I touched my roots, pushing them down to see
just how grown out they were. They were invading my dark strands
like the United States invaded small countries for oil. It was tragic.

Maybe I should dye my hair again? I felt like shit lately, and
getting my nails done would give me a little boost of confidence.
Maybe it was true, the montage they used in romance books and
movies where the woman has her Cinderella moment and changes
her appearance and—*poof!*—she forgets the boy and feels great
and lives her best life with her group of happy, single, amazing
friends—and another guy comes in and saves the day!

Insert eye roll here.

I didn't buy that shit for a second. It'd take a hell of a lot more than an appearance change to move on, but what I did buy was hair dye. Two tubes: one dark blond and one a shade darker to blend and break up the dullness that was contributing to my complexion looking so gray and dull. My skin had lost the little bit of color it once had, probably because I hadn't been outside much lately save for my walks to and from work. Loading up on vitamin D would take some time, but dyeing my hair had always been my restart button since I was first allowed to do it on my thirteenth birthday.

I'd gone through phases of pinkish hair, nearly fried my hair trying to have silver, and went from brunet to blond when I needed to completely escape and refresh. Since salons were so expensive, and I really needed to put my money into my house, I grabbed a mixing brush and bowl to make myself feel more professional and went on my way, hoping for the best, and only thirty dollars poorer.

An hour later, I stared at my freshly dyed, lighter hair and my bright-lavender nails in the mirror. As I looked at myself, I felt new. The tube said my hair would be a "golden walnut" color; I didn't know what that was, exactly, but I liked it. The lightness of it made my skin look a little pink, which made me feel more alive. Like the constant switching of hair colors, I'd always gone through phases of being the most confident girl in the room, to feeling like everyone in the room secretly hated me and was talking shit about me behind my back. Oh, the fun of overthinking.

My new hair reminded me of my hair when I was sixteen, a funny thought because I was literally wearing an old T-shirt from my high school as my PJs. It had a hole in the sleeve, and my shorts were the same color gray. With the texture of a soft towel, they were my favorite shorts and were tied to memories of comfort over the last few years. My hair and nails now done, it seemed like a good time to attempt my five-step skin-care routine, a major commitment of time and money.

Everything around me was constantly changing, now more than ever, and I was trying to just keep my feet on the ground. Austin was leaving soon; even though there was a chance he would be at Fort Benning for basic, I wouldn't see him until Family Day and graduation. Phillip would be coming home in the next few months, and I would be living alone again. Sometimes I secretly longed for it, to not have to talk with Elodie about the day or how I felt, and just sit in chosen silence or watch reality shows, turning my brain off without worrying about anyone else.

At the same time, I needed to get my shit together and focus on my life and career and holing up alone in my house wouldn't accelerate that progress. In reality, I didn't even have a career yet—I had training, but I needed more experience. I had no idea what my actual plan was beyond knowing that I didn't want to work for Mali forever. I needed to make more money so I could struggle less, save for the future, buy a decent car, and not hold my breath when I opened my electricity bill every month.

Who was I kidding? I didn't even know what I was doing this weekend, let alone with the rest of my life. I needed to get out of my own head. I was spending way too much time in there lately.

I shut off the bathroom light, went into the living room, and plopped onto the couch. I already felt accomplished, dying my hair, getting my nails done, and finally completing the overdue skin-care routine; I could now justify spending the rest of the day on the couch reading and watching TV.

Five minutes into my scrolling Instagram with *Boy Meets World* playing in the background, Elodie texted me. Thank God for being able to pause shows. She was going to a cookout after work and wanted to know if I wanted to go. There was a steak emoji, a beer, and a smiley face in the text.

Nope.

I started to type that I didn't feel like leaving my couch, but knew that would make her more inclined to push me to go, so I Googled things to do at Fort Benning on a Sunday. There was the local mall, a flea market, a craft show on post. I tapped my finger on the flea market even though it was twenty miles away and swiped through the pictures. I had lived here for years, but had never heard of it.

All outdoors, it looked like stall after stall was filled with stuff like tables and wood and lawnmowers. One guy even sold tile. I looked at the time in the corner of my phone. It was only one in the afternoon. I could get dressed, put on a tiny bit of makeup, and be out of the house before Elodie got home to push me into going to the cookout with her friends. Or even better, I could just put a bra back on, brush my teeth, and go in less than ten. At least my hair and nails were done.

I went with the second option. No one I knew would be at a random flea market twenty miles away on a Sunday afternoon. Most of them would be at the same cookout as Elodie. I bet Kael would be there, too, and an encounter like that was far from what I wanted on this refresh-and-self-care Sunday.

What I needed was to drive my car on the highway with the windows down and depressing-ass music turned up, to sing to myself, and maybe cry, on my way to buy something for my house. Maybe I would find a cool and unique lamp from someone's grandparent in Germany, to replace my IKEA lamp that I could find in all the matching houses on post. I loved the idea of secondhand furniture. The possible story behind each item made me giddy for some reason and allowed my recently dormant imagination to surge.

As I drove, I was getting more and more excited about what I might find, and about what I wanted my house to look like when it was all set up. I was nowhere near finished, but I hoped this little gem of a market would bring me good deals and easy assembly.

I looked in the rearview at my small backseat as I pulled into the lot. I wouldn't be able to fit much in my car, but maybe they had delivery? I had to know someone with a truck or big enough car, or maybe Austin did? Someone besides Kael, of course.

I stopped by the ATM at the closest gas station and pulled out two hundred dollars. I debated with myself about how much I might spend, so much so that by the time I got my cash, there were two people behind me waiting impatiently. It's not like I had the two hundred to spare, but I hardly ever spent money on myself and could justify a little shopping spree because I had just saved myself at least that much by not going to the hair salon.

When I drove into the dirt-paved parking, I smelled the food vendors first. I could always smell a taco a mile away. I parked as close as I could to the front, next to two massive trucks that made me feel like I was in Texas again. I shoved my cash into my small purse and climbed out of the car. As I got closer, looking past the gates to the stalls filled with rugs, jewelry, clothing, blankets, and big pieces of wood repurposed from barn doors, I wondered if two hundred would even be enough. My heart was racing in the good kind of way. This place was exactly what I needed today, and I wasn't even inside yet. Families crowded the parking lot and the entrance, excited kids, whiny kids, dads who looked like they'd rather be watching football, moms who looked like they hadn't slept in a week.

Finally, it was my turn, and I got my hand stamped at a counter, my cash pile going down ten more dollars for entry. I was surprised by how many people there were inside, a mix of military families and civilians. You could immediately tell the difference, of course. I scanned the crowd as I got a whiff of hot sugar and funnel cakes. This place was magical.

My first stop was a table covered in jewelry. I felt guilty because I knew I wasn't going to buy anything, I just wanted to look at it and admire it. I wasn't a jewelry person, but the deep-turquoise stones were mesmerizing and hard to walk past without stopping. The woman selling them smiled at me but didn't approach. She must get browsers like me all the time. She had a sweet smile, and I could tell just by looking at her that she had spent her life working herself to the bone.

The ring that caught my eye the most happened to be one of the cheapest. It was simple, just two thin silver bands, connected by a line of the same width up the middle. There was something about it that was calling to me, but it was twenty bucks and I really needed furniture and supplies.

I walked away with naked fingers and reminded myself not to get distracted by pretty rings or huge barn doors that I wouldn't be able to fit in my car. I walked past rows of wooden stalls and took in all the details, from the calluses on the fingers of the man selling the campfire wood, to the detail in an old painted shutter. I could see chips of the other colors it had been painted before the deep blue it now was. I didn't stop, I just walked past slowly, admiring everything.

Finally, I stopped at an old Airstream decorated with little cactuses and a huge water cooler full of lemons and limes and ice. They were selling pots of succulents and hanging plants. Adding more life to my house was essential, and I'd much rather be around plants than humans, hands down. I got a free drink in a biodegradable cup, then bought a couple of plants, took a picture of my two new babies that I really hoped I could keep alive, and sent it to Elodie and Instagram. Evidence that I had left the house that day.

Wasn't there the meme that said: "If it's not on Instagram, did it really even happen?"

I felt kind of lame right after I posted it and tucked my phone into my pocket. I sat down at one of the little tables and drank another plastic cup full of their water. Something about the aesthetic of fresh lemon and orange slices floating in mint-infused ice water on a hot-ass Georgia day made it the best water I'd ever had. I felt like I was at a spa, even with dirt covering my flip-flopped feet and my hair in a nest of a ponytail on top of my head. The longer I was at the market, the more I loved it. I mentally thanked Elodie for inviting me to the cookout that caused me to run to this place. It felt like the reset I needed—I was in a new town, with Golden Walnut hair, and beautiful plants to look after. The flea market felt so far from my house, from Fort Benning, even if it was only a thirty-minute drive. The drive there had been peaceful, only country roads and one little town with one gas station, a post office, and a couple houses spread out far enough that they wouldn't hear a peep from their neighbors.

I tossed my cup into the recycling bin and picked up my plants, ready to explore the rest of the market. I didn't really think it through, though, because the plants were actually pretty big, and I could barely see over one of them.

"Need some help with those?" a voice asked from behind me.

When I turned around, I almost dropped them both onto the ground.

CHAPTER **SIXTEEN**

Kael

Karina adjusted the plants in her arms. I reached to help her, and she took a step backward, nearly stepping into a pool of water to avoid my hand touching her.

"I got it," she repeated twice in a row, discarding my offer of help.

No surprise. She was a stubborn ass. No damsel in distress, and she loved to prove it, even if it made her blue in the face, or red in the arms, like she was now with the plants scraping her skin as she tried to distribute their weight. She had on gray shorts that were pretty damn short for the flea market on a Sunday. The thickness of her soft, exposed thighs made it hard to look up at the rest of her. The chances of two women having that body weren't likely.

When she first turned around, I thought it was my guilty conscience making me see Karina's face or body on a stranger's. A stranger with different hair than Karina had the last time I saw her just a few days ago. Watching her struggling to hold the pots was a little painful. I knew firsthand how heavy those fuckers were. One of them had big green leaves and a few purple flowers peeking out of soft soil, but the cactus had pebbles all around it and the pot itself was stone. The thorns on the cactus looked sharp as they poked at her arms again, and sure as hell wouldn't be fun to drop on bare legs or flip-flopped feet.

The first things I clocked about the girl were her thighs and bare feet. Not because I'm a pervy motherfucker, but because the soldier in me was wondering what the hell she was thinking wearing flip-flops to the flea market. Especially with the rain we had been having in Georgia.

"You're really not dressed for this," I said.

She glared at me.

Which made me smile. Seeing her, angry or not, shifted my mood drastically. Without the audience of her brother or Mendoza, I felt much more at ease with her—enough to talk to her at least.

"What are *you* doing here?" she asked, her eyes suspicious green slivers.

"Me?" I asked her. "I come here all the time. You clearly don't," I teased, looking down at her bare feet.

Her lighter hair color brightened her eyes, and something was different about her face. She wasn't wearing any makeup and I could see the little pool of freckles on the tip of her nose. I studied her as she looked down at the boots on my feet.

"See?" I said, stomping my foot lightly on the loose dirt.

She looked at me with an expression that was exactly the same as rolling her eyes, without actually moving them. Since it was an outdoor market, the ground of the entire setup was dirt. There was some occasional large gravel, which wouldn't be fun to walk in with only half an inch of rubber separating your skin from the ground. This time of year especially, the older stalls near the back fence had mud puddles the size of human bodies in front of and next to their tables and signs, even if it hadn't rained in days.

In general, the ground of the market was filled with dips and holes, random wooden posts, abandoned stalls . . . The place wasn't in the best shape, but that was part of why I liked it. We had that in common. Both of us were battered to hell.

"What are you doing here?" I asked again, still processing that Karina was actually there.

She finally stopped torturing herself and sat the plants down on the table in front of her.

"Fuck me," she groaned, wiping the dirt off her palms and onto her tattered gray T-shirt. She shook her arms in front of her body, and I couldn't stop myself from laughing as she assessed the damage to her skin. Her arms had some cuts, but nothing a little peroxide and a Band-Aid wouldn't fix.

"Me? What are *you* doing here?" she asked.

I pointed at her. She was in the mood to play games, obviously. "Well, me? I come here every weekend, so I know you don't. Are you going to take that as my final answer, or ask again? Now, your turn. What are you doing here in flip-flops and shorts?"

She frowned, making her brows move, and I noticed she just looked different. Well rested, maybe?

"So, what, now you're talking to me?" she snapped.

"I wasn't not talking to you before," I lied. She nearly growled at me, and it made me oddly excited. "So, how did you even find this place?"

She shrugged. "I found it on Yelp. And I need some stuff for my house, so I drove out."

"What are you looking for? I know most of what they have and who can give you the best deal. Did you get your plants from Kathy at the Airstream?"

I knew she had; we were only a few feet away from their sitting area.

Karina shook her head. "I don't know her name, but the Airstream lady, yeah."

She shaded her eyes with her hand and the purple paint on her nails caught my eye. She'd clearly been busy over the last few days giving herself a makeover, not that she'd needed one.

"Cool, she's been here forever. Her husband comes some weekends to help out. Nice guy."

What I didn't mention was that Kathy's husband had gone to Vietnam, and her son was now serving in Afghanistan. Serving in the military happened to be a family affair more often than not, but I didn't want to remind her of her brother's enlistment. Not while she wasn't throwing daggers at me for once.

Karina looked around at everything but me. I tried to do the same. I was in the middle of trying to detach her from my mind, too. I think I had gone most of the morning without thinking about her. Of course, I'd slipped a few times, but hey, no one was perfect. Running into her here of all places—it was wild, it threw me off, and I knew it was better for both of us to get through this awkward, random encounter as quickly as possible. But if I was being honest with myself, seeing her just felt so good. This was the second time in less than a week that we happened to be in the same place at the same time. She felt slightly less distant now than she had at the hospital, and I felt much more relaxed being somewhere familiar to me that wasn't to her.

"That's cool," she replied awkwardly. I nearly forgot that we were talking about Kathy's husband.

We stood in silence as people walked past with steaming coffee mugs and an older man carried a huge wooden door on his back across the grass. One of us would need to pull the trigger and say goodbye first. I looked over at her to see her staring directly at me. I certainly wasn't wearing my Sunday best, just casual clothes and my Army boots. She wasn't, either, but she looked fine as hell. I couldn't help but continue to stare at her legs, her hips, the sweat gleaming on her neck.

A couple more seconds of silence passed between us. Like the sun and the moon, dancing around until one gives in and tucks away for the night.

I waited, sort of hoping she would start going on about the plants, or she would yell at me for being a dick at the hospital, or her brother's enlistment. Something. Anything.

I finally broke the tense silence. "Well, nice seeing you. I'll let you get going, I need to meet a guy about some wood, anyway." I laughed a little so she would maybe get the "gotta see a man about a dog" reference I was going for.

She smiled at me, but it was vapid. No emotion behind it. A skilled chameleon who wasted her powers by using them against me. I needed to be the one to end the exchange before she had the chance to blow me off.

She cleared her throat and reached to pick the pots up again. "See you around."

"You can ask Kathy to hold them for you while you look around more if you aren't done shopping." I pointed to the silver Airstream.

Karina looked where I was pointing, and Kathy waved. "Hey, Martin! How are you, honey?" she yelled to me.

Karina's expression changed. She was now watching me closely and walked with me, right on my heels, as I approached Kathy, whose hair was pulled back in a ponytail, the roots gray but the tail red. Her wide eyes were colored with thick blue eyeliner and her nails were painted all different shades of the rainbow.

"I'm good. Getting some flooring and trying to head home before it gets too hot. How are you? How's Randy?" I asked.

Kathy smiled at the mention of her husband's name. "Yeah, it's a hot one." She looked up at the sky. "Randy's good. Hasn't changed a bit—never does. I'll tell him you said hi."

I got straight to the point for Karina so we could both move on with our days.

"Can my friend leave her pots here until she's ready to load her car?" I asked.

Kathy nodded. "Of course! Why didn't you tell me you were Martin's friend? So nice to meet you! I would have given her a discount!" Kathy wrapped Karina in a friendly hug that I knew she would be thrown off by and definitely wouldn't enjoy.

Karina managed a smile as she gently untangled herself in the most polite way. "Nice to meet you."

I didn't think Kathy noticed that Karina had moved farther away from her to avoid further physical contact, but I sure as hell did. In some ways Karina was so predictable; in others she was a complete loose cannon.

"Go ahead and leave the plants. I'll watch 'em for you until you're ready to leave. No problem!"

I picked the pots up and put them just behind the cash register before Karina could even think about telling me not to. An Army family approached the Airstream, checking out a row of hanging flower baskets, and Kathy excused herself to greet them by name. She was like that: she could meet someone once and remember their names, where they're from, what they bought or eyed before.

"Thanks. You didn't have to do that," Karina told me, her tone clipped.

I looked up at her as she was tucking a loose piece of her light hair behind her ear. Her face was bare and a little red from the sun. She wasn't going to look at me if her life depended on it.

I hated games, but if she wanted to play, I'd play. And to be fair, I'd started it at the hospital—she was just continuing it.

"See you around," she said flatly. It pissed me off instantly, but I didn't look at her as I turned my back to her and started to walk the other way. I waved my hand in the air in hopes of getting a rise out of her.

I had no reason to stay a second longer. Even if she got over me helping her brother enlist, there were too many dark corners to shine lights in when it came to the two of us. It's not like she would ever actually be able to trust me. Not me, not anyone. I'd heard it a million times now.

I got about three steps away before she said my name, and I thought about acting like I didn't hear it to save both of our sanities, but I couldn't resist.

"Yeah?" I said, barely turning toward her.

Let's get this over with, Karina. No drama.

"It's just so weird that you're here." She pulled at her lips, and I dared to meet her eyes. "Are you alone?"

I nodded. Why was she asking?

She tucked her hands into the pockets of her gray cotton shorts. We stood in the grueling sun and didn't say a word. I tried to stop myself from reading her, but I slipped and studied her expression, her nervously twitching lips. The anxiety I could feel from her was tugging at me, pulling me in.

"Are *you* alone?"

Why couldn't I walk away from her? I was a man of control; I lived for it. Yet I couldn't just walk away from Karina.

She nodded. "Don't you think it's weird? That I'm here? If you come here all the time? I didn't know that. I was just trying to get out of the cookout that Elodie invited me to, and I never really do stuff like this. You know I don't just seek out random markets in the middle of nowhere. But I did, and here you are . . ."

What did she want from me? Some sign that I believed in fate?

That her stories about the stars and the moon made destiny bring us here to make up and be together? She'd had a chance, many chances, to listen to the universe about me, but she'd run.

My instincts screamed to get the fuck away from there.

Abort the fucking mission, Martin.

Apparently, I loved wasting my time. And so did she.

"And? Now that destiny has brought us both here, you're going to stop pretending like you don't know me? At the hospital, you didn't seem to." She blinked. "You barely spoke to me!"

Kathy looked over at us and I ushered Karina to move out of her sight. Man, the last thing I needed was to have everyone in this place all up in my personal life. I'd been coming here alone, only bringing Mendoza a few times since I moved to Benning, so even having Karina here was going to get them all whispering. I wanted to keep my routine here. Hellos and goodbyes. Salutes and the occasional hug from someone who wanted to thank me for my service.

"Look, this isn't the place for us to hash this out. Neither was the ER."

Her chin jutted out and she stepped closer to me, hands on her full hips. Always a fight with this one. And her brother. It must run in their blood.

"When is, then? Or were we just never going to talk and pretend it didn't happen?"

"You love to do that," I reminded her.

And just as I went to take back the blow, she threw it back at me. "Me? That's *your* MO."

"Well, we have that in common." I put a little distance between us; I needed a breath to get a handle on myself.

"You're so annoying," she huffed, kicking her foot out.

"And you're not?"

Her cheeks had gone from pink to red. Her eyes were pure chaos and they became laser-focused on destroying me. She was Daenerys from *Game of Thrones*, skilled at taking weak men down. I would be next if I didn't stop this now. She felt I had betrayed her, that I was on the other side now, opposing her, so I was fair game to attack.

"How do you not think what you did was fucked up?" Her voice sounded much less rage-filled than her body language let on. I couldn't even tell which one was real. Then she added, "Or do you not care anymore?"

"I'm not happy with the way it played out, or all the choices I made, no. But that doesn't change the fact that I made them, does it?"

She shook her head. "You literally don't care. This isn't the time to be quiet, Martin."

Using my last name, it was clear she wanted to get a reaction out of me.

No way in hell was I going to give her one.

Well, maybe a small one.

I moved closer to her, towering over her.

"You're not going to believe anything I say and it's not going to make you forget what I did, or change it, so we're just wasting time here. You're going to have to get over your brother's enlistment before you can even try to forgive me for being a part of it. He's going to get off the hook because you're family, but I'll be punished forever. Someday you'll thank me, but it will be a long fucking time, I'm sure."

She scoffed, eyes filled with anger. I was pretty sure this girl fucking hated me.

I whispered so a family walking by didn't hear me, "I know you." I breathed onto her, so close to her face that I could see the rise and fall of her breath in her chest.

"You *don't*, and never will," she said back to me.

It hurt like hell, but I kept going. She wasn't completely in the right here and I was done taking blame for every single fuckup between us. If she wasn't so closed-minded about everything, both Fischer and I would have told her sooner, but we knew better.

"Look, I told you I was worried about him from the jump. He was fucking up, badly, and I knew that, but it wasn't my place to tell you about just how bad it was. I tried to do what I could, and then he mentioned the Army. He had been trying to join for a while back in whichever Carolina your piece of shit uncle lives in. I know a good recruiter who wouldn't treat him like complete dog shit, so I introduced them. When I brought you up and asked what you thought about it, your brother asked me not to mention any of it to you until he could explain everything himself. He's your brother, your twin at that, so I stepped out of it. I don't get in the way of family shit, Karina, and you two have enough shit to work out. It wasn't my place."

I wondered what she would say. There was a tiny, tiny possibility that she would realize I wasn't the villain in her story. She'd have to change the entire narrative she had created over the last few weeks, but it was possible she could be rational.

Instead of being rational, she jutted her chin up, crossed her arms around her body to protect herself further, and said, in the most assured voice I'd ever heard, "You lied to me. Not just about that, but since I met you, you've been lying to me about my dad, about your past, about my brother. You're a narcissist and a liar."

I looked around us so slyly that Karina barely noticed. We were already getting some attention. A few people were flat-out standing there staring at us, saying things that I couldn't hear. I stayed close to her so that our voices wouldn't travel. The conversation was beyond fucking inappropriate to have right there, right then, and I got distracted by the man who was paying Kathy for his stuff. He was visibly growing impatient as Kathy's pen scratched the old-school receipt pad. She changed pens and continued to handwrite the bill and tap her finger against the calculator buttons.

"I didn't lie," I finally said. "It's not a lie if I had your best interest in mind when telling it."

"Yes, it is. It doesn't work like that. You don't get to decide what I can and can't handle." She took a deep breath. "God, I'm so sick of people fucking doing that."

"Let's agree to disagree and finish this when people aren't staring at us?"

She looked around, noticing the vendors and customers eavesdropping.

"Don't count on it. I never want to see you again and I have a lamp to buy, anyway." She threw her arms to her sides. Her sandal landed on the tip of a branch that snapped up, biting her leg.

She didn't stop, or even flinch as it cut her skin.

Such was her determination to prove a point to me.

CHAPTER SEVENTEEN

Karina

It took everything in me not to make a sound when I tripped on that damn stick, and it cut my leg.

Kael was right. I was not appropriately dressed for this place. I moseyed through the market—screw him, I wasn't leaving just because he was here—but did everything in my power to not run into him again. I kept an eye out for his blue cutoff T-shirt as I went from booth to booth, taking my time to enjoy the place since now I could never come back. This was his territory, not mine.

Ugh, he was so damn obnoxious and rude and now the one time in weeks that I felt relaxed, he had to be there and ruin it.

Good thing he was a complete asshole to me; I was two seconds away from making the mistake of asking him if he wanted to continue to talk it all out. In my head, we could have been walking around, talking about everything, laughing even, like the couple standing next to me, holding hands and sharing a big cup of lemonade with only one straw. It must be so nice to have someone to just be around and share straws with, laugh with. No worry about trust or lies or being abandoned. Watching the relaxed couple made me feel even crazier for thinking I could have that with someone, especially a soldier. Not to mention that Kael was such a dick! I had never been exposed to the massively petty side of him, and never wanted to be again. The silent and steady, involved but inheritably distant Kael was at least tolerable. This Kael who didn't follow me when I walked away—not tolerable. And his immature little hand wave? Fuck him.

I should just leave. This place had been really fun at first and I'd been convinced I had found my new favorite place, but now knowing this was his stomping ground and that he came here "all the time" ruined it. In reality, I would have been better off sitting in Elodie's friend's backyard and pretending that their conversations were interesting and that I cared if they liked me. I mean I guess I did care, but I was too tired lately to keep reassuring myself that not every person secretly hated me or found me annoying. So, I could have just sat there, even if they all hated me and thought I was annoying after all; at least Elodie would've been there. And they would've had hot dogs and burgers, probably—another plus. This place had Kael, which was worse than hanging out with a bunch of Army wives and faking interest for hours. I didn't even get to try the tacos or funnel cakes that smelled so good when I entered the market. I had been starving but somehow now lost my appetite. In the last few minutes, this place had become worse than drinking room temperature hot dog water.

It baffled me that a few weeks ago I was letting this man crawl into the dark little spaces of my mind, those I rarely even visited myself, and now my stomach lurched at the thought of how embedded in my life he had become. For fuck's sake, hadn't I learned anything from my parents? I needed to learn to cut ties with people who were toxic in my life, instead of yearning for them. While it wasn't necessarily Kael who was toxic, everything about our circumstances was too full of bad blood; it had accumulated in way too short a time, and he was clearly still hanging out with my brother, choosing loyalty to him over me.

I didn't know why I felt so shocked, given that literally everyone in my life had always done the same thing.

I kept browsing and time at the market passed in a mysterious way. Eventually I forgot about Austin, Kael, and even my cell phone. I slid my fingertips along the back of a deep-purple satin wingback chair. Bright and exaggerated in its features, it made me feel like Alice in Wonderland. The chair was beautiful and funky, but I couldn't see it in my house. Even so, I ran my fingers over the metal buttons along the lining and across the smooth fabric of the seat again. The soft pastel color of my nails against its harsher midnight sky shade was beautiful.

While no one was looking, I pulled out my phone and snapped a picture of my hand on the seat of the chair. I used portrait mode so the background was slightly blurry and the light was focused on brightening and deepening the colors of the image. It was actually a really beautiful picture. I immediately looked around to see if anyone had noticed, I felt embarrassed as I tagged #fleamarketfinds. I didn't really get why I felt so silly taking the pictures when that's what life was now. Phones were beyond an accessory at this point, and most everything was documented at least a million times throughout the day. Even as I looked around, phones were in over half of the people's hands.

Glancing at the time on my phone, I realized it was almost 5:00 p.m. That seemed impossible to me, but when I looked about, some of the stalls were packing up their products into lockboxes and carts. At one of the stands toward the back, by all the trees, the guy running it was still talking to customers as he cut his locally famous, fairly priced wooden beams one by one, a line of people waiting their turn. Despite his gregarious approach, I assumed everyone else packing up meant the flea market was getting close to closing.

Kael popped into my mind when I saw Elodie's name on my screen and over a hundred notifications from Instagram. I tapped the app open and scrolled through my notifications, which were usually one or two a week at max. I had comments from person after person asking where I was, where they could get that chair, and to post more pictures. Estelle, my dad's wife, even commented that I had a great eye. Weird.

I went away from the notifications screen and typed Kael's name into the search bar, a newly formed but apparently unbreakable habit. Nothing new. The last picture was one I'd seen a ton of times both here and on Facebook, the one from his deployment with Mendoza and Phillip. The realization that he could sneak up behind me at any time hit me, and I slid my phone back into the pocket of my shorts. I hated the way that once I had opened my thoughts to him, he engulfed them in one passing breath. It was such a different reality than I thought it would be.

Kael was basically a fuckboy. I wanted to pretend he wasn't, but at the end of the day, he was. Him acting like a total douche today proved it. He wanted to float through my life and not stay, just like everyone else, and I would let him. I wanted nothing to do with him anymore.

Now paranoid, I looked around. The flea market was much less crowded than when I got there. Kael was probably gone; I needed to quit psyching myself out.

Out of the corner of my eye, I saw a white chair with a huge winged back in the corner of a stall. The upholstery looked like it had oil blotches on it until I walked closer and realized the spots were actually black embroidered roses.

My heart sank when I checked for a price and didn't see one. Not a good sign.

The saleswoman was sitting on a stool with her face in front of a small pink plastic fan. She had on a Bob Seger T-shirt, and I thought about my mom and how she always wore a shirt from one of his concerts, which my dad had often taken her to when they first got together. My mom used to sing "Against the Wind" in the car with her arm out of the window, rolling it to the sound of the music and the force of the wind. Funny enough, both the chair and the woman working reminded me of my mom. The saleswoman's hair was styled the same way my mom's had been, two long braids hanging over her shoulders and wild curls escaping each side, framing her face. Even the chair looked like something my mom would salivate over.

The woman caught me staring at her, and of course I made it awkward and looked away, then right back, as soon as I realized what I'd done. She smiled and told me to tell her if I had any questions, then started rearranging a bowl full of extravagantly detailed doorknobs. I nodded, thanking her, and touched one fingertip to the petal of one of the roses. The black flowers were embroidered with thick, soft yarn. I always yearned for random, cool furniture, but this was calling to me in a different way. It was just so amazing, the shape of the chair and the casual way the roses were scattered across the eggshell-white fabric. It looked both old and new, classic and trendy. It wasn't too loud, but definitely not subtle.

I sighed and thought about the money in my pocket. I had no way of knowing how much the chair would be, and it was impossible to guess at this flea market. Just today I'd seen an old, cracked cabinet for twelve hundred dollars and a beautiful antique desk for only forty right at the next stand, so there was really no way to gauge without flat-out asking and for some reason, the woman with my mom's hair intimidated me too much to ask. I was the kind of person who found so many simple things embarrassing, from crossing the street on a busy intersection—the countdown on the traffic light taunting me—to raising my hand in class. I had always been that way.

I noticed that a set of plates on the display table next to me didn't have a sticker. Most things in the stall didn't seem to have a price. Again, not a good sign. They were either expensive or she wanted to bargain, which I absolutely dreaded and couldn't do. I looked at the beautiful chair again. It would go perfectly in my living room; that was a good sign. I could move my couch over a little and turn the other chair to face this one . . .

I bit the bullet. "How much is this chair with the roses?" I asked the woman, my heart racing over the simple question.

She got down from her stool and walked over to me. Her cloth skirt flowed around her, the bottom of the dark linen covered in dusty dirt. I imagined that everyone, including me, would leave this place with a thin layer of dirt on their entire body. Beyond the similarity to my mother, there was something about her face that felt familiar, like someone from an old movie, when you couldn't recall what you'd seen them in before. Knowing how much of Hollywood had become scattered throughout Georgia, it wouldn't surprise me if she actually was.

"That chair, the upholstery is handsewn. It came all the way from Missouri. It was my granddad's and his old mistress hand-sewed the whole thing," the woman told me, just glazing right over the mistress part with a smile.

Her fingers were decorated with rings, and she had a bunch of long dangly necklaces hanging down and hitting poor Bob Seger in the face as she moved.

"You can have it for two-fifty. And that's a good deal. Two-fifty doesn't even cover the fabric; it's a steal. I can see the way you're looking at it, so I'm willing to go that low. I just get off on the fact that that bitch worked so hard on it for me not to keep it." Her sarcasm was thick with wit. I laughed a little.

I groaned. Of course, I couldn't afford it. I wasn't denying its worth, but it was just too much for me.

"Thank you, but I can't afford it right now," I said, looking at the chair as I backed away from her stall.

Ugh, it was so freaking beautiful.

My lack of extra spending money was another reason I couldn't imagine working for Mali forever. It kept me afloat right now, but by the time I was twenty-five, I wanted to be able to spend two-fifty on a chair on a random Sunday instead of feeling the burn of longing for something I couldn't have.

A voice caught me and the woman just as I was slipping away. "You can't do one-fifty?"

Kael stepped in front of me, his hands in front of his chest like he was praying.

"It's a very expensive chair, Martin. My stepmother handmade the upholstery."

Funny how she was mistress to me, stepmom to Kael. I loved the thought of women being honest with each other. She was a badass, I could just tell. It was also hilarious how Kael just happened to have this woman immediately charmed, and had for quite some time, by the looks of it. She was smiling, touching her long hair in a way that wasn't flirty, but made me jealous of how well she knew him. Just like the Airstream lady, she was all threaded into this life of his that I was oblivious to.

Everyone here seemed to have drunk an ice-cold glass of the Kael Martin Kool-Aid on a hot summer day.

Everyone except for me. I'd only had a sip. I craved more, but I knew it turned sour before it dripped on my tongue.

"I know, Ms. Rosa. But Karina here is living alone and trying to fix up her house."

I wanted to elbow him or tell her I was sorry that he was so obnoxious and loved to overstep, but her expression changed as he kept going.

Soon it seemed like he was actually winning the negotiation.

"Her brother's my close friend. He just joined the service . . ."

I felt a twinge of guilt until I realized yeah, my brother *was* going into the damn Army. If a cheaper chair was one tiny thing that made that a little better, then so be it. I'd also have to take the hit of calling my dad to ask him to drive all the way out here to help haul it back, which, apart from the fact that we weren't speaking, would add at least an hour of judgmental stares and snide comments about my safety, and my outfit, and how I wasn't being responsible going so far alone, how ugly and unnecessary the purchase was . . .

I was starting to wonder if the chair was even worth the head-ache and suffocation that would linger with me most of the day. And calling my dad wasn't rational, not after what we'd been through. But, then again, maybe Estelle would like the market. She seemed to like the picture I posted. But calling my dad was the last thing I wanted to do.

"Her twin brother, only twenty years old." I suddenly realized Kael was still negotiating on my behalf. Man, was he good at this. His charisma (when he felt like using it) made him impossibly alluring and hard to argue with.

Kael and Ms. Rosa went back and forth in twenty-dollar incre-ments, then five-dollar increments, eventually landing at two hundred. He was insanely smooth at negotiating. It was hard to look away. I really wanted the chair now and watching them barter felt sort of like a game, exciting and now I was even more invested.

"My dad's in the—" I began to say, but Kael stopped me with a gentle hand on my back. It was so obvious the way he did it, but his sweet friend Ms. Rosa didn't seem to notice, which was weird.

"One-seventy-five," he bargained.

Problem was, I only had just a little over a hundred dollars left.

"Kael, I only have one-twenty on me," I told him quietly.

"It's going to a good home," Kael told her, ignoring my warning of insufficient funds.

The tone he was using with her could sell carpet cleaner to a woman with hardwood floors.

With a couple more "pleases" and his huge, bright-white smile, she was so close to caving.

"Is she your girlfriend or something?" Her brow arched and she looked me up and down. I wasn't sure if she approved or not. I guess I'd find out soon.

"Sort of. I'm trying to convince her to be so if you could help me out . . . that would be great."

His smile was so infectious.

I caught the worst case and was smiling like an idiot when she finally caved. She broke out of character seconds later, smiling at him as he pulled out his wallet. She looked at me and I felt like she was in on some secret that I wasn't. It didn't make me paranoid like that thought usually did. Rather, it made me feel warm and made me smile shyly back at her. Ms. Rosa stuck her hand out for my cash and I placed it in her palm and watched as she counted it along with Kael's. I would go right to the ATM when we finished paying her and give Kael back every penny he'd put toward the chair. I didn't want to spend the extra money, but I really fucking wanted that chair, and I sure as hell wasn't going to owe him any-thing, not even fifty-five bucks.

I thanked her, Kael thanked her, and she hugged him. He truly did know everyone here, and I never even knew this place existed.

"Come around to this side more," Ms. Rosa said. "I know Mendoza can't come or sell here anymore, and I'm sorry for what happened . . . but we miss you on this side. How are you doing? I heard you got hurt."

She looked at him from toe to forehead and back to his leg, which made me really look at him. I realized he looked tired and a little dirty, as if he'd just done some sort of manual labor, a sweat ring on the back of his sky-blue T-shirt. He was so unfairly hot. Something about the casual confidence he exuded made me unable to look away from him. Ms. Rosa seemed to feel the same way I did. And she knew him and his friends better than I did.

Mendoza? So, Mendoza used to come here more often than I thought with Kael? Or sold something here, and now can't? I tried to make sense of it all, and what she said about his injured leg, while wondering how I managed to feel so close to him, but actually didn't know him at all. As far as I knew, Kael's leg was a little tender and ached sometimes here and there, but he was healing normally. At least, that's what he'd told me. I didn't know which of us had the real scoop, but I assumed it wasn't me.

"It's nothing." Kael bent a little to look down at his legs. "Just some soreness here and there. Who told you that, anyway?"

I noticed how sweet his voice was with her. And it sort of surprised me, no lie. I wondered how he knew her so well; Was it just from coming here on the weekends and visiting with Mendoza? So many questions, none of which made me feel particularly good.

Damn this stunning chair for being here today and damn me for not having any self-control and letting Kael help me.

"Your momma. She's been calling me. Well, she calls me here and there, but just the other day, she called by accident, but we ended up talking for a few." She gave him a knowing smile. She seemed like a woman who loved to gossip, but still had a pure heart and good intentions.

At the mention of Kael's mom, I perked up. He rarely talked about her, and I wanted to know if Ms. Rosa would give any clues as to why that was.

I knew he was a private person, but I wanted to know everything about him, while telling everyone, including myself, that I didn't. And I knew it wouldn't be coming from him, so it was one of my last chances to crack him open before he left my life for good.

The irrational, more curious side of me hoped he wouldn't just end the conversation or smile and sweetly nudge the topic away from himself, like he did with me most of the time.

"And you two just gossiped about me?" He was teasing her, and the smile he gave her was one I had never seen from him. "Nothing better to do?"

He looked like a carefree teenage boy for a second, like how I imagined him before the Army. It made me sad for him. I wondered how his mom saw him. And how she was. A tiny, little, small—very small, so small that I could easily see how stupid it was—part of me wished I could have been able to meet her. I wanted to see the woman who worked her fingers to the bone to raise such a morally sound man. Well, when it came to his views, not as a boyfriend, or whatever he'd been.

"That's what mommas do. I miss her sweet face coming in here with you. It's been so long," she said, looking at me with an expression that assumed I knew his mom and what she'd been up to. Ms. Rosa was sweet, but didn't have a clue.

A little sadness hit me again, and I missed a woman whom I didn't even know.

I really, really needed to get out of there. It must've been something in the lemon water from the Airstream that made me lose my good judgment.

"Well, I'll tell her you said hi when I talk to her next," Kael replied.

He looked down at his phone for a moment, then back up.

"It was nice seeing you, Ms. Rosa. I won't stay gone so long next time, but I do have to get going."

Immediately, I wondered where he was going. Home? The cookout? Somewhere else secretive people like him went to hang out and conspire how to confuse the rest of us?

Ms. Rosa hugged both of us. People here must really love to hug strangers. Giving me one more look over, she left me wondering if she approved of me or not. Not that it mattered, but I still couldn't tell by the time she left us standing by my pretty new chair.

"I'll go to the ATM now and grab the money I owe you," I said. "I have to figure out how to get this home."

"Don't worry about it," he said, shrugging.

His T-shirt was loose around his neck, exposing his collarbone and the full length of his shoulders to his fingertips. A hot chill ran over my entire body. His skin was gleaming with the warm kiss of the sun.

"What? Of course, I'm giving you the money back."

"It's what, sixty bucks?" he asked, shrugging.

"Fifty-five. I don't like to owe people anything, especially given our . . . circumstances." I metaphorically dug my flip-flops into the dirt.

He laughed lightly, kicking his boot against the loose dust at our feet. "Oh, I know you don't. I don't need the money back, even though you're going to force me to take it."

He looked up at me, so I rolled my eyes. "Are you ever going to stop acting like you know me when you don't?"

He cocked his head to the side. A little smile played on his lips like whatever he was going to say hung the stars. "I do know you, though."

"Barely."

"Well, I haven't been wrong so far."

I snorted. "Uhm, cocky much?" I straightened my back, trying to compete with his height. "Whatever you say."

Kael looked down at his phone again. I could barely hear the faint ring.

"I gotta go. You can give me the money for the chair later."

"Where are you going?" I asked before thinking. I wanted to slap myself on the forehead, but he was looking right at me with a curious expression that made my stomach twist.

His brows pulled in and he did that smile thing again and it made my stomach flutter. "To the baby shower," he said plainly.

Huh? Not what I expected, and I stood there stunned for a moment as his fingers tapped the screen of his phone.

"What baby shower?" I asked.

He looked at me like I was an idiot.

"Elodie's? I was wondering why you weren't there today, but figured you must've gone already and left or something."

Kael looked around at the people closing up their stalls. A man in a football jersey waved at him as he walked by carrying a folding table.

"What do you mean Elodie's baby shower? I haven't even started planning it yet."

"It's Tharpe's wife who planned it. Toni? She's saying it's a cookout so Elodie wouldn't catch on, but it's really a baby shower. Didn't they give you the invite?"

I shook my head. "Uh, no. They didn't."

I swallowed. My throat was so dry all of a sudden. I was embarrassed as hell and I wanted to disappear so I could process this.

"I mean, Elodie invited me to a platoon cookout, but I really didn't want to go . . ."

Then the embarrassment really flared up. My chest was on fire. I was the one who was supposed to plan her baby shower, or so I'd thought . . .

"Nobody told me it was a baby shower. No one even told me they were planning one. I don't have any of those women's numbers or contacts, anyway, but I would have helped . . . I thought I was planning it anyway. If I had known, I would have gone."

I wanted to cry.

Kael looked like he didn't know what to say to me.

"Oh," was all he said.

I wanted to snap at him, but this time my pain wasn't his fault. I took out my phone to text Elodie to apologize. I couldn't believe none of those women thought to invite me. Even worse: they threw a baby shower for her, and I had just assumed that I would be the one to do that. This was a clear, blazing message that those girls either hated me or didn't care to remember my existence at all.

"Do you wanna come with me? I'm going there now," Kael said.

I shook my head. "No fucking way."

"Why not?"

I blew out my breath. "Well, they clearly didn't want me there in the first place."

"It must have been a mix-up? They don't even know you, do they?" he asked seriously.

"I can't just show up uninvited. Ugh, I hate cliquey people. Whatever, I didn't want to go to that cookout, anyway. I'll have my own shower for her." I talked myself through the rejection I felt.

"Who cares what they think? Elodie's your best friend and lives with you. If anyone says anything, they'd be fucking stupid."

"People are usually stupid when given the chance."

He laughed. "You have an answer for everything, don't you?"

I pulled my lip between my teeth and nodded. "I'd be a great lawyer if I wasn't so empathetic and too poor for law school."

"Okay, Miss Empathy . . ." His voice changed to a whisper. "To everyone but me. Let's go to the baby shower for Elodie, not them. Plus, I can help you get that chair home? Your house is sort of on the way," he said.

It wasn't.

"I'll figure it out on my own." I blocked the low sun from my eyes with one hand. It was shining bright, just behind Kael's head and shoulders, but his broad body hid most of the light, except for where it crept around the edges of him.

He laughed. "Wow. You'd rather be stuck here with this chair with no way to get it home than ride with me. I didn't realize it was quite at that level," he said in a sad voice.

"I wouldn't have had the chance to tell you how I felt and it's not like you actually asked. You ghosted me." I rolled my eyes, arguing to lighten up the conversation. "Obviously it would be easier for you to bring the chair, but I wasn't thinking of you offering to take it."

"You know I will gladly help you—anytime," he said.

I wanted to tell him that no, I didn't know that. Not at all.

"I really wanted the chair and now, thanks to you, I have it, so whoever drives it home doesn't matter," I said in a dramatic way while hugging the back of it and sighing. "It's so beautiful."

"Yeah." He paused and I caught his eyes on my mouth. "It is."

I could feel my heart pounding. He licked his lips.

"Come on, Kare. Come with me. You don't want to miss her baby shower. I'm sorry they didn't invite you, but this is about Elodie, not them."

I rolled my eyes heavily. "Oh, don't you try that salesy shit on me. I'm immune to your charm."

He smirked at me, calling me a liar with his eyes. "Right."

"Besides, I don't know if I should go now that it's almost over. I was going to throw her one closer to her due date. I thought people waited until they knew the gender of the baby. They should have waited so people could actually know what to buy."

I looked up at Kael. He was leaning against a dining-room table set that was only eighty dollars for all six pieces. It looked at least a hundred years old and cool as hell with etchings of lines in the wood, marking family dinners, excited kids, memories made. Kael's finger traced along the edge of the table, collecting a tiny bit of dust.

"I have no idea why they did it now. I just found out yesterday, so I guess it was a last-minute kind of thing. I'm almost done with her gift. It's still got another week until it's ready, but I'm still going to stop by and at least show my face at the party."

I glared at him.

"Even though your baby shower would have been much, much better."

I smiled. So did he.

I looked around at the booths that were still open. "Ugh, and even if I stop by, I won't have a gift. What did you get her?"

"A crib," he told me, his voice lower and the cocky smile evaporating into the sticky market air.

I couldn't help but smile. "A crib. Wow."

"I'm making it, though, so it's taking longer than expected."

My mouth hung open. "You're making it, as in building it yourself?"

He nodded.

"Now I definitely can't show up with you, you're showing me up too much."

That was so sweet of him. I needed the reminder that he wasn't always an emotionless toy soldier, and that I wasn't a total crazy person for having seen something completely different in him once upon a time. Him building Elodie a crib for her baby by hand definitely did the trick of flipping my opinion of Kael. The thought of him coming here to buy wood to build a crib was pulling me to him emotionally. It changed something in the way I was looking at him, brought in a little light that I hoped Kael would put out with another lie before I was too far gone.

"Yeah. I'm sweet. I know." He wiped sweat from his forehead. "So are you going to stop being a brat and come with me or not?"

CHAPTER EIGHTEEN

When I first agreed to go, it was mostly the thrill of bickering with Kael that fueled the choice. It was also annoyance and anger that Elodie's friends hadn't even thought to invite me, or worse, maybe they purposely hadn't. I would find out soon enough.

My stomach ached with anxiety, already regretting climbing into Kael's truck. I was waiting for him, staring into the mirror, watching his body grow bigger and bigger as he got closer and closer in the reflection. He'd told me to wait in the truck while he did the work. I attempted to argue once, but the stinging from the cuts on my arms from the plants and the gash on my leg told me to shut it and I sat inside his car and watched him through the mirror. He was carrying my two new plants in both his arms. He was so solid, the body of a man who carried the world with him everywhere he went.

When he approached, I turned the music up while he fit both the chair and the plants into the back. I watched him play *Tetris* with it all for a few seconds, offered to help, but he ignored me. I thought about ditching out one more time before I snapped my seatbelt on and off out of boredom and checked my phone. Alerts for Instagram were still popping up from the picture of the purple chair. I knew the picture was good, but I didn't expect actual attention for it.

It was weird, this unfamiliar rush that came with scrolling down the list of somewhat familiar names. I usually didn't give a damn about these people; I just looked at their socials when I was bored. But now that I was fresh on their minds with my chair pic, I wondered what they thought about me and my post-high-school life. Hopefully they were under the impression that I had a lot more going on than I actually did. My senior year of high school was already three years ago, and it didn't feel like that much time had passed at all. Maybe because outside of putting a roof over my head I hadn't really done shit with my life beyond becoming a licensed massage therapist, which was great, but even that was over two years ago. In that time, Kael had deployed twice and many people I knew had long-term relationships, marriages, and some even had kids. I shivered a little even though it was hot as hell outside.

"Should we drop the stuff off at my house first?" I asked Kael when he sat down in the driver's seat. "You can follow me."

He turned the radio volume dial down until it was silent and shook his head. He took the bottom of his T-shirt and lifted it up to rub the sweat off his forehead. God, this car felt small, despite being a huge Bronco. I turned the a/c up higher. Not just for his comfort, but so he would keep his body covered.

"Not a chance." He smiled, wiping his face again.

I didn't look down at his bare skin, even though every part of me wanted to.

"Why not?" I asked.

"Because you won't go to Tharpe's house with me. You'll have me help you drop your shit off and you'll bounce. I know—"

He stopped himself before he said *you*.

"No way!" I laughed at his audacity for being so close to the truth. "I mean, yeah, I would maybe try that, but who knows? Maybe I go and we have fun?"

I caught what I said at the same time he did.

I stumbled to correct myself. "Not *we*. I meant *I*. Maybe I'll have fun."

He looked at me, skeptical, but his eyes were alight in a way that almost convinced me to tag along.

"Karina. You're honestly trying to tell me that you're willing to come? Because I can bring the stuff by, then drive there. You don't have to go. I just think it would be nice for Elodie if you were there. You're important to her, but I don't want you to be uncomfortable," he explained.

I blew out a puff of air, my legs fidgeting under my body, and ended up even closer to him.

"I'm going. Still feels like I'm intruding, though. But I can't go like this." I looked down at my ratty clothes. "My shirt has a literal hole in it." I poked my purple fingernail through. "I'd look like an idiot."

"You won't. Trust me," he said, like it wasn't weird for him to compliment me suddenly.

"Thanks." I met his eyes.

His breath caught in his throat and if he didn't mean to look at me like that, then it sure as hell felt like he did. Seconds passed as neither of us moved. Not one coherent thing passed through my mind. I could feel him, so close to me, all around me. The closest thing to the feeling was a hot bath with lavender-scented bubbles floating around the air, calming, refreshing.

He leaned in a little closer, and my heart picked up such speed that I worried he would hear it.

"See, we can be friends, after all." His words fell between us heavily.

I blinked, a little stunned and a lot ashamed that for a second I'd thought . . .

I don't know what I'd thought. I shook my head, scooting toward the window and away from him.

"We'll see about friends. Don't get your hopes up." I tried to keep my tone as playful and as far away from desperate as I could.

"Oh, I don't have any hopes, Karina."

He kicked his truck into reverse.

"What are you doing? I have my car here!" I yelled when he pushed the gas pedal down.

"I'm just driving you to your car," he told me, smiling a little as he turned the steering wheel. My hand clenched the handle on the door and I laughed it off, my heart pounding as we drove in silence except for the air conditioner blowing at full speed. Even the radio was off.

He drove a few rows over and parked close to my car.

"Thanks for the ride," I told him as I opened the door and got out. I heard his door open and watched him walk around to my car. He was waiting by the driver's-side door. His hand rubbed the top of his thigh as he stood there, waiting for me to get into my car.

"Is your leg bothering you?" I asked him, looking down at it.

I hoped not, especially because he had carried a heavy chair and plants for me. But my question only brought silence out of him. Even when he'd stayed over, he kept his leg covered. He kept his leg covered when he got massages and when he showered at my house; he always took pants into the bathroom with him to put on before he came back to my room. I had gotten so used to not asking that honestly sometimes I forgot about his injury.

"I'm fine. I'll follow you to your house." His key chain dangled from his index finger and he looked toward the highway about a hundred yards away from us.

He pulled on the unlocked door of my car, opening it for me.

"You shouldn't leave your doors unlocked here. Or anywhere." His brows pulled together and he rubbed his temple with one finger.

"I've been better about that," I said, sort of telling the truth.

"Right." He nodded to the open door. "I can see that."

I made a face at him as I moved by him to get into my car. He closed the door before I could even grab the handle and hit his hand against the door.

"You know, I liked when you talked less."

"I'm sure you did." He laughed, his voice farther away as he got into his truck.

The day couldn't have been further from what I'd expected it to be. I wondered if I would have still gone inside the market had I seen his Bronco in the lot. My head was still spinning from being so close to him in the car.

Gah, he makes me crazy.

I turned the radio on. A song was just ending and Ryan Seacrest's voice came on reading an ad for a dating app. The universe was taking jabs at me again. Thanks, Ryan.

I changed the station, then pulled up the directions home and propped my cell up in my cupholder so I could drive. Kael probably didn't need directions, so *I* probably should have followed *him* back.

I pulled out onto the road, Kael behind me. I couldn't believe those women had thrown Elodie a baby shower and hadn't invited me. I tried not to take it too personally, but that was pretty damn hard. I had spent the morning anxious over a damn cookout and was stressed enough at the idea of that. Being involved in their baby shower would probably have been worse because of the pressure of getting the gift, helping with the decorations, coordinating with people I barely knew. So, I didn't care out of a sense of being left out, per se. I was mostly disappointed that those girls threw the shower before I could. I was Elodie's closest friend. I mean, she lived with me. Unofficially or not, she slept at my house, on my couch, every night.

Elodie was probably going to think they cared more about her than I did. Toni, the girl who'd picked her up from the emergency room, likely decorated her on-post house for the occasion, and Elodie was probably so happy. Her house was probably bigger and definitely nicer than mine. I hated that these people had this power over me to make me feel so insecure. I didn't want to be that kind of girl, but something in my brain forced me to be.

I looked back at Kael's white Bronco following behind me. Looking at him made me feel steady for a moment. It calmed the rush of thoughts that were piling on top of each other as I drove. Unfortunately for me, I couldn't watch him and drive at the same time.

With every mile marker I passed, I felt more and more nervous about potentially dropping by the baby shower. I wasn't invited, and by the time we got back to my house, I wouldn't have time to get ready at all. I lifted my body to see my face in the rearview mirror. I didn't look like complete shit; little red specks of acne still covered my cheeks, but my skin was clearer today than it was the day before. I would only have time to throw some clean clothes on and possibly apply some mascara, concealer, and lip gloss.

By the time we pulled into my driveway, I had convinced myself not to go. He knew I would try to get out of going, I knew I would, too, but it still felt nice to daydream about going with Kael. I didn't think he would make a thing out of me canceling, more than just the typical *told you so*, but I didn't care about that nearly enough to be tortured socially. He waited by his truck until I unlocked my front door and propped my screen door open.

"I'm surprised your door is locked," he called from the edge of the driveway.

"Are you sure you don't need me to help you?" I offered as he unloaded the stuff.

"Nah, just keep the door open!" he yelled back.

My neighbor Bradley walked out onto his porch, looked from Kael to me, nodded politely, grabbed the newspaper that was lying there, and went back inside. I wondered if he knew he could read all that online. He seemed like the kind of guy who wouldn't realize that or at least wouldn't care to.

I nodded to Kael, and he lifted the chair out of his car. I popped in to move the old chair I'd been using out of the way, and as he walked into my place, I tried to think of something to say. Whenever he was around, I found it hard to not fill the silence, even in my small living room.

I pointed to the spot in my living room where my other chair had been moments ago, and he gently placed it there. Kael eyed the old chair in the corner.

"You're not throwing that out, are you?"

I nodded. "Yeah. It's old and creaky."

"It's so comfortable, though."

I laughed, remembering Kael's long legs dangling off the edge of it as he slept with it reclined. That felt so long ago. I wondered if we were thinking the same thing. It felt like we were.

"You can have it if you want?"

His face lit up. It was more of a reaction than I expected over an old chair that I'd taken from my dad's when Estelle remodeled their house.

"Let me pay you for it." He reached for his wallet. "Or just take that cash you owe me from the chair. Chair for chair."

"Chair for chair?" I teased him. "You're getting ripped off here. But I'll take it as long as you know that."

"I'm aware." He smiled. "I like that one. I slept like a baby in that thing."

I imagined Kael sleeping in a sleeping bag on the desert floor, his body having to adapt to the extreme climate change during the nights.

Kael looked at his phone right as I said, "Take it. Be my guest."

I waited a couple seconds while he texted someone. Finally, he looked up. "Last chance to go to the baby shower?"

"As jealous as I am of the fun you'll have, I have to . . . I have stuff to do. It's almost over and I don't have a gift or anything. I don't even have real shoes on."

Leaning against his new chair, Kael looked at me. "Okay," he said, exhaling a deep breath with the word.

"Okay?" I repeated.

"I can tell them you said hi." He shrugged.

"Then they'll know you saw me. I don't want that because Elodie might feel bad and I'm tired and have been out all day and—"

He lifted his hand to stop me. "I get it. I won't mention your name. I still think you should go to give them all a big fuck-you. I do have to go, though, since it's almost over."

"Go ahead," I said too quickly. My neck started to prickle. I wanted this confusing day to end.

"Okay?" He laughed softly. I liked that he wasn't pressuring me, but also kind of wanted him to at least try to convince me. God, I was all over the place.

"I'll drop the plants inside before I go, though."

He was on his phone again. I wondered if he'd really just found out about the shower and whoever the distraction on his phone was and if they were there waiting on him. I wasn't a part of the platoon's little group like he was, so I didn't know much of anything.

Whether he spent a lot of time with them or not, he was at least in the platoon and was friends with a lot of the guys. My mind started down the path of a conspiracy theory that Elodie must have told her Army wife group about me and Kael and my chest started to burn.

"Karina? You good?" Kael asked.

His voice brought a slice of reality back to me. My mind always went to the most extreme places. I wished it wasn't like that, but it always had been.

"Yeah," I said, my voice tight.

Kael would notice it. I knew he would, and when he then looked at me, he would say something, his lips touching my ear, like when he woke up in my bed telling me—

"Are you sure, though?" he asked. "Not talking about me and you. I'm talking about you, just in general." He stood in my doorway, still as a statue with his square jaw set.

I nodded. "Yeah. I'm just tired. Today was a long day . . . well, the month has been long, and I have to work in the morning, and shower. I'm fine. Really."

Kael sighed and rubbed his fingers over his smooth chin. "Okay. See you around then?"

"See you around then," I repeated.

He hesitated before he spoke. "Karina?"

I looked at him. "Yeah?"

"Your hair looks really good like that," he said, pointing toward my head. Self-consciously, I ran my hands over my hair.

He grabbed the old chair he was taking by one arm and wrapped his other one around the back of it. I stood there, not sure what to say outside of a mumbled "Thank you."

He carried the chair out of the living room without looking back. I left the door unlocked so he could bring the plants in and waited in the kitchen until I heard the door close again. I was all over the place and he was confusing me more than ever. I was supposed to hate him, to never even consider speaking to him again, yet the smile on my face wouldn't fade. I pulled the door shut tighter and locked both locks. I put the TV on and turned the volume up so I couldn't hear Kael's truck roar away from the curb. Now that I was in my little house again, alone, the plants were way less exciting than they had seemed earlier, most of their magic lost.

The chair was still as beautiful as ever, at least. I sat down on it, touching the fabric as I tried to relax and not think about the baby shower, and Kael, and how damn weird the day had been.

CHAPTER NINETEEN

Kael

The baby shower turned out to be more beer bottle than baby bottle vibe. Essentially, it was a backyard barbecue with a few baby-themed decorations here and there. Which was fine, but it hardly differed from the typical *Good Luck!* theme of an on-post BBQ.

When I first pulled up to the house, I wished that Karina would have agreed to come with me. Or that I would have stayed at her place just a little longer or talked to her more, asked her more questions about how she was and what she'd been up to. Part of me liked to have her as my little secret, but that was selfish; I hadn't introduced her to the guys' wives, but I knew the women would like her attitude and maybe even be inspired by her independence. I knew these wives weren't her crowd, but they weren't that bad, and at least Mendoza and Gloria would be around. If Karina would at least try to be friends with people, she would actually like Gloria. Their van was parked in front of the house, right next to Lawson's green Mustang. Lawson was that kind of fucking guy: patriotic Army stickers decorated his bumper like he bought them in bulk and a pair of fuzzy dice from the whack era of the 2000s hung from the rearview.

I rang the doorbell and Tharpe's wife, Toni, answered immediately.

She was a tall woman, mostly legs and a big smile. Her cheekbones were harsh but pretty and her eyes were blanketed with lack of sleep, or too much to drink; I couldn't tell just yet.

"Martin! I can't believe you actually came!" she said, hugging me. She smelled like a keg of beer and the glittery body spray my sister used to wear when she was in middle school.

I pulled away, but with a smile. "Thanks for inviting me."

Toni's brown eyes were pretty bloodshot, as were those of the other women on the back porch standing with Elodie. I walked by their separate clusters, waving, and stopped to double-kiss Elodie, who was describing to Fischer her love for American television. They were having the classic *Friends*-versus-*Seinfeld* debate. I shook Fischer's hand and looked around the yard, wondering if his sister would tell him I had been with her today. Everyone else was huddled in different pockets on the sloping grass. The food table, the grill, the sitting table. About twenty-five people in all, though I would have thought it would have thinned out more by this time. The yard smelled like tobacco and gristle from the grill.

"We have plenty of food left," Toni told me. "And drinks. Beers are here." She pointed to a blue plastic cooler on the ground.

"Thanks, I just ate," I lied. I wasn't hungry. I was fucking *worn out* and wanted to lay my ass in my bed at the soonest possible convenience. My leg was throbbing as I stepped off the deck and started walking down the hill. I was driving so I declined the beer too.

"Martin." Mendoza patted my back with a beer bottle in his hand—the one that wasn't fucked up.

He was leaning against the wooden fence and Gloria was sitting a few feet away in a chair, a can of Coke in her hand and her eyes on the kids playing in the yard as I walked over to say hi. They were running around with a bunch of bubbles and through a sprinkler with some other kids I didn't recognize. When Mendoza's kids saw me, two out of three came across the yard to say hi. Viviana, the middle one, ran up and wrapped her arms around my legs. My right leg ached when her bony arm pressed against it, but I couldn't bring myself to say anything to her. She was just so cute, so I smiled down and tried to keep a straight face.

I had been painless until a few minutes ago, when the rush of adrenaline from seeing Karina had faded away and the ache popped back up and the burning crept into every thread of my muscle.

I looked up to move my focus to anything else. I had plenty of experience avoiding pain. That's what war was: finding ways to not acknowledge the pain you were experiencing. You couldn't focus your brain on anything but Army-taught instincts and the grue-some art of war. If I thought about that, even for longer than a few seconds, I would remember the young girl in her hijab carrying a little boy's dead body in her arms . . . his face covered in dirt and blood. There were so many casualties every day that the boy could have been her brother, or she could have just found him on the street. I blinked to get that shit out of my mind. The pain, it was the pain that I associated every war memory with and sometimes when I wasn't paying attention, it would hit me. I'd been having these flashes more often the last few days. Maybe it was the fresh-ness of the encounter with Karina's dad, or Mendoza yelling about the unfairness of it all as he punched his hand through the glass of his back door.

It wasn't that I didn't feel the overwhelming, crushing guilt of war, but I could rationalize my choices for the most part. I didn't know how, or why, I was so lucky to not completely snap like some did. *Not yet, at least.* I didn't understand what I was doing, while I was doing it. That's what I told myself. I was back in the tent again;

I could almost taste the salt on my sweaty lips and smell the thick smoke in the air from the latest IED explosion. My skin started to prickle as I traveled back and forth between reality and my trauma.

I'm here, at Benning. Home. A drive from my ma and sister. A drive from Karina. I'm not there anymore.

I thought about what I was told in group therapy, to breathe. To count and breathe and look down at my feet, grounded to the green grass here at Fort Benning, not the dirt in Afghanistan.

"Martin! Hi! We were waiting on you so long! My daddy said you weren't coming, but I knew you would!" Viviana practically shouted, wagging her little finger in disapproval. She stood in front of me and lifted her arms into the air. Her face was morphing into the little girl from my memory in front of me.

I had to snap out of it.

Fuck.

"Hey, Daddy! I told you he would come! I'm always right!" she yelled across the lawn. Her voice was right below me, but sounded like she was talking through a tunnel.

I thought about today's events as a way to bring me back to the real world. The hours I spent polishing wood for Elodie's crib, the surprise of seeing Karina, how she looked going from stall to stall with no idea I was following her. I could feel her calmness as she browsed through the market. I missed the energy she brought to me.

The pull back to reality wasn't instant or easy, but it was close enough to come back to the present as I had to once again step over my past.

"Helloooo!" An impatient Vivi jumped in front of me, and I tried to play it off like I'd ignored her as a joke as the feeling came back to my legs, my grounded boots on the grass.

I laughed, and looked ahead, purposely ignoring her for a

second, then stuck my tongue out. I lifted her into my arms and pushed the pain back into the past. I was stronger than it was. Holding her right now proved it.

Viviana's legs wrapped around my waist. Fuck did holding her hurt, but I ignored the screaming of my muscles. I knew I shouldn't have lifted the plants, or the chairs, but at the time it felt so good to have my strength back. I was not used to this weak body yet; I refused to ever get fully used to it.

"Who told you I wasn't coming?" I asked her, pointing at her dad, who had now moved on to liquor, straight from the bottle. "I told him I would be late." I dipped her body down and she squealed. I barely noticed the pain.

The youngest boy, Julien, had been waving to me from near the back fence for a minute before I noticed. I waved back as his sister continued wiggling in my arms. Julien didn't seem to want to leave the bubble machine he was playing with. I couldn't blame him. A stream of fresh bubbles wafted past his face, a few catching on the dark curls hanging down his forehead. He laughed and I took a relaxed breath, watching the happiness on their youthful faces. Then I looked back over at Mendoza, a father who had even more demons than I did. I knew these kids' lives weren't always this full of laughter and sunlight. There were mostly dark and stormy nights, with the stress of unpaid bills and their dad's on-and-off absence due to the Army.

When parents come in and out of their kids' lives, it impacts them. I knew some of the best, strongest parents who did everything they could right, and I still saw the difference in their family when they would come back from deployment. You adjusted to life a certain way and then they came back and threw things off balance and a new routine began. No matter how happy the soldier's family would be to have them home again, the transition was always a struggle that no one really talked about, and it was fucking complicated. Plus, now they had a whole new beast to deal with in his PTSD episodes. His bandaged hand was a fresh reminder for us all.

"They're so messy." Viviana pointed to a group of five soldiers I didn't seem to recognize, beers in their hands, rowdy before the sun was even down. She was too mature for her age, but with her mom's strength and fearlessness to call people out, even adults, I didn't worry much about her.

I hated being around fuckers like them. Lawson, he was almost as bad as Jones and the rest of the rednecks in our platoon. I was one of two black men, Mendoza was the only Hispanic, and the rest were white dudes from Boston, Alabama, Kentucky. Some were cool as hell, some not so much.

I found it funny that none of them noticed me staring at their backs. They didn't feel eyes on them like a good soldier should. It never really turned off, that instinct. Not for me, anyway.

"I was working on my present for the baby," I whispered into her ear.

"What's the present?" she whispered back, not so subtly.

"You can't tell anyone, okay?"

While I waited for her to agree, we both looked at her oldest brother, Manuel, or little Manny, as we all called him. Standing there, he was the opposite of his sister's sweet, toothless smile. He met me with a stone expression. He liked me, too, but he wasn't affectionate like Viviana. Mendoza had told me many, many times that little Manny felt his absence during deployments most of all. More than his wife Gloria, even. He looked like a spitting image of his father, dark hair, dark eyes, worry heavy on his mouth.

"Tell me, tell me!" Viviana finally said, her childish excitement loud and clear, and right in my ear. Thank fucking god I could barely hear out of the right one most of the time. Rocket blasts night after night would do that.

Little Manny couldn't hide his smile any longer as his sister giggled. Gloria had walked over and joined us. She looked tired— *beautiful*, but like she needed to sit down and not move for hours. She was more made up than usual. I was used to midnight Gloria in her pajamas or sweats, panicked as her kids woke up from their father's screams. In the sunny backyard, she was wearing ripped jeans and a black T-shirt tied up to show her stomach, a jacket around her waist. She had makeup on, a lot of it. Like she was trying to cover up her exhaustion.

She looked good, though; she always did. Half of the guys gave Mendoza shit for how hot his wife was and how hot he was not. When they wanted to know how he got her, their being high school sweethearts always came up, and people nodded jokingly.

She loved him, though; man, did she love him. I didn't know if I had ever seen people love each other like they did. They were the definition of ride or die.

"I'm building a bed for the baby. A crib," I told Gloria's mini-me.

Gloria nodded at me, smiling at her kids. She was looking at Julien and speaking in Spanish.

"Can you make something for me?" Viviana asked.

Her mom and I laughed together. "You always want something, little girl," her mom teased. "Don't be a beggar."

"What do you want me to make you?" I asked.

She thought about it and wiggled down out of my arms. "I don't know. A bed? Or a princess chair?"

"Princess chair? Got it."

"Martin! Get the fuck over here! Stop playing with the kids and come have a beer!" Mendoza yelled.

Mendoza's daughter ran over to him, and I followed behind her.

She climbed onto his lap and wrapped her arms around his neck and his heart around her finger.

"What's up, man? About time you got here," he said by way of fucking with me.

"I was at the market," I said, and his face changed.

"You still go there?"

I paused, looking around. No one except Elodie could have heard us if they tried. But to be honest, she would need to get used to this kind of shit once her man came home, because he would be bringing a lot of baggage with him. I wouldn't say this to him or her, but his getting her pregnant was a bad fucking idea. For her, mostly, but also for him—he could barely take care of his own damn self, let alone a wife and a baby.

When Phillips told me how they got married fast, I lost my shit. I thought he was joking, that he met this hot French girl online and was going to just date her briefly as an online sex thing, like most dating that happened during deployment. The last thing I expected was for him to get her pregnant and move her across the world to Georgia.

I wasn't trying to be a dick, but it was way too soon for him to have a baby. He was a baby himself.

But then, it was none of my fucking business, so after my initial surprise, I kept my mouth shut.

"Uhm, Jerry Seinfeld is one of the best and most successful comedians in American history . . ." I heard Fischer say to Elodie.

Elodie looked happy, content, and nothing like she had in the emergency room. I had texted her after I saw Karina and Austin leaving and stopped by her room. I really wanted her to be okay; she had a tough road ahead.

"I'm not saying he's *not* great. But the humor in *Friends* is the best. It never gets old, it tells a story with each episode! It helped me a lot with my English, actually." Her French accent made me immediately agree with her, even though I otherwise knew *Seinfeld* was the superior comedy.

"And Jerry Seinfeld has nothing on Adam Sandler. He's America's—" Elodie began to say. I turned back to Mendoza as she entertained Fischer, explaining what on earth Adam Sandler had to do with the argument.

Mendoza looked impatiently at me.

"Yeah. I still go there. I usually stay on the supplies side, but today I ran into Ms. Rosa. She asked about you," I told him.

Mendoza's eyes were cloudy from the dark liquor in his hand. His jaw tightened. I was either pushing a hot button or he would at least feign being chill about me still going to the market even though he couldn't. I knew he cared about her.

"How's she doing? I can't believe Randy won't let me back in. I thought he would get over that shit by now, man."

"Yeah, one normally just gets over you driving through their fence and booths," I said, lightly, like it was funny.

But when it had happened it was terrifying, and Mendoza was so hammered that day that I thought he was going to continue on and drive right onto the highway after demolishing the fence. Mendoza had been chopping wood for Randy, Rosa's husband, and had almost cut his own fingers off, which made him get pissed and go to leave. He shifted into the wrong gear when he tried to back up, ramming his van into multiple stalls of home-building materials. And it didn't stop there—when he panicked, he drove straight toward the trees, barely missing Randy's car, and going straight through the fence. It was a miracle the insurance covered it. A miracle and some lies.

And that happened before the second tour to Afghanistan and all the shit we saw.

And the shit we did.

Mendoza took a long sip from the bottle. "Yeah, but I told him I'd work for free, cleaning shit up there. So I don't get it."

I shrugged. "Give him time. It's only been a few weeks we've been back."

CHAPTER **TWENTY**

An hour into my time at the cookout masked as a baby shower, a few more people had taken off, leaving only a handful of us in Tharpe's backyard. All of the kids were long gone, save Mendoza's.

The pack of young privates were taking shots of Maker's Mark straight from the bottle. Jack Daniel's and Maker's Mark: two things you could always find at a gathering of soldiers. The red wax seal of the Maker's bottle had been tossed into the grass. Mendoza's son Julien grabbed it with his little hand. Gloria, while also holding a sleeping Viviana on her lap, picked it up before he could put it in his mouth. She reminded me of my ma, never sitting down or clocking out of her maternal shift. She always did so many things at once. I had even seen Gloria eat lunch while breastfeeding *and* telling a guy off who'd complained about her feeding her baby in the restaurant. Gloria spoke her piece while sipping her iced tea *and* feeding Julien, and the man reddened and scrambled away before she even raised her voice. Personally, I was more grossed out by him talking with a mouthful of rare steak, his saliva flying out of his big-ass mouth than by her covered feeding—but, sure, go off, sir. She got to him before Mendoza or I could even start.

"Be careful, my love," she told Julien, tossing the top into a bowl full of mostly broken pretzel sticks.

"And y'all need to be careful. This is supposed to be a baby shower. If my kid chokes on anything you throw on the ground, I will be choking you." She looked around at all of us, even me, who was completely innocent.

I watched as she looked for her husband and sighed when she spotted him taking another drink. He had moved on to Coke and bourbon and was shooting the shit with the privates. I knew a few were tankers from another platoon in the company, but didn't know them by name. He was far from ready to leave, even though his wife looked beyond exhausted.

"Gloria." I waved to get her attention. "You can go. I'll make sure he gets home. It's late, and I know the kids have school in the morning."

She looked at him and then to Julien sitting next to her, little Manny standing nearby, and Vivi in her arms. While he shared his father's name and was undoubtedly his mini-me, little Manny's nickname also came from his parents calling him "little man" and somehow it changed to little Manny and stuck, despite him being the oldest child.

"Are you sure?"

"Yes. You know I'm more than capable of getting his ass in bed." I smiled, though we both knew it was usually far from funny when I dragged him in after a hard night.

Tharpe's wife was sitting at the table, trying to keep her husband from getting another beer out of the cooler. As he leaned forward, the plastic chair wobbling under his weight, she pulled on his shirt to bring its legs back to the ground. She huffed and puffed but didn't say anything. I was pretty sure she was embarrassed by Tharpe's behavior. I sure as hell would be.

"Would you stop? The kids are asleep, and we're at home. Chill out," he told her, swiping at where her hand held his shirt.

By the look on her face, I thought she was going to backhand him, but she just pulled her arm away and stormed off into the house. She slammed the door as he lifted the cooler top and shoved his hand into the melting ice and freezing water.

Gloria looked from the back door right at her husband. "You know what, Martin? I'm going to take you up on that offer."

She stood, shifting her daughter on her hip. Vivi woke up and wrapped her legs and arms around Gloria's body.

"Little Manny, can you help me get your brother in the car? Grab that bag," she said as he agreed. "Manny!" she called to her husband. "I'm taking the kids home."

"What! No, stay. *Babyyyy* . . ." He held his arms up, reaching for her.

She hesitated for a second, but ended up giving in to him, smiling at her idiot husband. He was her idiot. And mine. He was a good dude at the end of the day.

She put Vivi down and walked over to him.

"I'm tired. Martin's bringing you home. Stay, babe. Not too late." She wrapped her arms around his neck. His hands rounded her ass, and she licked his lips. They were always like this, all over each other in public. I looked away as Karina popped into my head, her hands running over my cropped hair, her teeth tugging at my earlobe as she climbed on top of me. Even just kissing her was more intimate than sex. I rolled my shoulders, trying to get her out of my damn head.

"Oh, I'll hurry home," Mendoza said, biting his lip. "Can y'all believe that's my wife?" Mendoza roared, clapping his hands as Gloria strode away.

Little Manny rolled his eyes. He looked so much like his dad it was crazy. His broad nose, the shade of his skin, the wide shape of his jaw.

"They're gross," I told him.

He agreed with me; even without a smile, I could tell by the way his mouth twitched that he wanted to laugh.

He was a stubborn little shit sometimes. Just like his old man.

Mendoza kept his eyes on his wife as she said goodbye to everyone else and kissed the back of his daughter's head. As they walked by, he fist-bumped the boys. He was so gentle with Vivi, but tough with the boys. It was how he was raised, the same way that I was, even with a single mother. Boys had to be tough, girls were delicate. Treat them accordingly. I knew firsthand how toxic the idea of what masculinity and being a "man" was. It had the power to eat a man alive and had been destroying families since the beginning of time, especially in my community growing up. So many single mothers who were struggling but no one ever seemed to say "absent fathers." It was all "single-mother households" instead of absent father.

I sat quietly, waving goodbye to the kids and Gloria, drinking a Sprite from the can, and listening to the conversation the circle of guys were having. Most were single soldiers, and those handful who were married had worn out the patience of their wives, many of whom had left already.

"I mean, we're going to go to war with Iran. It's going to happen in the next couple years, especially under this administration," one of them said.

I took them all in, what they were wearing, how drunk they appeared judging by body language and speech. Fischer's voice was in the background debating with Elodie; he was only a little buzzed. He had spent the whole hour since I arrived with Elodie, which I much preferred to him getting wasted with the rest of the group. I listened to their conversation even as my main focus was on the group of privates. My brain was trained to clock every detail of my surroundings, whether I meant to or not. Whether I wanted to or not.

"Don't talk about your boss like that," one of them said. He seemed the youngest, and looked eerily similar to the cartoon character Ferb. Red hair, sort of triangle nose. A straight-up cartoon character.

"He wasn't the boss I enlisted under. I don't want anything to do with his bullshit propaganda and fearmongering," another said. He was lanky, sort of square-nosed. The Phineas to his companion's Ferb.

"Fearmongering? He's opening our eyes up to all the shit the government does! And he's giving more jobs and protecting what this country is supposed to be."

Ahh, good old talk about the president. It was always a sore spot for soldiers and their families. Legally, we weren't even allowed to talk about the president publicly because of our contracts with the Army, but it usually didn't stop people from actually doing it.

"Fearmongering? Come on—that's a liberal-ass stance to take. Even for you," Ferb said.

"First of all, I'm not a liberal. I'm usually a conservative, until this election. But this dude is a straight-up child and so fucking embarrassing. Throwing temper tantrums on Twitter all damn day like he doesn't have anything better to do. He's wack, and you're wack for defending him. Didn't your grandpa serve in World War II?"

The short one nodded.

"Imagine how he would feel if he was still alive. Seeing all these neo-Nazis marching the streets and being encouraged by the president? Not just any president, but someone who is *proud* of how

he escaped serving in the military? Not only that, but he also dis-
respected John McCain, a prisoner of war. What would he say?
Huh?" The soldier's eyes were shining with the kind of gleam only
passion or whiskey could give. He had both running through his
veins.

"Fuck off with this talk. We are supposed to be brothers here,
why are worried about some lazy piece of shit in office when they
aren't worried about us? Only worry about each other," Mendoza
said, waving his drink around the circle of men, butting in before I
could decide if I wanted to or not.

Mendoza approached them. One was looking down at his
phone, barely paying attention to what was happening around
him. This baby shower could break out into a brawl, and he would
barely notice—it seemed like it was about to. The other two were
looking at the Ferb kid.

"He wouldn't be happy," the tall one continued. "He would be
wondering *what the fuck* he risked his life for if we were going to
go right back to this. People in the streets doing literal Nazi salutes
while claiming freedom?"

Mendoza interrupted again before the other guy responded,
"So do something about it instead of being the government's puppet. You bitching about it doesn't change it. You wanna change
shit? Go fucking actually do something about it instead of sitting
around bitching about some shit that we can't control. We're on
their payroll, the blood is on our hands."

I stood up from the table and walked over to the group. It was
getting too heated for the amount of alcohol everyone had had, not
to mention this was supposed to have been an event celebrating
Elodie, yet Fischer was the only one actually talking to her.

"We can change it by voting, and not putting up with this shit,"
the taller guy said.

Fischer and Elodie had fallen silent and were watching the guys' heated exchange. Elodie's hand was on her stomach in a protective sort of way.

"*Not putting up with it?* How you going to manage that, huh? You are the government's *property*. There's no choice whether to put up with something or not. You do what you're told. Just like the rest of us," said another private who looked like he was fresh out of basic.

Tall guy spoke again. "Why don't you ask him about the wall? You want that wasteful wall built, don't you? Tell Mendoza that. Look him in the eyes and tell him that."

I stepped into the middle of the circle. "Okay, okay, guys."

Mendoza's face hardened. "I'm from fucking Cali, bro. My family is from Mexico. You're ignorant as fuck. Like the wall. You need to watch your mouth." He reached out and ripped the whiskey bottle from one of the soldier's hands.

This was going to get ugly. I could feel everyone's adrenaline winding up. It was affecting me, too. My body was morphing into fight mode as everyone's body language had changed. I tried to toss water over their fire. One trip to the ER this week was enough.

"You're still going to deploy, you little bastards," I said. "And you'll be sitting over in that goddamn sandbox bickering about the same shit. And who's going to have your back?"

They looked at each other.

"It's sure the fuck not going to be the president or any politician. Doesn't matter who the president is, this shit has been going on since before we were born. This is what's important, not some fucking Oval Office that knows us by a number. Even if you die, it doesn't matter who the president is. To him, his biggest reason for not wanting you dead is because death tolls influence his stats during his term. Not because they want you alive. And not just him. All of them. *We* are all we have, so stop turning on each other before you get all of us killed next time we deploy."

"We aren't deploying. Last I heard, they're pulling troops out," the quiet tanker said. I knew by the symbol printed on his shirt. There were soldiers who just never turned it off and branded themselves as soldiers in every part of their lives.

I laughed. "Oh, yes, you will. Maybe not in the next six months. But your orders will come soon enough. Now, vote for who you vote for, and stand up for what you stand up for, but stop ruining Elodie's fucking baby shower."

I looked specifically at the tall kid.

"But don't let your politics stop you from doing your job. We're the boots on the ground. Not them. So stop letting it divide us so everyone doesn't get killed, because guess what?" I looked at these boys who wanted to be men so bad. "At the end of the day, some people will just be on the wrong side of history and that's their burden to carry. You had your reasons for signing up, we all did, now either shut the hell up or go to a bar. This is a goddamn baby shower."

Some of these kids were total shitbags and I knew it must have boiled their blood to be told to shut up by a Black man, but I dared anyone to say anything to me that was out of line. I learned within my first year enlisted that arguing with other soldiers over politics wasn't going to change their minds. People usually needed to actually see shit for themselves to open their minds, and even then, some people just didn't change. But one thing was clear: in the Army, political arguments got you into nothing but a fuck-ton of trouble and could ruin your career or get you killed.

"Yeah, well, from what I heard you won't be deploying, either." The tanker smirked, looking down at my leg.

He turned to the other guys and they all smiled; the tall one even laughed. My hands clenched at my sides. So, everyone knew that I was disabled now. Word traveled to them and got them thinking they were better than me now because of my injury. I was no longer Martin, the twenty-one-year-old E5 who saved lives and got promotions and medals faster than everyone else in the company. I was the useless vet now. A disposable, disabled, Black, useless veteran.

Mendoza rose up, pressing his bottle into the tanker's chest. My mind was in fight mode, but my body was still.

"You better watch your fucking mouth. All of you." His whole body shook as he threw the bottle to the side. It shattered as it hit the concrete patio.

Toni had come back outside and she screamed as the glass flew near her feet.

"What the fuck?" Tharpe rushed to Mendoza. I moved between them before Tharpe could lay a finger on Mendoza. Tharpe would thank me later. His wife, too.

"Guys, guys, guys." Fischer pushed through, grabbing Tharpe's shirt. "Come on. Look at her," he said, nodding to Elodie. "It's her baby shower. You fucking idiots."

Elodie seemed worried even as she smiled, looking across the group of us men. She was scared, I could sense it.

"Don't you know we're all doomed anyway?" Fischer continued.

He reminded me of his sister and her idea that doom was imminent. I guessed both of them were taught by their mother and her stories threaded with promises of punishments from the sky.

"Back down or get off my fucking property," Tharpe threatened Mendoza, the beer giving him extra courage.

"Watch your fucking boys, then. I guess you didn't tell them who the fuck I am, because they wouldn't be threatening me if they knew." He raised his fist, still wrapped in a bandage, and slammed it against the palm of his other hand.

"None of you want to fuck with me!" he yelled, hitting his hands together again. I reached for his arm and yanked him back.

He stood still, not fighting me. He was homed in on them. Mendoza lifted his hand up, looking straight at the boys, and used two fingers to make the shape of a gun. The tanker flinched as Mendoza pretended to pull a trigger, clicking his tongue.

"Stop! Oh my god. Stop it!" Toni shrieked, grabbing hold of her husband as he tried to step to Mendoza.

Elodie's eyes were wide, shocked, as she stared at them. She had probably only seen the sweet Mendoza, not the man with his finger on a trigger. If she thought this was bad, maybe she wasn't really ready for Phillips to come home after all.

"Fuck this. I'm going. Come on, Elodie," Fischer said to her. "You guys are all dicks. Elodie, I'm gonna get an Uber and I'll take you home."

"Where are you sleeping?" she asked him, concern clear in her voice.

I wondered the same.

"Martin's," Fischer said, seeming to realize that I was still here. He seemed overwhelmed, but didn't want to be in the middle of conflict. Basic training would beat that out of him. I hoped he kept some diplomacy to him. It would help him in the future as a leader if he stayed in and stepped up.

"Let's go. I'll take you both. The party's over anyway." I looked around the mess of the yard, glass shards, chip bags, paper plates everywhere.

"We'll take Mendoza first, then you," I said to Fischer and Elodie.

"You can leave the gifts here and I'll bring them by later," Toni said, motioning toward the table. There weren't many gifts, and none were too big. Just a few bags and one box wrapped in polka-dot paper.

"We can take the gifts," Fischer said and started collecting them.

Elodie was quiet as she hugged Toni goodbye and she grabbed two small gift bags to carry to the car. Toni apologized, saying how she would have driven Elodie home, but couldn't because the kids were asleep—not because she had had at least a bottle or two of wine to herself just since I'd arrived.

The boys dispersed, saying shit under their breath. I didn't give them attention. I'd go to their commander and tell him how shit his soldiers were. That was the way to really fuck with them. My heart was beating violently, and an unfamiliar feeling sat on my chest. Was I afraid of these boys? It felt like I was, but I had no reason to be. Was it embarrassment because of my injury? Fuck this.

"Let's go get more booze before the PX closes," one of them said as they walked past. I tried to calm the racing inside my chest and stared them down to appease my pride as they left.

"Fuck them. I'm sorry, Toni, but fuck them." Mendoza hugged her and I followed both of them inside, Elodie and Fischer behind me. I looked at Toni, her makeup smeared now, her hair frizzed and wild. I felt bad for the woman. She had a part to play, and she was trying. Her husband couldn't care less about her most of the time, and I knew he'd fucked a medic during our last deployment. More than once. I'm sure she knew what kind of shitbag her husband was. It was so obvious that she was absolutely suffering. I wondered if he was suffering like the rest of us. Like her, like Mendoza, like me. Hell, like Fischer, even if his trauma wasn't from the Army yet. Tharpe was no angel, but we'd gone to hell twice together and that changes a man.

His wife stood there, staring at him, her eyes heavy and tired. She'd made a life out of being a military spouse, from Family Readiness Group meetings to cookouts to play dates with the other wives. I was a single soldier, and even so I still knew she was a busybody who liked to gossip and buzz around. But she did a lot for us, always sending care packages and making sure our company had the best cookouts and shit. Her husband was right on the fence between being a total prick and not. He wasn't my favorite, but he wasn't the worst. We had lived together with six other guys during the first deployment. I didn't have a lot of one-on-one time with him since there wasn't much free time during war; he spent his with a group of medic girls who were usually average-looking, but, in a desert, while you were trying to stay alive, they were suddenly the hottest women on the planet to a group of horny men. Phillips, Mendoza, and I stayed out of trouble and out of the medics, literally. Of all my boys, only Phillips was left in Afghanistan. Damn. It was wild to think of him over there, starting over, working with a new group of people like nothing had happened. I hoped he was behaving, especially while watching his pregnant wife struggling to try to carry what was left of her cake to the back door.

The rest of us came home after the last mission. The one that not only wiped out half of our guys, but most of our minds.

And my body.

The mission we weren't supposed to think about or speak about.

The one Karina was entangled in now, no matter how hard I tried to keep her away from all of it. Her dad's mistakes were chasing both of his kids down.

"Let's go. Cab's leaving!" I told them as Elodie one-arm-hugged Toni for the third time.

Fischer grabbed the rest of the bags and followed Elodie out the front door. He was clueless about the shit his dad was covering up and I was done meddling in the Fischer family's drama and needed to get as far away as I could. I lifted up the polka-dot box and tucked it under my arm. I wanted to get the hell out of there and into my bed. The day had gone on for too fucking long.

"See you around. Thanks for having me," I told Toni as I passed her.

She sighed. "Thanks for coming." Her hand lifted halfway into the air before she gave up, sensing my *do not touch me* vibe, dropping it to her side.

It was almost ten, and I had an appointment in the morning. Fischer was due to demo the bathroom of the other side of my duplex while I would be at a discharge meeting where they taught a group of us soldiers how to fill out job applications. Lowe's. Home Depot. Local police forces. Security jobs. Those were the options they gave me for my future. At just twenty-one and with a heavy diagnosis of post-traumatic stress disorder and a fucked-up leg, not many places would jump at the chance to hire me.

The back of my truck was partly full again with the gifts. Mendoza was standing by the open trunk.

"Sorry, hands are full," he said as I approached.

He had taken a bottle of Maker's Mark from the table without my noticing. He took a swig of it.

"You're putting that shit away while I drive or you're not getting in," I warned him. I wasn't about to get arrested or assaulted by the MPs—again.

Elodie told us that she wanted to sit in the backseat in case she got motion sickness, and Mendoza wanted to sit up front so he didn't have to contend with a pregnant woman who might get carsick. Fischer slid in next to Elodie and I turned on to the street that would take us to the other side of post, a short drive to Mendoza's housing village.

"What a bunch of douchebags," he said when the four of us were in my truck.

"On the floor," I told Mendoza, looking at the liquor still in his hand.

"Okay, Jesus. You're worse than my old lady," he said, groaning, but obeyed.

"They weren't so bad. Just toward the end," Elodie said, trying to make the best of her ruined baby shower.

I knew that Karina should have been in charge of it.

"They were lucky I didn't want to put that bottle down." Mendoza fake-punched the air and Elodie giggled in the back.

"You better put those fists down before your wife whoops your ass," I said, nodding to his house when we pulled up a few minutes later.

Gloria, now in her pajamas, walked down the porch and toward us the moment my tires touched the driveway. I guess she'd heard my exhaust rumbling as we drove up. That was the only thing I hated about my truck; it was fucking loud.

She wrapped her arm around her husband's back as we all told them good night. He was slurring now, drinking from the bottle the second he was out of my car.

As their front door shut, Fischer's eyes caught mine in the rear-view mirror.

"Should we be worried about him?" he asked, his voice soft.

I put my gearshift in reverse and looked back at him.

"Yes, we should be," I said, wondering if I would be back there later that night.

CHAPTER **TWENTY-ONE**

Karina

"His kiss was sweet enough that when he kissed me, the salt in the water around us turned to sugar," Elodie said, reading aloud from a little poetry book I had bought when I lived in Texas.

She'd found it in the couch that morning when we were vacuuming under the cushions. We had been cleaning the living room all day and getting ready to paint. I even moved the furniture. Elodie obviously didn't move any heavy stuff since she was pregnant; instead she dusted every part of the room and helped by tidying the books on the shelves under the TV, wiping each one down with a rag and whatever brand of nonchemical Lysol she'd found at Target. It felt good to clean things out, but it was already late in the day, and I hoped my enthusiasm wouldn't burn out before we had our planned movie night.

I had this urge for change lately. I needed it. I was unsettled, I could feel it, and I knew that I wouldn't be able to feel at ease until the space surrounding me was different—like I could erase the memory of Kael, of my ex, Brien—of everything. The dark colors in my living room needed a refresh, kind of like my new hair and my new chair.

Elodie and I both had off work today because Mali had closed the spa for the week while her daughter was having a baby. I had just gone on my Starbucks run of the day to make us feel extra-productive and pinned a bunch of pictures on a Pinterest board without knowing that all of my Facebook friends could see every single one. They seemed to like what I was posting and my phone kept going off as they repinned or saved the stuff I was finding. Of course, on my tiny budget, my house would never look like the Pinterest board of my dreams, but anything would be better than the random blend of décor I had collected over the years. Some of it would stay, but most needed to go.

I had entered a new phase. As of today, the new carefree, light, and airy Karina who didn't overthink everything was going with the flow and focusing on her own life. Spending hours on Instagram looking at motivational, self-help, and mental-health memes inspired me. So, it was tan and light-gray pillows from Target, a concrete table decoration (even if I wasn't exactly clear on what it *was*), and anything that had a "chill" tone to it (whatever that felt like in the moment).

I began to paint the walls a crème brûlée color from some old paint cans that had been under the kitchen sink since I bought my house. The original plan had been to paint the entire living room and kitchen today, but it ended up taking way longer than I expected.

As the paint dried, I dragged the couch across the floor and moved it to the wall that separated the kitchen and living room. Over the last few days since I had found the flea market, I had been subtly moving things around. Today was the payoff; we took the painter's tape off the baseboards and plopped down on the clean couch. I had successfully distracted myself from obsessing over Kael for a few days. He came and went inside my mind, but I was almost at the end of it—I hoped.

After a short rest, and some more vacuuming, Elodie returned to the little poetry book and became fascinated with it. I went through a poetry phase when I was eighteen-ish and had spent an entire summer thinking I was going to either become a poet or marry one.

"She was the electricity that kept me going. But what I did not know was that I shared her with him. His ghost claimed more of her than I did, until they vanished together."

"How melodramatic," I huffed, remembering how deep that little book had felt when I'd read it over and over that summer. Back then, every poem had spoken to me personally. Now it all sounded so different. I had tied my own meaning to it back then, when my problems seemed so small compared to now. At that time in my life, I had no clue what love was. Not even close.

"Oh, come on, Karina. Don't be such a downer." She pressed the little book to her chest. "These are beautiful."

"Sure." I snorted. "I loved them when I read them, but I'm done wasting my time chasing some fairy-tale man who doesn't exist on planet Earth."

Elodie rolled her gorgeous eyes. The blue cotton romper she was wearing made her eyes even brighter than usual. She was stunning in a casual, breathtaking way. Inside and out.

"No duh. But we can at least pretend and read poems and things to make us long for it. Romance has to live somewhere, even if it's not in our lives." As she said it, she slid the book onto a shelf between my old textbook *Trail Guide to the Body* and another poetry book that I last recalled seeing covered in dust.

"How are things with Martin?" she asked with her back to me, rubbing a cloth along the entertainment center.

"The same as before: nonexistent." I tossed the pillows back onto the couch. The living room was almost done and my back and head hurt.

She frowned. "But even after the other day? He hasn't called you or anything?"

"What do you mean the other day?" I'd never spoken so fast in my life.

Her eyes widened. "Uhm, I mean . . . the market?"

Great, so Kael had told her. Jealousy, annoyance, embarrassment, violation, all rose up.

"He's a good man, Karina. You're not thinking clearly and he's too stubborn. Both of you are."

I got really defensive, really fast. "He doesn't give a shit about me, okay? So no, he hasn't called or texted or come by and he's not going to."

Her face turned sad. "I'm sure that's not why he—"

"Elodie, look, we are friends. You're maybe my closest friend, but I don't want to talk about Kael. Not with you, not with anyone. How many times do I have to tell you this?"

I could talk about some stuff with Elodie, sure. Some personal shit about my dad. Sometimes little things about my mom. *Whatever* about my brother. But the idea of her, or anyone, knowing every part of my life made me want to vomit. I didn't like people knowing my weaknesses, and I didn't like Elodie reminding me of Kael or smiling and giving me false hope while asking about him.

"I'm sorry, but I won't be able to get over it if I keep talking about it," I told her.

Her face was full of concern for me. It was a confusing experience, the way the tables felt like they were turning; normally it was I who worried about her, not the other way around.

"Who do you talk to, then? Because you just stay alone in this house and you don't talk to anyone. You need to make an online dating profile. Or at least use Instagram more."

"I talk to people . . ."

In truth, I didn't have anyone I wanted to *bother* or trust with my problems.

"Who?" She smiled, softly testing me.

I sat down on the couch, leaving the middle cushion open between us. "Who cares? Also, I'm not dating on an app or on Instagram."

She rolled her eyes. "Instagram is an app."

"Shh." I waved my hand in the air.

I knew I had to meet her in the middle; with her being overly emotional and me wanting to bury my feelings, I had to find the balance. I did it with my mom a lot, and with most people, except Kael, whose name was gaining way too much power in my house right now.

"I'm not *concerned* really . . ." Elodie paused and looked around the room, to the painted wall, to the new chair. Then she looked me up and down. "But you're redoing the house and your hair and style . . ."

"Yeah? *And? You're* having a baby with a man you barely know. Things are changing everywhere." As soon as the words came out, I bit my tongue. "I'm sorry. I shouldn't have said that."

Elodie, on top of being the most gentle person I'd ever met, was also the most understanding. She just nodded and moved on, despite my awful words to her just seconds ago.

"I just want you to be happy, okay?"

"I am happy. I got two new clients this week and I have purple nails and fresh hair, and that chair. I'm good." I pointed to my favorite item in my house, but even that had the memory of Kael embroidered on it.

"Purple nails? Now you're reaching." She looked at her phone and laughed. "You should date online. Toni asked me if you're on Tinder."

"Why is Toni talking about my dating life? I don't even know her." I lifted my body a little to sit on my knees on the couch.

Elodie acted offended. "It came up. Someone asked if you were single. She was actually complimenting you. Chill out."

"*You* chill," was the only thing I could say.

Stupid. But I was defending myself. She was the one talking about me with her lame-ass friends.

She shrugged her slender shoulders. "I'm chill. I'm just checking on you." She didn't seem pissed; her response was calm, if forward as hell.

"Well, I'm fine, okay? You and Toni don't have to worry about me. I'm fine. Can she go back to planning baby showers and cook-outs and whatever bullshit she does all day? I don't like the idea of you and Kael and Toni and God knows who else just sitting around talking about my life, okay?"

Elodie's smile went away. "You're being way too judgmental about them. You know, she told me she invited you to the baby shower on Facebook and you didn't even open her message."

"Facebook? I don't even check my messages on Facebook, Elodie." I threw my hands up and let them drop at my sides. "What the hell is happening with the world that Facebook is the only way to send baby shower invites and Instagram is used to meet men?"

It wasn't Elodie's fault that she saw the good in everyone, even me. She was smiling again. We rarely argued. In fact, I could hardly remember ever even getting annoyed with her. She was one of the very few people I felt that way about.

"I'm just saying. I also invited you before I knew it was for the baby. And Toni just wants you to like her, that's all."

"Why would she care if I like her? She doesn't even know me." And I had no desire to get to know her. "What's with these women?"

"Because you're, like, the cool girl, so she wants to impress you."

I laughed. "Me?! The *cool girl*?"

"Yes. Since you don't care if they like you, they want you to like them. Not like me—because I wanted them to like me, they didn't. You are all . . ." She slowly shook her shoulder-length hair back and forth like she was in a shampoo commercial and changed her voice to what I assumed was supposed to be mine. "All 'I don't care.'"

It sounded deep and ridiculous.

"And you dress all cool and you got Martin's attention, when everyone thought was going to stay single. He never even looks at other girls, and trust me, they *all* look at him."

"What do they know about me and Kael? And how?"

Ugh, news always traveled so fast around posts. Benning was no exception. I hoped Elodie wasn't the one telling them about my personal life. I trusted her, and it never even crossed my mind that she would talk about me with her new friends. I purposely stayed out of friend groups because of these types of issues. I preferred my drama to come from television or a romance novel.

"Not much. Just that he was into you and you ended it. But when people don't know the story they make up their own."

That was so true. My mom had a saying: *the gossiping mouth is never full.* Or something like that.

I stood up from the couch. "Yeah, well they aren't going to get any details. There aren't any, anyway."

"Okay." Elodie raised her hands up, smiling in defeat. "Fine."

"Thank you." I gave her a sarcastic smile back.

I busied myself by moving my new chair over a few inches, then back to where it was in the first place. And then I half pondered where it should really be, and half ignored my well-meaning roommate.

"So can I make you a Tinder profile?" she asked.

"No, oh my god." I shook my head. "No way. I don't want to date right now."

She raised her brow. "Right now? Or ever?"

"Both." I laughed a little.

Who knew my dating life was the topic of everyone's fascination, including Elodie's? What was it about dating that measured a woman's value in life?

"Ugh," she groaned, throwing a pillow at me. "You're killing me."

"You're killing me! On top of that, you said your baby shower totally sucked and everyone was drunk, so I definitely wouldn't take Toni's advice on anything life-related."

Elodie laughed as I tossed the pillow back at her but was quiet for a few moments before she spoke again.

"People are supposed to be connected to each other, don't you think?" She asked the question backward, the way she did with some sentences.

She clearly felt some way about my dating life, even though I had assumed she was too busy to even be paying attention.

"What do you mean?" I just had to ask against my better judgment.

"Well, people are supposed to be in love. That's what we're made for. Quite *literally*." She smiled. "It makes us feel good to have someone to share with. I'm not just talking about men. I mean friends . . . family. Just people in general. It makes me worry for you that you don't have anyone like that. You said yourself that I'm your closest friend and you barely tell me anything about your life. Your brother is leaving and he said—"

"My brother?" I cut her off, shocked that she even knew this. "So your friends and my brother and you all just sit around and talk about me?"

Elodie shook her head. "No."

"Well, it seems like it. Not everyone is comfortable with everyone else knowing about their personal life." I hit one hand against the pillow on the chair to make it stand up better, admittedly a little harder than necessary.

"Not everyone is the same or wants the same things. I have a lot of shit going on and the last thing I need is to be *connected* to someone. I'm connected to enough people who cause enough problems in my life so you, my brother, those women, and Kael can all stop worrying about me before I completely lose it. I need to worry about myself and myself only right now."

Truth was, I had never been a person who needed to be surrounded by friends or to date. Kael was an exception, but I was never the one to make the plans with the few friends I had throughout my life.

When I looked at Elodie, her brows were slumped, her full lips pouting. She was genuinely sad for me, I could feel it, but that didn't mean I was going to agree with her just for the sake of her pout disappearing.

"Just be happy, Karina, okay?"

"I will be." I didn't know when that would be, but it had to be someday, right? I wiped a bead of sweat off my forehead with my forearm. I needed to shower and today was hair-washing day. I was on day four of dry shampoo, and I was so glad to have a convenient way to get out of that conversation with Elodie. "I need to jump in the shower. I'm tired and sweaty."

She sighed and turned to face me, adorably lifting her shoulder to hide her weak smile, still a little upset.

I nodded and headed to the hallway with my phone in my hand. As I reached the bathroom door, I turned to Elodie, who was still looking at me. Her voice rang out through the hallway and she kept her eyes on her hands resting in her lap.

"By the way, we're going camping tomorrow! I already told everyone you would come and it's for your birthday and Austin's and it's Austin's last time with his friends and all of us together, so please don't fight me on it and just agree!" Elodie sounded like a deflated balloon by the time her speech was done.

I was so tired of hearing about this damn camping trip. "I'm not going." I shut the door behind me but could still hear her as she yelled, "YES, YOU ARE!"

I sank against the door and my body felt heavier than ever. I knew I had lost the camping battle and it wasn't even worth arguing over.

CHAPTER **TWENTY-TWO**

The morning had come. I felt the sun peering into my window to mock me, heat rising up my chest and on my bare thighs. My fan broke last night, because of course it did. I opened my eyes, slowly, covering them with my arm as a way to block the burning light that was forcing me to get up. It had finally arrived: the Friday of the inevitable peer pressure–fueled excursion where I would either be completely miserable and anxious, or I would . . . well, I couldn't see any other option when it came to being forced to be social with a group of Kael's and my brother's friends. Out in the woods of Georgia of all places. I checked my phone, only one text from Austin, a group chat that I hadn't volunteered to be a part of. Everyone else seemed to be excited—a lot of beer and tent emojis, along with a few flames, covered my screen.

I rolled my eyes and lifted my heavy body out of bed. I could hear Elodie in the kitchen speaking in her native tongue, presumably to her parents. My duffel bag sat on the floor, ready to go. I had packed in a rush last night and wondered whether I should start over. Had I packed enough clothes? Toiletries? Dignity? Confidence?

The last two were a for sure *no*, but I was determined to go through with this. It was important to my brother and Elodie, and it was just a few days, after all. Miraculously, it happened to fall on the week when Mali's daughter was due to give birth, so neither Elodie nor I had to worry about work, which was my first and last excuse. Elodie's doctor told her she was more than fine to go camping, but to make sure she wasn't too close to smoke and stayed away from alcohol, which seemed obvious, but apparently some people needed to be reminded, even while pregnant.

I opened my dresser, grabbed one more T-shirt, rolled it up, and tossed it in. Even though I would be in the thick Georgia woods and was by no means planning to dress up, I wanted to be somewhat cute. I hoped that at least one of Kael's friends would tell him that I looked good, even in the woods with no makeup on. I was trying not to make this whole thing about him, but ever since I'd seen him, I'd even go so far as to say I felt at ease with him; it was jarring. And even though Kael wouldn't be joining the group, I wanted to stay fresh in his mind.

I checked my phone one last time before going to the shower. My plan was to blow-dry and style my hair today and hope it would last with a little help from dry shampoo over the next three days. Humidity would surely kill my plan, but I was determined to try. When I got out of the shower, Elodie was standing by the front door, dressed, and bending down to put her sneakers on.

"I'm going to run a few errands. Toni asked me to get some things for the trip," she told me, grabbing her key chain from one of the hooks on the wall.

"I'll go with you," I offered. My hair was done, and I had the time since I was packed and ready, anyway. It annoyed me that Toni had asked the only pregnant person going to get things last-minute for the trip, but I was trying to give her the benefit of the doubt because she had a billion kids and was probably stressed and packing last-minute herself.

"Actually, Austin is coming over to go with me. He'll be here soon." Elodie's eyes left mine like she was nervous.

"Oh." I paused.

"Ice and things are needed . . . all heavy things so I need his help."

"Okay, well that's probably better, anyway. I'll be here when you guys get back, so if one of you can text me, I'll just come outside. Are you all packed?"

She nodded and she pulled her bottom lip between her teeth. "Um, actually, Karina, we will use my car for the coolers so last night in the group chat, we all decided who will ride with who . . ."

The fucking group chat. Of course, I'd muted it and hadn't read a single message as too many to count came in.

"Really? So, who am I riding with?" My heart began to race immediately. I didn't know anyone except Gloria and Mendoza.

"I think the Mendozas. Is that okay? I'm sorry my car is so small. If you want to drive yourself, you can, but you said you needed an oil change and since you didn't reply, I said Mendoza's would be best?"

I nodded. "Yeah, that's good, actually."

I wasn't one hundred percent comfortable with them, either, but I didn't want to risk driving my car alone for hours to an unknown campground when the engine light and oil light were both on. My motto for the weekend was supposed to be "go with the flow," but it seemed like it was going to be harder to do that with each minute that passed.

A little voice in my head reminded me that maybe, just maybe, I could get more background on Kael from his closest friends. I knew it wouldn't change anything, but it would satisfy my curiosity and masochistic tendencies. I wasn't even sure what I was looking for, anyway.

"It will be fun. I promise." Elodie smiled, making her best effort to convince me. I nodded and shooed her out the door. I was already committed to going, so I didn't want to talk about it anymore.

After she pulled out of the driveway, I wondered how I was supposed to know what time the Mendozas would be there to pick me up. I wasn't someone who thrived with zero plans. I cursed at my ceiling as I sat down on the couch and opened the group chat. There were too many messages to scroll all the way back, so I scanned for a pickup time, but didn't see anything. I decided to wait a bit and if they hadn't shown up, I would text and just ask.

I finished getting myself ready, a tiny bit of tinted moisturizer and a few dots of concealer along my cheeks. I didn't want my breakout to get worse, but wanted to look as fresh as I could manage, at least the first day. I sat my packed duffel by the door and scrolled through my phone. My Instagram account was still picking up steam since I'd posted at the flea market; even my random photos from months ago, a blurry one of the tree in front of my dad's house, an orange night sky in traffic with headlights that looked like fireworks speckled across the small image, were getting a lot of comments and likes. About fifty-ish each, which was a lot compared to the three or four here and there that I was used to.

I didn't understand it, but a little rush crept in with each comment complimenting my photos. I was glad I only had a couple posts of myself, mostly blurry or with an object covering my face, one a bouquet of flowers, one a plate full of waffles from a brunch with Elodie almost a year ago. I was far from confident enough to post selfie after selfie like most of the women I followed; I admired and envied their confidence, even if it was just what the algorithm wanted me to see. I scrolled through the likes on the waffle photo out of pure curiosity and almost dropped my phone as I brought it right up to my face to make sure I wasn't seeing things. Kael had liked the picture. I clicked on his profile, and it was private. The last time I checked was around the time we first met, and he didn't have an account. His profile seemed rather new, only three followers and he was following zero. I couldn't see the followers since he was on private, but it made me feel uneasy that he had an account now. I wasn't sure why; maybe I didn't want him to have access to the thousands of women on the app, and since Elodie told me that people were now dating people they met on the app . . . what if that was his reason for making the account? The thought made my stomach turn, and I wrapped my arm around my torso as if I could hold myself together.

It had been about twenty minutes since Elodie left so I texted to ask if she had any idea when the Mendozas would be coming to get me. I was ready to go. My anxiety was creeping in, and I was beginning to get intrusive thoughts like, *What if this whole thing is some kind of setup and Kael will actually be there, maybe—even worse—with another woman? What if someone gets too drunk and starts a fight that turns into more?*

What if . . .

What if . . .

What if . . .

Elodie's response popped up on my screen at the exact moment that I heard the noise. That familiar engine rumble that I had grown so used to. I longed for it; I hated it. I jumped up to my knees and peered out the front window. Kael's truck was pulling up, stopping in its usual spot in front of my house.

I rushed to the mirror on the wall while quietly cursing at myself for doing it, though I couldn't seem to control the impulse. My mind began to race as I heard his truck shut off. I pushed my ear against the door, hearing the car door close. What the hell was he doing here? Austin wasn't here; Elodie wasn't here.

As Kael got closer, I took a few deep breaths. The knock at the door startled me, even though I knew he was there. I opened it quickly, too quickly, as if I had been waiting at the door, which I had, but he didn't need to know that. He was dressed in joggers as always, form-fitting at the top and down his thighs, bunched around his ankles, showing white socks to match his always white sneakers, and a black T-shirt hung lower than the white hoodie he wore on top. His skin was glowing, flawless and freshly shaved. Same with his head. He looked so much like a cool, unbothered guy from a Gap or Nike advertisement. I both enjoyed and resented the view.

His body language was somewhat awkward as he stood at the bottom of my porch, but he still had his head high, confidence thick in his shoulders. In the bright sky behind him the clouds were thick. It was about seventy-five degrees, but the air had a hint of a chill to it, making me think I might need more than the thin cotton long-sleeved shirt and jeans I was wearing. I needed to grab a hoodie before I left.

I tried my damnest to be patient as I waited for him to tell me what he was doing here, but it lasted merely a few seconds.

"My brother and Elodie are both out: they left to go to the campground. They had to pick up some stuff on the way, so Mendoza—well, the Mendozas—are coming to get me anytime."

He shuffled his sneaker against the overgrown grass on the edges of my sidewalk. "Um, actually, I'm here to get you."

"What do you—what?" I held on to the doorknob to steady myself.

"Yeah . . . I'm supposed to drive you. A few guys ended up showing up at their place, apparently there was some miscommunication in some group text chat you all have. But I was the one with the least amount of bodies in my car, so . . . here I am?" Kael raised his arms in the air at his sides, like he was saying, *Sorry, I don't want to drive with you, either, but we don't have a choice.*

"I thought you weren't coming?" I said, puzzled, wondering when the hell that very important detail changed.

He half smiled, but it wasn't a kind or teasing one—it was uncomfortable. "Yeah, well, I also thought you weren't coming."

I gasped sarcastically. "Great."

He held up his hands in front of his body. "I meant, I didn't know you were coming. I don't have a problem with it, and I'm not saying I didn't want you to come. I just didn't know . . . if you're uncomfortable with me going, I can still dip out. I didn't mean to stress you out or ruin your weekend if you thought you wouldn't have to see me."

I had two options here—well, three:

1. I could cancel altogether and have my house to myself for three days with zero chance of Austin or anyone else stopping by.
2. I could go but tell Kael to stay back, since he'd offered, anyway. Whether or not it had been a genuine offer wasn't my problem.
3. I could just go and try as hard as possible to keep my distance from him. This would be the worst option for me, and probably for him, but better for the group. No drama, no one left out.

"It's fine," I said, deciding to lie, to try my best to act like I didn't care if he was coming or that I had to spend two hours in the car with him alone. "I don't want to make you uncomfortable, either. Are you good with me going? They're your friends, after all."

Kael nodded before he spoke. "Nah, it's cool with me. I don't think we should let our . . . I don't know what this is anymore." His hand waved between us. "Whatever it is, it shouldn't get in the way of everyone's weekend. We got along fine at the market. Well, after you laid into me a bit."

He was lucky that he smiled right away because our interaction at the market was far from me "laying into him" the way I had planned to and thought I wanted to.

"I was being nice." I matched my fake smile to his and watched his face light up as he laughed. The sound still gave me instant butterflies, but it felt a lot nicer than the hole I'd felt lately. I laughed with him, knowing this whole weekend could turn into a disaster at any point.

"Right. Well, I appreciate it."

We were bantering, borderline flirting and I felt my feet slipping near a very dangerous edge with him. I didn't want to be manipulated by my attraction or connection to him but standing there in the doorway I felt the same sense of comfort I always had with him. If we could just erase—

No. No. No, I repeated in my head.

"I'm ready when you are," I told him, turning my back to go inside to grab my bag. I heard the door creak, and when I looked up, he was standing next to me in the living room, arm out, expecting my bag.

"I can carry it."

"I know," he said, gently grabbing it from me before I could sling the straps on my shoulders.

It was a bit heavy because of my few books, my clothes, and boots. It was nothing for Kael, of course, who could lift me up and put me over his shoulder with zero trouble. The thought made my cheeks hot, so I looked away from him.

"Let's go?" I asked, surveying the living room to make sure I wasn't forgetting anything.

Kael walked past me. Where the heck was he going? I followed him to the kitchen and across it to the back door. He locked both locks, the top one made a rusty sound as Kael gave me a look that was clear as day.

"I was going to lock that." My white lie came out defensively.

"I know you sometimes forget. I wasn't trying to step on your toes. Just habit, I guess."

Truth was, I had totally forgotten about the back door, and if he hadn't checked it, it would have stayed open the entire time I was gone. Kael's soldier mentality came in handy quite often. There was a time when things were good between us when I stopped having to worry about my surroundings. When he was with me, I knew he would always open doors, walk on the outside when we walked together on a sidewalk, check my seatbelt, and make sure the doors were locked, my phone alarm was set to wake up for work, and the oven was turned off after making dinner. The small things that dramatically improved my mental clarity and day overall. He made things so easy . . . until the day he made them unbearable by taking away the comfort and security I had yearned for my entire life. In just a few minutes' time it was all undone.

"Can we go now?" I was growing angry over things I couldn't change, and I didn't want it to affect the drive. There was already enough tension between us.

He nodded, looked around the kitchen and asked me if the lights were all off. I ignored him and he flicked on the porch light just as we exited the house and made our way to his truck. He put my bag in the trunk and slammed it shut. I wasn't sure if I should get in the backseat or the front, but he walked up and opened the passenger seat door. It wasn't an Uber, after all.

I buckled in and he asked if I wanted to plug my phone in for music. I shook my head. He didn't need to hear all the breakup, "sad bops" as Spotify called it, playlists I'd been blaring lately. We drove in silence for a few minutes. He turned the a/c on too high, but I was too uneasy to say anything, so I pulled my sleeves down to cover my hands. Of course, I'd forgotten the damn second hoodie.

"We're picking up one more soldier on our way. Somehow, I became the taxi. She lives close by, so it won't take long."

"She?" I blurted out, my chest instantly aflame.

I tried not to look over at Kael but did anyway. His hand rubbed over his chin like answering was going to be painful. To him or me? I wondered.

"Uh, yeah. Turner. You've met her a couple times now."

"Turner? The one from the mall?"

He nodded. I wanted to slam my head against the hard glass of the window.

"Really?"

"Yeah."

I took a deep breath, trying to remain calm and not overreact. Whose bright idea was it to have me and a woman who clearly liked him, or at least was attracted to him, ride together? The thoughts I labeled as intrusive earlier came rushing back—this had to be a setup. Someone in this group absolutely was getting off on making this as hard for me as possible. My mind split into two parts, one that believed this whole trip was a massive setup, and one that kept telling me that was ludicrous, that no one on this trip was even bothered enough by me or thought enough about me, even in a malicious way, to notice or care that this pairing would make me feel miserable.

According to text-filled posts on Instagram, I was both a self-sabotaging insecure avoidant and a massive narcissist who assumed everything and everyone was considering and plotting around me when they weren't. Self-diagnosing was easier now because of random unqualified people posting their *if you do these three things you're A, B, or C* lists.

"She was supposed to ride with the Mendozas, too," Kael finally said.

I put my knees up, my dirty shoes on his seat, and nodded. I didn't say another word as we drove to pick up the woman whom Kael had known longer than me, who was prettier than me, and who hadn't had her heart torn apart by him the way I had.

CHAPTER **TWENTY-THREE**

Kael

I've met many women in my life, from married eighteen-year-olds who were too young and too lonely to be expected to make logical choices, to girls I went to high school with who wanted to do more with their lives, but ultimately couldn't get out of their situations due to lack of resources or support from their family. Sometimes both. I've met women at bars whose eye contact and shiny lip gloss made my cock hard, but, after two minutes of hearing them speak, their minds made me excuse myself to the bathroom and never come back. I've met widows who cry at the mention of their dead husbands' names and drown themselves in cheap vodka because the pain is too heavy.

I've known strong women like my ma, who would do anything, literally anything under the goddamn sun for me and my sister. I've talked to women born and raised in Afghanistan who, despite their country being blown apart day by day, still had a hope for a better future for their daughters. In a way, sometimes I felt like I was living a double life, one raised by a hard-as-rock but gentle woman, and now one full of rowdy men who don't talk about their struggles or hardships. Out of all the people I'd met, I'd usually found them easy to handle, and simple to empathize with, read, and understand. Except Karina.

I couldn't for the fucking life of me understand what she was thinking inside that thick skull of hers and I never knew what she was going to do or say next. She had told me since we met that she was predictable, boring, and that her life was small. Yet there was nothing routine about that woman. She was headstrong but so sensitive. Her sense of self was both bold and fragile. I wasn't happy about the current situation, either, driving with both Karina and Turner; I knew the tension would be thick.

Karina handed me her ID as we pulled up to the main gate of Benning, which was the one closest to Turner's barracks. She didn't say anything, but I heard her sigh as she slid the card into my palm.

The moment I pulled up to Turner's barracks, Karina got out of the front seat and moved to the back before I could even ask why. I could tell she didn't like Turner, and this whole driving-them-both thing had been really bad judgment on my part. Now that Karina was sitting in the back of my truck on our way to a three-day camping trip, there would be no escaping her or how badly I wanted to talk to her. I wanted to ask her how work has been, how she's been, if she's been going to her dad's house, why she dyed her hair again . . .

Even if she got on my nerves like no one ever had, I couldn't help that she made me feel alive, and interested in something—someone—for the first time since I'd left the battlefield.

Turner waved as we pulled up, bouncing down the grass and pavement and approaching the truck. I could tell she was also surprised to see Karina in my backseat, but even so, she smiled brightly at both of us.

"I'm so glad there are more women going on this trip," Turner said to Karina as she threw her camo duffel into my trunk. I stayed seated, not wanting Karina to get the wrong idea if I helped Turner with her bag the same way I'd helped her. Karina smiled, nodding to be polite.

The music was interrupted again by the sound of Turner's phone ringing. I regretted giving her control over the music instantly, but her phone ringing every few minutes when I was already on edge was not helping. Karina was staring out the window, lost in the maze that was her brain. I wondered if she was upset that I'd let Turner play DJ, but in my mind, she had no right to be since I'd asked her first and she'd said no. We must have been twenty minutes into the drive—four or five songs along in a playlist from the early 2000s. As Turner sang along to "Irreplaceable" by Beyoncé, Karina continued her silent streak. I wished I could go back to two hours ago when Gloria called me to ask if I could drive the two women. I should have found Turner another ride.

I knew if it were just me and Karina in the car, she wouldn't have been able to keep herself from talking and I'd much rather be listening to her voice than Turner's off-key singing into a nearly empty water bottle. Turner was dressed in a tight shirt that hung just above her waist, showing off the honey skin on her stomach and even tighter jeans with holes cut all over them. If it weren't for the thick flannel over her, she would freeze during the night. Outside of work she liked to dress as feminine as she could since she spent over half her time in a baggy uniform.

I tried to just focus on the empty highway ahead of me, but Turner's voice and phone ringing kept distracting me in an irritating way.

"You can answer that if you need to," I finally told her after the third time the same name popped up on my dashboard screen.

"Nah. He'll just think I want him more. You know how men can be when they're not ready to give up. Or do you think me ignoring him will just encourage him?" she said with a sigh.

"Actually, I have no idea, really," I replied after she stared at me expectantly.

"Right, because it's always you who is getting chased." She pointed a finger at me and shook her head.

Her hoop earrings dangled. Turner's cropped black shirt was so low-cut that her bra was peeking out on both sides, and I could feel how uncomfortable her tight jeans must have been just by looking at them. Her shoes were black and had some kind of metal balls on them, while Karina's dirty white Air Forces and baggy jeans made much more sense. They were quite the contrast to one another. Karina's hair was now in one of those clip things that looked like teeth and she wore a simple, long-sleeved shirt. I couldn't help but notice that the cotton of Karina's shirt was rather see-through and I didn't like the idea of the men at the campground being able to see the outline of her body, her bra, the deep curves of her waist. I knew they would all look and I couldn't blame them, even though it made me want to strangle them before it even happened.

Why was I even comparing them?

"I'm bored. Tell me about your most recent ex?" Turner asked me from the passenger seat.

"Mine?" Nervously, I looked in the rearview to see Karina's reaction, but her face was set in stone. She met my eyes for the tiniest of a second, and then looked out the window again. It annoyed me that she was sitting in the back, but she made it clear she didn't want to ride shotgun by the way she yanked open the back-door handle of my truck before we fully decided who would sit where.

"Yeah. Well, yours, too." She nodded toward Karina. "Dating these days is so freaking hard, you know? No pressure if you don't wanna tell me, though." She turned her body to Karina as she spoke.

I was going to tell Turner to leave Karina alone, that she wasn't the kind of person who wanted to share her personal life with a random girl she barely knew or liked, but before I could, Karina's brows raised and she shifted in her seat.

"Actually, I'm fine sharing." I was surprised by her response, but certainly ready to hear it. I arrogantly assumed she would talk about me, especially since Turner had run into us more than once now, so I was pretty shocked when she said the name Brien. I unplugged Turner's phone from my cord to turn the music off. *Yanked* would be a more accurate description.

"We dated on and off for a little bit. We weren't as serious as I thought we were and, looking back, it was such a juvenile relationship that it's almost embarrassing." She laughed. A soft and sarcastic one, but she laughed.

Turner was smiling warmly, clearly very interested in Karina's love life. "When did y'all break up? Did you end it or him?"

Karina's expression in the mirror told me that she already regretted engaging in "girl talk" with Turner. Since Turner didn't know her well enough to tell, she believed Karina's faux-interested smile. Her voice was soft and thoughtful.

"Hmm. I broke up with him the last time. He cheated on me, and I still dated him after that, more like hooking up, I guess. But eventually I realized there wasn't a single thing about him that I actually enjoyed. I created a person in my head who I wanted him to be, but it became too unrealistic of an expectation and eventually I had to stop. That's a bad habit of mine, creating good personas for people who don't deserve it."

That felt like a blow specifically for me, and Karina talking about hooking up with someone, especially that shitbag Brien, made me want to drive my truck off the side off the road.

"Wow. Yeah, I know what you mean by being attracted to the *idea* of someone. This guy, Reed, the one who keeps calling is my most recent ex and God, he's in victim mode right now, but he did the opposite of your situation and just pretended to be whoever he thought I wanted him to be, while he was actively on Tinder and in many girls' DMs on Insta and Facebook."

Turner talked so fast that it was a bit hard to keep up with her, but Karina had leaned up closer to the front seats and seemed to genuinely enjoy the venting session.

"But the lies became too much, and I couldn't stand it. I wouldn't have been that pissed if he had told me he didn't want to be exclusive. I *fucking* hate liars more than anything. Like, how hard is it to be honest? Of course, now I'm the bad guy, even though he's the one who lied over and over. Lying is just something I can't forgive, and I can forgive a lot."

If I heard the word *lie* one more time, I would jump out of the moving truck.

Karina made a noise and nodded in agreement. "Yeah, it's hard when you trust someone. Not to mention the loneliness you feel after getting used to the comfort of that person."

"I can promise you I'll never do that again. Being alone is one million percent better than being lied to and cheated on," Turner said, rolling her eyes.

"Yeah, I suppose so," Karina agreed. "There are a lot worse things than being lonely."

The rest of the drive was full of Turner talking randomly and Karina sitting mostly quietly in the back. Turner plugged her phone back into my radio and every once in a while, she would turn the volume up painfully loud and sing along again. No matter what song was playing, I couldn't stop replaying what Karina had said about Brien. How could she say he was her most recent ex? And right in front of me? When we stopped for gas, she didn't even look at me as she climbed out of the back of my truck. She and Turner surprisingly seemed to become fast friends as they locked arms and went inside the gas station to pee. I knew she was still really pissed at me and probably wished we had never met, but her denial was ironic; the topic had turned to lying but she'd lied to Turner and basically denied ever being with me. When they returned, Karina held a yellow bag of peanut M&M's in one hand and a bottle of water in the other.

She also had a small plastic bag of additional snacks hanging from her wrist, and when I began to drive, she silently put a blue Gatorade and a pack of Starburst in my cupholders. She knew from before, during our "not dating" period, that I loved them and it made me soften a little to know that despite her not wanting anything to do with me, she took the time to grab me these things. Turner didn't seem to notice and was guzzling a bottle of Coca-Cola singing along to a Jonas Brothers song. Her music taste was all over the place—another thing she and Karina had in common.

The small sign to enter the campground was so covered by overgrown brush and unruly bushes that if I hadn't been following my navigation, I would have missed the small dirt road. The dark green trees were tall and hardly any of the setting sun could pass through their branches. The woods were thick, and the smell of fall was in the air as Karina rolled down the back window and stuck her head out. I continued to drive slowly but kept stealing glances at her carefree, relaxed expression in the side mirror. There wasn't a paved road in sight now and the dirt under my tires formed a cloud of dust behind us even though I was driving less than twenty miles an hour. We passed a couple rows of small, empty wooden cabins with not a single car parked by any of them; the place looked nearly abandoned. I wondered if Karina would feel uneasy with the slightly horror-film vibe of the place, but when I looked at her again, her face was tilted toward the massive trees, and she smiled softly. She rolled her window halfway back up, I guessed to keep some of the dirt out, but she seemed unfazed. Turner was humming, scrolling on her phone.

"Who chose this place? It looks like shit," she commented as we slowed down to pass a man stepping out of an RV.

He was shirtless and holding a beer bottle. The setup around his old, rusted RV made me think he was living there, with folding chairs and a table, trash, a grill, and an American flag dangling from the awning. I would bet my life that he was a vet. I could easily spot one, one wounded fucker to another. As we got closer, he waved at us and I nodded back as we passed by. I could see he was wearing a black POW hat; I was right about him. I hoped living out here was a choice, and not because it was his only option. I shook my head to clear my thoughts; I had enough of my own shit to worry about and he wasn't my problem. I wouldn't end up like him. There it was: the lingering fear of being one of the thousands of homeless veterans across the U.S. My obsession with saving my money and owning property stemmed from the statistics and my own fear of ending up that way. Owning a piece of land in this country was the only way to ensure freedom. The government could take our bodies and alter our minds, a greedy apartment building owner could increase our rent, sell the building and kick us out, but no one could take away a paid-off home or piece of land. Karina knew that, too, and that's why she held her home so close to her heart; it was one of the first things I realized we had in common.

There were a few more RVs scattered randomly across a flat stretch of field and a couple of kids who couldn't be older than ten rode their bikes past us. There was an empty pool with a fence around it and a big CLOSED FOR MAINTENANCE sign that looked to be years old hung across the entrance gate. Most of the land was grass or dirt. Finally, tucked in a corner of the field next to the thick woods, away from the campground's other cabins and RVs, was a small cluster of tents. As we pulled up, I recognized Mendoza's van and parked a little bit away from it. Since I was going to be sleeping in my truck, I wanted some space. Again, I wondered where Karina would be sleeping and who was responsible for bringing and putting up the tent she would be in. I was eager for Turner to get out of my truck so I could have a moment alone with Karina. I also wanted to grill her about what she had said to Turner, completely dismissing our relationship while indirectly talking about it.

I didn't want to start the weekend arguing with Karina, but I was more than a little salty about it. Brien being considered her last ex drove me fucking crazy. She drove me fucking crazy. Yards away, Mendoza and Gloria were clearly already enjoying the time being kid-free and that brought an instant smile to my grumpy face. More so for Gloria, who never seemed to get a break. There were a few other soldiers from our platoon, and a few others I didn't recognize were standing around a firepit, filling coolers with ice and beer, and unloading their cars and trucks with all the essentials.

Turner popped out of the truck and left her bags in the back, rushing over to greet everyone. Karina was much slower, gathering her mental composure, I assumed. She sighed and opened the latch on the door. I just sat there looking down at my half-empty Gatorade bottle and unopened Starburst. When I heard her sneakers hit the ground, I got out of the driver's seat and turned to her. She was typing on her phone screen and then put it in the front pocket of her jeans and adjusted her hair clip as I watched her from behind. I stared at the back of her neck, remembering how it smelled, how the sweat on her skin tasted early in the morning.

"Why did you tell Turner that Brien was your last ex?"

"Huh?" She turned to face me and pushed her arms through

the straps of her book bag. It looked too heavy for her, but that wasn't my problem. She wouldn't let me hold it for her if I tried, anyway. She shrugged her shoulders to move it up farther and let out a grunt.

"In the car, you said Brien was your last ex-boyfriend."

She gave me a look that said a million words, but the loudest one was *and?*

"What did you expect me to say?" Karina was walking now, slow enough for me to keep up, but she definitely wanted the conversation to end as soon as possible.

"Well, I thought you would say it was me. I know she works with me, but—"

Karina's hand shot up to stop me from continuing. "I didn't say Brien because of you, or whatever your relationship with her is. I said his name because it's the truth."

"But what about me, about us?" I began to feel deflated, to say the least. The way she was looking at me was like I had just told her that the sky was green instead of blue.

"Us? We never dated."

With that gut punch, she approached the small group gathered around and smiled when Gloria handed her a beer from the cooler. She downed half of it in one gulp and I kicked my sneaker against a stump of wood. Why the fuck had I agreed to this in the first place?

CHAPTER **TWENTY-FOUR**

Karina

By the time the sun went down, our camping site had become much livelier and more crowded. I worried about who else might be coming. And where the hell were Elodie and my brother? I had agreed to a small trip with the handful of people I'd already met, and had expected to be staying in a tent with Elodie. I had planned to drive here with my brother and Elodie, but somehow got stuck riding with Kael and Turner of all people. And my duffel was still in Kael's truck. The ride wasn't as awful as I expected, and Turner was quite funny and kind. Maybe that had a little to do with the fact that she was being much nicer to me than in our previous interactions and a lot to do with the fact that she didn't flirt with Kael in front of me like I thought she would. My only impressions of her until then were territorial encounters, but maybe that had also been in my head since I was obsessed with Kael focusing his attention solely on me. That, and Turner's unapologetic confidence that made me realize I was even more insecure about myself than I'd been aware of.

The woods around us were thick, tall trees with massive trunks and leaves scattered all over the ground. Outside of our group, there weren't many people here, but I liked that. The sky was beautiful, and the trees felt like a shelter from the real world, like we had gone to another state, and not just another county. I was glad the pool was closed, even though it was too cold to swim anyway. When I looked around, all I could see was tree after tree and a few picnic tables a short distance from where we'd set up a fire and a grill that Mendoza and Gloria had brought. I was beginning to feel at ease; my anxious and intrusive thoughts were fading and less frequent. I stopped wondering what would happen if one of the massive trees fell over and crushed our campsite, or if one of the guys got alcohol poisoning and no one could drive him to the hospital. I was finding myself laughing at jokes and breathing slowly, my shoulders falling into a comfortable position as I stared at the crackling fire. Maybe that was because I was sitting next to Gloria on a big, uprooted tree trunk. We'd had beer after beer, and had now moved onto tequila shots. I was on my second one and she was on her . . . fifth?

"See, this isn't so bad, right?" she asked me, touching her little lime-green plastic shot glass to mine.

I wasn't sure, but she could hold her liquor like no one I had ever met.

I got the feeling that she could read me better than most people and oddly, it didn't scare me or make me want to hide from her. Gloria's company was so easy, though I barely knew her; she had that kind of personality that made you want to be like her, but not in an envious way, and she didn't make me feel small or out of place. She didn't force me to talk when I had nothing to say, and so far, she had made sure I was never left alone on the log for too long. She hadn't said a word about Kael, except during his brief appearance when she teased him for overcooking the burgers, and rolled her eyes when he threw a bun at her. She picked it up blew the speckles of dirt off, and took a big bite, making us all laugh.

Mendoza came over at least once every five minutes or so to kiss her, pet her head, rub his hand down her back. He even kissed her neck once in front of us all and neither of them cared. I found my face getting hot and wondered how on earth they kept that kind of passion after so many years.

My parents barely kissed or hugged, and Estelle and my father absolutely didn't show public affection. I was taken aback by the way I sort of craved it while watching the Mendozas. I thought about Kael walking over and licking his warm tongue against my neck, sucking at the base of my ear while I giggled, and knowing that later when no one was around, it would go even further. How incredibly nice would that be. My ears began to burn and not from the fire, so I stopped thinking about the ridiculous things I would never have in life. I'd gotten a brief taste of intimacy, and it had blown up in my face, so I shouldn't have been daydreaming about it.

Kael had disappeared after he helped Mendoza grill our first round of food and it seemed like I was the only one who noticed. I scanned the small crowd. Everyone looked slightly different with the orange flames illuminating their faces and bodies. Their voices were louder than before, a direct result of the alcohol. I felt invisible but seen at the same time, The air was getting colder, but I didn't want to seek out Kael, wherever the hell he went; I knew if I just kept drinking, I would get warmer and warmer. Fall had always been my favorite season, so I didn't mind.

There were only a few other people outside of our group at the campground—I'd say fewer than ten. Because of this and how vast the woods were, it felt like we had the place to ourselves. I was actually sort of relaxed, which I hadn't felt in a while, but the more relaxed I was, the more my mind drifted to Kael. Where had he run off to? What a coward, coming all the way here just to hide in the woods somewhere. I scanned the wooded area, analyzed where everyone who I did know was, but didn't see Turner. Despite our bonding on the ride here, I really, really, reealllly hoped she wasn't with Kael. All signs pointed to them being alone together somewhere, but I was almost too intoxicated to care.

Almost.

"Can I have another?" I asked Gloria over the crackling of the fire in front of us.

Austin and Elodie finally pulled up in Elodie's small car, the tires crunching over the dirt and sticks as Mendoza threw another log into the fire. Austin got out of the driver's seat and was welcomed by shouting and cheering; clearly everyone was happy that the life of the party had arrived. Elodie was met with hugs and exclamations:

"Here, sit down."

"Are you hungry? We already ate, but there are hot dogs, burgers, and sausages over on the table."

"Are you sure you're not too cold?"

"Is it okay to camp when you're pregnant?" an already hammered soldier asked.

I wondered where they had been all this time and planned to ask her when we had time to ourselves and the group was distracted with other shenanigans.

As Elodie sat down in the folding chair next to my giant log, Austin wrapped a thick dark-green blanket around her shoulders, and she thanked him with a smile. Her presence added to the warmth and comfort I was feeling thanks to the burn of tequila in my stomach. I recognized most of the faces by now; nearly all of them had been at my brother's party, which felt like ages ago. As Elodie told me how pretty their drive was, my brother brought her a can of Sprite and, in a shocking turn of events, he turned down the tequila Mendoza offered, saying he didn't feel like drinking. I nearly keeled over. He must have been hungover because he never missed out on the opportunity to drink. Either way, I was glad he wouldn't be, even if it was only for one night.

"Really?" Mendoza was as surprised as I was.

Austin nodded. "Yeah, really." He opened his mouth and poured a bubbly can of Coke down his throat like he was chugging a beer.

"Whatever, more for us." Mendoza patted my brother's shoulders and smiled an endearing, caring smile. In my head, I wrongfully assumed Mendoza or the other guys would taunt Austin or pressure him to drink, but not one of them did. Maybe they were all trying, or at the least not standing in the way of him attempting to get his body and mind in order before he left for basic?

For the first time, the thought of my brother leaving didn't burn my insides. I found myself looking around the group. Nearly all of them had been strangers until recently, but as I listened to the laughter and the shared stories about their lives, the highs and the lows, from the births of their babies to the constant near-death experiences they all shared, I began to feel like I was a part of something, like a chosen family.

And thank goodness my real family had *finally* showed up.

"What took you guys so long to get here? Did Austin get you guys lost?" I asked Elodie when my brother was out of earshot.

Her eyes followed him, and she shook her head. "We, uhm, we couldn't find the . . ." She seemed to be struggling with her English.

"It doesn't matter," I interrupted her as she continued to stammer a bit. "I'm glad you guys made it and I'm actually glad you made me come."

This brought a huge smile to Elodie's face, and she sat back, relaxed compared to a moment ago. I had to admit that so far I was having fun, but with the whole weekend ahead of us it was maybe too soon to speak. Nonetheless, looking over at Elodie with the warmth of tequila in my chest made me glad she'd guilted me into tagging along.

"Your cheeks are red. Aren't you freezing?" Elodie nudged my knee with her finger as someone suggested we play hide-and-seek across the campground.

"It's the alcohol. I'm okay," I lied.

When I was distracted, it'd been easy to not focus on how cold it had gotten, but now that she'd asked, I felt the chill all the way from the top of my scalp to the tips of my toes. My anxiety made me deny the smallest, not complicated things in life. Like now, why wouldn't I just say I'm cold? I couldn't bring myself to, just like I couldn't complain when I got a bad haircut, or the nail tech burned my hands with too-hot towels.

Elodie lifted the corner of her blanket and offered for me to come sit closer to her, but I shook my head, declining. I had to pee, so I would decide how to warm myself up when I got back. I scanned the darkness around us, looking for a wooden structure that resembled a bathroom. I hadn't been paying attention to anyone going and I'm sure most of the guys used the woods like soldiers would.

"Do you know where the bathroom is?" I finally asked Gloria. She squinted and the corner of her eyelash stuck.

"Ugh, these damn things." She pinched her fingers across the corner of her eye to mold her fake eyelash back down to the black line of eyeliner. "I think it's there." She pointed ahead, but I couldn't see anything. Instead of telling her that, I just nodded and thanked her, getting off the log before I peed my pants.

"I'll be right back," I told Gloria and Elodie.

"Want me to walk with you?" Gloria offered.

Even though it was dark, and I wasn't familiar with the space, I wanted to go alone for some reason. Without wanting to admit it,

I knew I was hoping I'd see Kael. If I saw him with Turner, would it hurt worse or help with my attempt at closure? I was a glutton for punishment, apparently, so I stuck my nose in the cold air and walked toward the darkness.

CHAPTER **TWENTY-FIVE**

Kael

Staring into the black of night was one of the most calming sensations for me. I never liked the dark much before deployment, but after seeing the sky light up with rocket after rocket, missile after missile, forming an explosion of never-ending fireworks, I had reached a turning point from being afraid of the dark to desperately longing for a silent, still, night of nothing. We were told to get used to it, to put headphones on, but it was fucking idiotic to tell us to put headphones on and cut off our sense of hearing while getting fired on. I'd heard more horror stories about people who'd fallen asleep wearing noise-canceling headphones, only to wake up to the ground shaking and everything burning.

Bringing myself back to the woods, I rolled my neck in an attempt to release some of the tension. I shut my eyes, trying to listen for Karina's voice in the distance. Not only was she being extremely quiet, the guys were being loud as hell, drowning out my chance at hearing her. I wanted to join them, but I didn't have it in me to be so close to her in my world. It felt like the more I pulled back from it, the further she got pulled in. I didn't like that. Not one fucking bit.

I heard the crunch of sticks near me and my back straightened;

my senses perked up, on high alert. Of course, I knew we were just at a campground, not on a mission in the desert, but my body would never fail to go into flight-or-fight, usually the latter.

"Ugh, where is the damn bathroom?" I heard a voice say.

It was Karina. I recognized it immediately.

"It's so damn cold. I need to get my bag from Kael's truck. Where the hell is he, anyway?" she grumbled to herself. I laughed, genuinely amused by her complaints.

"What was that?" she questioned the air around her.

"Right here," I said, jumping off the back hatch of my truck and landing with my feet on the dirt.

"What the hell!" Karina nearly shrieked. She hadn't been expecting me here, which made it funnier. I laughed again, this time louder, and lifted my phone into the air with the flashlight on.

"What are you doing out here in the dark? You scared the shit out of me," she said, wrapping her arms around her chest. She must be freezing in just a long-sleeved shirt and jeans.

"I'm just avoiding the crowd. What are you doing out here? Where's your coat?"

She stepped closer into the light of my phone flashlight, just close enough that I could see her roll her eyes.

"I didn't bring a coat. I didn't bring anything useful, come to think of it," she told me. Her voice sounded slightly slushed, like she was buzzed but not quite drunk. The idea of her being drunk around so many rowdy men made me uneasy, but it wasn't my place to tell her that, and lord knows if I did, she would surely put me in my place.

"Of course you didn't," I whispered to myself, rubbing my hand over my mouth and chin. She was probably too worried about everything and everyone else to pay attention to what she would need.

"You brought books, though?" I asked. I could tell when I picked up her bag that she had brought at least two.

"How do you know that?"

"Your bag."

She scoffed. "You went through my bag?"

I shook my head. I leaned back into the bed of my truck and turned on a small overhead light. "No, no. But I carried it. I can tell what's in a bag without going through it. Especially if it's something obvious like books. When were you planning to get reading time in?" I smiled at her.

"They're more of an emotional support thing than thinking I'd be able to read. Plus, I didn't have a clue what to expect. I've never been on a camping trip that didn't involve my parents fighting or Austin and my dad trying to kill each other."

Ahhh, there it was. The effortless stream of thoughts that fell from her lips, comforting me even more than the rocketless sky.

"This is more of a sleeping party in the woods than camping. Whose tent are you sleeping in?" I asked her out of curiosity and a bit of worry. I'd loaded her tiny bag into the car so I knew she didn't bring a tent and from the anxiety rolling off her right now, I could read her mind and knew she hadn't thought that through.

"Uhm." She looked back toward the campground. The fire was burning bright, voices carrying to us even a couple hundred feet away.

"Whatever you do, don't agree to sleep with Mendoza and Gloria. They will fuck with you in there and think they're being quiet."

Laughter mixed with surprise filled the air between us. "Good to know. Maybe my brother and Elodie brought one? I really, really suck at this."

Silence fell between us. "You need a coat first before we figure out where you'll sleep." I reached back to open my duffel bag and grabbed my thickest hoodie and a blanket, handing them to her.

She stared at me, reluctant, but her guard was mostly down. I could tell that I didn't have much longer with her in many ways, but this moment, just the two of us in the darkness, felt so good. I hated the way she had that effect on me, but while I was in the center of it, I loved it.

"Take them. And don't you have to pee? The bathroom is pitch-black, FYI, and I saw Turner go in there with Gunner, the guy who looks like he should be in Hollywood, not the woods in Georgia," I pointed out as she grabbed the hoodie from me and wrapped the blanket around her body. She shivered. I wanted to tell her to come closer but didn't.

"I didn't see anyone like that, but what are they . . ." The realization hit her, and she smiled. "Ohhh. I'm glad Turner is occupied," she said, surprising both myself and her.

"You are?" I asked, looking into her eyes.

She nodded.

"And why is that?"

Karina shook her head. That was all I was going to get, but that was fine with me because I knew exactly what she meant even if she would never say it.

"So, where should I pee? I'm dying here. I waited way too long and have been drinking . . ."

I pointed to the closest spot hidden in the trees.

Her mouth fell open. "In there?"

I nodded.

"But it's dark. Like dark-dark."

"There's no one in there. Plus, I'm right here. I'll keep an eye out. You'll be okay."

The fear slipped from her face, and she nodded slowly,

considering her options. I knew Gunner and Turner were absolutely fucking in that bathroom and I knew Karina did not want to see or hear that.

"Ugh. Fine, but make sure you don't let anyone come over there. And if I'm not back in five minutes, I got eaten by a bear."

We both laughed as I assured her that I would avenge her death if a bear ate her.

"Just call my name if you need help, and here—" I handed her a proper flashlight and a roll of paper towel. She put the blanket on the bed of my open truck.

"Wow. You've come prepared."

I agreed. "I mean after years sleeping in the woods, the desert, you name it, I know what to bring."

"Thank you, Kael."

She smiled at me and I felt my chest ache. Maybe she was starting to hate me less? Or was she just in a good mood because of the alcohol and environment? Whatever it was, I would take it. I watched her as she walked past my truck and into the beginning of the line of trees.

"Be careful, Karina," I called out to her, and she lifted the flashlight below her face and beamed at me again. For the next few minutes, I would pretend that our relationship wasn't destroyed and that she loved me the way I loved her, even if she would never know.

CHAPTER **TWENTY-SIX**

The moment the flashlight came back on, I heard Karina cussing at the sticks and debris breaking under her shoes. She wasn't dressed to go camping, but that was hardly a surprise: she was chronically unprepared. With my back against a thick tree, I waited for her to come out of the woods.

"Everything good?" I asked in a quiet voice, trying not to surprise her as she emerged from the tree-covered darkness.

"Yeah. I mean as good as it gets peeing in the pitch-black woods," she groaned as she stepped closer and approached me.

Grabbing on to the blanket that was slipping down, she lifted it up to cover her shoulders. I leaned forward to help her as she tilted her face upward, looking directly into my eyes. I shivered, though my body felt warm. The soft light from the back of my truck cast a shadow across her cheekbones. She didn't look away; she just kept her focus directly on me. I wondered which one of us would look away first. Even the darkness didn't dilute the intensity. It felt like months since I'd had her attention like this, solely fixated on me and only me. She looked like she wanted to say something, and God I hoped she would. I didn't trust whatever the hell would slip out of my mouth right now.

"I—" she whispered, and her tongue dipped down to coat her lips.

Her eyes moved to my mouth, and I couldn't stop myself from assuming her mind was going to the same place mine was. The way she tasted, the warmth of her tongue, and the way she kissed. It was always this way with her; she was so tempting without even realizing it. I wanted to kiss her again, to press my lips against hers. I wished I had known that the last time I kissed her would be the last time. There wasn't so much as an inkling of finality then. Now that the strings had been untied and our relationship had unraveled, I found myself still captivated by her. Karina had a way of putting me in a trance. It was something I had never experienced in my lifetime, and I had been through a lot.

"You what?" I finally asked after a couple more seconds of silence, trying my damnest to be in the present and to stop fantasizing about the past.

She broke eye contact. "I-I don't know," she admitted with a shrug. "I feel like I'm not mad at you right now and I'm trying to figure out why that is. It's confusing me. Like, I should be so pissed, I shouldn't want to be around you, and especially not alone and thinking . . ." She paused and stared at the ground. "What am I even saying?"

I studied her. "I don't know, what are you saying, Karina?"

With hesitation, she exhaled the night air. "I-I just . . . I missed you, I guess." She looked toward the trees. "And since I don't want to be stupid and say anything I'll regret, I'm going to go back to the group now, have another drink, and try to forget what I just said. Can you do the same?"

I shook my head. "Not a chance."

"Kael." She sighed.

"Karina." I gently touched her elbow over the blanket. "This might be the last time we're together like this and I'd much rather those be your last words to me than what you said earlier."

I assumed for a moment that she was as lost in thought as I was, but her eye roll said otherwise.

"You're seriously still annoyed about what I said in the truck? I was just speaking the truth. We technically didn't date."

"We spent every moment that we could together, we shared parts of ourselves that we hadn't before . . . what exactly is 'dating' to you, Karina, if that's not it?"

"But you never asked me to be your girlfriend. technically," she insisted.

I lifted my body up to sit in the bed of my truck. My sneakered feet dangled above the ground. "Do people still do that? Ask someone to be their girlfriend or boyfriend?"

She looked uncertain, like I had caught her in a trap. She knew she was being petty, but I could tell by her body language and from our history that she was going to stick to her guns on this, even if it was immature and ridiculous. I was *also* being immature and ridiculous in hopes of having just a little more of her time and attention. This time with Karina was feeding something in me that I hadn't realized was starving.

"Some people do. Romantic ones, anyway. Plus, if we were dating, it would have been worse that you lied to me. You realize that, right?"

There it was. I knew it was coming. "Yeah." I couldn't disagree with her. She was right and I wasn't going to gaslight her or try to manipulate the truth.

"Good," she huffed, crossing her arms under the tan wool blanket. "At least you know."

I sat and she stood in silence for a few moments. She hadn't run off yet, which was all I could ask for. I knew there was nothing I could do to change what had happened, but fuck, the possibility of this weekend really being the last time we would spend time together, even if I hadn't expected her to speak to me, was the only reason I'd agreed to come on this nightmare of a trip in the first place.

"Can you do me a favor? One I don't deserve, but for the sake of potential regret haunting both of us . . ."

Her face was pinched with skepticism, but her silence encouraged me to keep talking.

"Would it be possible for us to try to pretend that the last few weeks didn't happen? Like I'm not the person who fucked you over? If you say no, I get it, but—"

"Let me guess . . . *it's the last time we will see each other*?" she said in a deepened tone that I guessed was supposed to be mocking mine.

I nodded.

"You know what? Let's do that."

Her agreement shocked me. I wanted to be sure she actually meant it. "Really?"

"Yeah, really. Mostly because I really can't stand any more tension or drama or stress. And I'm already stressed enough being here and not knowing anyone. I don't want to hold on to my anger. I can feel it sitting there, inside of me, and I really, really can't handle it right now. I'm still not okay with what happened, and I will *never* understand why my brother did what he did, or why you went along with it, but I've decided that since it's done and I can't fix it or change it, I'm going to have to accept it. I'll never forgive you, but I can pretend to for the next forty-eight hours."

Processing her words, the amount of *never*s she used stuck to me, but I needed to take what she was offering, and she was right; she would never understand why I did what I did, even though it was for her. I had resigned myself to being the villain and in a plot twist, I was now getting a free pass for forty-eight hours. It felt too good to be true, but I'd take it. Even a few hours would suffice, and the time was ticking for us, for me.

"Deal, then?" I reached my hand out for her to shake.

Her hand slid out of the opening of the blanket wrapped around her.

"Deal."

Karina lifted her body onto the back of my truck and sat next to me. As she surveyed the inside, seats down and covered with blankets, her eyes went wide.

"Whoa, you've got everything here." She picked up my charging port and turned it around in her hands.

It was a thick black-and-orange box with a charge that lasted for days.

"This looks intense." She put it down and I watched her glance from the outlet to my laptop and to the white screen hung up against the window. "Is that a projector screen?" she asked, her voice like she had just found a pile of diamonds.

I nodded. "Didn't want to be bored out here."

"This isn't the same truck I rode here in . . . it looks like the setup for a date. The lights, the screen . . ." There was a sarcastic tone to her voice that was almost an accusation.

"Nah, no way. Who would I be dating out here, anyway?" I had to ask.

Karina's nose scrunched up and I knew she didn't want to admit even an ounce of the jealousy she was clearly feeling.

"You know who."

A small laugh shook my shoulders. God, this woman was infuriating, but so damn charming. She practically hated me now, but her jealousy made me happy, as fucked up as that was.

"The only person I have any desire to date is you."

She jerked her head toward me so quickly I thought it might pop off. "Shush. Don't say stuff like that."

I shrugged. "You brought it up."

I was like an attention-deprived child, causing distraction just to get a rise out of her. She rolled her eyes again and didn't give me the satisfaction I was craving.

"So, if you're not planning on spending a romantic night in the back of your truck, then what's with all this?"

I shook my head. "I have this stuff lying around, I use it to keep myself entertained. No romance involved."

"Why don't you just hang out and drink with everyone then? Isn't this supposed to be one last hurrah for my brother, anyway?"

I rubbed my hand over my leg. It wasn't hurting for once, but I guess I had formed a habit. "I see your brother every day, lucky me," I replied. "Someone has to be sober when there are so many variables."

We both looked toward the noise coming from the campsite. Hollering, laughing, the ruckus was getting louder by the minute.

"You're the one who decided to take my brother in."

"Touché."

"But you're right about the drinking. I kept worrying about what might happen out here, but then I drank tequila and beer and more beer. I was pretty buzzed, but now it's wearing off."

"Yikes. That's a very direct way of calling me a buzz kill," I teased.

Her smile grew and she shook her head. "Not what I meant," she said, a few pieces of hair falling out of the clip and onto her cheeks.

It was hard not to reach over and tuck them behind her ears. Her hair looked so soft and my mind remembered way too clearly how it smelled like vanilla and soap. It was more smooth than usual, which was weird, considering we were in the humid

Georgia woods. She always looked beautiful, but I preferred when her strands were wild and unruly, like her mind and spirit.

She caught me staring at her, but it wasn't as awkward as it should have been. She stared back at me, and it felt like neither of us knew what to say. I was afraid of pissing her off and dredging up the past, so I waited for her to make the next move. She shivered and tried to cover her legs with the blanket.

"Please tell me you have more clothes in your bag. It's going to be warm during the days, but freezing at night."

"Your truck has been holding my bag hostage and I forgot to bring a hoodie." She sighed.

"You can have mine." I began to take it off before she could stop me. My body always ran hot, and with not one, but two portable heaters aboard, I had no intention of leaving the truck.

She must have been really damn cold, and put my hoodie on without an argument.

"You can take one of my heaters with you to your and Elodie's tent when you get settled there."

As much as I didn't want Elodie's pregnant body to be cold, I was much more concerned about Karina. She was chronically cold, and I cut myself some slack for putting my friend's pregnant wife second. Elodie seemed well enough taken care of since Fischer had appointed himself in charge of her lately.

"Why are you being so nice to me?" Karina's voice was cautious and soft.

"What? I'm always nice to you—" I stopped midsentence. "At least I try to be."

Her eyes left mine and landed on her crossed legs where the blanket was. My white hoodie was too long on her arms, but she already seemed warmer and more comfortable than she had a few minutes ago.

"Well, I guess I better get back to the party. Elodie is probably wondering where I am . . ." she said, making me wish I would have started a better conversation.

"Doesn't seem like we're missing out on much."

In the distance, I could see Mendoza and Gloria hugging, Elodie sitting in a chair with a sleeping bag wrapped around her body, and Fischer standing next to her like a guard dog. There weren't many other campers around us and for their sake, I was glad. The fewer people, the less chance of something going down.

"What were you going to watch on that thing?" Karina pointed to my mini-projector.

It was a little bit bigger than my hand and I had gotten it on Amazon before my last field training. It came in handy when we were out in the middle of nowhere in Louisiana with no cell service and no Wi-Fi. I ended up being the hero with downloaded episodes of *Breaking Bad* that we projected onto the side of the Humvee during our downtime.

I shrugged. "Not sure. I downloaded some episodes of *Arrested Development*."

"Random." Karina laughed a little and repositioned her body, perching herself a few feet closer to me.

"I needed some nostalgic comedy to balance my life out."

"Is *Game of Thrones* too full of murder and rape for you?" She raised her brows. I knew she meant it to be funny, but she, as always, was dead-on.

I nodded. "Actually, yeah. Yeah, it is."

Even in the dim light of the rear of my truck, I could see the flush across her cheeks. She lifted her hands up, and the long sleeves of the hoodie fell down a bit.

"I'm sorry—I was joking, but it wasn't funny. I didn't mean

to—" Her index finger slid over her thumbnail again and again, an anxious tic she had.

I reached over and put my hand on hers to calm them out of habit. She didn't move away, sighing, and her hands remained under mine. "It's fine, really."

Looking down at both of our hands, I smiled a bit. "Is this fine?" I asked her, clearly talking about the fact that we were touching for the first time in weeks, and it felt like years. Even though she had agreed to let bygones be bygones for the weekend, and I was slightly taking advantage of that, I wanted to make sure she was okay with me touching her. I was a fuckup when it came to Karina, but I respected her consent above all.

Karina nodded. "Do you think it will ever go away? Your memories, I mean. Will you always suffer?" Her voice was sad.

My first reaction was to laugh it off or downplay it because I didn't want her pity, but there wasn't any in her voice, only genuine worry. She was one of the only people who wasn't blood-related to me who worried about me; my battle buddies did in their own way during deployment, but mostly to keep the body count down.

"Honestly, I think it will always be like this. Not being able to watch violent shows, play certain video games, see the fireworks on the Fourth of July, relax by a burning fire. I'll likely never get a good night's sleep, not without you, at least, and I—" The warmth of Karina's mouth silenced mine.

The surprise of her sudden affection would have knocked me over if I hadn't been sitting down. I let the undeniable physical pull between us completely take over. Wrapping both of my hands around her waist, I pulled her onto my lap as her hungry mouth tasted and teased mine. Every nerve in my body from my nose touching hers, to every vertebra of my spine as we lay back, to my hips pressed against hers, was wildly alert. I threaded my fingers through her hair, unclipping it, and felt her soft curls fall across my cheeks and neck. She began to rock her body slowly against the hardness of my cock. Confusion and longing wrapped around her name as our breaths became one. She brought her hands to my face, touching me as if to make sure I was really there. There was a slight tremor to her touch that excited me as she traced my jawline, and down the base of my throat. I gasped and she groaned, swallowing my sounds.

There was no way of knowing how far this would go; it was completely up to her. I kissed her with intention, knowing that I didn't want to be soft if this really might be the last time, while thanking whatever god there was for gifting me this second chance. Karina's hands reached under my T-shirt and she dug her fingernails into my skin.

"Touch me," she whispered into my open mouth. "Kael, touch me."

I gripped her ass with both palms as she started undressing herself. She lifted the hoodie off first, then her shirt and I kissed down her neck, across her chest as she pulled at my T-shirt to take it off. I pressed Karina's soft body against me and used my upper body strength to flip us over gently, hovering above her as her mouth sucked at the bare skin on my shoulder. I wanted to tear the rest of the clothes off her body and bury myself in her. I had completely forgotten where the hell we were, who was around, or what fucking planet we were on.

Her thighs wrapped around my lower back, and she lifted her hips, whining and biting down on my skin. "Do you—" I began to ask her, but couldn't finish the sentence because her hand reached into my sweats and gripped my cock. She moved slowly, pumping me while nodding.

"Can you close the back?" she asked me. I nodded, desperate to keep her hand on me, but knew we needed the privacy.

She was panting, pulling her jeans off as I lifted the latch on the back of my truck and tapped the lights off one by one. I glanced over to the campfire to make sure no one could see us. Not that I gave a fuck, but for her sake. I was only a few inches away from her body lying across the back of my truck bed when she grabbed a hold of me, her strength surprising me. Her hands were no longer unsure as she took my boxers down, pushing my pants out of the way. She was vibrant and needy, and it was making me dizzy in the best fucking way.

Karina hooked her finger through the dog tags dangling from my neck and pulled me to kiss her. Her panties were soaked, and I gently stroked my index finger across her, circling the pool of wetness through the thin cotton. Her hips jolted up and I pressed harder, keeping my finger steady, knowing it would make her even more frenzied. Once my fingertip was soaked with her need, I brought it to the small space between our mouths. Before I could taste her, she wrapped her lips around the tip of my finger and sucked gently. I almost came from the boldness of watching her taste herself.

I couldn't wait a second longer, I yanked her panties down, pulling them off her thick thighs and tossed them aside. Her body was warm when it met mine and my cock twitched as it slid into her, and I held on to her back tightly as it arched with every movement I made. I wanted to fuck her slowly, to savor the whimpers and the feeling of filling her entire being, but it was hard to control myself with Karina. I rocked into her, pulling out, pushing back in, while gently pressing and circling her clit, knowing exactly how to make her come. She bit my shoulder again, this time harder, and I wrapped my hand in her hair, pulling as the pressure in our bodies built and built, losing balance and logic and everything in between as we both came, breathing and cursing one another's names.

CHAPTER **TWENTY-SEVEN**

Karina

The rise and fall of my chest matched with Kael's as he rested his head in the curve of my neck. His dog tags were cold, despite how warm his body was, and I could feel his heart pounding against my skin. I wasn't sure how we'd got here, or if it was a horrible idea or not, but something had possessed me to kiss him, to touch him, and to go as far as to hook up with him . . . in the back of his truck of all places. I didn't care that Elodie, my brother, and a group of all their friends were close by. I barely thought of them long enough to have Kael close the back of his truck. It was too soon to regret what had just happened and honestly, I hoped I never did. It felt so good, not just physically, but mentally and emotionally, to be close to him.

As if on cue, he lifted his head up to look at me. It was dark, but his eyes were bright and gleaming. He rubbed his nose against mine and it made me laugh in a childlike way. I loved how free he made me feel, like it was okay to giggle and not worry about being quiet or reserved.

"That was uhm, unexpected?" He smiled and kissed the tip of my nose.

I nodded my head, agreeing with a matching smile.

"What even happened?" I joked, but was asking the question to myself, really.

"I have no clue. That was all you." Kael leaned up on one elbow and studied my face.

I knew him well enough to know he was looking for a sign of panic, regret, anger, but he wouldn't find it. In that moment, I just felt warm and calm and at peace with myself, with him, despite everything we had gone through. It didn't make sense and I wasn't going to torture myself to break down exactly why I'd kissed Kael in the first place. Deconstructing that would ruin the only happiness I had felt in weeks. Stopping myself from self-sabotage or ignorance—maybe a bit of both—was bliss. In any case, that was progress.

I took a deep breath and Kael kissed across my cheeks in a soft line. The windows were slightly foggy as I looked up, and his body blanketed mine, so even if someone approached, they wouldn't see me. I didn't care enough to want to move, anyway, and I was enjoying the feeling of his warm body on mine. I loved the way he didn't just climb off me after getting what he wanted. Being in such a vulnerable state and having a man roll over as soon as he came was the kind of neglectful trauma that made me terrified to be close to anyone, but Kael had never done that, and I couldn't imagine that he ever would. I didn't want to think about the women he had been with before me or would be with after me—even the brief thought of it made it hard to breathe. I hugged his back tighter, burying my head into his neck.

"You okay?" he asked, always able to read my mind.

I nodded. I wondered what he was thinking, but didn't want to ask. The silence was so enjoyable that I closed my eyes, focusing only on the present and Kael's breath. It was cut short by a sudden chorus of shouting. Kael's body stiffened immediately and he lifted himself up onto his knees and wiped his hand across the window to see what was going on.

"Motherfucker," he groaned, reaching for his clothes. I had never seen him get dressed so quickly.

"What's happening?" I pulled my panties up my thighs and yanked my legs through my jeans. I grabbed Kael's hoodie and didn't bother to put my bra back on.

"They're about to fight." His voice was calm, but I could feel his energy shifting into protective peacemaker mode. He brought his hand to my cheek, brushing his thumb across my mouth. "Stay here. I'll be back, but you need to stay in the truck."

He knew damn well I wasn't going to stay in the truck, and he wasn't the least bit surprised when I followed him out and we walked toward the group. Mendoza and another guy called Warren were in each other's faces, both yelling in Spanish. I couldn't remember if I had met him at my brother's party or not, but I knew that he and Mendoza had been laughing together earlier by the campfire. I looked around to clock Elodie and make sure she was away from the chaos, but my brother was a step ahead of me and had his arm around her shoulders as they backed away from the scene. Kael went right in and immediately grabbed Mendoza's arm while Gloria reached for the other. Warren brought his hand down to grab Mendoza, but it landed on Gloria's arm. She yelped at the impact and before I could blink, Warren was on the ground, Mendoza on top of him.

"Manny, stop!" his wife screamed.

Kael grabbed hold of Mendoza's shirt to pull him off, but to no avail.

"I'll fucking kill you!" Mendoza yelled as his fist landed on Warren's jaw. Kael tried again, and this time he had more success, but Mendoza was like a bull, blinded by anger, and he shoved

Kael backward, making him trip over a pile of branches. I rushed to Kael's side, but he was already back on his feet and going for Mendoza again.

A couple of the guys had joined Kael to break up the fight. The look in Mendoza's eyes as they dragged him away sent a chill down my spine. He was a completely different person right now, his eyes black, mouth twisted, the corner of it dripping with blood. Gloria was quiet now, a blank expression as she stared at her husband and Kael walking away. The two of them disappeared into the dark woods.

Warren got to his feet and stepped toward Gloria. I moved between them without a trace of fear in my body. Kael would have wanted me to.

"I'm sorry, I didn't mean to touch you. I was trying to get him off me and didn't see you." Warren held up his hands.

"It's fine," she said, touching my arm as she spoke. Her hand was ice-cold; I could feel it through the thick cotton hoodie. When he repeated his apology, she waved him off. "I said it's fine, just go—"

The resolve in her voice further proved how used to this behavior she was. It made me sad for her, her children, and her husband.

"You should go," I told Warren, who was holding his jaw.

I reached for Gloria's hand and laced my fingers through hers, leading her away from Warren and toward the log we had been hanging out on earlier in the day. It felt like days had passed, with so many changes since the sun set.

"Where do you think they went?" I asked her, nodding toward the woods where Kael and Mendoza had gone.

"Hopefully Manny fell into a fucking ditch and got some sense knocked into him." Gloria leaned forward and grabbed the bottle of tequila from the dirt at our feet. She drank straight from the bottle and wiped her mouth off, hissing as the liquor made its way through her. When she handed it to me, I almost declined, but figured she could use a drinking partner right now.

"Do you want to talk about what happened? I understand if you don't," I asked, sizing up her comfort level. If she wanted to pretend nothing happened, it wasn't my place to press her for information. I was just glad that the fight was broken up before it escalated any further.

"Same shit as always. Stupid soldiers picking at each other until one of them gets violent. I fucking told Warren to stop pushing Manny's buttons, but he didn't listen and got his ass beat. And my husband can't control himself," she said, sighing, and was still relatively calm considering what had happened.

"This is the reality of being married to someone with PTSD. He was never like this when we were young. He always had a temper but with every deployment, his mind got more fucked up. He goes in and out, in and out. Sometimes I feel like he's slipping away and I'm afraid he will disappear completely or drink himself to death."

I let the vulnerability of her words breathe between us before I responded. The tequila bottle was nearly empty and all of Gloria's lipstick had faded; her eyes were bloodshot in the light of the fire burning in front of us. She leaned into me, resting her body against my side. I could feel the relief leave her small frame as her shoulders fell, starting to shake.

"Sorry, I'm not usually a crier," she said, wiping at her eyes. I tightened my arm around her shoulders and used my free hand to press against the base of her neck and gently squeezed her trapezius muscle. It was rock-hard, and a moan fell from her lips as I pressed my fingers into it, repeating the motion.

"Do you mind? Your shoulders are so tight," I asked her. I couldn't help but notice how badly she needed the relief.

Gloria shook her head, and I stood up, moving behind her to

use both of my hands on her shoulders. They seemed to be carrying the world and were resistant to my kneading fingers. I felt the tissue separating as Gloria rolled her head back.

"When was the last time you had a massage?" I asked after a few minutes of working on her.

I leaned in to see her face. She had stopped crying and seemed to have slipped into the trance that only a massage can bring. It was one of my favorite things about my work, seeing the transformation in my clients' faces when their brows relaxed, their jaws unclenched, their breathing slowed.

"Never," she replied, her voice nearly lost over the faint crackling of the wood in the fire. It was nearly out, and everyone had disappeared into their tents. I wondered where Elodie had gone, and if she had set up a tent for the two of us, but wanted to focus on Gloria, who had helped me settle in and needed someone right now.

"You've never had a massage?"

She shook her head, and I moved my hands down to her shoulder blades, finding the tight knots and rolling my thumbs over them, pushing upward. "I can't afford massages. I can barely afford groceries most months."

I immediately felt like crap for asking such a ridiculous question. As if a mother of three on an Army salary could afford the luxury of treating herself to a massage regularly. I knew better, but hated the reality and wished that health insurance covered natural body treatments as freely as they handed out addictive narcotics.

"Little Manny wants to play soccer next year and I don't know how we're going to afford it. It's not even like I can work; childcare is impossibly expensive. It's fucked up, but that's life. We'll make it work. We always do."

It made me sick to my stomach that her family had sacrificed so much and still she had to worry about paying for her son to play a sport. It was wrong and made me enraged for her, for the hundreds of thousands of families who barely got by. Growing up, I had been so spoiled once my dad became an officer; his big house and steady paycheck felt like a million dollars to my mom and me and Austin, but the reality for most enlisted soldiers was very different from an officer's family.

"I'm sorry for asking such a stupid question."

Anxiety bubbled in my chest, heavy with guilt. Gloria waved her hands and reached up to touch my hand on her shoulder. Her hands were warm now.

"Don't worry about it. The free massage is making up for it."

I could hear the smile in her voice.

"You can come to see me at work anytime and I'll treat you. I know from Kael that you don't often have a sitter, but if you do, I'd love to give you a free massage, really. You need it and I appreciate everything you've done for me."

She turned her body around to face me and I couldn't read her expression.

"I haven't done anything for you. I see why Martin is so in love with you," she said with a laugh. "But you shouldn't be too quick to do things for people who are kind in the moment. It stresses me out thinking about how badly people will take advantage of you."

Her advice was a bit harsh. My eyes stung a bit, but she did have a point. I wasn't used to people being so blunt and outside of Elodie, I barely had anyone looking out for me. With the exception of Kael.

"Take advantage of me, do you mean like Kael did?" I asked Gloria directly, trying to match her confidence and straight-forwardness. I wanted to know how much she knew about our situation, or whatever the hell we were. My cheeks burned wondering what she would think about me hooking up with him less than an hour ago.

She shook her head. "Nah, not Martin. He can be a fucking idiot, but he loves you. I know you're probably worried as hell about your brother, but . . ." She paused and licked her lips, and I tried to catch my breath. "I'm sorry to say this, but sometimes people need the help and structure of the military to get their shit together. I love your brother, too, and I know it's scary, Karina, but he will make a good soldier."

Her words burned in my chest, but soothed my mind at the same time. I didn't ask for her opinion and I didn't expect her to know that I was pissed at Kael for helping my brother sign his life away. It was strange how everyone else seemed to be on the same page about my brother enlisting. Did they all know him better than I did?

I barely had the bandwidth to process her thoughts about Austin, let alone the fact that she thought Kael loved me. Did he tell her that? Before I could ask her, Kael and Mendoza approached us.

"There you two are." Mendoza's voice sounded like a car that was out of gas.

His fiery rage from earlier had completely disappeared and he looked almost sheepish. He smiled as they got closer. Kael's expression was neutral as if they had just gone for a causal walk. He was limping slightly as he patted Mendoza's back. I thought about the pile of branches Mendoza had shoved him into and wanted to slap Mendoza for possibly hurting Kael; even if he was back to himself now, it made me see red.

Gloria stood up and her husband wrapped both of his arms around her body. "I'm sorry, baby. Are you okay?" he asked, his face buried in her thick hair.

She pushed at him, but not with enough strength to budge him. "You fucking asshole. I told you to stop hitting people."

"I know. I know." Mendoza squeezed a giggle out of Gloria as he lifted her off her feet. When he put her down, she was looking at him like he hung the moon, and he was looking at her like she was every star in the sky. I even started to forgive Mendoza because of the way he was with his wife, so openly and completely in love. They seemed to forget they weren't alone, or maybe they didn't care.

"Let's go to bed. Straight to the tent. If you so much as look at Warren or anyone else, I'll bury you in these woods," Gloria threatened.

"Good night, you two," the Mendozas called back to us as they made their way to their tent, hand in hand.

I didn't know how on earth she had gotten used to the chaos. I found it so unsettling, but as Kael's soft eyes met mine, I decided that being around him, even in the midst of all this, would be worth it. Once again, I was in awe of the way he handled everyone, and since he was always looking out for other people, he needed someone to look after him. That someone should be me.

CHAPTER **TWENTY-EIGHT**

Kael's truck was more than comfortable. Between the heaters, the pile of blankets, and the warmth of his arms around me, I slept like a baby. When the sun came up, I was surprised that I didn't wake up one single time the entire night. I was so comfortable lying on my side in the crook of his shoulder. His arm gently brushed my skin under the T-shirt of his I ended up sleeping in. He was awake when I opened my eyes, but both of us stayed quiet, enjoying the early-morning silence. Kael's other hand stroked my hair, and I hugged his body tighter. I'd missed waking up with him more than words could explain.

Eventually the group woke up and voices got louder. I heard the clanging of what sounded like pots and pans and could smell the fire, then food. The smell of bacon always reminded me of Saturday mornings when my mom was in a good place. She would wake up early, start a pot of coffee, and blast music through the kitchen as she made a complete and utter mess everywhere, from the counter to the sink to the floor. Her attempts at making shapes out of pancakes always failed, but everyone knew that ugly pancakes tasted the best—at least, that's what Austin and I told her.

The one thing we hadn't had to lie about was the deliciousness of the pile of bacon, crispy with a paper towel soaking up the grease. My brother and I always started eating it directly from the plate before the rest of the food was done. Everyone in the house, even my father, preferred overcooked bacon. It was quite literally one of the only things all four of us agreed on. My mom's epic and highly secret recipe included sprinkling brown sugar on the meat and putting it in the oven while it was still cold. I was getting hungry thinking about it and being able to smell the food cooking at the campfire made my stomach growl.

"Hungry?" Kael asked, kissing my forehead and hugging my body.

I nodded, head buried against his chest. "I don't want to get up but I'm starving, and the smell of bacon is killing me."

He rolled onto his back and lifted my chin with his fingers. Last night seemed like such a blur. After the fight happened, we went back to the truck and used our bodies to communicate instead of words. His frustration was clear as he bit at my skin and I'd felt it melt away as I climbed on top of him, circling my hips until his body tensed, eyes clenched shut, and he came, pressing me against him until his breathing slowed and he fell asleep. I'd counted his breaths, exhausted from the vast range of emotions we had both gone through in just one night, and passed out shortly after.

"Let's get some food," Kael suggested.

I lifted my body up and stretched. Muscles I had forgotten existed ached—the good kind of sore.

Kael put on the same kind of outfit as he wore yesterday, but in gray. I looked down at his white hoodie in my hands. "Will it be weird if I wear this? What if they all notice?"

The edges of his mouth turned up into a smile. "Who cares? They're all going to see us walking up together anyway. Unless you wanted to go out there separately and pretend you slept in the woods?"

He had a point, and Elodie would definitely ask me where I'd slept since it hadn't been with her. I didn't have any texts or calls from her, so maybe she already knew? Maybe they all already knew? I began to worry about everyone's perception of me, their potential stares and opinions making my hands ache. I pressed one of my fists together, digging my nails into my palm to distract my mind.

"No, no, no." Kael's voice was soft as he undid my hand. Little moon shapes from my nails were already there. "Hurt me instead, then." He opened his hand and held his palm up out to me.

There wasn't so much as a hint of judgment in his eyes as he held mine. He knew my coping mechanisms better than I did myself, and, as always, he tried to shield me from myself. I lifted his hand and kissed his palm.

"Let's go eat," I told him, pulling the hoodie over my head.

No one even looked up as we approached the group around the campfire. Gloria was handing out paper plates to the people sitting at the picnic table. There was a pan with enough scrambled eggs to feed an army in the center, a paper plate with fried eggs, another pan of sausage, and a bowl of potatoes, peppers, and onions. It smelled so, so good and my stomach grumbled as I sat down across from Elodie. Mendoza walked over with another skillet of freshly hot and still-popping-in-the-grease bacon and sat it in front of Warren. His jaw was swollen, and he had a bloodstained mark under his bottom lip, but the two of them seemed to be fine now. Next to Warren was my brother, who was unusually quiet as he handed Elodie a bottled water, taking the cap off for her.

"I missed my sous-chef," Mendoza told Kael, his mouth full of meat as he spoke.

ANNA TODD

"Seems like you got along just fine without me." Kael grabbed a piece of bacon and popped it into his mouth. He sat down next to me and nodded at Elodie, telling her good morning. She smiled, narrowing her eyes as she looked back and forth between me and Kael.

"Good morning, you two," she said through her impossibly huge grin. She didn't try to hide her smugness or her joy at the conclusion she had obviously come to about us.

"Morning." I smiled back, widening my eyes to tell her to shush, and that I would explain later.

"Where did you—" my brother began to ask me, but Elodie's elbow nudged his side and stopped him midsentence.

"Ow," he whined. I expected him to call us out, but instead he grabbed the empty plate in front of him and began to shovel eggs onto it.

"What do you want?" Kael whispered to me, pointing at the food.

Gloria carried over a bag of bread and asked which idiot had brought a bag of bread, but no toaster. No one confessed and she said she was going to feed it to the birds.

"Anything," I said, eyeing the warm food. The morning air was a bit cold still and steam rose from the table as everyone began to eat. "Except the bacon," I added, noticing that Austin also left out the bacon since it was soft. Elodie seemed to love it; she barely finished chewing a piece before she put another in her mouth.

As I ate my eggs, I looked around at the group again. Everyone was getting along, talking about some sports team and planning a group outing to a football game in Atlanta. Hearing about Atlanta made me remember that Kael and I still had so much unfinished business to talk about. What did our hookup mean for us? He had his hand on my thigh under the table and had barely taken his eyes off me since we sat down, so clearly things had changed. But what did that mean for his plans to go to Atlanta? I tried to distract myself from worrying about the future or the past and only focus on how steady and warm his touch was, how beautiful his eyes were when the sun shined across them, turning them from rich midnight to golden-flaked espresso.

"Happy birthday to you! Happy birthday to you!" rang out around me and I looked up to see Gloria carrying a sheet cake toward the table. It had a row of lit candles, their small flames wavering as she sat it on the table directly between my brother and me.

"Happy birthday, dear Fischer," everyone sang, Elodie, Kael, and a few others I didn't see adding, "and Karina!"

Kael clapped his hands as everyone cheered for us. I felt a little embarrassed by the attention, but realized this was the first time in my life I'd had a group of friends sing "Happy Birthday" to me. For our entire lives, our birthday always felt like Austin's birthday, but today, even though these were his friends, I didn't feel like an after-thought as I blew out the candles. Gloria's arms wrapped around my shoulders from behind and she kissed my cheek. "Happy birth-day, Karina. I'm so glad you're here," she said into my ear.

I almost burst into tears as Elodie jumped up and hugged me, too. I wasn't used to this much affection and I was worried what would happen if I let myself get too used to it.

CHAPTER **TWENTY-NINE**

I told Austin I would go to dinner, even though I didn't really want to be around my dad or Estelle, like, at all. I was going out of pure guilt piled on by others, and the fact that my brother might not be around for any more birthday dinners together. As much as I didn't want to be there, I needed to do it for him . . . we were twins, after all.

The preciseness of the dinner hour was hanging over my head. In the past, it always bothered me that the time couldn't be changed, that I couldn't just cancel, but I never did anything about that. It was just something that had to be done, and I'd accepted it. But skipping these last few weeks felt like a good change, like a power stance that I was taking against my dad and the very particular order he forced onto my life. He was damn lucky that I was even going to his house after what happened the last time I saw him. If I had it my way, I would choose to avoid him as long as I could, mandatory family gatherings and funerals being the exception.

"If they have any leftover sweets, will you bring me some?" Elodie asked me as I attempted to pull my sweater over my head and slip my feet into my shoes at the same time.

I refused to dress up tonight and wore a Harvard sweatshirt I'd bought at H&M to try to re-create Princess Diana's casual street style. It didn't look anything on me like it did on her, but paired with black knee-length shorts and dirty sneakers, it was comfy and would do the trick of annoying my dad and making Estelle cringe.

I promised to bring Elodie back a snack as she lay down on the couch and blew me a kiss. I rushed out of the door and started down the steps, but turned around and used my key to lock the door. Kael's constant reminders were finally working. I missed Kael, even though it had only been two days since I saw him last. We texted a lot, but I was practically working from open to close and he was busy with discharge meetings that would take up most of the week. Today I barely made it off work in time to shower before the approaching hell of a dinner at my father's house. I played a random playlist on Spotify that was named "studying when you're miserable but don't wanna fail." The title drew me in, and the slow, folksy instrumentals worked, making me focus only on the drive and not on my anger toward my father.

My dad's house was the same as it had always been. The same overdone landscaping with random little trees and mismatched flowers planted by Estelle out of boredom, yet never maintained. The same flags flying high on the pole. The same driveway that made my mind race with last-ditch excuses to not go inside. I slapped my hands against my cheeks gently, enough to bring some color to my drained face. I had to stop letting this house and its inhabitants demoralize me. I didn't know exactly how to do that, but I had to figure it out or my dad would ruin my life like he had my mother's.

Everything in my life was changing: my brother was leaving, Elodie's due date was creeping closer each week, Kael and I were attempting to restart our . . . I couldn't finish the sentence. I didn't know why it was so hard for me to just call it a relationship, but we hadn't had the official talk yet, so for now, it didn't need a label. With so much change as of late, I hoped the intimidating dynamic of dinner with my father would also change for the better. As much as I kept preaching to myself about change, change, change, there I was, right back at Tuesday-night dinners. Everything inside their house was predictable. Though Estelle had replaced a few things over the last couple years to bond herself to the house and settle into her new last name, the house was mostly full of the furniture my mom and dad had collected over their life together. Old picture frames that my mom had bought were now occupied by his new wife's face. I had never really thought about how much of my mom was left in that house, but as I got out of my car, I wondered how Estelle felt about being surrounded by my mom's ghost, or if she even thought about it that way at all.

As if they were moved by an actual ghost, the front curtains drew back to reveal my dad standing there watching me. Austin was next to him, his shadow much more imposing than my dad's. Austin waved and my dad said something to him, making him smile. It was almost eerie to see them together, both smiling from the window. Austin looked so much like my dad right then that I had to look away or I would bolt back to my car and take off.

I would bet they were bonding over Austin's recent enlistment. I wondered when my dad had found out and I hated how happy he probably was that my brother was following in his footsteps.

I could gag.

I walked across the grass and when I got to the door, Austin was there waiting, wearing a white Nike hoodie and sweats. Immediately I knew they were Kael's. I had taken a shower after work, but refused to go the whole nine yards of blow-drying, or applying mascara or foundation. I twisted my wet hair into a claw clip and put some moisturizer on. I wanted my outfit to bother my dad, but even he was dressed in more casual clothes, wearing loose-fitting blue jeans and a burnt-orange T-shirt. Was I in bizarro world? Estelle and her usual dress or cashmere would be my last hope to look underdressed.

"Yo." Austin threw his arm over my shoulder and hugged me as soon as I stepped into the house. He smelled like a fresh sip of beer and faint cologne. His eyes were bright, no circles under them, no blotchy hangover spots on his cheeks or neck. Whatever the hell Kael had been doing with him was working. Lately, my brother had been looking better than I had ever seen him.

My heart began to swell until my dad's voice sounded out, the same old gray concrete it had always been. "Karina, I'm glad you could make it."

"Like I had a choice, really," I said into my brother's neck.

"Be nice," he replied under his breath.

Hearing loud cheering from the TV, my father turned and pointed, his hand on my brother's shoulder as I tried to unwrap myself from his embrace. "Ah, look. They scored."

"Since when are you into sports again?" I whispered to my brother, who was still hugging me to him.

"Since now." He shrugged. "Glad you came."

Austin finally let me go, and I checked the time on my phone. I had only been there for two minutes. It was going to be a long night. Especially with everyone acting like nothing had happened. The elephant in the room. I followed behind them and stood next to the couch, staring absentmindedly at the men knocking into one another on the TV.

"Kare, come in and get settled," my dad said. "You act like you *didn't* grow up in this house."

"I didn't grow up here," I reminded him, but walked farther into the living room, nonetheless.

He didn't reply, but I could tell by the look he gave me that it pained him not to snap back at me. I wondered how long it would take for one of us to bring up what had happened between me, my dad, and Kael. I didn't know how long I could just pretend like we hadn't had a massive blowup and hadn't spoken in weeks. The anger inside of me mixed with the crunching sound of football pads on the television made my head hurt. I looked for the remote to turn it down a bit, but it was sticking out of my dad's front jeans pocket. During my childhood, my dad always held on to the remote—literally—when a game was on. It drove my mother mad, so mad that once she grabbed one of his shiny golf clubs and smashed it into the brand-new TV we'd bought during tax season. Both of our parents' screams filled the air as Austin and I ran down the porch and to the park at the end our block. Austin dangled upside down on the monkey bars and I sat in the mulch, picking up handfuls and throwing it as we debated which one of our parents would win the fight that day. By the time we got home, my dad was in their bedroom and our mom was asleep on the front porch swing, an empty bottle of wine on the steps.

Years later, these types of memories still freshly echoed in my mind as if they had occurred recently. So much so that as I stood in front of my father's blaring TV, I could hear the sound of the creaking metal chains of the porch swing. I wished I could afford to go to therapy again, but now that I was turning twenty-one, my health insurance from my dad's retirement was about to disappear, so there was really no chance. As Austin and my father chummed it up like old pals, I considered telling my dad I would send him the bill for my much-needed therapy.

I wondered if deep down he thought he had lived his life the way he should have and had done right by his children, or if he even gave a shit. It had always seemed like his career and reputation mattered more than anything else in the world.

I had never seen my brother and father this way. They were usually at each other's throats or making awkward small talk that Austin would later complain about. Our father had never been affectionate with either of us, purposely keeping his physical distance as long as I could remember. And this evening, neither of them had mentioned the thing that had to be bringing them together, which was my brother following in his footsteps and enlisting. I wondered when Austin might have told him, how he'd reacted, if Estelle had smiled along, proud of Austin for the first time since she'd met him.

On cue, Estelle walked into the living room to bring my dad a beer and stopped to say hi to me. She seemed different tonight, maybe because it had been a while since I'd last seen her. Something about her looked more fresh than usual and she barely had any makeup on. She was wearing a long-sleeved linen shirt that was something between beige and gray and her hair was tied back in a ponytail. Was it casual Tuesday for everyone and I just didn't get the Fischer family memo?

"You look gorgeous," she said. "So stylish. Reminds me of when I was in my twenties."

"Thanks," I told her, trying not to sound as startled as I was. Her face was sincere even though I was basically wearing pajamas to the family dinner.

"I like your hair like that, too. It really brings out your eyes," she added.

She reached to touch my hair, and I jerked away, but didn't exactly mean to. She looked at me, not able to hide the hurt on her face, and I lamely apologized with a small smile. I didn't mean to hurt her feelings, she was the least of the villains in the house at the moment, but that didn't mean I wanted her to touch me or caress my hair.

"Would you like some wine?" she asked me, her expression back to one of a smiling, pleasant host.

I nodded, even though I wasn't in the mood to drink, but I wanted to accept at least one thing from her after rejecting her.

She smiled a little, keeping it a beat too long to not be fake, and that just made me feel more awkward. Her eyes were on me—they were one of her best features, but they always gave her emotions away. They were the color of warm honey, set deep in her face, with long, dark lashes fanning against her cheeks. My brother's gross friends always said how hot she was. Austin hated the hot stepmom jokes, but I'm sure my dad loved having a beautiful wife dangling from his arm. While my mom was a stunning, energetic woman whose spirit just jumped out at you, I had never seen my dad parade my mom around like he did Estelle in her pencil skirts and tight dresses. Strangely, I wished I could stop judging Estelle so harshly. I hated the way it made me feel to think so negatively about anyone, especially as she stood there with a defeated expression, trying to get along with me while knowing I had never accepted or liked her.

The men in the house continued to ignore me, and to break the tense energy with Estelle, I followed her into the kitchen when she went to get my wine. She didn't need to wait on me the way she did my dad. Their house had a lot of rooms, but they were all shoved together. There were so many things hung on the walls: his awards, mass-printed paintings of flowers, old family photos—it made me laugh that one of the frames still had the stock photo of a random family in a field inside. It would never be filled the way Estelle wanted, with a photo of the four of us, or maybe she didn't give a shit and just liked the frame. The kitchen had a slight theme:

white plaster bowls full of fruit, bread loaves half eaten and their bags half full, twirled and clamped shut with mismatching clips.

The clutter and wall art made the house feel like it was closing in on me. The decorations were mostly tones of brown; a big cabinet that had belonged to my grandma on my dad's side was full of trinkets scattered around the shelves, neat enough to look decorated, but still cluttered. I recognized them all; they had been with my dad long before Estelle came into the picture. I was no Joanna Gaines, but if I had the kind of money my dad did, I would update my home with new things that made me happy, not just wives. I wouldn't keep decades of memories only because I didn't feel like bothering with moving them.

On the kitchen wall, near the fridge, there was a painting of a comet flying through a dark starry sky that my mom got at a garage sale when I was a kid. It followed us from house to house, kitchen to kitchen. Estelle standing in front of it as she uncorked a bottle of red wine felt wrong, but again, it was my dad's fault, not hers. She probably didn't even know that it'd belonged to my mom. I watched Estelle pour the wine slowly, as if she was lost in thought the same way I was.

I politely took my glass of wine and slipped into the dining room. My head was spinning as I took a deep breath and tried to stop thinking about my mom. In the next room, Austin and my dad talked loudly about the game. I guessed my father and brother's relationship had changed recently; I'd assumed that Austin hadn't been here, but it was becoming clear that he had. Long enough for them to become best buds. It made me envious that no matter what my brother did, my dad was proud. Even when Austin got steady C's his entire academic career, as long as he was still playing football, he was a star student in my father's eyes. Austin, with his average grades, got more praise and shoulder pats that I ever did . . . his favorite dinners made, trips to Dallas to see the Cowboys play in person. And now that he was going to be a soldier, my dad must have been over the moon.

No matter how many A's I got, or how many science fairs or spelling bees I participated in, my dad either didn't notice or didn't care. I used to daydream of devising plans to get my father's attention and approval, like running away or smoking a stolen cigarette in the house just to have my dad notice. Being yelled at was better than being ignored. It only got worse after Mom left; at least she would cheer for me when I brought home a good report card or finished a project. When she was mentally present, she made me feel seen, but as I got older, those times were few and far between.

"That's a goal! Hell yes!" my dad shouted from the other room, pouring salt in my wound.

I continued to reminisce about the unfairness of how my dad treated my brother. In my memory, I could hear my dad telling Austin he was destined to play sports at a state college and would "really make something of himself." Not once had my dad ever asked me what I wanted to do in the future, let alone encouraged me. My mom told me once, with vodka on her breath, that my dad wished I were a boy. Once the words were out, she covered her mouth and tried to take it back, but I would always remember the honesty in her voice when she said it. Now that I was more grown up, I was beginning to realize that my dad had issues with women in general, and not just the perpetual disappointment directed at my mother and me.

I pulled out my phone, about to text Kael to complain about all of them, to bitch about Estelle's awkwardness and how my brother did virtually nothing and was still the golden child, to ask him what he knew about my dad's awareness of Austin's enlistment. I was so relieved that things had changed between Kael and me;

even though our future was unclear, I was okay with that, for now, at least. I had gone from a brand-new, Instagram-quote-loving girl who didn't pine over stupid soldiers with trust issues, to hooking up with Kael in the back of his truck in the middle of the woods and then missing him every second he wasn't by my side. I wanted him to be the first to text me tonight, but I knew he was busy, so instead of complaining to him, I swiped out of my text messages and tapped on the Instagram icon.

I had a lot of notifications again; the market cactus and the purple chair picture were still the most popular out of my tiny grid and my followers were growing daily. Strangers were commenting for me to post more often, asking me where the chair was from and how much I would sell it for. The internet was so strange.

As Estelle brought in food from the kitchen into the dining room, I asked if she needed my help, but she politely declined. Each dish she carried in looked and smelled so good, and I was suddenly starving. Austin and my dad finally waltzed in as Estelle sat her gravy boat in front of me, still oblivious that its origin was offensive. I pushed it away, toward the center of the table, and made a mental note to accidentally break it someday soon. Austin plopped down across from me, and my dad took his usual seat as head of the table. Estelle began to busy herself with carving the chicken, something my dad used to do for my mom, who would get grossed out and become a vegetarian for a week whenever she attempted to carve any type of meat. Estelle didn't seem to mind as she skillfully and silently sliced through the crispy skin, the smell of lemon and pepper rising with the steam from the dish.

Since no one was talking and I didn't care about manners or etiquette today, I continued scrolling on my phone. I tapped on my photo icon and looked through the album, wishing I took more pictures of my experiences in general, and not just because of

Instagram. I only had two random pictures from the camping trip: one of the fire, and one of a yummy breakfast. I should have taken some snapshots of Gloria, of Elodie, of Kael . . . and my brother with our joint birthday cake.

Family dinner began and continued around me. No one said much or seemed to care that I was completely checked out for most of it. My dad popped the top off a fresh bottle of beer that Estelle brought him, situating himself with elbows on the table as he took a sip. The chicken was good, as usual, and the mashed potatoes sucked, as usual. Estelle hated butter and never used it, and potatoes without it were practically a sin. The table decorations were on point though: maroon silk napkins with shiny silver rings around them and everything. She had neatly arranged place settings with silverware and wineglasses at every seat of the eight-person table despite there only being four of us. The chandelier kept flickering overhead, giving me a bit of sensory overload.

We were almost done with Estelle's gourmet meal, and for once my dad hadn't bombarded me with questions and passive-aggressive insults about my life choices, my job, and the way I was dressed. Likely he was too fixated on his golden boy becoming *a soldier*! He must be glowing with pride and not the least bit concerned what his daughter had been up to. Maybe he didn't want to cause a fight, considering we still hadn't so much as breathed a word about what'd happened between us and Kael. Even Austin had stayed silent about it. My father wasn't acting like someone who had ruined a group of men's lives, like they all didn't hate him to death, like even doctors at Martin Hospital didn't have mysterious vendettas against him. Not that I thought he was going to bring up the faults he'd collected or war crimes in the middle of dinner, but still. The smooth, unwavering expression on his face gave me chills. He was a master at faking.

"So, Austin, how are you making money to support yourself these days?" My dad finally broke the silence, his eyes dancing around the table. Despite knowing it was coming, the last thing I wanted to talk about was my brother and the Army.

Austin sighed, wiping at his mouth with the fancy silk napkin. "I'm still working with a friend right now. Fixing up a duplex. Like, flipping it, basically."

I looked at him, beyond confused about his response and why he didn't mention enlisting in the Army. I moved a half-eaten baby carrot around on my plate as Estelle asked my brother another question.

"Does it pay much? This sounds like a good opportunity, Austin." Estelle kept right on talking, not halted by my dad, who raised his brow. "Even if the pay isn't much, it could be a good chance to learn if it's something you're passionate about."

Austin nodded and set his beer bottle down in front of him. I noticed he had been nursing the same one since I arrived. "Yeah, my friend Martin is really good at real estate and demo. He's good at the business stuff and the physical stuff."

I almost choked on my food as they casually spoke about him. Like my dad and Kael hadn't had a screaming match in my living room just weeks ago, each threatening one another as I stood in disbelief. I watched his stone face closely. He didn't blink—he just continued to act like he didn't know that Kael was Martin, the friend my brother was talking about. I was so confused, but my gut told me to stay quiet for now, even though I had a million things to say.

My biggest question: Why was everyone talking about Austin's future flipping houses when he was weeks away from leaving for basic training? My dad and Austin hadn't mentioned the Army yet? Was he keeping that from my dad and Estelle? It was beyond freaking creepy how good of an actor my dad and my brother both were in the moment. The fork my dad used scraped against his nearly empty plate. There wasn't much left, but he seemed determined to get every last morsel of food. I really hit the lotto with my parents, didn't I? An absent mom, a cold puppet master dad.

My brother went on, "It's a pretty good setup. I get to have a roof over my head."

He looked at our dad and their eyes met. "What do you mean a roof?"

"Yeah, Martin's letting me stay with him since I'm between places right now." Austin would have usually made a snarky comment about how my dad was to blame for his misfortune in life, but he didn't. He was keeping things matter-of-fact, even if he was leaving out a massive detail about his life lately.

"He is? Well . . ." My dad's throat sounded a little dry.

"Yeah. He's a good dude." Austin nodded.

I could sense it was becoming harder and harder for my dad not to say something about Kael. He used a lot of self-control, and I watched him bite his tongue. He was clearly up to something.

"Well, this is a good in if we need any repairs or remodeling done," Estelle chirped, clueless.

"Right." My dad looked at Estelle and then me. The tone of his voice was more bitter than the tequila I drank straight the weekend before.

CHAPTER **THIRTY**

"Are you still hungry?" Estelle asked my dad. He grumbled a yes and she stood up to place another piece of chicken on his plate. He didn't even look at her as he changed the subject and started talking to Austin about an industrial plant in the Midwest that had had an explosion over the weekend. Estelle slid my dad's refreshed plate right under his arms without him moving, like some well-choreographed dance. She then picked up his beer bottle and shook it gently, lifting it to the light to see how close to empty it was. After determining that her man-child was fine, she sat her chin on her wrist and stared around the room, not once noticing that I was staring at her. I wondered what she was thinking about: How happy she was here serving my father, or running away like my mother had?

Her being domestic wasn't the issue. It was that I knew my dad gave little to nothing in return. Yes, he paid the bills, so he got a pass for that, but I had never once seen him say thank you or anything that wasn't superficial. He was never appreciative of the fact that she cooked every meal he ate and washed every single dish he touched. I felt for her in that regard, and I wondered if she had known this would be her life once she married my father. I knew so little about her past that it was hard to say whether her life had gotten better or worse since. My eyes trailed down her neckline from the dainty heart-shaped diamond dangling over her chest bone to the big diamond ring on her left hand; I guessed she was just fine in this captivity. Maybe I was being too judgmental again.

"I made some pies for the FRG. Saved an extra one. I remember your friend likes pie."

I was startled by Estelle suddenly standing behind me.

Austin jumped in before I could respond. "Is it cool if we take it back for Elodie? She loves the stuff, and you know me and Karina really don't care for sweets."

"Oh, sure." Estelle's voice was cheery. "I can pack it up. Your father needs to watch his sugar, anyway." She sauntered into the kitchen.

Even I was playing a part today as I sat there and passed up dessert, a frosted cherry pie with sugar coating caramelized on the edges of braided dough. It had the kind of smell that I imagined came along with happy childhood memories of running through tall grass in the evening air, a smiling mother calling for her children to come in for a treat. It was always someone else's mother, though, not mine. This cherry pie was Elodie's favorite—she would devour it when I got home. I snapped a picture of it while no one was paying attention and sent it to Elodie. She immediately replied with a tongue out emoji. I moved the napkin ring and tilted my phone a little and took another photo from a different angle, just to entertain myself. I posted the image to my Instagram for the hell of it and watched as my phone lit up again and again. I ignored the notifications until I saw Kael's name pop up. I clicked his profile, and it was still private. I meant to ask him about liking my other posts, but with everything that had happened during the camping trip, there had been no time to bring it up.

I heard aluminum foil tearing and as my dad finally said my name, I flipped my phone over and laid it face down on the table.

"Karina, how is Eloise, anyway?"

So now he wanted to act like I existed? At least he'd chosen a topic I cared about and unrelated to my job.

"Elodie," Austin corrected him before I could and made a face at my dad when he wasn't looking.

"She's fine. Still pregnant." I shrugged. I didn't want my dad to know much about her, and I went into protective mode as I thought about the connection my dad likely had to Phillip. There was no reason to tell him more than whatever he already knew.

"She's such a pretty girl. Like wow. Stunning," Estelle called from the kitchen.

Austin nodded. My dad, too.

"Yeah, she's really beautiful," Austin said. He lifted his beer and took a drink.

"Yeah. She is. But she's also kind, considerate, brave, and a really great friend to me," I informed them. Elodie was stunning, of course, but that was the least interesting thing about her.

"Her husband will be home soon, right?" Estelle asked, setting the pie-to-go in front of Austin.

"What?" Austin sounded surprised.

My dad snapped his head toward his wife. She batted her pretty eyes at him and shrugged. Maybe she didn't know that this was a sore subject for all of us.

"I heard he was coming home soon," my dad added.

"How would you even know that when Elodie doesn't know when he's coming back?" Austin asked indignantly.

It seemed he knew more than I thought he did about the whole situation.

I leaned forward even more. "I thought he was supposed to come home in a few months. And, as I'm sure you know"—I looked directly at my father—"he was deployed with Martin, or Kael, as you guys know him. They're all in the same platoon."

My dad took up my challenge and stared straight at me. His crepe-like skin was blotching with patches of little red spots around his nose.

I picked up my wineglass and finished it in one gulp. I was ready to go.

"Well, we hope he returns safely to his wife. I hope all the boys do," Estelle said sweetly.

"Don't we all," Austin sighed into his beer bottle.

I wanted to add, *yeah, well most aren't so lucky*, but decided to keep working on my exit strategy.

The tension in my dad's shoulders had gone down but I still felt more than on edge. I was ready to leave twenty minutes ago, but had assumed there would be some sort of birthday cake, or singing, or a thoughtless gift of picture frames with positive quotes in an even more thoughtless party bag stuffed with tissue paper.

"Anyway, now that you've got yourself a job, maybe a car next?" My dad's attention had not surprisingly gone back to my brother.

"I don't know, maybe . . . maybe not."

"Why not? A car is an essential part of growing up," my dad told Austin, as if he was only the one who had ever considered this. How arrogant.

Austin's eyes rolled and it made me happy to know he wasn't totally on my dad's side.

"It's just not a priority for me right now. Maybe when I have kids or when I can afford a decent one."

My head spun a little at the word *kids* coming from my brother's mouth. I was certain I had never, ever heard him even mention having children. Maybe he really was growing up?

"Hm. You should reconsider." My dad continued to push his opinion.

"Maybe. Anyway, can we talk about something else, literally anything else? The game, the weather, the fucking—I mean freak-ing—economy at this point would be better."

My dad turned to his attention to me. "What about you, Karina? How's work going?"

Ugh, here we go.

"It's actually great. I've been working more and more hours and am thinking about signing up for a training course soon. Oh, and I got a raise," I lied, but just about the raise.

I just felt like I had to have something a bit more impressive than nothing.

"Training course for what? How many ways can you rub your hands on someone's skin?" My dad's tone was full of mockery, and he nearly laughed, like he'd told an impressive joke.

I groaned and dug my fingernails into my hand to stop myself from flipping over his fancy table and telling him to go fuck him-self. "Actually, there are many different practices and techniques from all over the world and they're always changing. My career field is growing and growing. Wellness is becoming a part of more people's lives and I know it's only going to get bigger and bigger as an industry, so I want to try to stay on top of it."

Even after my speech, my father was unfazed. I didn't know why I bothered to waste my breath, but I meant every word and I would bet money that Estelle will be the perfect consumer of the ever-expanding wellness industry.

"Who do you think won the game?" my dad asked Austin, completely changing the subject. I didn't care this time.

I reached for my phone and texted my brother to ask why he didn't bring up the Army and when the hell we were leaving, but the ding from his phone came from the living room, so it was pointless. Austin and my dad continued talking sports while Estelle absently stared into the abyss.

CHAPTER **THIRTY-ONE**

Maybe I had been wrong about the potential birthday celebration. I was getting off easy and would be able to get the hell out of there soon. It felt like I had been there for ten hours instead of nearly two.

"You're riding back with me, right?" I asked my brother while Estelle distracted my dad with talk about the upcoming maintenance on their RV.

"I have a ride coming," he responded.

My dad gently poked at Estelle's arm and she stood up. She excused herself from the table and walked into the kitchen, retying her ponytail on the way. My dad got up to follow her without any explanation, but I was more than happy they were giving Austin and me a second alone. I waited for my dad's footsteps to make the floor creak like they always had before I opened my mouth.

"Have you not told him about the Army?" I asked my brother, whispering so neither my dad nor Estelle could hear me.

He shrugged. "I'm waiting."

"For what?" I flicked both of my palms out in question.

"I dunno. I just don't want to deal with it right now. I don't need another headache and him knowing my business doesn't mean shit to me. I'm just trying to get along with him tonight because he seems to be in a good mood for whatever reason."

I nodded. I agreed with him, so I couldn't really argue there. Plus, I did like knowing something my dad didn't.

"Wait, so if he doesn't know about your enlistment, why the heck is he in such a good mood?"

"No clue." He shrugged again. My brother shrugged his shoulders more than anyone I had ever met. It was a big part of the way he communicated in his own carefree way.

"Something must be up." I tapped my finger on the table to emphasize my point.

"Maybe his retirement came through sooner than expected?" Austin suggested.

"Ugh. I hope not, but wouldn't be surprised if he got his way. He always does." I made a grossed-out face. I wished things didn't come so easily for our father—even just this once.

"Maybe Estelle's from a loaded family and one of her parents died and left them an inheritance."

I shook my head. "No way. If she was from a rich family, she'd never put up with Dad."

Austin laughed, covering his mouth to keep our speculative gossip down. "True. Maybe he took a life insurance policy out on her and is going to off her," he whispered and pushed his hair back, tucking the longer bits at the sides behind his ears, a habit left over from childhood. "Or maybe it's the opposite," he added.

I was laughing now, too, even though our humor was twisted. We got that from our mother for sure. I pushed his shoulder. "You sound like Mom, making up stories," I told him.

We both laughed a little, but the blanket of loss covered us within a few seconds, and we fell silent.

His white hoodie had a tan smear by the neck that looked like makeup. I hoped he wasn't worrying about hooking up with women right now. Worse, I hoped the makeup had rubbed off on the hoodie while my brother—not Kael—was wearing it.

"That's Kael's, right?" I pulled the cotton collar at the base of his neck.

"How did you know?"

I stuck my nose in the air and looked toward the kitchen to make sure Estelle wasn't lurking. "I know everything, haven't you learned that by now?"

My brother, with a mature and rare tone, leaned his head close to mine. His blue-eyed gaze poured into me, and I swore I could read his mind, so I wasn't the least bit surprised when the words came out. "What's up with you two? I know something happened when we all were camping."

I reached for my nearly empty water glass. "Nothing."

It was Austin's turn to push me. "Bullshit. Martin's miraculously become pleasant to be around the last few days, smiling and shit. I've never seen him check his phone so often and I know y'all slept in his truck together." My brother raised his brow.

"Tell me whose makeup is on your shirt first." I pointed to the evidence.

Austin's face went pale as he looked down at the mark.

"Please, for the love of God, tell me you haven't been seeing Katie after all the trouble she caused."

He shook his head so fast that I thought it would fly off. "Nah, nah, nah. But I've been wearing this outfit lately, not him, so stop being jealous," my brother teased me. "Actually, the jealousy kind of suits you, so keep it up."

Saved by the bell . . . well, the cake.

Estelle had her hands full, carrying a medium-sized cake in

covered in white icing with more piped icing and pearly candy around the bottom edges.

"We got you two a little something for your birthdays. Nothing big. Just a cake and ice cream," she said, setting the cake on the table. Our dad trailed in slowly behind her, and returned to his seat at the head of the table, placing a tub of Neapolitan ice cream directly in front of his placemat.

The reflection of the candle flames lit up Estelle's face as she passed the lighter, one by one across, all twenty-one of them. When she was finally finished, she began to sing "Happy Birthday." My dad's voice was lazy but after twenty birthdays with him, it would have broken the tradition if he'd acted excited. Austin was smiling and singing along, and I mouthed the words, to be polite. I thought about all my different birthday memories, from my mom dancing around the kitchen with a jar of store-bought icing, letting us dip our fingers into it and getting high on sugar before school, to my most recent favorite just last weekend with Kael clapping along and Gloria hugging me.

At the campsite I felt calm, warm, and seen. In this stale house, I just felt itchy and uncomfortable and out of place. Relief washed over me as the birthday song finally ended. I tried not to make eye contact with anyone as I let Austin blow out all of the candles. He found the humor in continuing to have to blow and blow, but I was too emotionally drained to care to even try.

Estelle smiled, proud of her little show. Even my dad seemed to enjoy the moment as he handed her a cake knife.

"Ladies first," she said, half smiling as she slid a piece of the cake onto the clean porcelain plate in front of me. At times she was sort of sweet and I could tell she was really trying. I simply thanked her, continuing my attempt at being nicer to her.

"Happy birthday," my dad said. "I can't believe you two are

going to be twenty-one. Man, I can remember the day I brought you home. We kept mixing you up the first couple days."

It was a nice sentiment, but my dad slipping on the mention of "we"—something he was normally very careful about, usually preferring to ignore the fact that my mom ever existed—caught me off guard. I really, really didn't like when he brought her up, even without using her name. I didn't know which would be worse: being the ex-wife who was still missed and pined after, or being nameless in conversation, an obliterated ex. The latter felt worse, like being an old couch you had memories with, but no attachment to as you put it on the curb and replaced it with a brand-new IKEA one.

"What did you to wish for?" Estelle asked.

"I wished for a car," Austin joked, dipping his finger into the icing, like he did with every cake, whether it was his or not. "And world peace," he added.

"And you, Karina?" my dad asked me.

I wanted to ignore him. It was hard to decide whether I should be sarcastic or genuine with my response. I had a million reasons to be pissed at my dad right now and after years of playing nice, I had reached my threshold. For the last few years, I had tried to work to internally resolve my anger toward him, but he didn't make it any easier.

"Same as Austin, world peace," I said, mentally only half there, half in the past reliving every battle I'd ever had with my dad.

Sometimes I would argue with him over simple things like using the dishwasher on the wrong setting, but other times, there would be an explosion, like what happened with Kael. One thing never changed: whatever the fight or war was about, my brother would inevitably get a lesser punishment and better treatment than I would, no matter the circumstances. But for the last couple years, I had been a dutiful daughter, showing up like clockwork every single Tuesday for family dinner. Until recently when Kael encouraged me to set boundaries with my dad. Kael, Kael, Kael. If Kael had been here, he would have taken me out of this torturous room full of fake words and even phonier smiles.

"Did you make this cake?" Austin asked Estelle. He took a huge bite and crumbs fell from his lips.

"I wish!" She laughed, serving my father second to last. A highly unusual sequence. "It's from a bakery just outside of post. Owned by an Army wife. Everything there is spectacular."

"Yeah, this is good," Austin agreed, speaking with his mouth still full.

My brother's phone rang from the other room. He popped up and went into the living room to grab and answer it. His voice carried back into the quiet dining room.

"Yo, I'm almost done." He paused. "Yeah, I'm here. You can come inside for a minute. I'm eating my birthday cake, but I'm almost done. Just come in for a sec."

While my brother finished his call with whomever he had just invited in, I dug my fork into the icing, coating it, and almost took a bite until I smelled the citrus.

"Is this lemon cake?" I used my fork to poke the cream-colored dough with yellow speckles throughout. I could smell that it was.

Estelle nodded proudly, beaming. "Your father's favorite."

Of course, neither of them had remembered or cared that I not only hated lemon cake, but it made my throat itch and nose run. Though it was my birthday, none of that mattered since it was my dad's favorite.

Austin looked at me when he put the phone down and took his seat at the table. I somehow knew who it was before he said it.

"It's Martin."

I looked to my dad, whose face hadn't changed. I thought about my dad and Kael screaming at each other in my house, their words flying around my head as I began to slightly panic. I wondered again how much my brother really knew about Kael and my dad's history. We all seemed to be talking around it, but avoiding the issue. The conflict.

Was Kael really going to come inside my father's house? My dad appeared to be unmoved, but I wondered how he would react when Kael walked in. Would the smooth general sitting at the head of a big table stay unbothered, or would he turn into the shouting, unhinged man who was in my living room just weeks ago?

It wasn't lost on me that he was eating the slice that happened to have my name written in neat green frosting. He tore into it, chomping with his mouth half open, crumbs falling from his thin lips onto his orange T-shirt.

Gross.

Kael's impending arrival was having an effect on the way my father took up space in the room. His presence was shrinking and I felt more powerful, knowing that Kael wasn't afraid of my him the way the rest of us were. I had no idea what would happen when Kael walked through my father's front door.

A roaring noise interrupted the room, and everyone's heads turned toward the living room window, where Kael's rumbling Bronco could be seen pulling up.

"That's him." My brother looked at me. "We've got plenty of cake left," he said, avoiding eye contact with our dad. From the little he knew about my father and Kael's altercation, Austin had to be uneasy. I certainly was—I wanted to warn Kael, to rush outside and stop him from coming in, but I sat still, wanting to see just how long my father would continue to ignore the situation and pretend that the two of them didn't have a screaming match in my living room just a few weeks ago.

I shot a glance at my father. "Yeah, we do have a lot of cake left. Don't we, Dad?" I purposely poked at his faux calm.

The expression *if looks could kill* was the only way to explain the way my father was glaring at me.

He wiped his mouth with his napkin, but missed a smear of bright-green frosting just below his lips.

He didn't look away from me as he said, "Yes, we sure do."

CHAPTER **THIRTY-TWO**

Kael

"Fuck." I tossed my phone onto the leather of the empty passenger seat.

Why wasn't Fischer ready to come outside when he knew I was picking him up at nine and that I was never late? The agreement we'd made for the ride was that he would be waiting on the sidewalk when I pulled up. Joining their dysfunctional family birthday celebration was not a part of the plan, and Fischer knew I would not want to go in that damn house. He was the one who texted me before he even got there saying the wanted to get the hell out as early as he could. I instantly felt guilty for not texting Karina that I would be here. Now that we were back to talking regularly, I should have warned her that I would be stopping by, even if I hadn't planned to come inside.

It annoyed the shit out of me that Karina was back here for a family dinner, but I knew it was to celebrate their birthdays. One thing about Fischer that I hoped the Army would kick out of him was his lack of consideration for other people. He wasn't malicious about it; he was just fucking clueless at times. I'd die before I admitted it, but sometimes I wished I could be a little more like him and not carry the burden of always worrying about everyone else before myself. I had instinctively done that for as long as I could remember, and it was only becoming more of an issue the older I became.

Fischer didn't know the gritty details of what went down with their dad and me, but he had to know that his sister and father had a strained dynamic, to put it lightly. Based on that alone he shouldn't have asked me to come in—especially not if he knew that Mendoza's mind and soul had been smashed by his own father; that would have devastated him. I knew how much Fischer loved Mendoza, and I didn't have the heart to tell him.

I couldn't believe I was at this man's house again. It would be my fucking luck that I had taken in *his* only son and had fallen for *his* only daughter. And I cared so much about the two of them that, at this point, I couldn't use them as a way to hurt him.

I grabbed my phone as I got out. One text from Elodie. I paused to read it, stalling because Karina was inside. I closed out Elodie's text and typed in a **K**. I thought it would be the right thing to do, to text Karina and cut through the tension before I even stepped into the house. My fingers hovered over her name, just a couple taps on the screen away, but I couldn't do it. I put my phone back into the pocket of my joggers and walked up to the porch.

Officer houses were overdone and big as hell compared to the tiny barrack rooms most soldiers lived in. All the housing neighborhoods were the same, duplicated homes lined up in rows or across cul-de-sacs to reward the soldiers who moved to higher ranks and went to college in exchange for their sacrifices for the country. They deserved it—and way more.

But the officers . . . that was still a hard pill to swallow, knowing that so much of the money to support them came from the bloodshed and sacrifice of others, while most of them kept their hands clean. War was what the United States was built on, and men like

Karina's dad profited off a system that started as something to be proud of, something we are told is to protect our freedom. The thing was, that system had now ruined so many people's lives and had become an excuse for a lot of motherfuckers who benefitted from privilege and a two-tiered system. So many of them didn't have to do the groundwork to make a lot of fucking money.

Growing up, I had always wanted to be a soldier, and none of the politics mattered to me. I only knew that I wanted to do something I would be proud of, something that my sister and ma could be proud of. I'd wanted to help the American people feel safe and secure, while earning myself a steady paycheck and getting healthcare, maybe even that college degree the recruiter had promised me. That was my standard line, but deep down, the number-one reason had been to get my ass out of Riverdale before I ended up in the wrong place at the wrong time like a lot of the guys my age did. There weren't many jobs, even less education, and the hardships I witnessed as the child of a single-mother household drove me to escape that town and do something that would make my ma's life easier. It wasn't her fault that my sperm donor got to run off and take no responsibility for me. Even when he was around, he wasn't really around, and my sister's "dad" was even worse. Must be nice to be a man with no responsibility and get to run off. Mothers don't get that chance . . . except Karina's.

Karina's story was in many ways the opposite of mine, but somehow we bonded over our abandonment. I knew exactly where the man who'd helped create me was, but she had no idea where her mom, who had raised her from childhood, had gone. I didn't know which was worse, and we had spent hours lying together, tangled in the sheets and in our minds, trying to decide. It angered both of us that her dad would be set for life—he'd live off a retirement package while I had to live with my fucked-up body and mind.

His would be a mostly carefree life while thousands of men and women continued to serve, and to struggle to make ends meet. Don't get me wrong, soldiers deserved to retire and retire comfortably, but evil men did not. I knew all too well that he had blood on his hands and death on his breath.

I lifted my head back, closed my eyes, and tried to remind myself that I wasn't like him. I did my fucking best. Most of the people I knew weren't like him. Checks and balances were still mostly intact when it came to the Army's battle of good and evil. Karina's dad could keep his shiny new truck in the driveway, his glowing career achievements, and his fake-ass honor as long as he took his retirement and kept his boots on the ground here, and not hurting anyone else. If I had to, I could live with that, but only because he was Karina's father.

Hell, here I was about to go into his house, with his whole family inside. I hated that she was related to him. It wasn't fair that she didn't have a good dad. She was so pure and generous to the people she cared about, even if they weren't deserving and nine times out of ten they would disappoint her. Still, deep down she desperately wanted her father's approval, though she was too proud to ever say it. I lived with the chip on my shoulder that I got fucked over when it came to my dad, but I'd take a ghost over a demon any day.

I looked at the house again. "Fuck meee."

I rang the doorbell. In short order, the latch on the lock turned and Karina's stepmom was standing there, looking more like a museum guide than someone opening the door to her own home. She was styled like so many officer's wives on post: the hair, the clothes, probably at least three Michael Kors bags in her closet. Her eyes were bright, but something was different about her than I remembered. Tonight she was more casual, wearing little jewelry, less makeup.

"Martin, hi. Welcome, come in." She smiled, waving me inside.

"Thanks." I nodded, unsure of what to do.

"We're all in the dining room having cake. Glad you're here."

"I'm sure everyone is," I said, without her detecting my sarcasm. Dark humor reminded me that I probably couldn't run, anyway. My leg had been extra-fucked since tripping over the weekend. I tried not to look at my mangled, scarred skin, but I could tell it was going to swell up the moment I hit the ground.

She led me inside and I shut the door behind us, before following her through the living room and into the dining room where Karina sat next to her brother, her arms spread out before her on top of the dining table. She was frowning, looking at an untouched piece of cake on a plate in front of her. She stared at it blankly . . . then her eyes dragged up to mine.

She didn't break eye contact, but nervously tucked her hair behind her ear. I had thought about her every hour, every day, since we left the camping trip two days ago. We had driven back together, just the two of us, after Turner got a ride with the guy she hooked up with. We hadn't done much talking because she'd ended up sleeping over half of the time, but that'd made me relax, knowing how drained her social battery must have been after the weekend and that she was comfortable enough to sleep while I drove through the winding country roads. She'd been out of juice, but I was recharged by her. Tonight, she looked so fucking good, even barefaced in a crewneck sweatshirt; her eyes were bright with excitement to see me. She used to get dressed up when she went to her father's dumb dinners, but maybe her getup tonight was to prove a point that she didn't want to be there. Karina always found ways to express herself through her appearance like changing her nail or hair color when something in her life felt out of control, wearing an old T-shirt attached to some memory, or a bright-yellow sundress she'd ordered online to match her mood. Unlike me, who assumed the same uniform and identity every day, on my body and inside of my mind.

"What's up! Glad you came in!" Fischer yelled to me, throwing his hands in the air. "Dad, you know Martin who I was talking about earlier."

The man himself sat at the head of the table, his lips in a steady line. He nodded his head once, like we were both teenagers meeting in a damn schoolyard. My chest began to rise at the sight of him just sitting there silently gloating while I had to pretend that I didn't want to rip his fucking throat out. If I didn't love his daughter and son, maybe I would have actually done it. When Karina stood up and said my name, I could barely force myself to look away from her father even though all of my being wanted to answer.

"Kael, come here." Her voice was gentle, leading me away from my anger and into her aura. She was like the soft wind right after it rained, like the gentle touch of damp grass in the spring. She was the opposite of her father, an empathetic woman who cared more about me than her father's opinion. She rounded the table and grabbed my hand, leading me to sit on the other side of her. When I sat down, I could feel my heart rate slowing, my body coming out of flight-or-fight. Still holding my hand, she brushed her thumb over mine and I counted the times as I waited for whatever the hell was going to happen next.

"Would you like some cake?" Karina's stepmom asked me.

"No, I'm good, thank you," I answered.

I wondered if Karina and Fischer's father was realizing that his daughter and me were back on good terms. Could he tell by the way she'd greeted me? Did he see the way she looked at me? Was he aware enough of his daughter's emotions to know that he could no longer come between us?

Fischer laughed. "Come on. Sometimes we can have our cake and eat it, too." He tried to be funny, but given the circumstances it was hard for me to muster a smile, let alone laugh at a corny joke. He knew his dad disliked me, even if he didn't know all the reasons why.

I looked at the cake; not even half of it was eaten. It was extravagant and over-the-top. Like the cake, the Fischer family seemed perfect—a perfect example of appearance meaning nothing. It was all a façade, a Hollywood-level backdrop.

The cake said *Happy Birthday Austin &*—Karina's name had been eaten. I looked at her plate, but there was no sign of the green icing. What was left on her dad's plate was smeared with it. He *would* eat her fucking name as if it were *his* birthday cake. Even if I was on the brink of death from starvation, I wasn't going to touch that fucking cake.

I looked down at Karina's unashamed hand on my thigh. She was slightly digging her nails into my skin, not enough to hurt, but enough to keep me mentally present. Being back in this house with her felt like a decade had passed since the last time. Fischer's party, Karina and me upstairs in her old room, her skeptically checking my ID card to see when my birthday was. I'd barely known her then; now I couldn't know her more.

The slice of cake on her plate had little flakes of yellow and I could smell the lemon as I inspected her picked-at dessert.

"Is this lemon-flavored?" I meant to ask only Karina, but of course the overzealous wife responded first.

"Yes! With Meyer lemons. They're so popular now, have you tried them?"

I shook my head and looked at Karina, who seemed to be amused and anxious at the same time.

"Apparently no one remembered that I don't like lemon cake."

She said the words into my ear, but I knew at least her brother could hear.

I shot a glance at Karina's dad, just to see his expression as his daughter was leaning into me, near my neck. He looked like he wanted me to die on the spot and that filled me with an indescribable joy. Fischer looked at me and at his sister, a silly stupid grin on his face. His tune had changed drastically over the last few days. I knew he was rooting for us.

"Want a beer?" Fischer offered.

"I'm driving." I pulled out my car keys, dangling them on my index finger.

He nodded his head. "I was telling my dad how good you've been to me."

Karina was staring at me, waiting for my reaction. I didn't want to give her, or any of them, one.

"Thanks. Yeah, he's been working really hard to help me get the duplex done before he leaves."

"Where are you going, Austin? Another camping trip?" the stepmother asked.

Everything went silent, Karina's hand squeezed my thigh, and I realized I had dropped a major fucking bomb on the table.

CHAPTER **THIRTY-THREE**

Karina

My mouth fell open.

Holy shit.

The color of Austin's skin was slowly turning red, creeping up from his neck to his forehead.

"You're not going back to your uncle's?" our dad asked. His brows crinkled together and I could tell he was mentally going through a list of places Austin could be off to, but none of them were the Army . . .

Austin shook his head. There was no way out of the truth of it all except for Austin flat-out lying to our dad. He had been doing that very well all night.

"I'm not going back to . . ." my brother started. "I, uh . . . I joined the Army." Austin's words dropped onto the table. My dad's eyes nearly blew out of his head, and Estelle made a noise I'd only heard in movies when someone's surprised.

My dad cleared his throat. "You *what*?"

Kael sat still as stone next to me. From his expression, I could tell that he was as surprised as I was that Austin had kept his enlistment a secret from our dad.

Austin sighed, pushing his plate away. "I enlisted. I've been working with a recruiter. I was going to tell you—"

My dad stood up. "*When? When* were you going to tell me? Because you've been here for hours and just had the whole dinner at my house and didn't say a damn word about it. You said you had a new job doing construction demo!" He pounded his fist against the table. The plates shook and his beer rocked, almost falling over.

Estelle jumped to her feet. "Honey," she warned him, looking at Kael and then my brother, and finally me. This outburst was surely not what she had planned when she was sticking twenty-one candles through the delicate icing of this fancy birthday cake.

Austin was silent. Kael's leg began to shake under my hand, and I felt like I was back in my teens preparing myself for Austin and my dad to go at it.

"I shouldn't have expected anything less than lies from you," my dad spit as he moved toward my brother.

Kael's body pushed against my touch as he tried to stand up, but I did my best to stop him. There was no use getting between my father and brother, and Kael—of all people—really, really needed to stay out of it.

"Anything less from me? I thought you would be proud! And it's not like you've set an example or encouraged either of us when it comes to our futures." Austin stood up from the table to face our father. Even though he towered over him physically, I knew my brother was at least a little afraid of our father. He had always been, but right now Austin was somehow holding his own.

"I haven't?" our dad responded in disbelief. "I've worked myself to the bone to provide for you. Both of you," he added, seeming to suddenly remember I was sitting there.

"Yeah, maybe you did when we were kids, but not so much for

the past decade. You preached to me about joining the service ever since I can remember, and now that I've done it, you're pissed? What changed?" Austin interrogated the proud and arrogant man standing in front of him.

"You must have done this to spite me," my dad hissed. "If that weren't the case, you would have and should have come to me to help you do this."

"Your help will always be the last thing I need."

Our father looked as if Austin's words had truly wounded him.

"That's hardly your tune when you call me for money, drunk off your ass, or when you begged me to let you come back here to Benning!" My dad's voice was getting louder.

"You sent me to live with your loser brother and barely spoke to me the whole time I was gone!" said Austin. "Through high school, you only gave a fuck about me when it was useful to you. If I had turned out to be the football star you dreamed of, I bet you wouldn't have shipped me off. You can deny it all you want, but you've always been a shitty father and you always will be. I'm tired of pretending otherwise, and so is Karina, who you stomp all over, even worse than me. She just puts up with it." His voice matched my dad's in volume now.

I didn't know if I was glad my brother was standing up for me or if I was offended by him basically calling me a doormat for our father, but a spade is a spade.

Dad grabbed Austin's arm with swiftness and I couldn't keep Kael down any longer. He rushed between them, something I was growing used to seeing him do, placing himself into conflict between others—often my brother.

"Calm down, both of you. You need to calm down. Fischer, let's take a walk," Kael insisted in a stern voice.

I expected my dad to scream at Kael, push him, maybe even

punch him. But he didn't; he seemed to slowly control his rage as Kael stood there to challenge him, right in his face. This was Martin, the soldier that my father knew and hated. It was mutual.

"Thank you for your concern, Sergeant Martin. But this has nothing to do with you. Stay out of my family's business. I'm not sure why you're even here in my house," he said, seething.

"Your family's business involves me, unfortunately, so I won't be staying out of it." Kael's voice was steady, and he sounded more like Sergeant Martin than I had ever heard him.

"And just how does my family's business concern you?" my dad shot back, his temper surging to the level it had been with Austin.

"You know why." Kael kept a flat tone that I knew was meant to provoke my father, to drive him further out of control.

"No, I don't think I do." My dad took a final step to Kael—any closer and his nose would be against Kael's chest.

"This isn't the time and place to get into all of it. But your family is my business." Kael turned a little and pointed to the birthday cake and burnt-out candles lying on the table with blackened ends. "Your son has become like a brother to me, and you should know better than anyone that enlisting is going to ensure his future, and that's why I helped him out."

My father scoffed. "His future? Like yours? I saw your medical discharge paperwork, Martin. Do you know how hard it's going to be to get a job out in the real world? You're still a kid with a disability, not to a mention a PTSD diagnosis." My father's grimace turned into a smile as he continued, "I guess we'll see you at Home Depot stocking shelves . . . if you're lucky."

Kael kept his face neutral. I had no idea how. I wanted to scream, to flip the decorated dining table over and break every single dish in the house.

"You have no idea what I'm capable of." The threat was clear in

Kael's voice as my father physically stumbled backward a few steps before turning his attention to Austin.

My dad pointed his finger at Austin, who was panting, standing a few feet away from Kael and my father. "You went to him instead of me? I've been in the Army longer than any of you have been alive. And you?" he snarled at me. "Did you know? Were all of you in this together?"

I was frozen and before I could thaw, Kael spoke for me. "She didn't know. Stop directing your anger at the wrong people, especially your daughter."

My dad's focus went to Kael, then to me, and back to Kael. "I told you to stay the hell out of it. Just because you befriended my son doesn't give you the agency to—"

"And I love your daughter. I love her and there's nothing and no one on this planet who's going to get in the way of that."

My dad's beady eyes blinked so fast I couldn't keep up. I looked at Kael, declaring his love for me in such an honest and bold way, and my heart leaped. I felt like the room was spinning and everyone except Kael and I had disappeared. I didn't care what my dad or Estelle thought, only what Kael did, and *he loved me.*

"Love?" my dad scoffed. "You're skipping town as soon as your paperwork goes through. Karina knows that. Both of you are foolish children who—"

I stood up, ready to go head-to-head with our dad when Austin pushed his way back to him. "Enough! Fuck, that's enough!" my brother shouted. "It's already done, and I don't need your fucking approval. We may all be kids to you, but our lives aren't yours to decide. Both of us fucking hate you."

Expressionless, our father tried to reach for Austin, but gave up as Austin backed away, bumping into the display cabinet and knocking over the nostalgic trinkets on the glass shelves.

"Do you even know what this means? Did you even think this through?" our dad roared. "Do you know how many enemies our last name has? *Huh?*"

The room rocked with the words from his mouth.

Enemies?

I thought about the doctor who'd asked my brother if he was our dad's son. I thought about all the people involved in the incident in Afghanistan and how many people wanted to see my father's downfall. It chilled me to the bone thinking about how many more skeletons were hiding in my father's walk-in closet.

"*You* might have enemies, but I don't. I did this for myself. Not you, not Karina, no one except my fucking self." Austin snatched his beer, drank the last sip, and looked at Kael. "Let's get the fuck out of here."

Austin grabbed Elodie's wrapped cherry pie from the table and stomped through the dining room as everyone except Kael stood stunned, unsure of what to do or say. He looked at me with worry clear across his face.

"Please take him home. I'll be fine," I reassured him.

He leaned in, kissed my cheek, and followed my brother out of the house. I considered going with them, but couldn't move.

The front door slammed shut as they left, and Estelle jumped in her place.

"Did you know about this?" My dad's attention turned to me.

I thought about telling the truth just to pour salt into his wounded ego. But I just shook my head.

"And what's this nonsense about you and Martin? Are you in some kind of relationship with him again? Didn't you learn your lesson the last time?" he asked me straight.

I waited a moment to respond, not only because I was still processing everything that had just happened, but because I wanted to give my dad an adult response, something he couldn't swat away like a pesky fly. I glanced at Estelle, who I had nearly forgotten was there. She looked like she was going to pass out or vomit any second. Her usual calm demeanor was so easily rocked and it was obvious how out of her league she was when it came to coping with our family problems.

"Is this your way of trying to get back at me?" he insinuated, making it all about him before I even had a chance to answer his questions.

"No. None of this is about you. Not everything is about you," I said in the clearest voice I could manage.

He looked at me as if he was examining whether I was a liar, like himself and his son. I braced myself for his snarky, snakebite-in-words to hit me, but he just sat there. I didn't know if he was waiting for me to continue or if he was trying to control his temper.

"I'm not going to talk about my personal life with you. We've never had that type of relationship. I love Kael and nothing you say about him will change that. If you can't accept that, if you can't stay out of Kael's Army stuff and stop causing problems, I'm going to have to cut off all of my contact with you." I looked him dead in the eyes.

I could tell he was surprised to hear such directness from me, but I was full of adrenaline from watching Kael and Austin tell my father off. It gave me confidence to push back.

"I don't know if you even realize what you're doing, or if you're too blinded by your pride, but you've been pushing away everyone in your life and tonight you made it so much worse. I'm no longer going to pretend to be the perfect daughter you expect to show up every Tuesday night. If you can't accept me and love me the way I am, I won't be coming around anymore. I mean it." I did mean it. I was beginning to understand the choice my mother had to make, and that gave me a sense of freedom and terror at the same time.

CHAPTER **THIRTY-FOUR**

I was standing on the porch, rummaging through my purse trying to find my keys, when the door opened, and someone walked out.

To my surprise, it was Estelle.

"Hey," she said, stepping closer to me.

"Hey." I looked at her.

"Can we sit down for a minute?" she asked, her voice soft.

I nodded, though reluctant to sit on my mom's swing with her.

When Estelle sat down, the swing creaked under her weight. "I'm sorry for how your dad reacted. He was just so shocked and hurt that no one told him."

"Is that why you're out here? To make excuses and apologize for him?" I felt bold enough to be direct with her, just like I had been with my dad.

Estelle's face became sad. She shook her head slightly. "No. He's upstairs. I wanted to catch you before you left to see if you were okay."

"Oh." I let the silence simmer for a moment. I didn't know if I wanted to be vulnerable with her. But she was reaching out to me.

"If you want me to go away, just say it. I know you don't care much for me, and my comfort is not going to replace what you should be getting from your father . . ."

"So, you're not on his side?" I asked her.

She gave a small, wry laugh. "I'm not on anyone's side. But I know how it feels to have a strained relationship with a parent and regret it later in life. It hurts me to watch all of this and know that there's nothing I can do."

"You could do something, though? He's your husband, not your commander."

She sighed years' worth of sighs and turned to face me. "He's a very stubborn man." She looked away from me, to the lights bordering the manicured lawn, and blankly stared into the night.

"Can I ask you something?" I didn't wait for her to say yes before I went on. "Why do you put up with him? Do you really love him that much? I'm sorry, but I just don't understand it."

Estelle closed her eyes, her long lashes brushed against high cheekbones. "I wonder the same thing sometimes, but I remember the man I fell in love with. The man who loved fiercely, who laughed at my silly jokes, took me places I had never dreamed I'd be."

It was hard to imagine my dad laughing and even harder to imagine Estelle joking or having a sense of humor at all. It made me sad to realize time and time again that I didn't know this woman even though she'd been in my life for years now.

"It's not only about the vacations or the comfortable lifestyle, though it may seem that way," she said, her voice just above a whisper. "I know the man I fell in love with is in there, even if he shows up less and less often than he used to. I choose to believe that, whether it's naïve or hopeful, or just plain stupid."

I never thought about her perspective or imagined for a second that she might also be in pain while living with my father. I had judged her and thought she'd done this to herself, knowing what she was getting into, but how could she have? Why hadn't I given her the benefit of the doubt or shown her even a bit of compassion since I'd met her? Was it because of my mother, my father, my undealt-with trauma of loss, all which weren't her fault?

"I don't know what to say . . ." I explained to her. "I'm kind of surprised by all of this."

She nodded in agreement. "It's understandable and you don't need to feel pressured to say anything. You and I have hardly had a meaningful conversation since we met, so I'm sure this is as overwhelming for you as it is for me."

The swing below us rocked gently and I allowed myself to press my back against the familiar wood. I wondered if Estelle had even used it since she'd moved in, so I decided to ask her. "Have you ever sat out here? I don't know if you know this, but this is sort of my comfort spot. Has been since I was a kid. My mom's, too . . ."

I hadn't meant it as a reminder of what was my mom's and what wasn't, so I hoped she didn't take it that way.

"You know," she began, joining me in leaning into the swing and letting her feet lift off the ground. "I haven't. I knew it was your mother's from the photos I'd found and from your father when he'd had too much—" She stopped midsentence and I wanted—no, needed—her to continue. It was unlikely we would ever be in this position again with one another.

"Please keep going," I practically begged, assuring, "I won't tell my dad anything you say or anything. I'm not that kind of person."

She seemed a little afraid and fumbled her words at the beginning, but nevertheless, she continued, "I've found your father out here talking to the wind more times than I'd like to admit. Mostly, I just stand at the door and listen to him talking to a ghost, but sometimes I can't stand it and go back inside, pour some wine, and try like hell to forget about it."

"Ghosts? Like soldiers he's lost?"

She shook her head and leaned forward a bit, rubbing her palms against her jeans. "Your mother."

The breath from my lungs evaporated and the swing felt increasingly unsteady. I repeated her words. "My mother?"

Nodding, Estelle went back to staring ahead. "He talks to her more and more these days. Sometimes out of longing, sometimes desperation and intoxication. I've never mentioned this, not even to him. I know this puts you in an uncomfortable situation and I'm crossing a line here, but please don't repeat this. It just feels nice to tell someone, anyone . . . even his daughter."

I shook my head, both to promise her and to try to make sense of what I was hearing.

"I can't imagine what my father would possibly have to say to my mother. I'm surprised that he would even care or remember that she loved this swing."

"He remembers more than you think, Karina. He just won't say it. and I've come to terms with her presence even though she's gone. I do hope that, as the years pass, your dad, your brother, and you, will make more space for me, in your lives and in your hearts."

"I'm sorry I've been such a bratty teenager."

She smiled. "You have no idea how badly I've wanted an angry teenage daughter."

"Really?"

She nodded again, this time with more excitement.

"When I first met your dad and he said he had two teenagers, I had this whole different picture of our life in my head." She covered her mouth with her hand and laughed lightly at what she was saying. "I remember being so excited when he told me he had kids—not afraid one bit. I thought your brother would probably be closer to your father, but I would still try and bond with him over sports or cook all of his favorite foods. But *you* . . ." She pointed at me and shook her finger. She looked more alive than I had ever, ever seen her. She was almost a different person altogether. "I had this whole fantasy in my head where I got to actually be somewhat of a mother to you. I couldn't wait to get our nails done together, to go prom-dress shopping, to talk about boys—I certainly had a lot of experience to share—and to support you through your first breakup. With every month that went by, I told myself that you just needed a little more time. I knew you must miss your mom more than I could imagine, so I kept waiting for the day to come, when we could build a bond, but that's not how it works. I just wished it did."

I could feel my perspective changing as she continued, her eyes blinking away tears.

"I thought about all these scenarios, but not once did I think it would be like this, where I barely see or know you, and your brother and your dad are always at each other's throats."

I could see something in her, something sad and hopeless, but still *alive*. In my head she had always been a villain, she was the reason my mom left us, and all she was doing was trying to fill a huge gap in our lives that could never be filled. No matter how many elaborate dinners she stuffed us with, she just didn't belong. No one did—because our dad deserved to be miserable and alone there in his big house.

It was so quiet outside that it seemed like even the crickets had stopped their song to listen to us.

"I'm sorry your mom isn't around now to see the woman you've become, and I know I'll never replace her and that's not what I'm trying to do," said Estelle. "I just wanted to tell you how I feel because I never have and I'm so sorry for that. I do care about you so much, Karina."

I was sorry, too, that my mom needed to leave her family to find her peace. I couldn't forget that my dad, not Estelle, was responsible for that.

"You don't have to say anything. I just wanted to get it off my chest. Go take care of your brother and I'll take care of your dad," she said, standing up from the swing.

I waited until she was at the door and almost in the house before I called to her. "Estelle?"

She turned back to look at me.

"Thanks for telling me all of that. I'm processing it, and I don't want to say the wrong thing, but I do appreciate it." I spoke as sincerely as I could. It was true and she didn't deserve the confusion of whatever flustered words would come out of my mouth if I tried to make sense of all of it right then and there.

She nodded. "I'll take it," she said, her face breaking into a smile as she walked into the house.

CHAPTER **THIRTY-FIVE**

Kael

I pulled my truck up to Karina's curb. I had planned for Fischer and me to drive back to my place, but he was determined to bring that damn pie to Elodie, and anyway, it gave me an excuse to check on Karina. She likely would not be back yet if she had stuck around to nurse her father's ego for a little while after her brother stormed out. Fischer and I had stopped by the PX for him to grab a couple things and I needed a new broom. We'd killed some time and to my pleasant surprise, Karina's car was parked in the driveway when we arrived.

"I wonder what he said after I left. That motherfucker." Fischer was still angry at his dad for his reaction to the news and had been fuming ever since.

"Let's go inside," I encouraged him, pointing to the porch light that I'd fixed several weeks ago.

We got out of the truck, and I chuckled as we walked across the lawn. Karina's silhouette appeared in the doorway, an hourglass counting down the precious few days I had left before my time in Benning ran out. I'd become accustomed to those countdowns, of time running out, when I wasn't sure if I'd even make it home, or through my next mission, or survive breaking down camp without being ambushed and blown to pieces. I used to believe I wouldn't live to see the ending of things. But there she was making me more hopeful.

She was now in pajamas, a tiny green tank top that only covered half of her soft stomach, and little matching green shorts. If her brother wasn't here, I would pick her up and carry her to her room, take off those barely there clothes, and let all of the anger and chaos disappear.

"Do either of you want some wine?" Karina asked as her brother approached the doorway and I stepped onto the porch.

Fischer shook his head. "Nah." He held the pie in both hands and had been acting like the damn thing was a breakable piece of thin glass, barking at me to slow down over bumps and turns as I drove there.

"Just beer. If you have some." I shrugged. I planned on staying long enough that the one beer wouldn't do any harm by the time I had to drive back home—that was, if she didn't invite me to stay the night, which was what I really fucking wanted.

Karina's hair was tied back at the bottom of her neck with a different color of clip than she'd worn at dinner. This one was green to match her pj set and it made her eyes bright and almost mossy. God, she was beautiful.

"I'm so glad you're here." She sighed, hugging me right in front of her brother.

All pretenses were gone, and I was more than okay with that. I inhaled the scent of her hair and the sweet smell of her invaded my senses as I hugged her close.

"Are you all right?" I asked.

She nodded into my chest. "Just exhausted, but I'm so glad you're here."

"Hey lovebirds, where's Elodie? She said she was home," Fischer asked us.

Karina leaned a little away from me, but kept her arms wrapped around my back. "She's in my room."

"I thought for sure your dad knew he had enlisted." I looked down at Karina." I wouldn't have said anything if I thought otherwise."

Karina's green eyes studied me. I wouldn't blame her if she didn't believe that.

"His reaction surprised me," Karina said. "I thought he would've been ecstatic over him joining, honestly. I figured he would pat you on the back, Austin, and pop champagne. I'm confused why he acted that way."

"Because he wants to be in control of everything and everyone. Once that slips from him, he doesn't know how to handle it." I responded, matter-of-factly.

"You really are a soldier who studies his enemy," she said, playfully pinching at the small of my back.

"Did he say anything after I left?" Fischer asked his sister with his eyes closed.

She shook her head. "No, he went upstairs and never came back down. Like the coward he is. But . . ." She stopped for a second and looked at me. "I did have a moment with Estelle that was kind of nice. Confusing, but nice."

"Dad's a prick and now you're bonding with Estelle. That's so boring," Fischer grumbled, leaning his back against the couch.

"I'm not here for anyone's entertainment," Karina said, looking at both of us.

"I'm going to your room to hang out with Elodie. I need to unload this pie," Fischer announced as he walked into the kitchen.

I heard familiar the rusty rattle of the silverware drawer and looked over at Karina and she looked at me. I guess we were a pretty boring pair from the outside. So much so that Fischer would rather hang out with a pregnant Elodie than with us. No objection—I wanted the alone time with Karina.

Karina's hands were wrapped around the wine bottle as she sat down on the couch cross-legged.

"You're watching *Twilight*. Again?" I asked her when I heard familiar music coming from the television.

"Yes. It's my happy place," she explained.

"Right." I laughed and chose the new chair, the one I haggled with Ms. Rosa for at the market, and sat down.

Fischer had left his phone on the coffee table and the screen lit up with a strand of texts, but I couldn't see whose name it was and really didn't give a shit. I leaned forward to turn his distracting phone over and reached for the book on the table. It was a book of poems. I skimmed through the pages.

"I'm still confused how you can be the most skeptical person I've ever met, but you love poetry and fairy tales." The poem on the page in front of me was about a lying, betraying lover. I turned the small pages. The next was about unrequited love.

Not the time to read this, I thought to myself, and tossed it back onto the table.

"I never said I like fairy tales," she corrected me.

"Yes, you did. Not only that, you also tell them all the time."

She turned her body to face mine. "Is that a complaint?"

The little smile on her face had me wondering if she was already a bit buzzed.

"No, ma'am. That is not a complaint."

She laughed at me and lifted the wine bottle above her head to check how much was left.

When she looked over at me, I was staring at her mouth. She caught me.

"Want to go to the porch?" I asked, a little scared that she might throw something at me.

Instead, her face lit up and she nodded, grabbing her wine and a blanket, and pushed herself off the couch.

"Aren't you cold?" I asked as she sat down on the cement and crossed her legs again.

Karina shook her head. "Nope. This thing is thick." She held up the corner of the blanket she was sitting on and covered with. "Want some?" she offered.

I nodded, even though it was warm out. It was in the sixties and I loved the perfect fall weather.

"Tonight was a shit show. I would never say this to my brother, but I'm actually kind of glad you told our dad off. I know that's selfish, but it felt good to not be the disappointment or the one who was pissing him off, for once."

"You're the least selfish person I've ever met," I reminded her as I sat down next to her.

She reached for my hand.

"Oh, and get this. Estelle and I had this weird moment on the porch where she was talking about how she dreamed we would be close before she met me and I think she meant it? It's confusing and I'm still reeling from it. But it made me question how much I've judged her and how awful I've been to her. It's really my dad's fault. Not hers. She just married him, imagining a completely different and new life than the one she has."

Even though I didn't care for Estelle, knowing that she and Karina had found a connection made me happy for her. I knew how badly she needed to be heard and seen by the people around her, especially her family.

I felt the warmth of her body move near mine as she lay back and stared up at the sky, still holding on to my hand.

"The worst part is it made me miss my mom even more. I don't know what's wrong with me lately, but even though my thoughts are all over the place, they keep coming back to her. I miss her more than ever, but I can't figure out why."

I lay back next to her and dangled my feet off the edge of her porch. It was like I could see her words floating with the stars.

"But she was so fucked up in so many ways. The more I think about it, the crazier it makes me. I keep trying to analyze my mother's choices and her life. Like her friends . . ." Karina paused midsentence. "Did she even have any? I don't. I have you, Elodie, and my brother . . . but soon, all of you will be gone."

My stomach lurched. She was right.

"Elodie is here—she just won't be living in your house." I tried to take a little of her anxiety away.

"Yeah, for now. But once the baby is born and Phillip comes back, I'll barely see her. Plus, chances are high that they will get stationed somewhere else. Then what will I do? Austin will be gone, too, and I'll be here in this house by myself. I'll have no one. I'll go to work and come home to an empty house."

Anxiety was coming off her in waves. I wanted to calm it. I hated how alone she was in this world. She deserved to be surrounded by people who loved her.

"You have me?"

She let go of my hand to pick at the stitching on the blanket between us. Her silence made me lose my breath.

"For how long, though?" she asked me, her eyes looking toward the night sky.

"I wish I knew the answer."

She sighed into the silent night air, then rolled over, propping herself up on one elbow. I stayed on my back, watching her closely. The tips of her hair fell onto my face as she tried to clip her curls back up. I brushed them back with my fingers and she closed her eyes.

"Every aspect of my life feels uncertain, and I can't handle you being a part of that. I keep trying to just ignore the reality, our reality, but it hurts. I wish you could be my stability," she said, then pointed to the brightest star above us and closed her eyes.

"I'd like to be," I told her, wishing on the same star. I continued to run her hair through my fingers and she dropped her head down to rest her chin in my palm.

"Are we just hurting each other more by doing this?" she quietly questioned.

I didn't know the answer. If it were anyone else in our position, I would say they were crazy, wasting their time and energy, and to cut their ties and run the other way, but when it came to Karina, I couldn't do that. And to my very pleasant surprise, she couldn't seem to, either.

"Maybe, but it's going to hurt either way." My words were ludicrous, but they were true. "We might as well go as far as we can, right? Isn't that what life is about? Love and pain, happiness and suffering? Who says we can't be happy until the suffering begins?"

Karina's eyes shone as they filled with silent tears. She blinked them away before one could fall and lay back down, resting her head against my pounding heart. All I could think about was how good it felt, like getting a bandage with numbing cream wrapped over a fresh, bloody wound. My heart was pounding, more afraid of the future than I'd ever admit, but at least it was still beating . . . for now.

CHAPTER **THIRTY-SIX**

Karina

That Thursday, my birthday eve, I was sitting on the couch, scrolling on my phone, looking at a picture I had taken of Kael asleep in my bed. I moved to Twitter and the first thing I saw was a collage of celebrity red carpet photos at a movie premiere. I lifted the phone to Elodie to show her an up-and-coming actress who starred in one of her favorite Netflix movies, and she squinted to see from where she sat on the other end of the couch.

"She looks so pretty; How much does it cost to look like that?" I sighed, zooming in on her clear skin and sleek hair.

"Your skin is beautiful." Elodie scooted a little closer to me to look at my screen again. "And, her dress is hideous." She giggled, then looked down at her own outfit. Black Nike shorts that certainly were mine because none of Elodie's clothes fit her anymore and an oversized T-shirt that I could have sworn was Austin's, with a stain that looked like hot sauce or ketchup. I had a three-dollar overnight hair mask on, and we both had sheet masks stuck to our faces. Elodie's was sliding down her nose and some of the serum was dripping down her neck.

I was in pajamas, too, an old T-shirt from my brother's football days and cotton shorts, legs stubbly. I wiped my dirty phone screen clean with the bottom of my shirt.

"Look at us, how glamorous we are, judging the most beautiful people in the world." I rolled my eyes, zooming back in on the actress's complexion. I mean, seriously, not one pore showed on her perfectly contoured face.

"Speak for yourself." Elodie stuck her tongue out at me and waved her hand over her messy blond hair. "Once this baby is out, it's over for all these girls. Even the Jenners." She flicked her wrist, laughing.

She had a way of making me feel special, like a normal girl with a real best friend.

"I can hear you from the kitchen," Austin said, making his way into the living room with a bowl of cereal in his hand. "You two are beautiful, don't be ridiculous."

He sat on the floor next to the couch in front of Elodie, and she eyed his cereal bowl.

"Want some?" he offered, holding it up to her. She nodded and he dipped the spoon into the bowl—Cheerios and milk with sugar, the way our mom always had it. Austin spoon-fed Elodie and if they weren't my brother and my best friend, I would have felt like the third wheel.

"If I had the money, I would be prettier." Elodie spoke while the cereal crunched between her teeth. "They have lasers for everything now. And Amazon has these little sucker things that make your pores and stretch marks disappear." She lifted the bottom of her shirt to show the thin purple marks on her pale skin.

"You don't need it. I do. Plus, pores don't shrink. Didn't you learn that in training?" I teased her.

"Why are girls like this?" Austin moaned, turning to his phone, his fingers tapping away on the screen. "You two are being so weird right now."

I started typing into the search bar on my Instagram.

"Well, because women on the internet look like this." I showed him the latest bikini picture of a popular Instagram model living a lavish life with a surgically crafted body. I followed her only as a point of comparison with myself: while she was in Bali on the edge of a mountain in a tiny, tiny orange bathing suit, I was sitting on my couch with cheese-puff-stained fingers, wishing Kael would text me like he'd promised to. I had barely heard from him today, even though he said he would text me when he got out of his discharge orientation that supposedly ended at seven o'clock, already an hour ago.

"No one looks like that in real life." Austin grabbed the phone from my hand and tossed it onto a pillow on the floor. "Trust me, I've met girls online and when we met in person—" Elodie shot Austin a look of disgust and he stopped midsentence. "Just saying, don't compare yourselves to edited photos."

"You don't get it because you don't have the same pressures that we do," I explained, peeling the now-dry sheet mask off my face and tossing it onto the table. Elodie did the same, but she balled hers up and put both of ours into her empty snack bowl.

It was beyond fucked up how much I criticized my own body, my mind, my emotions, whereas I was quick to defend Elodie when she put herself down. I knew the unattainable beauty standard was beyond toxic, but I couldn't help it. So many people had paid a lot of money to brainwash me through media and marketing since childhood, and my obsessions were nearly impossible to undo.

"Well Martin seems to like you, orange-stained fingers and all," my brother laughed. I used my cheese-puff-stained middle finger to flip him off.

"Speak of the devil," he said, looking to his side, toward the front door.

I popped up off the couch. "Kael! You're here."

I didn't care to hide my excitement as I wiped my fingertips on my shorts. If I hadn't missed him so much, I would have been embarrassed by the hardened mask on my hair or that he may have heard the conversation with my brother and Elodie.

"I rang your doorbell." He shrugged. "But it must be broken."

I sighed. Of course it was.

"I'll add it to the list," I told him as he closed the door and started to take his boots off.

"How'd it go?" my brother asked him.

Kael was focused on Austin and that gave me the opportunity to take him in without anyone noticing. He was wearing his ACUs and his clean-shaven face highlighted his sharp jawline and intense dark eyes. I studied him as he knelt down, his fingers hooked around the laces, to undo the heavy tan boots on his feet.

"Fine. It ran long because some dumbass kept asking the same questions over and over."

"So? What's the verdict? Good news, bad news, no news?" Austin pressed him for information.

"Come on! Tell us!" Elodie pleaded.

Apparently this appointment was something they both knew about? When he mentioned it to me, Kael hadn't made it sound important. I felt a sting of jealousy.

"Well . . ." he started to say, looking directly at me. "They're letting me out of the Army. With a medical discharge."

"Fuck yeah!" Austin put the bowl on my table and sat up taller, kneeling now. He cheered like he was watching a sporting event.

"I'm pretty much all cleared, just have some reintegration

classes and physical therapy to complete, but they're letting me out. I can't believe it." He closed his hand over his chin, halfway hiding his smile.

I suddenly wanted to be with Kael without an audience. He looked so youthful and elated with the close proximity of freedom beaming off him. His optimism was infectious, even I had to fold my lips in to stop from grinning. I was just about to say something when Austin stood up to hug Kael, breaking our eye contact. He hit his hands hard against Kael's back and I wiped at my eyes, selfishly wishing Elodie and my brother weren't here.

"Just like that? No strings attached?" Austin asked when Kael pulled back from him.

Seeing Austin's brotherly affection toward Kael surprised me every time. I had never seen him like that with any of his other friends and acquaintances. Their relationship made me feel like someone else was looking out for Austin and that gave me a little peace of mind.

On the other hand, it made me sad knowing they would more than likely drift apart and eventually lose contact once Austin left for basic training. I didn't want to think about the date approaching; it was coming up very, very soon. My stomach knotted at the thought. There was so much change happening around me, I wasn't sure how much more I could handle.

"I'm not stupid enough to think there aren't any strings attached. This is the United States Army we're talking about here," Kael said in a clipped tone. "But I'll take what I can get. At least it's one step closer. It came faster than I thought. Even my first sergeant said someone must have pulled some strings."

"What happens now? You're not moving away yet, are you?" Elodie asked. "Phillip will be back—" Her meek voice was more of a plea than a statement.

Austin looked at her and then at me. I couldn't read the expression on his face.

"Atlanta's been the plan for a while now. It's just a question of when. I thought it would be months before I heard anything about getting discharged." Kael paused. "It takes some guys over a year to get out, but here I am. I haven't had time to process what happened today."

He walked around the couch, closer to where I stood, and his uniform socks left marks on my old hardwood floors that I knew I wouldn't ever want to erase. Sometimes when I looked at him, I felt like he belonged here, like he was going to be a permanent part of my life. His stamp was already all over my house, from the shower to the porch light to my bed.

"I am happy for you," Elodie exclaimed, "but I don't want you to go. You were my first friend here." She stood up to hug him, squeezing his hand, which was so much bigger than hers. I looked away as he rubbed the other hand across her back.

I stood there in front of the couch, the back of my calves pressed against it. Like a needy child, I wanted it to be my turn.

"I'm not going far. Atlanta's just a drive away. Don't worry." He kept on assuring Elodie.

My eyes shot up at him. I knew he loved Atlanta, and I knew I couldn't force him to stay near me in Fort Benning—a huge trigger for his trauma and PTSD. But hearing him say it again and again had me panicking a little. His departure was a constant thought in the back of my head, especially now that we were in whatever kind of relationship we were in. Both of us did our best to avoid the topic outright, but here it was staring us in the face. I wondered just how limited our time was, and if I would wake up one day and he would be gone.

Austin's voice interrupted my depressing thoughts, "Have you told anyone else yet?"

"No. I came straight here," Kael responded, looking at me. Not at Austin, not at Elodie.

I was so relieved that he'd come here first. Austin and Elodie celebrated Kael's news like he was family—and there I was, the brat in the corner, too lost in her head to join in but full of internal commentary.

"Everything is going to be so different without you here," Elodie said, "Both of you." Her voice cracked a bit and Austin sweetly patted her back.

I knew Elodie would miss Austin, too; he had become like a brother to her since he'd been back. But she would have her baby and her husband soon to fill her life. I hadn't heard her and Phillip fighting since before the camping trip. Even if things were rocky between the two of them, I was sure it would get better once he was back home by her side.

I wanted everything in Elodie's life to go well, to be full of happiness and laughter, sunlight and peace. I would be losing my twin, and my best and pretty much only friend, by the time Phillip returned. I had already lost my mother, I wouldn't mind losing my father, and now Kael was leaving, too. So much change. So much chaos. I went from wanting to congratulate Kael and wrap my arms around him and pull him into my room, to wishing we had never gotten back together. But then, a moment later, I wanted him to hug me and never let go. These circular thoughts made me dizzy.

"I need to call my ma; I haven't told her yet," Kael said, pulling his phone from his uniform pocket and walking toward the front door.

I nodded, still not able to say a word.

"Wow. I can't believe he's getting out." Austin spoke over Kael's mumbled voice on the porch. My brother's head began to hang as he said, "All of this is starting to feel real. Me leaving for basic, Martin getting discharged . . ."

"Stop talking about it, you're making me and the baby sad." Elodie looked at him, and then at the clock hanging on the wall. "Oh, no. it's almost eight and I need to run to the PX before they close."

I had told her I would go with her when she mentioned it this morning. Now that Kael was here and we had so much to talk about, I regretted my offer.

"I got a coupon for one of those fancy video monitor things and it expires tomorrow," she explained to Austin who looked confused over the urgency of going tonight. She looked at me, then toward my front door to Kael. "Do you still want to go?" She knew me well enough to know that my mind was on Kael right now and the last thing I wanted to do was go to the PX.

"Uhm . . ." I started to reply.

"I'll go?" Austin said to Elodie, either to save me or just to get out of the house. Regardless, I was grateful for the interruption.

"Yes." She smiled. "You can go with me since *she* has other things to do," she teased, nodding toward Kael on the phone outside. "Plus, you can help me carry stuff. Oh, I also want strawberries and that whipped stuff . . . what's it called again, Karina?"

"Cool Whip."

She smiled and walked over to the coat rack on the wall near the door. She threw a hoodie on over her pajamas and slid her feet into a pair of dirty white platform sneakers. She always looked so effortlessly adorable and stylish.

"Do I have anything on my face?" Elodie asked, patting her fingers against her dewy, freshly masked skin. I shook my head and she smiled.

I could see out the window that Kael was walking around my

yard now, his Army uniform blending in with the dead grass. He turned around and was smiling—a smile that warmed me from the inside out. I couldn't begin to imagine how happy his mother was; it almost brought me to tears.

"Let's go now, please? Are you ready?" Elodie tilted her head, smiling at Austin.

He nodded. "We'll be back."

"Do you need anything? Want some more cheese puffs?" Elodie asked as she shoved her keys and phone into the front pocket of her hoodie.

I shook my head. "I'm saving money, remember?" I reminded her right as Kael walked up the porch steps and opened the door.

"Where are you all going?" Kael asked my brother.

"Elodie and me are going to the PX," my brother replied.

Elodie grabbed on to Austin's sleeve, practically dragging him out the door. "We need to go! The store is closing!"

"When do you think they'll be back?" Kael checked the time on his phone. "He'll need a ride to my place, but I can text him to have Elodie drop him off there when they're done." He looked around the living room, his attention focusing on every little detail of his surroundings, as usual.

It was one of the things I found most fascinating about him. Instead of a single book, Kael was an entire library. The sheer amount of information he had stored in that brain of his could probably change the world if he shared it more. His intelligence made him magnetic, quick-witted, and wise. It also made him annoying and cocky and irritating at times, but not right now. Right now, he was fascinating, and mine, and we were finally alone.

Kael and I were the sun and the moon, slowly rotating around one another in the middle of my living-room floor. I hoped his mind was going to the same place that mine was.

"So, what now?" he asked me.

I shrugged, slowly stepping a little to the right as he did the same to the left. We were dancing. Our minds, our bodies. I wondered who would pounce first.

The circular thoughts were back, making me dizzy. I walked over to the window and looked to see if Elodie and Austin had left.

"They're gone." I breathed a sigh of relief.

I had been dying to have a moment alone with Kael since he showed up at my house. Even though I had seen him on Tuesday night, I'd missed him so much. He stepped toward me and leaned his arm on my new chair from the flea market. For the rest of my life, I'd never be able to look at that chair without thinking of him. If I were the type of girl who believed in destiny or serendipity, I would see the day at the flea market as just that. It was the day that began the road back to us for Kael and me. But we were soon going to be divided again, not by deceit or secrets, just by life and the fucked-up way the universe decided it would be.

"I'm sorry I told all of you at the same time. I wanted to tell you about the discharge alone first, I tried to call you, but you didn't answer," he said, lifting his other arm toward me.

I looked at the couch and coffee table for my phone. "I don't know where I put my phone. It's okay. I'm just glad I didn't find out last," I said quietly.

"Come here, Karina." Kael's voice drew me to him like I was being hypnotized. He wrapped his arms around me, one by one, and I looked up at him and he studied my face.

"I really am happy for you. I know how important this is," I said with a warm smile.

"Would you come with me?"

It took me a few seconds to understand what he was asking. "Come with you to Atlanta?" I repeated slowly, separating the words with a half second between them.

He nodded. "I know you have your life here, but selfishly, I want you to come with me. I don't want to be away from you."

"Could you stay here?" I knew the answer, but if he could be hopefully selfish in this moment, so could I.

Kael shook his head. "I can't. I can't be here in this town, at this post. I don't know that I'll ever be able to move on with my life as it is, but I can't live here in this graveyard. I want to be with you . . . fuck, I've never wanted anything more in my life and I don't know how the hell I will leave, but Karina, I have to. I hope you understand that."

His words, carefully crafted and honest, hurt me to the bone. I wasn't hurt by *him*, but by our reality. It felt so unfair. I would never ask him to stay here, to suffer and be reminded of the hell he had been through, but I knew I couldn't leave this place. I had many reasons, from my house to my work, to not being ready to take the risk of losing my independence for the possibility of love. Kael and I had grown together in our own little bubble, and then it had popped. Imagine how messed up things would be if I sold my house, moved to Atlanta, and we broke up again? The world was wide, too wide for me to even contemplate.

"I know your brain must be in overdrive. But you don't need to worry about any of this right now, especially not today." Kael brought his hand up to touch my cheek.

The rough calluses on his palms brushed against my skin and I let out a sigh of relief, even though there was no resolution.

I knew that nothing would change today, but it wasn't easy to forget everything that would be taken away from us. I was genuinely beyond happy for Kael to be released from this place that was like a prison to him, no matter how it would affect me. I'd choose his peace and freedom over my own needs any day, even if that meant breaking my own heart. The expiration date for us was approaching right at the time when everything felt so perfect—too perfect. With each passing second, we had less and less time together. The comfort and healing in my life—that he had made possible—would be gone. Long distance was the only viable plan, but hardly a solution since that rarely ever worked in the end. My head began to ache; a high-speed train of worries plowed through my brain.

Kael's hands were shaking a bit when he brought them up to the base of my ears. He cupped them over both and kissed my forehead. My shoulders dropped.

"Shhhhh," he whispered against my forehead before pressing his lips against my skin.

It worked like magic. Like noise-canceling headphones. My mind had gone from running through a screaming stream of increasingly worse possible scenarios to complete and full silence. I closed my eyes, gripping the starchy material of his uniform covering his arms. I held on to him, and he kept my ears covered as he dipped his head down, bending to line his eyes up with mine. I pulled at his uniform and kissed him hard. His mouth was warm and tasted like lingering coffee with a hint of sadness. I opened my mouth farther, more desperately. His hands went to my hips and he squeezed them, our bodies pressed against the side of the hard chair.

Kael's hands pushed the thin fabric of my pajama shorts up on the sides and he massaged the thick pockets of flesh between my hips and thighs. I moaned as he unlocked the part of me that was touch-deprived, salacious, and melting into him. He hitched one of my legs onto the arm of the chair, spreading me open, and slid his fingers across me. I was already soaking through the fabric and the moment he touched me, I ripped at his uniform jacket, pushing it down his arms and onto the floor. His tan T-shirt was still on, but the definition of his body was easily seen under it. I lifted it up over his head as fast as I could. His touch immediately found me again, this time he slid a finger inside, slowly pumping, then adding another. I held on to his back, my nails digging into his beautiful skin. I was frenzied, adrenaline pumping through me, but Kael was moving slowly, tenderly kissing and licking my neck, breathing my name into my ear, making goose bumps cover my entire body. His fingers were moving slowly, teasingly, and it just made me need him more. Gently, he moved me to the front of the chair and sat me down, his skillful touch staying between my legs as he used one hand to pull my shorts and panties down one leg without fail. I could feel my body building to bliss as he dipped his head down, gripped both sides of my ass and pressed his warm tongue against me. I tried to grip his shoulders, but my mind and body were out of control. I clawed the sides of the chair, saying his name as I came, his tongue swirling and swirling. I thought I might pass out from the pleasure as my back rose, my legs stiffened, and waves crashed over me as his lips sucked my already throbbing clit. I was so sensitive but didn't want him to stop. I needed more. He was so composed as he lifted his head up, slowly circling me still, his lips glistening under the light. God, he was so beautiful.

"Happy birthday, Karina," he said, kissing the inside of my thighs as I slowly came back to a much more blissful reality than I had been in when he first arrived.

"I love you," I told him between breaths. His eyes caught mine and I could tell they were full of surprise. For two people who felt so intensely for one another, we didn't say the words as often as we felt them. I knew how he felt, and he knew how I felt, and that's what mattered.

Kael rose to his knees, and I wrapped my thighs around his back, pulling him closer to me. He kissed my cheeks, both sides, and my lips. I could taste myself on him as he spoke into my open mouth.

"I love you, more than anything." His words were simple, but I felt my eyes stinging as he kissed me again. The ache in my heart was healed . . . for now.

CHAPTER **THIRTY-SEVEN**

"Happy birthday," Kael whispered before I even opened my eyes.

He had stayed the night and his warm body was wrapped around me; the heat from his skin was more intense than the sun creeping across my bedroom.

"I'm so over my birthday," I groaned and blinked my eyes open. His head was on my chest, our bodies tangled together.

"And why is that?"

"We already celebrated twice, at the campground and at my dad's, and honestly the second one really made me never want to acknowledge my birthday again for the rest of my life."

"But I got you something. Should I return it?" Kael asked me in a low voice.

"You did?" I sat up a little and he lifted his head to look at me.

He nodded. "The materials are in the back of my truck. Well, some of them, anyway. The rest are at my place."

"Materials?"

He nodded again and kissed my bare shoulder. I shivered and he kissed my skin a second time.

"What kind of materials?" I asked him. I had no clue what he could be up to.

"Well . . ." He licked his lips and squinted a bit as the light cast across his beautiful face. "Let's get out of bed and I'll show you." He took me by the hand and gently dragged me out of the bed. I grabbed a hoodie from the floor in case Elodie or Austin, or both, were in my living room.

I handed Kael his shirt and he slid it over his head. The house was silent as we walked down the hallway and into the living room. Kael led me to the front door and opened it. I was confused, to say the least. He stepped out and I followed, standing awkwardly next to him, wishing we were still in my bed, but excited about whatever he had planned for me.

"I know how much you love porch swings—"

I almost squealed before he finished.

"So, first I'm going to build you a small deck, and then hang a swing on it, that is, after I fix the crumbled edges of your porch. It's in pretty bad shape and—" I covered his mouth with my hand, and he playfully bit my palm.

"Are you serious?" My eyes stung with emotion. I slung my arms around his neck and squeezed him, making both of us tilt back a bit, but his strength kept us from falling backward off my porch.

"Kael! This is . . . that is . . . I have no words." I kept hugging him.

I wanted to tell him that he didn't have to do all of that, that it would take so much time and so much energy, but I wasn't going to let my anxiety get in the way of such a thoughtful, albeit outrageous gift. He was bringing one of my dreams to life, my own porch swing on my own porch. I was so thankful I could have burst at the seams.

As Kael started to unload a toolbox and long wooden boards from the back of his truck, I watched him for a bit, still in awe that he had given me the best gift I'd ever received.

"Do you need help?" I asked him while sitting on my butt on the porch steps.

"Don't even think about it. Go take a shower or lie back down. Don't lift a finger." He nodded toward the house.

I couldn't help but smile. So, this is what it was like when someone did something for you just to make you happy, without the goal of getting something in return.

"Fine. I don't want to go back to bed, but I'll take an everything shower," I told him, pushing my palms against my knees to stand up. My thighs were delightfully sore from our night together.

"An everything what?" he asked, dropping an armful of wood next to the porch.

"It's like an everything bagel, but in shower form. I saw it on Instagram. It's basically every possible step of a shower, double shampoo, shaving, body scrub, and wash . . ." I went on, thinking about the woman whose nighttime routine I watched daily. If only I had a nicer bathroom, and maybe more self-confidence, I could film my self-care.

"The internet is a weird, weird place," Kael groaned with a hint of amusement.

I stepped down the stairs to stand in front of him. "Speaking of the internet, you should follow me on Instagram." I put a hand on my hip. It was a little sore, too. I stretched a little, twisting my torso. Kael looked pleased.

"Okay?" he said simply, pulled his phone from his pocket and handed it to me. "Passcode is 0917."

I lit up. I had never seen a guy give a girl their phone passcode so casually, but I had seen plenty of women finding insane infidelities on their partners phones. "I get to follow myself? How romantic," I teased, rolling my eyes, and Kael bent to kiss my forehead.

"That's as romantic as Instagram can get." He shrugged and got back to work without another word, leaving me holding his phone.

I was beyond tempted to look through it, from the photos to

the texts, but I stopped myself. Not today. I typed in the passcode and wasn't surprised that he barely had any apps, no texts, no little red notification dots anywhere. I opened his Instagram and began to type my name. It was already in the search bar. My heart did a little squeeze and I looked across the yard to him. Ugh, I loved him. Plain and simple, it was these tiny moments that made me love him more and more. I followed myself and couldn't help but click on the DM icon. It was empty. Did he delete his messages? Or was he the only person to never get a direct message on Instagram? *Okay, enough snooping, Karina.* I hit the side bar on his phone, putting it to sleep, and left it on the porch.

"I'm going inside!" I called to him.

He nodded, lifting a bucket out of the bed of the truck, and smiled at me.

I went inside and decided to make him breakfast in lieu of taking an everything shower. I wanted to do something for him, even small a small gesture, since he was going to be spending his time working on my porch. I checked my fridge to see what I had. There was a can of biscuits in the back, and I knew I had sausage in the freezer. Checking the expiration date on the can, I tried to remember the last time I made gravy and biscuits. Growing up, I had them at least twice a month; my mom had the best recipe. I'd learned it from her, and I'd only used it twice, both times for Elodie. I grabbed the roll of sausage from the freezer and turned on the hot water in the sink. It wasn't the best way to defrost meat, but whatever. I gathered the other ingredients—flour, milk, pepper—turned the oven to preheat, and played music on my phone, allowing myself to get lost in the game of house Kael and I were playing.

About thirty minutes later, I nearly jumped out of my skin when Kael came up behind me as I was stirring the sausage gravy. I was singing along to Taylor Swift, totally in my own world. He laughed, his breath warm against my neck.

"I smelled the sausage and had to come see what you were up to," he said, lips against my skin. I shivered as he pulled the neckline of my hoodie down a little to kiss my neck.

"I made gravy and biscuits and was going to come get you in, like, two minutes. Just need to add more pepper," I said, grabbing the pepper shaker, shaking it heavy-handed until a pile was on top of my gravy. My mouth was watering.

"Yum, thank you. What happened to your bagel shower?" Kael's arms squeezed my torso gently.

I laughed. "It's an everything shower."

"Right." I could feel him smiling against my cheek from behind me.

"I decided to be domestic and feed you instead." I playfully pushed my hips back against his solid body.

I turned the stove off and told him to sit down at the table as I brought plates and water, and pulled the hot biscuits off the sheet pan and onto another plate. Kael kept licking his lips and smacking his gums, a sign that the smell had him starving, too. I made his plate and hoped for the best. His eyes went wide when he took the first bite.

"Holy shit, this is so good," he said, his mouth full of a big bite.

I smiled, totally satisfied and proud of myself.

"Thank you. It's a secret family recipe," I whispered, cupping my hand next to my mouth.

"I won't tell anyone, as long as you don't tell my ma that these are the best biscuits and gravy I've ever had." He dove his fork into the rest of a biscuit. I was glad I'd made the whole roll.

My mind went to my mom as I took a bite. The taste was so distinctively her that it made my chest ache a little. It was comforting and painful at the same time. I needed to climb out of this spiral before it went too far.

"Speaking of your mom . . . tell me how excited she was?" I raised a brow, pivoting the conversation to Kael.

"My ma is too long of a story," he said. "She's happy about my discharge, but her health has taken a turn."

Concern shot through me. It wasn't like I knew a ton about his mom, but I did know how important she was to him. "Do you want to talk about it?" I asked, touching his face gently.

He shook his head. "Not today. Not on your birthday. Please."

I nodded once, agreeing to his wishes even though I was worried. I chewed my food slowly. "And Mendoza?"

Kael looked over at me. "Mendoza's having a shitty week, actually."

"Why? What happened?"

"Julien has some sort of problem with his eyes. More than needing glasses. They're talking surgery, potential blindness. Gloria is a mess." He looked at me, then winked to lighten things up. "I'm really bringing down the mood on your birthday."

My heart broke for them. Gloria must be in so much pain. I wondered if it would be weird to reach out to her, but decided that since Kael was telling me in confidence, it wouldn't be a good idea.

Kael's hands ran over his shaved head. He had a fresh haircut; I could tell by the way his hair was buzzed into a perfectly straight line around his neck and forehead.

"Is there anything they can do?" I asked, knowing it wasn't likely.

"Not really. Just depend on the healthcare system to figure it out. And Mendoza isn't great at depending on anyone."

"Except you," I reminded him.

He sat his fork down and nodded, a small smile taking over his face. "Yeah, except me."

I watched Kael's expression change as he sat quietly for a minute. I could tell his mind was drifting to more serious thoughts about his friend.

"I just wish he would see someone for himself. Not just Julien, but he really needs help. It's becoming more and more apparent with every episode he has. I've told him that more times than I can count. He's too proud, but it's not about ego, it's just the way he was raised—like me, to suffer in silence. Even with two therapists, multiple meds, and weekly doctor visits, I'm not fixed yet."

He tapped his temple and the tone in his voice made me shiver.

"Mendoza's losing control of his family's well-being, yet another crisis in his life," he continued. "When I met him a few years ago, he was a totally different person. Seeing violence, being in the middle of life and death, it'll fuck you up. It's really, really fucked him up. And now his kid's hurting. It's not fair."

Kael's jaw clenched and his throat moved as he swallowed. "And the worst part is, even if he wasn't a prideful motherfucker, he'd be crazy to say he needed help. He'd be terrified that if he says anything about how he's feeling or what he's going through, they will kick him out of the Army, and he won't be able to support his family. That's how they get a lot of guys to stay in. Mendoza has kids who need healthcare, and if these tests come back and say Julien needs more help, they'll need it more than ever. It's scary, thinking about life after the Army, even for me. I don't know who I am without my uniform." Kael looked down at his plate. "And I don't have anyone else to worry about but myself."

His words stung me a bit and he could tell. I had sat quiet and listening, eager for everything he was sharing with me. But this hurt.

"I mean financially," he clarified, and I relaxed a little. "My sister and my ma, hell, they would be fine if I died. They'd be better off with my life insurance from the government."

"Not funny." I pushed at his shoulder, finding his causal talk about death unamusing. "Do you really feel like that? Like you don't know who you are?"

He nodded. "It's fucking scary. I had this plan my whole life to join and stay until retirement, and now that I'm really getting out, it's hitting me like a ton of bricks. I'm so used to just trying to stay alive. I'm good at being a soldier—great at it, honestly. I don't know what else I'm good at or what will happen when I take this uniform off for the last time."

"You're great at remodeling and that's a huge market. Those rental companies, the ones who are using houses like hotels, are really taking off in big cities. I keep seeing them online." I didn't know what to say. I didn't have an answer for his big questions, so I pathetically offered some small encouragement.

Kael's soft smile turned into a grin.

"Thank you, Karina. I hope it works out the way I want it to."

I inched closer. "Me, too."

I couldn't look away from him.

"I think it's your dad who's been helping me get out earlier, by the way." He said it so casually, I almost choked.

"What?"

"Yeah, I don't know for sure, but I'm pretty certain it's him. No one gets out this fast without a senior officer pulling the strings. I asked around and nobody had a clue why this was happening. Only your dad knows my circumstances. I'll tell you when I know more, but I have a feeling it was him."

I was confused. "Why would he do it?"

The whole thing made me feel slightly ill. It seemed like a good thing, but my dad never did nice things for people without a selfish motive, and he surely wouldn't go out of his way to help someone he despised as much as Kael.

"Who knows." He shrugged. "I'm assuming he just wants me away from you as soon as possible."

"I don't like the idea of him meddling in your life. I mean, I'm glad it's to your advantage in this case, but there has to be a catch. I know my dad."

Kael looked at me closely. "How about for today, we just focus on what matters, which is you and me."

The silence ticked between us as he stared at me, locking eye contact and not breaking it. The hairs on my neck stood straight up. Neither of us were touching the food now.

I felt so content with him and so safe; I wanted to be closer to him, to make everything better for Kael. I didn't fully understand the complexity of what I was feeling, but I knew that I loved him.

Kael reached over and his fingers circled my wrists, and he brought my hand to his chest, pulling my chair closer to him. The energy between us had changed so quickly that I could barely catch my breath. One second we were eating and having a serious conversation and the next, sparks were flying and I was climbing onto his lap on the chair. His eyes held mine and he sighed, relief pulling his shoulders down. One of his hands went to my hip and the other pushed into my hair.

Every single cell in my body danced and hummed under the warmth of his touch.

His hand moved up my neck as we talked without words. He stopped at the base of my throat and squeezed very gently. I moved my body against his, my shorts against the thin cotton of his sweatpants. As I felt him grow harder, I dipped my body down farther. The friction felt like nothing I had ever experienced during my time on this earth.

His lips touched my jawline, peppering their way across to my desperate lips.

"Karina, I—" he began to say, still kissing me. The vibration of his phone in his pocket stopped my body from rocking against his.

He reached into his pocket and grabbed his phone, which showed Mendoza's name on the screen, and he ignored the call.

"What if he's in trouble?" I asked, climbing off his lap. I didn't move far; my body wouldn't allow me to.

His phone rang again. This time he picked up.

"Hey, what's up? You good?" he immediately asked.

He looked up at me. The way his pupils were so small that they were drowning in a sea of cloudy brown made me eager to touch him again. I looked at his hands and he lifted one up to my face, gently running this thumb across my cheek. I felt like I was dreaming. I hoped everything with Mendoza was okay, for his sake and Kael's, and selfishly, even my own since it was my birthday, after all . . .

Mendoza spoke for a few seconds before Kael moved the phone from his ear and tapped on the screen a few times. He touched the screen, sliding his thumb and pointer finger across it to zoom in and look closer.

"Holy shit. Where did you get that?"

I was staring at Kael, expecting him to look at me again. He didn't. I couldn't hear what Mendoza was saying to him, and the not knowing slammed onto my nerves as I waited to find out what was happening.

"Okay. Do not send that to anyone or even mention it until we find out who started this and where it came from."

What the hell is going on? The words burned in my throat, dying to escape my mouth. "Okay. Thanks. Keep me updated if Phillips reaches out to you." He ended the call, speechless.

"What? What's wrong?" My stomach dropped, thinking the worst for Mendoza or Elodie's husband. I was all around confused.

Kael lifted the phone, turning it to me, and my eyes blinked trying to make sense of what was on the screen. It was a picture of two people in an embrace in what looked like a parking lot. Within a few seconds it dawned on me what Elodie's husband had to do with this picture. Elodie was in it. And the boy in the blue jeans and T-shirt with the disheveled blond hair was Austin. I was staring at a photo of my brother and Elodie. Together. She was wearing the outfit she'd left the house in last night, and so was he . . .

They were standing next to her car.

Their arms were wrapped around one another . . .

Their lips touching.

"What the—?" I couldn't finish my thought when I heard what sounded like a car pulling into my driveway. I walked to the window to see an unfamiliar black car parked next to my house, and a driver opening the back passenger door. A solider climbed out, dressed in ACUs, with buzzed black hair. It took me until he reached the grass, walking toward my porch, to realize who it was, since I had only seen him in pictures.

Holy hell.

It was Phillip, in the flesh, with the worst possible timing on the planet.

A NOTE FROM THE AUTHOR

Hey you, thank you for picking this novel up and giving it a chance. Thank you for supporting storytellers and helping me continue to create and share my stories with the world. In such chaotic times, we often turn to music, novels, films, and knowing that my books are a part of that means everything to me. This story and its themes are very personally important to me, and I hope you feel that while turning the pages.

I originally wrote a version of this novel a few years ago, just like *The Falling* (the first book in this series), and during the pandemic, I reread them both and decided to rework, rewrite, and revisit the story. I want to make you—the reader—and myself proud with the books I put into the world, so I undertook the long process of rewriting and republishing it, so thank you again for allowing me to do that and for supporting my wild ideas. :P

Whether you're new to my work or have been reading me for years, I truly appreciate you giving your time and resources to support this series and authors around the world. In times of darkness, we turn to art, and being a part of that is everything to me. I can't thank you enough and I truly hope you enjoy this book.

ACKNOWLEDGMENTS

First of all, I want to thank you for reading and finishing this passion project of mine. I continue to be amazed by the support you give me, and for those of you who are new to my works, thank you for joining this community and supporting authors from all walks of life.

Asher: As you grow up, I continue to see your love of words and books and it makes my heart soar. You're the reason I keep doing this, so that when you're old enough, you will be proud of the person I am, the words I write, and our life together. I love you more than words and am so grateful to be your mom. You teach me so much about myself and one day, when you're much older, I will embarrass you by showing you all of my books. :P

Erin: You continue to be my right hand, left hand, and both hands at times. :P You always keep me sane and try to keep my wild brain organized. Not to mention that you're always here for me and Asher, and it means the world to me. Here's to the next ten years of friendship and growing Frayed Pages! Love you more.

Douglas: What started as a fan page and a friendship has now turned into building a company together, and I'm so grateful to have you on my team. You're creative, innovative, and one of my favorite humans. We've been through so much together and I'm so excited for our future. Love you!

Flavia: Working with you was one of the best choices I've ever made, but being your friend—more like family—has been even better. You constantly inspire and motivate me to go for all of my insane dreams. Thank you for being such an integral part of my life, work and not, and for always having my back. You're a badass and I love you.

Vilma: We've known each other since before my first book was released, and who knew we would end up this close—and not even because of our love of books, but for our bangtan and soul connection. I can't imagine these last few years without you. Here's to many, many more memories together and counting down until ot7 is on stage again. *sobs*

JW: The alien to my fairy. You've shown me what it feels like to feel safe, secure, and loved for who and how I am.

Anne: Editor, counselor, supporter, inspiration—a few words to describe how I feel about you, but of course they're not close to enough. I'm so grateful for how you cheer me on, encourage me, and work with me on bringing my imagination to life. Meeting and working with you has changed the way I view my career and my voice and I can't thank you enough. Making you emotional during our editing Zooms is one of the highlights of the process. <3 Thank you for everything.

All of the fan pages online: I see you, I hear you, and I appreciate you. You do so much for me and lift me up and encourage me every single day. <3

Semra: Thank you for everything you do, in front of and behind the scenes.

The family group chat: You know who you are <3 What began on a beautiful night in NYC on the rooftop of a hotel in Brooklyn has changed the way I trust (in a good way) and has given me a sense of community and safety and support. I love you all so so so fucking much.

Kristin: Here we are, again, haha. You've been there for me since day one, literally. My career wouldn't be the same without you cheering me on, keeping me sane, and talking me off MANY MANY cliffs. :P Thank you for always being the calm in the storm and continuing to believe in me a decade later. You're the only person I would trust to drive across the entire state of Florida in a torrential downpour. ☺

Maeve: Thank you for always making things work, even when they're constantly changing. Your adaptability and positivity are so admirable and make my life so much easier, haha! I've loved building this imprint with your help and can't wait for the future.

Tina: Thank you for all of your work to bridge the gap between all of the projects and deadlines, and communication and miscommunication. :P I'm grateful to be able to come to you. You're such an important part of the FPxWP team and I appreciate all of your hard work.

Deanna: Thank you for always being so cheery and patient and making it work under the most insane circumstances. You're literal sunshine and I looking forward to continuing to work with you.

Delaney and the Wattpad team: Thank you for everything you do to help grow the imprint behind the scenes. I'm looking forward to the many, many exciting things to come. ☺

Aron: *unicorn emoji* Here's to the next thirty years. :P

The sales team: Thank you for your hard work to get the books on the shelves! It doesn't go unnoticed and is so, so appreciated!

ABOUT THE AUTHOR

Anna Todd is the *New York Times* best-selling author of the After series, which has been released in thirty-five languages and has sold more than twelve million copies worldwide—becoming a #1 best-seller in several countries. Always an avid reader, Todd began writing stories on her phone through Wattpad, with After becoming the platform's most-read series with over two billion reads. She has served as a producer and screenwriter on the film adaptations of *After* and *After We Collided*, and in 2017, she founded the entertainment company Frayed Pages Media to produce innovative and creative work across film, television, and publishing. A native of Ohio, she lives with her family in Los Angeles.

@annatodd

@imaginator1D